G000123174

PORTRAIT OF MAUD

PORTRAIT OF MAUD

June Barraclough

This first world edition published in Great Britain 1994 by
SEVERN HOUSE PUBLISHERS LTD of
9–15 High Street, Sutton, Surrey SM1 1DF.
First published in the USA 1994 by
SEVERN HOUSE PUBLISHERS INC., of
425 Park Avenue, New York, NY 10022.

Copyright © 1994 by June Barraclough

All rights reserved.
The moral rights of the author have been asserted.

British Library Cataloguing in Publication Data
Barraclough, June
  Portrait of Maud
  I. Title
  823.914 [F]

  ISBN 0-7278-4596-9

All situations in this publication are fictitious and
any resemblance to living persons is purely coincidental.

Typeset by Hewer Text Composition Services, Edinburgh.
Printed and bound in Great Britain by
Redwood Books, Trowbridge, Wiltshire.

Contents

PRELUDE

1988

Prelude

Maud Crichton, an old woman of eighty-three, was admitted in the spring of 1988 to the Dedlock Grange Nursing Home, a pleasantly large house near a small village in England's East Midlands.

'The nurses here are all stupid,' she said many times to Matron. Matron never replied to this rude remark but tried privately to make allowances for her new inmate. You could not help feeling sorry for her, with no close relatives and hardly any visitors, not counting the solicitor and the doctor, who came regularly.

One autumn afternoon a few months after her arrival at Dedlock Grange, Maud was dozing after the plain but wholesome lunch, provided on trays in their rooms for those who did not wish to join the others in the Dining Room. On waking she found the shreds of a dream still adhering to the walls of her mind. There had been something comforting but surprising about it. It seemed to have taken place in a school where she had once taught but also in an Art Gallery and a large garden. With the part of her mind that was now awake and intermittently active, she groped round the contours of her memory. But trying to force an explanation for the strange happiness that seemed to be connected with those dream places only made them dissolve and disappear, leaving her only with a conviction that she must in her non-dreaming existence once or twice have been happy. This conviction was accompanied by the knowledge that her present life itself was a waking nightmare. The sudden and rational recognition of her non-happiness had surprised her, and tears of self-pity pricked at her eyes, finally splashing down on to her black dress. If only Ma were here. She would remove her from this place, take her home, look after her properly . . .

The tears and with them the memory stopped as suddenly as they had arrived and Maud groped for her spectacles, which someone must have removed whilst she dozed. Finding them in her lap she put them firmly back on, but they slipped on to the bridge of her nose. Her hair had come down again. She must have help in pinning it up again and forcing it back into its coronet.

She grasped the arms of her chair. Her lunch tray was gone. The same someone must have removed it. She straightened her back and cautiously extended her right leg, then her left, before slowly pushing herself up and taking three steps to the electric bell-push by the side of the dressing-table, leaning on it with all her might. Then she went back to her chair, folded her hands on her lap and waited for attendance.

Her dream was gone completely now, whatever it had been about. Soon she forgot she had dreamed and forgot she was not happy and waited for a nurse to visit her whom she could tick off for not doing her hair properly that morning . . .

PART ONE

1904–1929

Chapter One

Margaret Livingstone Gray had finally been allowed to wed. She was thirty, and bonny, and several young men and not so young men had looked upon her with interest and approval. But not before her thirtieth year had she considered allowing one of them to alter her status of spinster schoolmistress. The reason was that she was Preacher Gray's daughter, and therefore special. Andrew Gray had not planned for his youngest daughter ever to escape his clutches, though he would not have put it quite like that. A widower, he had, after the marriage and departure to Canada of his elder daughter, depended upon Maggie to housekeep, keep his accounts, look after him – his clothes, his food, his general welfare – and to serve as buffer between himself and his erring flock. It was only because he had fallen under the spell of Widow Jessie Irvine and realised she might do for him all that Maggie did – and more – that he had finally given his consent to a marriage between his daughter and Angus Crichton.

Maggie was not in love with Angus, though he had shyly courted her on and off for years, but the advent of Jessie had left her feeling hurt and jealous and aggrieved. She knew the time had come for her to leave her father's house and make a home of her own.

Preacher Gray was well aware what sort of man his new son-in-law was: he'd provide a modest home for Maggie and remain under the thumb of his father-in-law. Any small extras which the Preacher thought to visit upon him and his bride would serve only to make Angus grateful, for he was still only a journeyman worker.

Preacher Gray's first wife had died when the youngest of his six children, Margaret, was ten. But he no longer recognised

7

two of his sons, Hamish and Daniel, Hamish having broken the oath of temperance in a spectacular manner and the other, handsome Dan, got a woman into 'trouble', and not married her. Soft-hearted Margaret did see them now and again; she was torn between the respect and awe she felt for her father and the love she had for the two scapegraces who had treated her kindly in a childhood that had not been remarkable for occasions of happiness. The two other brothers, James and Stanley, were, like their father, strong Free Church of Scotland. They were each married to a good Christian woman of the circuit.

Possessed of great rhetorical skill and an incredible memory Preacher Gray hypnotised his congregation as much as inspired them. He was not a really handsome man but when his dark eyes flashed folk trembled, for he had the air of an Old Testament patriarch and his glance bore into their very souls. If this was not enough, one growled exclamation prevented any further rebellion.

Maggie did take a little dowry of her own to Angus Crichton on her marriage, money saved by generations of her own mother's family, thrifty Lowlanders, left specifically for her – but only if she wed. These savings she intended to use eventually to set up Angus, perhaps in the cork or jute line, and for the education of her own bairns. For the present Angus was content to continue as carpenter and the couple began married life on the southern edge of the city in a small dwelling of one storey but with a mansard room above.

Their first child, a girl, was born a year after the wedding and christened Maud Livingstone Gray Crichton. Maggie had at least had her own way in this. Angus had stood by as Maggie's father thundered she should be named Margaret like Maggie herself and her own dead mother, but Maggie had tremblingly stood her ground, not quite daring to say that Maud was the name of the heroine of a poem she had read but limiting herself to murmuring that it was the name of one of the King's nieces. At this the Preacher bristled the more until she remembered that one of the Canadian cousins had that name among others. Gray did not like the look in his daughter's eyes and felt a little giddy at such unexpected opposition, so 'Maud' she was, and M L G Crichton appeared on the cover of her first exercise book, Maud

Crichton on her own private notebooks a little later where she was to detail in her neat copperplate her Grandfather's sermons and sayings.

As she grew out of babyhood Maud was even bonnier than her mother though with a look of slight hauteur. If anything softened Preacher Gray's habitual fierceness, it was his granddaughter's ways. She remained the only girl child among his grandchildren, for when Maggie and Angus had completed their family four years later the two others were both boys, Malcolm and Duncan, one dark and sober, the other red-headed and noisy.

For several years Maggie was too relieved to have escaped from her father to complain about lack of money, though she never admitted this to herself. Maud was the apple of her eye and she dressed her as beautifully as she dared, having been brought up to believe that finery was the work of the devil. The child enjoyed being showed off to her mother's old friends and revelled in her lacy collars and clean-smelling linen. She appeared biddable, was certainly less trouble than Duncan and even quicker-witted than Malcolm, and repaid her grandfather's early tutoring by doing brilliantly at school, being marked out for the Academy in the City whither she could transfer with a scholarship at the age of eleven. Maggie was aware that she poured all the love into her daughter that she could not truly feel for Angus. She had been adored by her own patient mother and still mourned her untimely death, and she had never felt truly loved since, however fond her husband had always been of her and still was.

'Ye have my brains, Maud,' Preacher Gray would often say to his granddaughter – 'Ye mun use them in the sairvice of the Lord.' As a little girl Maud adored her powerful grandfather who yet preached that women were for the service of their menfolk, as the Bible had writ. She did not see herself yet as one of the women. Twice on Sunday they would trail down the lane and take the tram to his kirk which was always full of worshippers. She watched him in the pulpit and was proud of him. As she grew older she paid more attention to what he was saying and puzzled over it. She learned that the Bible was the sole authority; that Man was totally depraved after the Fall from Paradise when Eve had tempted him, and she knew that her grandfather took it for granted that women tempted men and were unreliable. But on earth God's will reigned supreme in spite of appearances. You were saved in the end only by His Grace; all was apparently already laid down – you had no will of your own, were saved to be one of the Elect, or you were not. She puzzled mightily over this. As long as you didn't know whether you were saved or not you had to play safe, say your prayers, do what God and Grandfather bade you and hope you would escape divine wrath. She had the impression that her grandfather thought he himself was saved all right, though he insisted you would know only after you were dead. But, she wondered, if some were saved and some were not, what did it matter what you did? She kept her question to herself.

Another thing she found hard was her family's attitude to enjoying yourself. Almost everything pleasant was forbidden or at least disapproved of: bracelets and earrings and fine clothes, rich food, playing ball on Sunday (though that was no hardship to miss), or in fact doing anything on the Sabbath but attending the kirk and reading the Bible, and maybe a few improving books. Ma did not even knit on Sunday. It must be kept different from all the other days of the week.

As Maud grew older and eventually went to the Academy she discovered that one or two of the girls there did not appear to believe all this. They were not members of the feared and hated Catholic Church – nothing so exotic – but were less Godfearing Presbyterians, or Episcopalians. Rose was one of them, the child of an English businessman, and Maud at first feared for Rose's soul. But nothing bad seemed to happen to her or to other school acquaintances whose grandfather was not God. Of course, they might die young, and then what? Maud toyed often with the notion of dying young; she hated the ugliness of women who grew to a great age, grandmothers of large families like some of their neighbours. Maud heard that women were to be modest, dutiful, upright, temperate and thrifty. When she was about twelve something in her rebelled against all this, and she suffered several months of headaches and loss of appetite. The headaches were however ultimately diagnosed as the result of extreme shortsightedness and too much reading, and spectacles were procured. Then suddenly there seemed to come a clarification of herself and her place in the world. Her appetite picked up for a time, to become a problem again two or three years later when the rigid control she exercised on herself erupted into a passionate resistance to food. Enjoying your food too much was a sin, the sin of gluttony; the Elect ate sparsely. Was she trying to prove herself one of them? All through the war food had been in short supply and shopping was still a struggle, but though Maggie put the best pieces of stew in front of her daughter, tempted her with dumplings and apple turnovers, Maud was unable to finish her portion, though she picked at it a little.

'I dinna understand it. She was never a finicky wee bairn in that way,' said Maggie in despair to Angus. Preacher Gray was approached to get some sense into her, since the doctor found nothing physically wrong. The Preacher was cornered by Maud on a visit with her mother to her grandfather's house.

'The good book says, take no thought for your raiment, Grandfather?' she started.

'Aye, it does that.'

'And food is also an occasion for indulgence?' she went on.

Maggie stared at this strange daughter of hers who now looked almost a woman.

'Ye're no a saint, child. We're not called upon to starve ourselves,' he said after a pause. He enjoyed his own plain table kept so well by his second wife.

'The Elect enjoy their food then?' she enquired.

'The good things the Lord has seen fit to bestow upon us are all verra well in moderation,' he replied.

'I eat in moderation,' she said calmly.

'Ye mun no worry your Ma,' he said. 'Eat and be thankful and praise the Lord for the morsels that enter your mouth.'

She looked at him intently. He is not consistent, she thought. But she had done it. She could be one of the Elect if she wanted.

After this her appetite picked up again though she was not a big eater, was really rather indifferent to food.

Clothes were another matter and by the time she was fifteen she enjoyed looking at the goods displayed in the shop windows of the city, especially the jewels at the gold and silversmiths. She had become sceptical about all talk of the Elect and the Saved but kept her own counsel. Although still small she had almost grown to her full height and was still doing extremely well at the Academy. 'Maud has rare powers of analysis' said one report.

Maggie and Angus did not quite see eye to eye about their clever daughter. The mother wanted Maud to have the chance of escape from domestic drudgery, but the father, though proud of her brains, could not quite trust a woman who wished to do nothing around the home. Maggie had never asked her to do the dirty work, nor to cook, though Maud spent hours darning tiny holes in her stockings. That was 'lady's work'; Maggie would grasp Maud's hands occasionally as she sat at the table by the window in the parlour and exclaim admiringly: 'White as snae! – aye, ye've the hands of a lady.' Maud was complacent about them but a little guilty that her mother's hands were so work-worn for a woman who had been a teacher. 'My hands are the hands of a scholar,' she thought, and worked away neatly at her darning after she had tired of pushing her fine new fountain pen, a present for her fifteenth birthday, across virgin pages rapidly filled with her tiny, regular, beautiful script. Latin and Greek were her favourite subjects, especially Latin. Here was a language with all its ends tied up, that you could neither change nor improve, that stayed the same for ever. All you had to do was to learn its rules, and occasionally bend them if you wanted to show how clever you were.

It was at the end of this year, 1919, that something happened that shook Maud whilst at the same time confirming her own powers: she came down with the Scarlet Fever. It was most unpleasant; they had shaved off her hair, fumigated the house and carried her away to the Isolation Hospital. Maggie was beside herself at first, but Maud made a good recovery, rather enjoying the fuss once she was out of danger.

'Thank the Almighty it was not the Spanish Influenza,' said Preacher Gray. That was also raging at the time and claimed many deaths through eventual pneumonia. But Maud was more worried about her hair than dying. Her grandfather had always called it Woman's Crowning Glory and she had worn it in long brown plaits to her waist, aiming to put it up in a year or so.

'It will soon grow again,' Maggie comforted her.

'Oh, Ma, I am ugly,' she wailed. She took to wearing a little black straw hat as she lay on the couch in the parlour getting her strength back. 'Vanity of Vanities,' was all her grandfather said, which Maud thought horribly unjust when he had used to make such a fuss of her thick, dark locks. In her heart of hearts she was vain. She refused to have any visitors till the hair had grown back several inches, and lay reading in the dim light, the small hat on her head tied round her chin with a black bow Maggie had confected in case the headgear should slip.

One Saturday afternoon in early summer everyone else was out when there was a knock at the outer door that gave on to the lane. At first Maud ignored it but then heard the door pushed open and her Uncle Dan's voice.

She stood up, her book pressed against her chest as Dan shouted: 'I've come to see ye, Maudie.'

She hated being called Maudie, indeed she did not like her first name at all, so she did not at first reply. Eventually 'Ma will be back in an hour – come back then,' she said, but not raising her voice. Dan pushed open the door of her sanctuary and stood there grinning. For some reason or other she had always rather liked Uncle Dan better than Uncle Hamish who had no conversation to speak of and drank too much. Dan, she thought, was rather silly but quite kind. She sat down again on the couch and he stood there looking at her.

'Hello there,' he said in an irritatingly jocular fashion.

'Hello, Uncle,' she replied, looking down once more at her open book to make it quite clear she found his visit unwelcome.

'I hear that you and your wee hat will not be parted,' he said, entering the room and taking off his own flat cap.

If there was one thing Maud could not bear it was to be teased, and she was angry that he spoke to her in a wheedling voice as if she were a small child.

'You hear right,' she answered coldly. He sat down uninvited on a stiff-backed horse-hair stuffed chair by the window and contemplated her.

'How old are ye noo, Maud?'

'I'm in my sixteenth year,' she replied after a pause, and then looked down at her book again.

13

'Is that so? Well, ye're an awfu' fine lassie now and the fever will have made ye grow tall, ye ken. It speeds up the growth.'

What nonsense he talked, and yet there was something in his eyes, some pleading look that excited her.

'Will ye no take off your hat just the once? I'd like fine to see your face better.'

'I'd rather take off my glasses,' she said. (Then I couldn't see your stupid face properly, she thought.)

'Aye, take them off. Too much study's not good for a lassie.'

That made her angry. He'd never done any studying himself as she well knew.

'Your Ma was a good scholar,' he added. 'She taught the bairns. And she was bonny too – like you.'

'Ma never wore glasses,' said Maud. 'There – does that satisfy you?' She took off her spectacles and folded them, laid them on her closed book and sat, straight-backed, still wearing the hat. She had on a skirt that just peeped over her ankles, and a green silk blouse that her mother had made her to cheer her up on her return from the hospital. She heard him catch his breath, but could not now see him clearly.

'Ye're beautiful, Maudie,' she heard him say. He got up and stood before her, a small man with rather fine brown eyes but with hair beginning to thin, and ill-fitting false teeth.

'Will ye give your old uncle a kiss?' he said, hoarsely now. She felt at a disadvantage sitting down so stood up, moving away slightly from him, one hand on the back of the couch.

For a moment they stared at each other. Then – 'Don't be disgusting,' she said coldly.

'Och, it's disgusting I am now, is it?' He grabbed her other hand. She was not frightened, not even surprised, having gathered enough about Dan's proclivities from her father and mother's whispered conversations to know that he was what they called a Ladies' man. But Ma would be furious if she found out that he had had the temerity to ask her to kiss him, even if Ma did not know how little of the child remained in her. She quickly wondered if she could turn this visit to her own advantage but as she was thinking this over he made a sudden grab at her and planted a hot, greedy kiss on her neck.

14

'Oh, Maudie,' he said. 'I've been wanting to do that lang sine.'

Should she slap his face? No, it would be better to behave in a coldly angry way and order him out of the house. But she was alone and might remain so for another hour.

'I don't suppose you would like me to tell Ma about that?' she said, flicking her finger on her blouse collar as if to remove the contamination. He stared at her, his face flushed. 'Don't dare touch me again, Daniel.'

'Aye, but you're beautiful when you're angry,' he said and walked to the window, turning his back on her for a moment. Then he turned round again. 'Isn't a man allowed to kiss his own niece then?'

'I'm not a child,' said Maud.

'Remember when ye were only a bairn you used to sit on your Neighbour Nicholl's lap? He told me himself – "That wee lassie kens a thing or two" he said to me. "She'll be a flirt, mark my words".'

'How dare you?' breathed Maud, thoroughly annoyed. 'That horrible old man – I hated him dandling me. I told Ma . . .' She took a breath. 'I'm no flirt – and I don't encourage people to take liberties.' Now she sounded dignified and he was a little abashed, but something made him persist.

'Ye might not encourage them maybe – but ye canna help it. It's writ on your face, Maudie. However, we'll say nae more about it, eh?' His face, which had been red, was now pale. Perhaps he realised that he had given himself away and put himself into her hands Maud sensed what sort of a kiss he wanted to give her, and the knowledge made her draw herself up and look at him coldly. He was what they called a dirty old man.

'If I wanted kisses I wouldn't be going to you for them. Her alluding to the kisses she might want incensed him, though he flinched. 'I'll say no more about it – on one condition.' She fingered the bow on her throat.

'And what's that?' His voice sounded anxious. He would not have wanted this conversation brought to the ears of his sister. Maud's voice softened a little now she realised she had him in her power.

15

'Give me the money to have my picture taken when my hair's grown back.'

He whistled. She had a cheek – and perhaps there might be something in it for him one day. He was sure he was not the first man to snatch a kiss. In this he was wrong for Maud's looks were not the sort to attract callow youths. She rather frightened them.

'Your grandfather doesna approve of photographs,' he said, looking at her keenly.

'I know – but I do – and I want one. Next Hogmanay perhaps?'

'If I do will ye give me a kiss at Christmas?'

She bit her lip with vexation. Men were very persistent, she realised. 'Certainly not. But if you don't want to give me a little present I'll tell Ma when she comes back what you've just been trying to do.'

'I havena done anything bad, Maud – aye I'll give you ten shillings – but you must show me the picture.'

'If it's any good,' she replied coolly.

'I'd better go,' he said, having himself come to the realisation that there was more in this niece of his than met the eye.

'You can make a cup of tea in the kitchen,' she said – 'I have my book to finish.' And she sat down again, opened the book and bent her head to it, then thoughtfully put back the glasses.

After a moment's contemplation he went out, banging both doors behind him. He was shaken, knew he'd better be more careful in future. When he had gone Maud put the book down and stood at the window. Her neck, where his lips had lingered, seemed to burn. She was trembling. Yet she'd got the better of him and he wouldn't try it on again. The skirmish had both excited and depressed her. Were all men like Uncle Dan underneath?

That evening she was moved to take off her hat and brush her short hair which felt silky and soft.

'Oh, by the way, Uncle Dan called,' she had remarked to her mother when Maggie returned. 'But as you were not in he didna stay.'

16

It was the first time she had not told her mother the whole truth. She was growing up.

A much worse encounter was to disturb Maud Crichton two years later in the carriage of a train. She was on her way back from an interview at the university over the bridge and had been alone in a compartment until a dull looking man in his forties got in at the last station before the terminus. She stared out of the window, aware that he was staring at her. Maud was used to being stared at. But as time went on her neck felt uncomfortable from trying not to move, so she turned round to the other window. As she did so she glimpsed him out of the corner of her eye and heard a soft sound as though breath were being slowly exhaled through teeth. Her glance had caught the man's hands which were on his lap, between them peeped out the end of something like a stiff, pink sausage. He uttered no word as she fixed her gaze on the other window and the passing scenery, but began a soft moaning. What should she do? He did not seem about to touch her; he was as if alone in the compartment, was apparently oblivious of her. And what could she say to the driver if she were to pull the communication cord and stop the train? She stared fixedly out of the window, revolted, and yet curious, as the breathing became more rasping and uneven and then, suddenly, stopped. The train was just about to enter the station. She must stand up and gather her attaché case, in which were certificates and testimonials and references for the scholarship application, from the rack above. But the man was quicker than her. He stood, buttoned up his fly, turned to look at her as he began to lower the leather strap of the carriage window to open the door from the other side, the train slowing down now, and suddenly put his tongue out at her, leaning back near her face to do it. A horribly waggly, red tongue. And then the door was fully open and he had jumped out and walked off. She remained for a moment sitting motionless, the hairs crisping on her neck, and then stood up slowly, weak-kneed. For some reason or other she found she was crying, and this annoyed her. Was this what they called common assault? Was there something odd about her that such an ordinary-looking man, who had not been ill-dressed, should expose himself? But

17

she was both horrified and fascinated by that gasping pleasure he had made for himself in her presence.

Maud, unlike many young women, was acquainted with the facts of life through her reading, along with older women's talk of the 'they only want one thing' variety. But that man had not wanted to do anything to her, only to have her as a passive spectator. Yet he had hated her; that was why he had put his tongue out at her. She felt slightly sick. The incident quite drove the memory of her university interview from her head as she sat in the tram on the way home, fearing all the time the man might reappear. Then she bade herself sternly to forget it, to say nothing to anyone, but she could not forget his face and that dirty, lolling red tongue that seemed to have licked her soul. Did it often happen to other young women, this sort of thing? There was nobody she might ask, for she had no intimate women friends of her own age and it would only upset Ma.

Maud began to see the masculine sex as weak, a prey to passions it could not and scarcely wanted to control. Women must always have had to put up with this weakness, which was also men's strength, since most women appeared to want a few children. But why were there so many families with too many? Men were irresponsible and this irresponsibility might be exploited if women were going to survive their onslaught. A woman might learn to twist them round her little finger. Not wanting something for yourself you might have everything – admiration and money and power. Maud had always enjoyed admiration. If men were sometimes weak they also had strengths women did not appear to possess. Above everyone she loved her mother, and Ma had always told her ever since she was a wee girl that she was somehow special. She knew she was, but also despised her need to believe it. One part of her nature was truly ascetic and stoical. She enjoyed being praised for her academic achievements, but her greatest pleasure was to feel able to praise herself, knowing her judgment was good. There were other qualities for which she could be liked, even occasionally at school – her ready wit for one. Her looks though seemed either to lead people on or to enrage them. But she could not help the way she was made.

Like the Roman Empresses who fascinated her, she was both

18

beautiful and clever, but imagined the empresses would despise people, so easily gratified by the bestowal of a kind word, or even a kiss. They wanted her approval, these people – Ma, and even Malcolm – just as they thirsted for Preacher Gray's approval. Their needing this gave her an empire over them which she had never consciously sought.

Maud naturally kept such thoughts to herself. Even as a small child when her grandfather had been stern with her, she had eventually realised he was not all-powerful and could know nothing of her secret doubts. Angus, who might have given Maud a stronger base from which to launch herself into the world, had always approached her tentatively. Yet she had never been a child who appeared to lose her temper; tantrums had not been events in her childhood. As Maud grew up she felt there was no point in striving to please her father, for the praise of a weak man was not worth having. Maggie praised her, sometimes injudiciously, but she forgave her mother that. Even Uncle Dan, who since the scene in the parlour had kept out of her way except to smuggle that ten shilling note into her hand the following Hogmanay, was not a worthy admirer. She needed a man whom she could admire to admire her. The 'Studio Portrait' had come out quite well, but she had shown it to nobody and told Dan, when he dared to ask, that it was a failure. Sometimes when she looked at it it seemed to her that there was a quality in the expression of the eyes that she did not recognise as belonging to her. She knew she was beautiful, and could not imagine growing older and losing those looks. How terrible it would be to live on and lose them thereby becoming another person. That the old often lost their wits too did not worry her, in spite of her grandfather's advancing senility.

After that incident on the train the summer had come, though it was the usual dull and rainy one, and she had left the Academy where she had been Dux of her class for two years running. She had not preened herself over that. Work was her badge, her emblem. More than her physical self it was what she thought defined herself to the world outside. 'Maggie Crichton's clever daughter', who was set to do great things. But she was not conceited. On the other hand she despised the girls in the Academy who spent their time crimping their hair and chatting about clothes and laddies. All their efforts were directed towards catching a young man one day. If Maud took trouble over her appearance it was for her own sake. She liked to be clean and tidy and neat, but the sleek, well-groomed look she worked for was to raise her above the contrivances of other women. You did not buff your nails or wash your hair for the sake of men. If they liked the way she was, that was a separate thing.

Sometimes she was torn between her desire to do well in her academic work and her occasional need to relax at the 'flicks' or with a novel. She liked the strong plots and intrigues of the highly coloured romances of the late Victorian age, though she did not believe in their heroines' virtue. Heroines took risks that appalled Maud but fascinated her. She never quite saw herself as a heroine of this sort, nor as a young wife or someone's sweetheart, more as an 'older woman,' though it might seem absurd. What did clever women do if they did not wish to marry? – could you earn your living as a female scholar, or a sort of Mother Superior in the knowledge stakes, with loving acolytes?

She was awarded the best possible scholarship and was set to go daily across the bridge and start upon her serious classical education. She did not look forward to the actual new life with great enthusiasm except that it would give her more peaks to climb and more room to manoeuvre. She enjoyed doing work she was good at, but what she had seen of students had not enthralled her.

One afternoon she went shopping alone in the city searching for gloves. She was extremely particular about her dress and was trying to assemble a look that would mark her out as both fashionable – the way women in London magazines were fashionable – and yet different. It began to rain heavily and so she turned her steps towards the City Art Gallery. She might sit down there, for she was shy of entering a tea shop alone and was also careful with her small allowance. It was the sort of gloomy, cold day which caused many people to feel depressed, but Maud was of sterner stuff. It had begun to rain, which was a nuisance, for it would spoil her new scarf, but she put up her umbrella and was soon at the door of the civic pile. Not that she was a connoisseur of paintings, but she knew what she liked and was always eager to expand parts of her knowledge.

There was one picture which she had especially liked the first time she had visited the Gallery without quite knowing why. It was a large one on the first floor of the building: *The Return of Persephone*, it was called. She made her way to it now, having placed her umbrella in the receptacle at the foot of the stairs. There seemed nobody else around except a keeper sitting snoozing by the door of each long room.

The picture was on the wall opposite and she sat down on a bench in the middle of the room to contemplate it. There was all around her that pervasive smell of museums and galleries, a mixture of dust and polish. Now that she looked at Lord Leighton's picture again she remembered why she liked it. It had been an illustration in a book of myths her mother had given her when she was very small. On the left stood Demeter, her arms stretched out to clasp Persephone as she emerged, escorted by Iris, from the darkness on the right that was Pluto's. In the light of the upper world the figure of Demeter, was strong, mature and vigorous. Persephone looked as though she was swooning towards her mother out of the darkness into the light – her feet not touching the ground, for now, after reaching the air of the cave entrance, she seemed to be turning from a diver into a bird.

Maud liked classical subjects but this picture touched her more deeply. She liked the soft drapery round the figures of mother and daughter and the way Persephone's robe was echoed in the clouds beyond the cave opening. That the 'opening' led to Hades she was well aware. That very summer she had read her Ovid in which the story was told. Hades was also, she well knew, the name of Pluto's realm under the ground, inhabited by the ghosts of the dead. Maud shivered, as much from the cold of the vast room in which she sat as from thoughts of the tomb. She sat on, thinking about death, trying not to be morbid, and she was just about to go down and see if it had stopped raining when she heard footsteps in the corridor. A man dressed in a thick alpaca overcoat pearled with raindrops came into the room. Having stared around he made for a picture Maud had not bothered to study, a recent acquisition, something from France. Obviously

21

it was still raining, so she made the circuit of the room once more, cross that someone else had come, for she liked to be alone. She was concentrating on a picture of chrysanthemums in a vase, a rather messy picture she thought, when she became aware that the other occupant of the room was looking at her. She moved on, intending to escape whether it was raining or not, when the man said – and his voice seemed to echo through the gallery: 'Don't you like it then?' She turned in the direction of the voice, half afraid that here was another lewd lecher like the man in the train, but saw only a tall, upright figure with iron grey hair and an extremely handsome long face. The voice had been cultivated Scots but without the harsh accent of the region.

She thought, he is just being friendly, as we are the only two people here to look at the pictures. 'No – it's a mess,' she said. 'I prefer pictures that tell you something. This is not my sort of picture.'

'One day it will be worth a good deal,' he answered ruminatively, and came to stand by her side. 'Show me what you like,' he ordered.

'It's in another room.' Maud had no wish to involve herself in explaining why she liked the classical picture and made as if to go, when he added, looking at her in the same way he had been looking at the picture: 'Has anyone yet painted *you*?'

'Of course not,' she answered sharply, but her vanity was intrigued.

Hector Heron had in fact remarked her face as he had made the circuit of the room, and been astonished. She did not look as though she came from the city, and her carriage as she had stood before each picture, quite unaware of his glance, had impressed him. So upright. So erect. He was disappointed that her taste was not as well formed as her figure. 'Hector Heron,' he said, and bowed.

For some reason she decided to invent another Christian name for herself on the spur of the moment. 'Isolde Crichton,' she said.

'Isolde? That *is* an unusual name.'

'It is only one of my names,' she found herself explaining. 'I am called something else by most people.'

He smiled. He looked rather distinguished, she thought, and

wondered where she had heard his name, for she was sure she had heard it somewhere. Hector, she thought – leader of the Trojan forces during the siege. A noble name for a noble man.

'You look sad,' said this Hector.

'I was thinking of your namesake,' she said.

They should have called her Helen, he felt confusedly. It was not like him to feel confused, nor to talk to young women in galleries or museums.

'Names are strange,' he said. 'There have always been Hectors in Scotland. Isolde now – that is the first time I have heard it used up here.'

Maud felt ashamed. She must confess it was not really her name. As the man looked kind and interested – and rich – she decided he might be trusted with her real name. 'I just call myself that occasionally,' she said. 'My real name is Maud.' Now it was out.

He stared and said: 'Isolde is better, I agree – but Helen, that is a good Scots name and one that would suit you.'

For some reason she felt reassured rather than put on her guard by this remark and now she remembered where she had heard his name. He must be the famous Sir Hector Heron, the jute manufacturer. Well, well . . .

For his part Sir Hector was feeling suddenly rash. He looked at his watch. 'Why don't you come for a cup of tea at Hood's Rooms with me – and you can explain why you would like to be called Isolde.'

Maud hesitated. But what harm could come to her in the tea-rooms? He could hardly slip chloroform in her cup. It was about time she learned to look after herself. And he had said some rather interesting things to her. This might be her Great Opportunity. 'Thank you,' she said, lying politely – 'I was going there in any case.'

They went out of the building together, Maud looking straight ahead and Hector Heron occasionally stealing a sidelong glance at the finest profile he, a connoisseur of the arts and of all beautiful things, thought he had ever seen in his life.

He saw, as they drank their tea and Maud pretended to eat a

23

little piece of cake, that she was a poor girl, or at least one without pretensions to anything but brains and beauty.

'My grandfather is a minister,' she told him. 'And I want to be a scholar.' She answered his questions unaffectedly but candidly, he thought. He could have gone on listening to her for ever or at least using the listening as a pretext for studying the planes of her face, the high hollow of her cheekbones and the mobile softly modelled upper lip.

'You must refine your taste,' he said when he had drunk his tea. 'I have a house in Fife where I collect pictures – other things too – porcelain and furniture – you must visit me there and learn how to look at these things and compare them.'

What nonsense he was talking. She was probably perfectly happy to continue with the tastes she had been brought up with, did not need a middle-aged aesthete to teach her anything. She gave the appearance of a very self-contained girl. Maud said coolly: 'Thank you. I should like to do that. There are not many fine things around here – only dirt and dull people.'

So she was ambitious. Not surprising. He wondered if her academic ambitions were the result of a genuine interest in scholarship. He might make enquiries about her. Yet he felt somehow reluctant to appear a busybody. The girl was a bonus, he thought, a pleasant surprise for a rainy day, and he must not interfere in her life. He was stirred and a little disappointed when she half rose and said she must go, they were expecting her at home, and, she added: 'I have to buy a pair of gloves.'

'You like shopping?' he asked, for something to say, since he wanted to detain her a little longer.

Maud wanted to explain that the things she coveted were beyond her means, but stopped herself. Instead she said: 'I know what I like – I have seen some grey gloves which would go well with my new outfit. I have had to buy clothes for October, you see.' It seemed quite natural to tell him this.

'You must allow me to give you the address of my place in the country and I shall leave it to you to let me know when you might pay a visit there,' he said. 'It is not too far from your place of study – I'd like to show you around.'

He gave her his card on which she saw inscribed – Hector Heron – Garvits, Fife – and a telephone number. 'I have no cards,' said Maud. 'But the name is Crichton and you know where I shall be.'

With that he got up too and helped her into her coat which she had hung carefully on a peg provided on the large coat-stand that was in the shape of antlers. The few other tea drinkers did not look at them with any especial interest, a girl obviously being given a treat by an uncle or guardian.

He went out with Maud and doffed his hat as she turned to go in the direction of one of the two department stores the city could boast of. Would she contact him? Maybe some uncharitable folk might think he'd picked up the lassie, but he did not see it like that. It would be a pleasure to be able to contemplate such a face whilst showing off his place. There was nothing in it; he was not an ogre or a skirt-chaser – had never had a 'reputation' as ladies' man, though he had been painfully in love once or twice in his life. For her part Maud felt she had a secret, and Maud loved secrets.

Chapter Two

She had other things to think about in those few weeks that separated her schoolgirl existence from her new life as a student. In any case, she would not have acted quickly; it was not her nature to do that. She thought now and again of Sir Hector, looked him up in the Business Guide and let matters rest. Her mother was not told of the meeting, nor anyone else who might have been interested.

Maggie was soon to suffer a loss that usurped the place in her head occupied by Maud's future, or indeed any other concerns at all, for her father, Preacher Gray, had a sudden stroke. Her stepmother begged Maggie to come and help with the nursing and the running of the house, for he was expected to recover, and the visitors were numerous who came with hushed voices to extol their spiritual guide and mentor. Maud had to stay to 'look after' her father and brothers though Maggie came back each day to cook them an evening meal. The arrangement did not suit Maud at all. Why could not one of the daughters-in-law hold the fort for Jessie Gray? Still, she attempted to peel a few potatoes and to shop for the provisions that Maggie instructed her to buy, but it was a tedious business. She dusted desultorily also, but refused to wash clothes. 'Why not send them to a laundry, Ma?' she asked. Maggie could quite see that Maud was not up to many basic tasks and did not really want her to be, so she managed to run between the two houses and fulfil all her obligations, praying that the old man would either recover completely or be taken to his forefathers and not linger on as a semblance of himself.

Her prayers were granted, for one evening in early September Preacher Gray had another stroke from which he did not recover. Soon the whole family were on the way to say farewell to their dead patriarch, the good brothers and the prodigal ones, though one set did not speak to the other. Maud stood in his bedroom the night before the funeral with her mother and the second Mrs Preacher Gray. Maggie's elder sister Helen had been telegraphed but could not make the journey from Canada so only the local family was there to see him laid to rest.

She put her arms round her mother that evening and tried to feel sad, whilst remembering many salty phrases uttered by her grandfather. She could still not quite realise that he was dead through he looked dead enough in the coffin which stood on a long trestle in the room, waiting to be taken to the funeral on the morrow. A woman had brought lilies but Ma had said they were unsuitable and they had been banished to the parlour. Maggie was crying, perhaps from relief as well as sorrow. One by one the other members of the family came in to pay their respects. Jessie Gray was now completely collapsed. She had been under the thumb of her second husband for as long as Maud could remember and been treated more like a housekeeper than a wife, so that at first she simply did not know what to do with herself. Twenty years her grandfather had had this second wife who had never seemed like a grandmother to her, and the woman seemed nothing now her man was gone. He was a handsome man, Maud thought, even in death. They had shut his eyes and folded his hands under the shroud and there was a bandage under his chin. He looked peaceful.

The service the next day was attended by all the family and their children and in-laws, even Uncle Hamish, who cried copiously – hypocritically, Maud thought – but he might have imbibed too much whisky beforehand. Uncle Dan eyed her from his place at the side of the plain rows of benches and Maud thought she could afford to acknowledge him, but did it rather frostily.

She barely acknowledged the aunts and cousins who crowded round the table, though they all looked at her curiously, for she knew she had nothing to say to them and she always abjured small talk when possible. When they passed on to her after greeting her mother and step-grandmother, she bore the 'A fine man he was . . . aye Maud, ye've lost a fine grandpa,' with a slight bow of the head and a scarcely audible 'Thank

27

you'. Uncle Hamish had disappeared, quite likely he had gone to seek solace for his sorrows in another dram or two and she had no wish to say anything to Uncle Dan. She stayed by her mother until Maggie said: 'Ye can go home with the boys now, Maud – we've to clear up after all this lot.' She did not offer to help; they would all love a good crack together when the younger members of the family had gone. Grandfather's wife was now seated at the table dispensing further cups of tea, looking pale but dry-eyed. Still, Maud supposed he *had* been a fine man and had influenced her more than she had realised.

But the death of her grandfather marked a turning point in her life, the first time she had seen death, and the first time she had felt with her body as apart from known with her mind that neither would she live for ever.

The already familiar journey over the Tay Bridge was to become an integral part of life for Maud during the first three years of her university studies. She had been given the bursary to help with her living expenses and books but she had no desire to join a crowd of giggling Bejants and Bejantines. Ma's cooking and cherishing were what she was used to and it would save money to live at home. Also she would be freer in an existence divided between home and college than penned down in the confines of a women's hall of residence. She could come and go from home to university as she wanted, and if a time came when she wanted to be free of domestic or college surveillance she would be able to juggle between the two.

Looking round the lecture hall where she sat during her first few days after all the tedious business of registering and being introduced to other new students, Maud thought her fellows a motley crew. These boys and girls – she had better learn to call them men and women, she supposed – looked either callow or uninteresting. The girls for the most part wore their hair bobbed, and were just like the girls she had grown up with at school. She bent her head to her thick new manuscript book, resolving to say as little as possible to anyone except in the course of duty. She hated being in a crowd, hated not knowing her way around. But she was here to learn and learn she must and would.

Lectures were a waste of time when you could find the same

things in books. Unless they were outstandingly good, which had so far not been the case. From time to time she had found herself woolgathering, which would never do. Time for that at home or at the 'flicks' where she went to relax sometimes on Saturdays if they had a good film and no 'Buffalo Bill.' They were an interlude in a hard-working life and she seemed to need more of this sort of escape since the Preacher's death and in spite of her new found dignity as a university student.

She noticed some of the students had posh voices, and there were a few English ones too. Yet it was on the whole not such a change from the Academy as she had imagined. She could remain as self-contained as she wished; nobody could actually force her to join the revels that accompanied the many traditions of the place. There were busily thriving hives of activity around various "clubs", and little knots of friends frequented certain café or sat together at lectures, but she did not feel excluded. She spent most of her free time in the Library and thought the Preacher would have been proud of her; but she realised that others might find her attitude aloof. They would put it down to shyness.

She found the jokes of most students almost incomprehensible. She would return home at the end of the afternoon or early evening with a profound sense of relief, for she savoured her solitude, and at home they made allowances for her work. 'Crossing over' from college to home was like entering another country, although as time went on she was to feel she really belonged to neither. The great grey estuary and the sea beyond would claim her and she enjoyed the mournful sound of the foghorn on days when the Haar was blowing. The sea and the fog were not ugly, as so many things seemed to be. But the sands of the university town stretched for miles and she would sometimes wonder what it might feel like to walk away on them and never look back, and where she would arrive if she did.

She liked travelling, liked the train, and did not mind the journey or the walk at each end. Yet she suffered from chilblains, and the tip of her nose would grow pink from the cold winds that blew round the place. She was not the only young person to suffer in such a way. The large Hall of Residence for the women students that had been built about sixty years before was notoriously chilly, and fires were allowed only in the Common Room so that often the girls said they froze in their blankets. It was amazing that the Ancient Romans had bothered to conquer Scotland, said a wag. There were scarcely more than ninety students in each year and they were divided up into faculties only in their second year. Most were reading Classics, History, Modern Languages or English, though a few girls did read medicine and the sciences. But the first year students reading Arts subjects were herded together for a general year of culture, and to sort out the sheep from the goats, the Ordinary from the Honours. Maud had no worries about belonging eventually to the latter since she found few who shared her love of learning for its own sake. In this it was just like school. The male students indulged themselves in many varieties of sport and the women played Lacrosse, the richer ones intending also to take up golf. Maud thanked heaven that sport was not compulsory. She shared the Preacher's opinion of the players of ball games: that they were mad. 'Twenty-two folk chasing a wee ball up and doon a field – I canna imagine why they do it, for if they want air in their lungs they'd be better off taking a guid long walk.' As time passed Maud found that his words on this and many other topics kept echoing in her head. A girl named Jacqueline Livesey occasionally teased her about her intransigence. Maud did not like being teased but she put up with it from Jackie since Jackie was kind – and talkative – but not expecting answers, which would have been beyond Maud in some of her moods.

Miss Livesey came from a rich suburb in the city where the likes of Sir Hector lived, but she put on no airs and Maud discovered that she lived with relatives, was not herself wealthy. Maud did not know that part of the city at all, though she knew most of it fairly well with its shipyards and its smells from the jam factories and jute processing mills. The other great industry, the newspaper and magazine empire, was where Jacqueline hoped to penetrate, wanting, she confessed, to write stories less moralistic and less sickly than the ones that flooded the market. Yet she said she herself had not got used to the place yet – 'People look so ill here, you know,' she said to Maud, surprising her. Jackie had been sent to live in the city only two years before when her father's London business failed and he had taken her mother and younger sister to seek his fortune in Canada. Jackie had refused to accompany them, which Maud thought very brave. 'I belong to Europe,' said Jackie grandly. To her mother's family she had gone, to a grandmother and cousins who drew money both from the shipyard and the whaling industry. There was money on loan from them which Jackie fully intended to pay back through her own efforts. The family did not interfere with her, big braw cousins who had their own interests, which were not hers. But they were tolerant and kindly, although at first she had felt so home-sick that she had nearly packed up and gone to join her parents and sister in Toronto. Some stubbornness had made her stay, and now she was glad she had. She had begun to enjoy solitary walks when the sea mists came up and the warning on the lightship moored in the Firth moaned all day.

'It isna a "romantic" place,' said Maud.

'No – but it's somewhere I can start afresh and prove myself,' replied Jackie. 'I'd never have met Calum if I hadn't come here,' she added. Maud had heard a lot about Calum, a medical student idolised by her friend.

When Jackie started at the university she had immediately singled out Maud as 'interesting'. The first thing she had noticed, even before she had registered the perfectly shaped features, was her posture: a straight little back and flat stomach, and the carriage, of a pocket Venus.

The face had arched eyebrows over heavy-lidded brown eyes and a softly sculptured upper lip. The symmetry of her features was accentuated by the way Maud dressed her dark brown hair, drawn back behind her ears and then the thick braids looped round in the fashion known as ear-phones. Even the girls who had held out longest were having their hair bobbed now, but not Maud.

Jackie herself was undeniably pretty, with deep-set dark blue eyes, a short nose, a full and generous mouth and thick gold-brown hair which she wore in a fringe. She knew vaguely that she was passable to look at but felt Maud's looks were something quite other. She also on closer acquaintance sensed an aloofness, an air of *noli me tangere*, a remoteness which the

31

expression in Maud's eyes scarcely contradicted. There was a blankness in Maud's glance. Jackie thought what a pity it was that Maud was short-sighted and had to wear spectacles for everything but close work. Yet the spectacles took away only a little from the general effect since Maud took no half measures and they were black horn-rims, unusual for a girl to wear. Spectacles or no, Jackie could see she was an exceptionally beautiful girl. She found it odd that this word was not used of Maud by other girls, even her own friends. 'Oh, *Maud!*' they would say, as if that said it all; that she was different, a 'swot'; hard to get to know; gave nothing away. Jackie, who was observant, noticed that male students remarked above all the 'good figure' even when they had looked at her face. If they lingered on the latter they seemed both puzzled and intrigued, and then a little over-awed. Jackie saw that this annoyed them. Who was Maud Crichton to give them this feeling? A nobody, a day-girl, at the place on account of a special scholarship, not a pally, chummy sort of girl, probably cold-hearted.

Those, including Jackie, who sat with Maud in Professor Carmichael's Greek class were awed not by her looks but by her mastery of the language. She had a gift – that they could not deny – but it was allied to intense application. When she refused to take part in their social activities they were content to call her standoffish. Jackie heard them say so. They would have left it at that, she thought, but their glance would then return to her perfect bosom whose outline was visible even under the red gown and white shirt and black tie. A 'brainy' girl should not possess such a feature!

Maud continued not to take much notice of her fellows, though towards one or two she unbent sufficiently to lend a sharpened pencil or a ruler when they were in need. Nobody could guess what she was thinking in that small sculptured head so that it was quite a surprise to hear her voice in class. Though pitched low it sounded robust. Jackie was the only student with whom Maud conversed at length and this may have been because Jackie could have made an inanimate object listen to her and because she was not embarrassed by silences or diffidence.

She also found something mysteriously compelling about

Maud. If any of them were to be famous, she opined it would be Maud. Jackie had a romantic temperament, often invented mysterious lives and longings for people and was in every way Maud's opposite, though she imagined a mental sympathy between them. She would not take no for an answer from Maud, though she was never rude, and careful not to appear too curious. She was warm-hearted, interested in what made people tick without being a gossip, and she envied Maud most of all her nose which was unlike her own Plebeian proboscis.

Such a 'modern' young woman as Jackie Livesey might have been expected to irritate Maud, yet the latter appeared to find the other girl to her liking and perhaps envied the ease with which Jackie confronted the world.

'You have the grammar and syntax and I have the adjectives,' Jackie said to her. Maud knew that she was subtly underselling herself, for Jackie had ideas as well as adjectives and was clearly on the way to be more suited to composition in English than translation from Cicero. Miss Livesey was also an open rebel in this Puritanical society whilst Maud was a covert one, as usual keeping her thoughts to herself. Even Jackie did not know what these were, but Maud was not shockable, and this excited Jackie rather. She had noticed, right from the beginning of their acquaintance – Jackie did not believe one might yet call it friendship – that Miss Crichton, though excessively critical of others, was also critical about her own efforts, quite humble. Jackie admired Maud's analytic powers, and her industry, and foresaw that brilliant academic future for her which her own parents had wished for herself. But Jackie dreamt only of writing stories, or journalism of a literary sort, and was studying for an Arts degree to fill out some of the gaps in her own knowledge of which she was strongly aware. After the degree, and if she had not by then written a publishable story or two, well, there were plenty of newspapers in that city across the Firth, though no woman had as yet distinguished herself writing for them. She told Maud this and Maud looked quite encouraging.

One autumn morning Maud was walking along the causey from the station holding her new black attaché case stiffly with one hand and trying to stop her round-brimmed hat from being

33

blown across the road and the grass verge to the seashore below. A messenger boy was slouching along behind her whistling something rude, but she had not heard him, was too intent upon reaching her class in time. Occasionally a knot of male students would saunter by on the other side of the street, but nobody greeted her.

That morning she was to be lucky. She hated to be late, especially as it was not her fault that the train was often delayed in its high journey across the bridge. She followed one or two late-rising women students into the door at the back of the lecture amphitheatre and then went up two flights of stone steps to the 'circle' where she sat down upon an empty bench. She liked to sit alone on the highest rung of seats where she could have space for her case and her hat. It was cold, so she never took off her coat if she could help it, for then she would have to don the hated scarlet gown which was at present hanging on Jackie's peg at the women's residence. She knew that bright scarlet did not suit her and loathed the colour in any case. It gave her a sick headache and brought back memories of her grandfather's diatribes against the Scarlet Woman. Yet she could not entirely avoid it since students were supposed to wear their gowns when moving around the town and at lectures and classes. She would not have gone against regulations so completely as not to wear it when absolutely necessary, for she had been raised with an almost excessively meek attitude to authority, but nobody ever seemed to notice her in her coat at the back.

Once he got into his stride Professor Carmichael reminded her of Preacher Gray, though the latter would scarcely have dared to embark upon the subjects the classically trained academic did with wry authority. Did the other students understand what he was talking about? Maud did not think so. They took down all he said, but looked unenlightened, whereas she guessed what lay behind some of his allusions. Maud's passion was Ancient History and as she took down his swift chronology she allowed herself to muse over the true nature of those emperors and empresses who popped in and out of his lectures. Some women seemed to have wielded power even in those days – empresses anyway, and perhaps the lovers of

34

poets – but only for short periods of time amidst confused relations with fathers, brothers, husbands, sons. Yet they had been intelligent enough all those centuries ago to grasp it when the opportunity offered. Women did not seem to try that on nowadays. Men directed everything, except in the home, and women had to accommodate themselves to them. Maud did not consider herself a Feminist, and all that nonsense about the Vote left her cold. But what was the use of intelligence without riches? She did not expect ever to be rich (though she was extremely careful with the money she had) but she knew that she had plenty of intelligence and could not help thinking she might like to taste a little dominion one day. She pushed her thoughts away from Sir Hector – she had seen that he was attracted to her, seen it through his courtesy and kindness, but she had not yet decided what to do about it.

Most women wanted to be loved, she thought, as the next lecturer droned on about courtly romances in the Middle Ages. Or they wanted to love men. More fools they, for what was that 'love' they were always talking about but the simple workings of power – men's over women, if the women were not too bright, or even simpler, natural lust? Yet there had been women who had remained mysteries for men, women who had been worshipped or even listened to, sometimes respected, in more exciting times.

At eleven o'clock she listened to the last lecture of the morning given by an extremely fair young man with an English accent. But she was still thinking of those empresses. When all the students streamed out of the hall she recollected there would be a Latin prose to finish that evening when she had written up her notes. She always went through her notes religiously the day she had taken them down, but she loved doing Latin proses. There was something about manipulating this language that excited her, following the rules yet occasionally breaking them.

Later that morning she felt rather faint so went into a small tea-shop not much frequented by students. There Jackie Livesey found her, sipping tea, her hands round the plain white cup to warm herself, for she was always cold, as Jackie had noticed.

'Aren't you going to eat anything?' asked Jackie sitting down beside her and wondering if a cheese sandwich would see her through to the High Tea they were given at six o'clock. Jackie, who was perpetually hungry, thought that Maud never seemed to have any appetite. Yet Maud was not thin. It must be that her mother gave her a good supper in the evening after her tedious journey back home.

'No, thank you,' replied Maud. 'I was just thirsty – and cold.' She watched Jackie order her sandwich, her eyes looking over the rim of her cup, and then she put it down and pulled on her new gloves, ready to leave. There was no time to waste, so much to do. Then she realised that Jackie might think her rude to depart so soon after her own arrival and so put her hands in her lap.

'I'm going to get warm on the beach,' said Jackie. 'I feel like a bit of fresh air – a walk will do me good. Want to come?' Maud looked amazed that anyone should choose to walk on the beach when it was so cold, and she knew her friend would, as usual, be behindhand with her own work.

'No – I have to get back to the Library,' she said. Jackie smiled. 'Don't wait for me then – get back to your books. I intend to read myself for a few moments – a modern novel. I wish we could study what's being written nowadays instead of all that dry-as-dust stuff.' Maud smiled but said nothing.

Maud sat on in the Library, but this time thoughts of Sir Hector kept obtruding. She was in her usual chair and had a large Latin dictionary on the table before her. Meeting a man like Hector had disturbed her as well as exciting her a little. What destiny might be waiting for her if she went to visit him? The only time she could get away unobserved was at the week-end; she could always announce extra Saturday classes, she supposed. He might send his chauffeur for her, as his estate was some twenty miles away in the country. Perhaps there was a station in the village near his house? She made a mental note to study a map. Why was she thinking in these terms? Surely Ma would not mind if she accepted the invitation to see his house? But of course she would. His wife might not be there . . .

She wanted to start living an independent life of her own and switched her thoughts to Jackie Livesey who talked a lot about independence, but still more about her friend Calum Fyffe who was studying medicine and was in his fourth year. Jackie had told her how she had met him and got to know him in the city before she realised he was a student at the university she was to attend herself. He had been a vague acquaintance of one of her cousins, not a close friend, and came himself from Edinburgh, whither he intended to return. They got on well, though there was as yet nothing you could call romantic about their relationship. Jackie had always got on well with boys, liked to argue with them, and Calum, with his practical hands, long silences, and occasional flights of wild humour suited her well. She was sure he was going to make an excellent doctor and he was also the only person she knew who declared himself an atheist. Jackie didn't exactly call herself that, but said she disliked most of the manifestations of Christianity she had been brought up with. Jackie also thought she was a Socialist, but was not quite sure. She was a believer in 'Free Love' *and* Romance, hoping the two would eventually be found together. Though she had her introspective crises she was always ready to fall in love, aware too that young men did not give the name 'love' to the sort of feelings they had for young women. But Jackie imagined several years of intense love affairs, though she knew she might give her heart away in them. She told Maud all this too.

'Men look so stupid,' Maud had said – 'All pop-eyed and bloated-faced and breathing heavily when they are "in love".'

Jackie was rather horrified. Such experiences were not her own. Poor Maud. Perhaps someone had tried to seduce her?

Maud observed Jackie, so open in all her dealings and conversation, and rather marvelled at her. She talked so much about Calum that Maud assumed she must be 'in love' with him even if she did not realise it herself. Maud did not actually invite Jackie's confidences, but made an effort to listen if listening were required.

'You must meet him,' said the ingenuous Jackie. 'I'm sure you'd like him.'

Maud had told Jackie nothing about her own meeting with Sir Hector; maybe she would if it were ever necessary, if, for example, she needed an alibi. She was amusedly shocked at herself weaving alibis out of an invitation to sample the splendours of Garvits. Privately she called the man she had met in the gallery 'The Master of Troy'. She had always liked to invest people with nicknames but had so far not found one for Jackie Livesey.

She and Jackie saw each other almost daily in the tea-shop; their meetings were not arranged, for Maud would have scorned to arrange them. Jackie knew where she would be between lectures, that was all, if she wanted to talk. She was puzzled why Jackie should want to talk to her rather than the hosts of other young women she seemed to know already, but there it was, and she supposed she ought to have a sort of friend for herself. Occasionally she would wonder how Jackie saw *her* – it was a disturbing thought, that others might see you quite differently from the way you saw yourself, for it meant you abdicated control.

One November Saturday afternoon, after many weeks' indecision, Maud decided to write to Sir Hector. It was over three months since their meeting and she had heard nothing from him, until the day before there had arrived a postcard inside an envelope addressed to her at the University. It was a reproduction of an Allen Ramsay portrait and bore only the message: 'I have even better paintings than this at Garvits. Yours sincerely: H.H.'

She thought she might like to visit Garvits, about which she had now made detailed enquiries. She would have to go on a Saturday and return in the evening and would have to prepare the family by inventing an extra Saturday afternoon lecture. She wrote Heron a simple reply naming a Saturday in the near future. His answer came rapidly, addressed to her once more at the university. He would send his chauffeur in the Rolls to pick her up from the railway station in the university town; she would know him by the brown uniform and black cap. Very tactful, she thought, but why couldn't he come himself? Should she tell Jackie about it? There did not seem any real need; she was not going to be kidnapped. Sir Hector was a respectable man, a pillar of business and Scots society, and there was nothing remotely scandalous about their meeting again. The trouble was that she had never been a person who liked to instigate things. Whatever came of the meeting – and nothing at all might come of it – she would leave any further running to the man himself. Maud thought Sir Hector might be a solid future admirer whatever he was at this present moment, and as she had done absolutely nothing to make him want to see her again, felt innocent. Even if he had stared at her in a manner she could not quite admit to understanding.

The Rolls was already drawn up by the station entrance that Saturday afternoon and the man doffed his cap when she approached it. She wondered what description Sir Hector had given his servant so that he might recognise her – a "wee lassie" probably, except that he didn't talk that way. She got into the car, sat on the back seat and was wafted away. They passed a small village some miles further on before turning on to a narrower road. All around were fields and bare trees and the sky was pewter grey. She began to enjoy the ride though she never relaxed her upright position, one hand holding the hand rail at the side. There were small hills in the distance now, until the car turned again and advanced along a winding road. Then a large pillared gateway appeared and the driver slowed down a little and began a slight ascent. The drive was lined with conifers and she imagined a sort of Sleeping Beauty castle at the end of it, but there was only a granite lodge before the Rolls turned again and went up a broader road now and she saw Garvits appear sideways on. There was a gravelled courtyard and a terrace and a large door with iron hasps. The Rolls stopped and she saw the house door open and Sir Hector come out from it and wait for her to descend. No butler then, or whoever opened doors in books. She got out of the car, the chauffeur touched his cap again and then got back into the car, turned it round and drove off. She stood still for a moment, taking a deep breath, then walked towards him.

'Welcome to Garvits,' said Sir Hector Heron and stood back for her to enter his domain.

Grey, exquisite Garvits lay in the foothills in rolling green country only a few miles from the sea, a house rebuilt for a modern man of taste who had proved himself in the city and wanted to have examples round him of the things that money earned through three generations had acquired, and all in a building suitable for his own use and eventual retirement.

No harm had been done by making Sir Hector wait for her visit, thought Maud, but she was a little nervous even so.

He took her coat and then said: 'Let me show you the view from here – I think you will agree it's a splendid one,' and Maud followed him to the large window that gave out on to a terrace and then led the eye to landscaped lawns falling down smoothly to a flight of steps and a band of trees. But beyond the trees there were the hills and through the hills a tiny gap where might be seen the sea, distant and pale. 'We can have a look round the gardens later,' he said. 'If you are not too cold.'

He explained they would bring them tea at five o'clock; evidently discreet servants were around. Then he led her up a flight of stairs to a long gallery which ran the whole breadth of the house. Everywhere there were tables and chairs of the sort you saw only in museums or illustrated books on castles or palaces, yet the general effect was not one of ostentation. Pictures everywhere too, not just in the gallery where seemed to be his favourites. Yet she was determined not to appear too easily impressed.

'Look at this lady,' he said, stopping before a small painting that was hung at the side of a window alcove. Maud obligingly stared at the picture of an eighteenth-century woman dressed in yellow and wearing a high riding hat, and Hector Heron stared at Maud as she did.

'Does she remind you of anyone?' he asked.

'I don't think so.'

He cleared his throat. 'I thought when I saw you in the city gallery that you reminded me of someone, but I could not think who. Then when I got home I remembered. Now I can see you and the picture side by side – '

'But she has curly hair,' said Maud.

'The eyes and nose and cheekbones are yours,' he said as though she was just another picture.

She turned to look at it again, and he thought, the mouth too, but I mustn't say that.

'Mistress Susanna Urquhart,' she read off the title fixed to the bottom of the gilt frame.

'Aye – a beautiful woman,' he said shortly.

Maud thought, he collects beautiful paintings; does he also collect beautiful women?

'It's very fine,' she said. 'But I dinna see myself in it.'

He moved away. 'I'll show you some ornaments later. I don't like to have people watching *me* when I'm looking at pictures, so I'll leave you to it – just come down when you've had your fill.'

He was very polite and she felt he was treating her as an equal. But there was an inequality between them, existing not only because he was rich and she was poor and he was older. What was it? Perhaps that she had no taste? Or that he thought she had not. There was certainly little sense of equality between the men and women she knew. In Maud's opinion women who wanted to be 'equal' did so because they were not attractive to the opposite sex. And she was, and she was certain that Sir Hector found her so. She tried to concentrate on the pictures – bowls of fruit, landscapes, one or two cottage interiors, but was more interested in what he had said, so went back to the painting of Mistress Susanna. The woman in the picture was handsome but there was a look in her eyes which Maud had never seen in her own. Why did Sir Hector think the lady looked like her? – what did he see in her face? She felt a little at a loss. She would rather look at ornaments than pictures, for she did not quite know what to look for in pictures like these. Were they famous beyond Garvits? She wanted to know about possessions and ways of life not found in Ferry Lane, or even at the university, since such knowledge could always come in handy, but she did not want to change, or be changed. Had he invited her to Garvits just to improve her taste? Of course he hadn't.

When she went down to find him he said he would show her round the rest of the house. She looked thoughtful but was at first silent.

Hector too was feeling a little nervous. What was she thinking as she exclaimed politely over his Chinese clock and his seventeenth-century English oak furniture, and said the Chinese porcelain dishes were 'verra fine'? He suspected she did not know why those objects were there, arranged carefully in each room to show off their qualities or juxtaposed as contrasts. In his library she did stoop to read the titles of his fine collection of first editions, and appeared genuinely impressed. But his dining-room made her catch her breath.

'You eat here every day?' she asked in some wonderment.

He explained that he did not spend all his time at Garvits, only at the weekend and during holidays and that he had a flat in Edinburgh. 'We used to entertain,' he said, 'but since my wife became an invalid and had to go abroad for her health, I rarely do.'

Maud looked as though this explained quite a lot.

Was his wife still alive then? She dared not ask.

'There is so much here,' she said, gesturing at the silver-laden sideboards – 'I don't know much about silver and *objets d'art* – could I learn, do you think?'

'Anyone can learn,' he said, 'if they are interested – but it took me years to know what I wanted to collect.'

Years and money, she thought.

The dining-room was not a place she could feel at ease in. Yet she was impressed.

Hector was meanwhile searching wildly for an excuse to see her again. When she stood by his side he felt a shiver of delight mixed with a faint feeling of desire that had been a stranger for him for some time. Indeed he had hardly registered it as desire when he had first met her, so mixed had it been with the pleasure he took in just looking at her face. Now he had an aching need to pass his fingers over her cheek, lift her hair from her brow, stroke her hands. This was folly. He must calm down, never see her again – or contrive a different approach.

'I'm a dull dog – I don't really enjoy entertaining large numbers of people,' he said. She looked at him sceptically but understood. 'You haven't seen all my treasures yet,' he went on. 'You could come every other Saturday if you wanted to see more.'

'It would take a long time to appreciate it all,' she replied demurely. 'I didn't know that some people had so many possessions.'

'You haven't told me much about college – have you made new friends?' he asked as they moved into the drawing-room.

'Only one friend,' said Maud.

'You might bring her here with you one day,' he offered nobly – 'If it is a she?'

'Oh, yes, I don't have "boy friends",' said Maud looking as though butter wouldn't melt in her mouth.

'You surprise me,' he said, and smiled. At last the ice was broken. There was a softly glowing fire in the beautiful drawing-room and a small table set up before it piled high with plates of scones and oat-cakes.

'My cook makes them for me – you must eat your fill,' he commanded. Maud was not really hungry, nerves had undermined her appetite, but obediently she ate a scone and it was delicious. Surprisingly Hector himself poured the tea. It was scented yet strong, taken without milk. Maud, who did not like milk, liked the tea. She must leave soon if she were to catch the train which he said went across the estuary from the local station. The chauffeur would take her there. But she was now reluctant to go. She must pluck up her courage and ask him a question.

'Why did you say that the woman in the portrait looked like me?' she finally got out as he was pouring another cup of tea for himself. She looked into the fire as she said it and he saw her profile from a new angle.

'Because nobody knows what she is thinking,' he answered gravely.

'She is mysterious?'

'Aye.'

So he thought her mysterious too. I am not mysterious, she brooded, – am I? Not to myself. I know what I am thinking, but he does not, so that excites him. Should I cultivate this 'mystery'? Yet something unaccustomed, something she knew she had in her but had never brought to the surface moved in Maud. She was looking at a man who sensed the mysteries of others when he thought them worth knowing. And he was a mystery to her in a way that no one yet had been. For the first time she thought, we are all mysteries to each other. There was nothing she had to do about it; for him she had only to be herself. If I were not good-looking he would not feel I was interesting or mysterious, she thought. I did not make my own features. They came together – one chance in a hundred thousand, I suppose. As they both now stared into the fire Hector was thinking along the same lines: a fairy waved her wand at her conception and fused the elements into something new, something perfect. How beautiful her lips are – do they contradict her nature? For he was aware that Maud was not a "sensitive".

'Your looks, like Mistress Susanna Urquhart's, will even improve with age,' he said softly.

Like wine, thought Maud.

'Many girls have something when they are young – and it may continue if they know what to make of themselves and do not have too hard lives – the bloom of youth, they call it. But you – ' he turned his face to hers as she sat, hands in lap, listening to him with a slight wariness, those age-old eyes looking at him.

'You have classical looks, Maud. You don't smile much – You could be a statue in my garden – flowing robes would suit you. Classical features are not found very often – a sculptor might – ' He paused, must tread carefully. 'They improve with age, looks like yours,' he said again.

'I don't want to grow old,' said Maud as if in a trance.

'No – not old – I meant mature – your thirties, forties even – '

'I wish I were older now,' said Maud. 'I've never felt young.'

'Oh, don't wish that! – you are perfect as you are – I didn't mean to say all this,' he said distractedly.

'Have another cup of tea,' he went on in an ordinary voice. 'And come again in a fortnight. You haven't seen all my treasures yet.'

He had such an expression in his eyes, one she had not seen before, not in Uncle Dan or in anyone. She had wanted to be admired and he did admire her. But she wanted to be sure of his feelings before she let herself in for anything more. I am extremely young, she thought, though I don't feel young. To him I must appear a baby. But I have the advantage now and he is a very fine feather in my cap. Do men fall in love with women they hardly know?'

'I'd like to get to know you better,' he said as if echoing her thoughts. 'Of course you are busy, and so am I – but I'd like

44

you to come again – you haven't even seen the gardens yet.' He wants me to make it seem all above board, she thought, though it is not, and I don't mind. Maud stood up – 'I must not miss my train,' she said.

'No – of course not. Archie will take you to the station.' He got up himself and when she followed him into the spacious entrance hall, her coat was handed to her by a servant who appeared from the corridor at the back where they had not penetrated.

'Thank you,' she said as she pulled on her gloves. 'I've enjoyed looking at everything – you have been very kind.'

There was nothing more he dared say, since the chauffeur was ready with the car. He helped her on with her thick, brown coat and handed her her bucket-shaped hat. 'Goodbye then, Maud,' he said when the servant had gone away. 'Come in a fortnight.' With a sudden abrupt gesture he took her gloved hand and kissed it on the underside of her wrist.

She nursed it all the way to the station and sat in the train still feeling the touch of his lips on the small piece of skin between the pearl buttons and this time had to admit it was a not disagreeable sensation.

Chapter Three

Jackie had gone home on a weekend exeat and was sitting with Calum Fyffe in her grandmother's drawing-room. Calum was doing some of his practical hospital work but was free for an evening. They had been listening to records on the new phonograph. Not many were to Calum's taste. He was tired, though he had not admitted to it, so they sat down at each end of the long Chesterfield and chatted over a cup of tea and shortcakes.

'Don't you find them all gloomy and Puritanical up here?' Jackie was saying. '*You're* not, Calum, but then you're "foreign", like me. What made this so-called Lowland character, do you think?'

'Climate?' he suggested, his mouth full of biscuit.

'I'd rather say religion – but I expect rain and cold finished it off. Maud says they're all canny in the east and "canned" in the west of Scotland. She uses a lot of slang.' Calum was used to hearing the sayings of Maud. '*She's* not like that though – you must meet her. There's a paradox there I wish I understood.'

He said nothing, so she went on. 'Do things get less or more complicated when you grow up?'

'What does Maud say?' he asked ironically.

'Don't tease me, Calum – I asked a serious question.' But her eyes were sparkling.

'I don't think the Scots are different from anyone else,' he said after taking a gulp of hot, sweet tea. 'They have the same organs as the rest of humanity.'

'And they are often clever, and cautious – which they call "canny".'

'Maud sounds impossible,' he offered. 'Clever and – you

say – beautiful so she can't be good as well, or right about everything.'

'She fascinates me – don't you find some people just completely fascinating?'

'Where is the paradox?' he asked, interested in spite of himself, for he thought Jackie liked to confect mysteries round everybody.

'Oh, I don't know – that people should be almost unconsciously "conscious" of themselves – or is it the other way round? I thought of that yesterday and wanted to write a story about someone who was unaware of things, yet terribly aware of other people's weaknesses. There *is* something mysterious about Maud,' she went on.

'She perhaps makes things up about herself to be interesting?' he offered again after a pause.

'No – it's not so much what she *says*. She's possibly quite conventional about some things – I think she's usually got her own way at home.'

'Perhaps she was spoilt.'

'No, not in the sense we might mean. She's poor and she's not conceited, though she's so "guid at the Greek" as they say. You will see her next week – you promise? – We can all have tea together at the Hall if you pretend to be my cousin.'

'Why should you fash yourself, Jackie?'

'I just want you to like her.'

'She doesn't sound my type – I'll probably run a mile.'

'Oh, she can be quite ordinary – though I don't think most people like her. Maud's different – she dresses differently, I don't know what it is – there always seems to be a "line" to her.'

'Is she tall?'

'No, no – quite small really. A lot smaller than I am.' Jackie's inches annoyed her, particularly since Calum was not a tall man.

'I didn't know girls took such notice of each other,' he teased.

'Oh, we do – girls notice far more than you men do.' In fact Maud had once said quite dispassionately to Jackie that she was 'very pretty' and she had been touched, then thought

47

perhaps Maud did not like prettiness or thought it an unworthy quality.

'She says her Pa said someone must once have dropped a brick on her to stop her growing when she was thirteen. Have another cup.'

'From what you say she sounds to have a fairly high opinion of herself,' he said determined now to keep his end up in the conversation.

'I told her, you can always put your hair up and wear high heels,' said Jackie pursuing her own line of thought. 'But she talks mainly about her grandfather who was some sort of preacher – it's funny what an effect we find our relatives have on us, isn't it? Before I came to Scotland and left my parents I never thought about them. I didn't think they'd affected me much. But I think they do more than we think.'

What hidden depths did Calum have wondered Jackie.

'I'll have to push off,' he said. 'Thanks for the music and the tea, Jackie. I'll see you the week after next then – when I meet the ineffable Maud.'

After he had gone she watched his trilby-hatted figure stride confidently down the avenue till he disappeared at the corner. He was a lovely man. She could hardly believe her luck in finding him.

Hector had no business appointments the Monday after Maud's visit and decided to stay over at Garvits until the evening. This was unusual, and at first he rationalised it to himself that he had been overworking and needed another day in the fresh air of Fife. But he knew this was not really the case. He wanted to have a few more hours in rooms touched by the presence of Maud Crichton and where he might also receive some balm from his accumulations of beautiful objects which had never yet failed to provide him with spiritual solace on days when he felt justifiably depressed. His wife, Florence, lived in Switzerland, and his children were, for the present, on an extended cruise with relatives. Garvits was one of their homes too, but they did not choose to spend their holidays there, preferring the warmer climes which their father's wealth could afford to purchase for them. His wife was a different matter. For years even before the war she had been ill, and now he did not expect a lasting recovery from the melancholia which had arrived after the birth of both her children and engulfed her afterwards. It seemed there was no specific cure, though doctors had said a life free from worries of any kind might along with the processes of time effect an alleviation. So she was at present in Switzerland where the air was good for her and where resided experts in the burgeoning science of the mind. She seemed to prefer the attentions of doctors to those of her own husband. Finally he had admitted temporary defeat and became used to being a bachelor again.

He was proud of Garvits, which he had bought before the war, preferring it to the Scots baronial his grandfather the first rich Heron, had purchased in the last century. The war had been over five years yet there seemed no prospect of improvement in general for the majority of the people even though business had picked up. But how long could that last? America was the place to be, and he had almost gone there to open up another market for jute products which still provided the largest sector of employment for his workers and the largest part of his fortune. His father and grandfather however had salted away enough to keep him a rich man, quite apart from his own efforts, and he had preferred to turn his money into the purchase of beauty, a market which he felt sure would never fail.

He went out of the arches which led from his hall to the courtyard. It was sunny but with a nip in the air. He had reconstructed a house around the original one that had been there for several centuries and this facade of stone had been the first of his 'improvements' made at a time when he still hoped that Florence would soon take over the reins of housekeeping again and enjoy the place as he had intended her to. He hoped to retire to Garvits once his son could take over in the main office. Gavin was now seventeen, but would need far more guidance than Hector had ever had from his own father, and he knew it would be some years before he could give up the reins completely. He was conscious of a growing desire to retire completely from the business and devote the rest of his life to travel and buying beautiful objects. There might in the end be more money in a collection of paintings and furniture and bibelots, not to mention his porcelain and books, than in the capital amassed from the uncertain markets of this new post-war world. Gavin did not as yet care for such things as pictures or furniture. Hector had this taste from his own mother, who was still alive. As for Christina, who was fifteen, all she seemed to care about at present was riding.

He descended the steps that led to the terrace by the long windows of the room where he had taken tea with Maud, and then climbed up again to the Yew Walk.

He had not asked Maud if she was really interested in gardens; he somehow thought not. Not many young people were; it seemed to be something that came with middle age. He had hoped Florence would become a garden addict; it seemed an ideal occupation for one who suffered from nerves, but alas, this, like so many of his hopes, had so far remained a pious one. After his walk he still felt restless and went indoors again to the fire lit in his library. The telephone was waiting expectantly for him; there were business calls he ought to make. But he sat by the fire before rousing himself for luncheon which when he was alone at Garvits was at his own request simple.

His little French clock chimed one and there was a knock at the door. Mrs Archie stood there with the tray he insisted on having when he was alone. He smiled at Maud's idea that he might eat alone in state in the dining-room.

He despatched the broth with pleasure and ate a few pieces of toast and a piece of fruit. He had never been a gourmet; a good thing too, since it had kept him his waistline. He caught himself thinking – I am not an old man. I've been getting used to regarding myself as old. Stupid. Many folk would say he was in his prime. He was only fifty, still comparatively young. He had better pull himself together and order the car for Edinburgh. Mooning around was a mistake.

He decided on one further small tour of his treasures, for in spite of his self admonitions he still felt a mixture of depression and edginess which disappeared only when he tried to conjure up Maud. Alone he walked from room to room on the ground floor, and found himself still thinking of Maud, wondering what she had been like as a child. It was absurd – as though he had caught some infection from her that prevented his having her out of his mind for more than an instant. He ought to have gone on resisting the temptation as he had done for those first three months after encountering her, though even then she had constantly been in his thoughts. At this rate he would soon be a laughing stock.

The drawing-room was no better when he looked in the empty grate. The satinwood table was so highly polished he could see his own features in it. He paused at his picture of *Spring Lilac*, an Impressionist painting which he loved, but today it seemed to have a melancholy air about it. Would violet suit Maud? He shook his head, looked out of the window; the sun was still shining and the outside world beckoned. But before he prepared himself for his departure he went into his library where again everything was still and shining, and took out his first edition of *The Lady of the Lake* before shutting the door quietly and going upstairs for his leather case of papers. He would keep Maud a secret known only to himself. His servants would not talk – and what was there to talk about? Perhaps he ought not to have the girl visit again – yet what harm was there in it? He was not normally a man given to impulse but having once invited Maud to share his tea table that rainy day in summer it seemed that he could not help himself.

Jackie was down in the Common Room by three-thirty on the Wednesday waiting for the arrival of Calum. It was not so long before that chaperones had been *de rigueur* for the young ladies of the College, and women had had to sit apart from the men at lectures. Most of their tutors were men, but, now that a university education had been possible for girls for almost a generation and they were even allowed to take their degrees and not fobbed off with an inferior qualification, the staff had been swollen by the addition of a few women tutors and lecturers. One now hovered in the Common Room.

'I hear you are to take tea with your cousin and Miss Crichton?' she said, advancing to Jackie with a piece of paper in her hand.

'That is so, Miss McKechnie,' answered Jackie demurely. 'Miss Crichton will be in soon.' She looked out of the window and saw Calum Fyffe on the steps just about to ring the bell to enter the building. Male visitors were only grudgingly tolerated. She knew that Calum, however, had good manners and would charm such as Miss McKechnie. He was ushered into the Common Room just then and he said a pleasant 'Good Afternoon,' to the two women and shook hands with Miss McKechnie, bowing slightly as he did so.

'My cousin, Mr Fyffe,' said Jackie virtuously to that lady and even imagined a slight blush on her face. Calum was so handsome; she thought, even Miss McKechnie will be impressed.

A maid came in with a tray on which perched a teapot, cups and plates and she placed it with a rattle on a long table near the window. The room was featureless and rather cold, for the fire they lit there was never large enough. Jackie thought the tutor might feel she must wait till Maud arrived, but instead she said: 'Pleased, I'm sure, to make your acquaintance,' and went out rather stiffly, but leaving the door open.

'We aren't allowed to be in a room with a young man with the door shut,' whispered Jackie, giggling. 'Maud will be here in a moment, I hope.'

'Let's sit near the fire – can I pour you a cup of tea?' asked Calum, laughing too.

They heard a slight movement at the open door. Jackie looked round and saw Maud, hand on the door-knob, looking rather irresolute.

'Maud! Thank goodness – now we can shut the door,' she said. 'This is Calum – Calum this is Maud.'

Maud offered a rather cold hand and came shivering up to the fire. She sat down in the one armchair, one leg crossed over the other at the ankle. Jackie asked Calum to take round the cups. Then he pulled up two wooden chairs to the fire and offered Jackie one, after handing Maud her tea. Jackie sat down gratefully then and was for a moment silent. Maud drank her tea gingerly, Calum swiftly, before saying to her: 'I hear you are great at the Greek – that's what Jackie told me anyway.'

Maud looked surprised, Jackie pleased, that Calum had broken the ice.

'We haven't done much yet,' Maud answered looking into her cup. She looked inscrutable, thought Calum. He tried again. 'You go over home every day?'

52

'Aye,' said Maud. 'It's a wee bit warmer at home.'

Calum got up and looked for a poker to coax the fire into flame. 'You find time to enjoy yourself as well, I suppose, if you are at home? Jackie says there's not much going on here.'

'I've never been one for parties,' said Maud. 'I read at weekends and lie in a bit. I go to the "flicks" as well,' she added in an obvious effort to say something on which he might feel able to make a comment.

Jackie felt at least the conversation now had a subject. Maud was shy, she thought, and she could see Calum thought her an oddity.

'One day they'll do the sound as well,' he said. 'Doesn't the screen give you a headache though?'

Maud considered. 'No – I get headaches sometimes from reading – do you really think they'll have talking pictures soon then? That would be great!'

'It wouldn't stop your reading, Maud, would it? I know it wouldn't me – I'd rather read than look at pictures in the dark,' said Jackie.

'*I* don't get enough time for that,' said Calum. 'They say we medics are harder worked than any other faculty.'

'Didn't it frighten you when you began?' Maud asked, putting down her cup. 'Did you have to cut up dead people?'

'Och – at first it was a bit weird you know – but you get used to it. Living folk are harder to treat.' He laughed. Maud looked serious.

'I couldna do it,' she said. 'My grandfather always said he'd have liked to be a doctor but the Church called – a "doctor for souls" he used to say.'

'If you look after the body the soul will take care of itself,' said Calum a little testily. Maud looked surprised again, but put out her hands nearer the small fire which was at least a little brighter now after Calum's ministrations.

'Have ye brothers and sisters then, Miss Crichton?' he asked, thinking he had been rather rude and wanting to make amends.

'Aye – I have the two brothers – no sisters,' answered Maud.

'And you are the eldest?'

53

'Aye.'

'Calum always says you can tell whether a person is an only child or the elder or younger,' interposed Jackie. 'He guessed me aright.'

Maud was thinking, when can I get away from this conversation decently? Jackie's young man isna bad looking, but he's a bit of a bore.

'Calum is the only boy in his family,' said Jackie. 'That's why he is so bossy.' Calum laughed, but Maud frowned slightly. 'Calum – tell her about your theory of handwriting.'

Calum felt a little annoyed. 'Nay – Maud won't want to hear that.' He was used to acquaintances asking him for medical diagnoses – graphology was just a bit of fun.

Maud looked interested. 'Does neat handwriting mean a certain of sort person then?' She had that morning received a letter from Sir Hector in stylish script that looked more seventeenth century than twentieth. Nobody yet knew about her visit to Garvits ten days ago. She wondered if Calum had heard of the man, but was not sure how to ask without drawing down interest upon herself.

Jackie was now busying herself with pouring hot water into the silver-plated college teapot and could not see Calum as he replied: 'Psychology will one day tell us a lot about folk from things like their handwriting or the colours they prefer or their habits.'

Maud looked sceptical. 'I prefer green ink – does that tell you about me?' she asked.

'Maybe that you like to be different?' he answered, noting the soft hair that grew in the nape of her neck and was not caught up with the rest into the heavy braids. She had her ears pierced too, he noticed, and there were little gold rings in them. Had she had to fight to wear them?

Maud took her second cup from Jackie like a queen, did not fuss around with sugar and cream like most girls did.

'Liking to be different and being so – they are not the same then?' asked Jackie. Maud took off her glasses and wiped them with a lace pocket handkerchief.

'Oh, well – green ink – I suppose if you liked orange or yellow that would show something different,' he said teasingly.

'Yellow ink wouldna show on the page,' Maud answered, taking him seriously.

They all sat in silence for a moment, Jackie searching her mind for a new topic of conversation. Maud had not touched a scone but was drinking her tea, one cheek slightly flushed by the fire. Jackie looked at Calum and thought how handsome he was and how clever. Calum was also wondering what other topic of conversation he might introduce. He was brought-up used to talking to women. But he could think of nothing for the moment.

'There was a silly piece in the students' mag – did you see it Maud?' Jackie said – 'Comparing people to animals and flowers – it said Professor Carmichael was like a bear with his claws sheathed – at least they didn't say Carmichael just "Prof C" – '

'I didna see it,' said Maud. 'I don't think his claws are sheathed though. He says things he thinks nobody will under-stand and they all take down his words and don't think what he means – he is more like a two-faced baboon.' Really! thought Calum. But Jackie is like a very nice loyal young sheepdog, he thought. And this Maud is like a Siamese cat with a cold little muzzle – but the eyes are the wrong colour. Aloud he said: 'You are a harebell, Jackie, and Miss Crichton is a little like an arum lily.' He didn't know why he spoke such nonsense – it seemed stupid the minute the words were out of his mouth and it wasn't that she looked virginal as much as that she looked proud and her skin was very smooth. But he preferred harebells.

'And you are a thistle, Calum Fyffe,' said Jackie. 'And Maud is a bit of Scotch heather.'

'Mauve from cold,' said Maud, making an attempt at a joke.

They all laughed. Well at least now they knew each other, Jackie thought, as Calum said goodbye shortly afterwards and disappeared into the cold darkness back to his lodgings. Maud said goodbye too soon after his departure, having refused the need for a cavalier to walk her to the station. She had been bored, but they had meant to be kind, she quite saw, even if their ways of thinking and being were utterly remote from her own.

*　　*　　*

It was several days before Jackie could see Calum again for his studies were now mainly devoted to practical work in the labs some distance away. Soon he would be doing his final clinical year and would be away from the place altogether. Jackie was dreading this. Just the thought of Calum, knowing that he was in the same town and she might come upon him unawares, was exciting. She knew he liked her; whether that liking would be transformed into the sort of feeling she already had for him was something she set aside for the future. It was enough for now to luxuriate in his presence.

They both found themselves in front of Mackenzies cake shop one afternoon in the week following their tea party at the Women's Hall of Residence, The cake shop had a few tables at the back for the consumption of its goodies, and there was tea available.

'Thank you, Mr Fyffe – yes – I will,' she replied to his invitation.

Once seated with two especially buttery scones before them and two steaming cups of tea, Jackie said: 'Tell me what you thought of Maud.'

Calum drained his first cup before he replied. He turned his brilliant dark eyes upon her. 'An interesting case!' he said.

'What do you mean, Calum? – didn't you find her a beauty?'

'I think she's the sort of girl who would not be easy to get to know,' he offered.

'That's not telling me anything – didn't you think she has classical looks?'

'I thought she looked rather cold,' he said. 'But I'm only a mere man – I don't have female intuition so I couldn't guess what there was underneath.'

Jackie was disappointed and looked it. 'Do you mean cold and shivery or a cold nature?' she asked.

'Your common room was certainly rather chilly,' he said, not being able to find words for that set-apartedness he had at least noticed in Maud Crichton. He wondered if Maud had yet pronounced on himself. He had only to wait, for Jackie would be bound to tell him if she had!

'I noticed she'd a sharp tongue when she chose to use it,' he offered.

'But didn't you think she was beautiful?' Jackie asked him again eagerly. Odd, the way some girls were about looks. The suspicion crossed his mind that Jackie might want him to say that Maud was not as pretty as herself.

'Perhaps she likes to appear a bit distant,' he said. 'I suppose if I were a painter I'd paint her, but I'm not.'

'You *did* think her beautiful then?'

'I suppose she is quite – does she have many friends?'

'I think I'm her only friend here – ' she gestured out of the window at the town. 'But I'm sure she has some mysterious life elsewhere!'

'You're such a romantic, Jackie – she looked rather lonely to me – but from preference.'

'What did you mean – a "case" then?' she asked him, buttering another scone and biting into it. Jackie had been much affected by a philosopher who pronounced that personal relationships and love of beauty were the most important things in life.

'Well, I suppose she does look a trifle unusual, but there can't be much mystery about someone as young as we are, can there?

'Everyone is mysterious,' said Jackie, draining another cup of tea. 'And Maud even more so. Maud is certainly the wrong name for her – she should be called Helen,'

'The face that launched a thousand ships?' said Calum.

'And burnt the topless towers of Ilium,' continued Jackie. 'Yes – it's that exactly.'

Calum was amused. He didn't find Jackie mysterious, just interesting.

'Don't you think men would find her attractive,' pursued Jackie. 'Or do men like sirens with "it"?' She was treading a little dangerously, but could not resist trying to discover more about Calum.

He was about to say that the one thing he had noticed about her little friend was an extremely well-developed bosom, but he thought it was not the sort of thing he could say to Jackie quite yet.

'I expect she'd be a challenge to *some* men,' he said sagely, and laughed. 'But I don't know what they'd be letting themselves in for.'

'*I* think Maud has an "older man" interested in her,' said Jackie solemnly.

'Just an idea or do you know?'

'Just an idea – it's what I would think would be the case with a girl like her. But I don't think she's ever been – ' she was going to say 'in love', but that might make Calum think about the state of being-in-loveness and she was not quite ready to discuss that.

'Well, she liked *you*,' she said instead.

'Oh, good – ' he answered with a laugh.

Maud had actually said little about Calum, but because he was Jackie's friend and was trying to be pleasant, she said he had a Mediterranean sort of face with his dark, curly hair. It was not the sort of face that attracted her. Jackie was welcome to this young embryo doctor if that was what she wanted. He certainly looked a bit more experienced than the braw youths who sat next to them in lectures; Calum hadn't stared at her or said anything silly so she could tell Jackie she'd liked him. 'It must take strong nerves to be a doctor,' she added.

'Maud admires doctors,' said Jackie recalling this. 'I think she's rather squeamish herself.'

The conversation passed to medicine, to Calum's description of a case of over endowment of thyroid and from that to whether your nature was just the result of the physical state of your glands. Glands were much in fashion. Jackie did not like the idea that you were just a bundle of sensations, and said so. Calum did not like it either, but was still trying to form his own philosophy which had taken many knocks through the four years of his medical studies. Being young – although in Jackie's eyes a man, not a boy – he was unsure about the importance of feelings, but did not talk about his own.

'I must go – thank goodness it'll be Christmas soon, though I shan't get much of a rest. I've to help out at the Infirmary,' he said, as they went out. Jackie found it hard not to stare after him as he walked briskly down South Street. Had he *no* idea how she felt about him? Perhaps he found her odd, wanting to discuss Maud. He had squeezed her hand though when he left her outside the teashop – and she felt warm and comfortable for the rest of the day.

*　　*　　*

Maud's letter from Sir Hector Heron had made her rather meditative. 'You must soon come again on a Saturday,' he had written. 'Why not bring your friend – if she's interested in paintings?' She saw that he had decided to make an effort to behave in the way appropriate to an uninvolved kindly uncle figure. It might be a good thing; she had not yet decided what to do about him. Yet she did not really want to involve Jackie, who would treat the whole thing as a romantic adventure, that being her way. She would just have to mention it casually though he could hardly be presented as a 'friend of the family'. And Jackie could not get away as easily as she could, with her freedom to travel at the weekends and in the evenings. It might be a good idea to make him wait, and arrange for the visit after Christmas to be with Jackie, as he had suggested.

She was sitting in the window embrasure of one of the downstairs lecture-rooms waiting for a class to begin, pondering how she should answer his letter.

Just then a knock came at the door and she turned from her contemplation of the sky. 'Och, I thought it was Miss Graham,' said the voice of Catherine Campbell, one of her class who had the habit of arriving early and sitting at the front of the class making a great show of industry.

'No – it's me,' said Maud, stuffing the letter back in the pocket of her gown and marching to the back of the classroom where she had left her books and papers. She did not feel like a chat with this Catherine who was fat and had spots. Others arrived shortly afterwards so she was spared, and the class went on its usual way under the tutelage of Miss Graham who only asked Maud a question when nobody else could answer it. Maud removed her thoughts firmly from Sir Hector and put them on the path of Latin prose composition.

That evening she replied to Hector at home where she sat at the table in her small bedroom with her books. There was talk of Maggie and Angus buying a bigger house, now that Angus had finally set himself up as a cork merchant. Maud was not keen to move, though she might have a more comfortable room. Leaving would be the end of her childhood, she thought, and was superstitious about it. She sat for a moment looking down at the cobbled yard beneath, before applying her mind to Hector

Heron, who she guessed was trying his best to avoid temptation. Her parents knew nothing whatever about him and never would if it were up to her. Maggie still indulged her as a child but her father thought she was older than her years. She knew this from what he had said just before she went to the university. 'Oh, well, Maudie, ye'll do as ye wish, I know, for ye've an old head on young shoulders.' Had Uncle Dan said something to him about her?

But her parents were no problem and Hector Heron was. She would write saying she could not manage to get away till after the end of term but that she would ask her friend to accompany her in the New Year as he had suggested. She filled her new fountain pen with green ink. The pen was a present from Maggie for her first term and the ink was green for her own personal writing, it not being allowed for academic work. 'Dear Sir Hector, Thank you for your letter. I much look forward to visiting Garvits again to assist my aesthetic education, but I'm afraid that I shan't be able to get away before the end of term. I am a little behind hand with work. As you mention that I might bring a friend I shall ask Miss Jacqueline Livesey, whose grandmother lives in Broughty Ferry and who is studying with me in my year. I enjoyed our afternoon at Garvits and seeing the portrait of the Urquhart lady. Would Saturday January 3rd be convenient for our visit? Please let me know if it is not. I hope you will spend a happy Christmas and Hogmanay. Yours sincerely, M L G Crichton'. She put it in an envelope and stamped it to post on her way to the university the next day. Then she went to bed and slept dreamlessly.

On the morrow she went to seek Jackie out in her room. Jackie was ink-stained and flushed and a large pile of paper was at her elbow. Maud raised her eyebrows: 'Working, Jackie?'

'I was but then I got the most wonderful idea for a story. I'm calling it "The Nine of Diamonds",' she went on.

'Don't let me interrupt you,' said Maud.

'Oh, it's all right – I've done the first draft and it had better stay there for me to look it over tomorrow – I do have that prose to do.'

'I can help with that,' said Maud. Jackie looked surprised. 'I

came to ask you if you were doing anything on January third,'
Maud went on.

'I shouldn't think I'm doing anything – why?' said Jackie,
flinging herself on the bed and lying there, hands behind her
head and observing Maud.

'Oh, it's just I have a friend who's invited me and a friend
of mine to take tea that day and I thought you might care
to come.'

'Sounds mysterious. Where? Here or at home?'

'Neither. He has a house in the country, a beautiful house –
he's an art collector,' replied Maud casually. 'I've been before.
I thought it might amuse you – you know more about that sort
of thing than I do.'

'I'd love to, Maud. It's sweet of you to ask *me*. What's his
name?'

'Hector Heron,' said Maud, moving to look out of the
window.

So that's her secret, thought Jackie. 'I've heard of him of
course,' she said aloud. 'Is he on the Bursary Committee?'

'No – why?' Maud turned in surprise.

'Oh, I just thought he might be a benefactor to brilliant
scholars.'

'No – he's just an acquaintance of mine,' said Maud. 'I met
him in the City Gallery when we were both sheltering from the
rain.' It would be a nuisance if Jackie's undoubted usefulness in
enabling Maud to distance herself from Sir Hector for a time,
thus allowing him to see she was not so easily won over, ended
in the story getting round. 'Does your grandmother know him?'
she asked.

'I don't think so. Everybody's heard of him, of course.'

'Well, keep it quiet. I don't think he's in the habit of inviting
young women to view his treasures.'

'You can rely on me, Maud. My lips are sealed.'

Jackie, although a lover of talk, was not a gossip and could
be suitably discreet. Maud was aware of this and aware of her
friend's loyalty.

Jackie did not ask just then either what had led a middle-aged
gentleman to extend such an invitation to a girl he had met in
an art gallery. She could imagine why.

61

She would love to accompany Maud to Garvits, for the Heron treasures were a legend in the county. But Maud did not seem unduly impressed. What an inscrutable girl she was. For the moment though there was her own prose to finish.

'I shall owe you an invitation *and* some Latin sentences,' she said. 'What can I give you in return?'

'Ye're not going to get away with it so easily,' said Maud. 'I'll give you a tutorial. Now why have you put the Imperfect Subjunctive here?'

After half an hour with Maud as taskmistress, Jackie felt she had earned a cup of tea. It was fascinating to see how Maud's mind worked, selecting possibilities and combining them, abandoning them, deciding on matters of grammar and style and showing Jackie how to do so too. She regarded Maud's sleek head that was still bent over the book explaining the rules of 'quin', and thought how clever she was. Later though, when it was Jackie's turn to read aloud from a book chosen for their poetry course and she read from *Marmion* with a perfect Scots accent it was Maud's turn to admire. 'I couldna do better myself,' she said in genuine wonderment.

These sessions in Jackie's 'cell' as she called it, did not take place very often, since Maud eschewed too many interruptions to her own work, and visits to Jackie usually ended in Jackie's declaiming pieces of her favourite poetry. Today though Jackie had to write out her prose efforts, or rather Maud's improvements, so Maud was able to slip away. She posted her letter to Sir Hector and all she could do now was to await his reactions.

She walked down to the ruined cathedral and paused a moment to look at the graves in the kirkyard, wondering at the same time what Jackie's story of "The Nine of Diamonds" would be like. She had never had a fairly intimate woman friend before and it was a novel experience. It would be amusing to see what she thought of Sir Hector. Maud walked on and looked in a few shops, the prices of whose goods were out of her reach, loitering over the silk lingerie displayed in a small but highly select window. How she would love a silk nightdress; she could imagine the feel of the stuff against her skin. Many students in their scarlet gowns were hurrying by and she decided to go into the library until the class convened.

Now that Jackie knew who Maud's secret admirer was – and she was sure that was the reason for his knowing her, that he admired her – she was even more intrigued. Playing gooseberry would be a novel experience for her and she looked forward to the visit even more than to the Christmas festivities, though not more than she did to a dance she was invited to attend with her cousins, at which Calum was sure to be, even if he did not go so far as to ask her to accompany him formally. She dreamed of dancing eternally with Calum to some exotic rhythm, perhaps a tango or a Neapolitan song, was certain that one day it would happen.

Sir Hector had wondered as he fingered his Scott first edition in its 1820 binding whether *The Lady of the Lake* might be pointing at something of personal significance for him. Might he be a Roderick, the hero of that long poem, whom the heroine would never love? He groaned, put the book down and tried to concentrate upon his business papers. Never before had he found thoughts of a woman coming between himself and his work. It was unmanly. He even felt jealous of imaginary youths.

He had invited Maud to come with her friend on the day she had suggested during the Christmas vacation. He must have been mad to think of it, though it had been an attempt to rid himself of his obsessive thoughts about her and put the relationship on a sensible footing. But his thoughts would return to the picture on his tapestries, that judgment of Paris that might have instigated the Trojan war. How could he himself not choose, who already had business success and enough power as was decent for a man to have? Oh, he would choose the most beautiful woman in the world without a doubt. But that woman could not be his wife. He already had a wife.

Chapter Four

Christmas and Hogmanay were spent by Maud in the usual way with a good deal of chapel-going and not much fun. Chapel without Preacher Gray was more like going to a shareholders' meeting, she thought. As she sat supposedly praying, next to Maggie who *was* praying, she was thinking about Sir Hector and her approaching visit there.

Just after Christmas it began to snow. Large drifts were humped against walls and on gardens. At this rate they would not be able to get to Garvits at all. The plan was that she should explain that Jackie and she were invited to a university tea dance that Saturday afternoon and would return on the train. She was on tenterhooks all morning; she hated her plans being opposed by such a mundane event as snow, but fortunately there was no further fall that day and she set off to the train which was to take her to the village station nearest to Garvits and not, as Ma thought, to the university. Jackie was to get on at Taybridge also. Maud had dressed very carefully for the visit and was wearing her black lamb collar, best gloves and a new scarf of dark green under the warm winter coat. The hat was wide-brimmed and a present from Ma. Under the coat there was her best knitted costume of another green so dark as to be almost black. She pulled down the window of the compartment when she saw Jackie walking along the platform, stamping into the cold snow with her fur-lined boots, on her head a scarlet Tam o' Shanter. She saw Maud and trudged up to the door and joined her in the stuffy compartment.

'At least it's better than freezing,' said Maud. She was not wearing her glasses and the tip of her perfect nose was pink.

'At the last moment I thought I'd never make it,' said Jackie, shaking out her gloves which were unfreezing their ridges of snow where she had scooped it up for fun.

'The chauffeur will meet us at Cupar,' said Maud.

'I say, I like your scarf. Was it a present for New Year? How was your Christmas?'

'Not so hot,' replied Maud using an idiom learned recently from the sub-titles of the 'flicks'.

'Do you think we'll be able to get through the snow? There was drifting – ?'

'Oh, I think Sir Hector will see we do – he's probably got a regiment of slaves clearing the road for his Rolls,' said Maud complacently.

It proved an almost accurate forecast. Although there were no 'slaves' needed on the public highway, the drive up to Garvits had been cleared. The chauffeur was as he had been before a silent figure; what he thought about his employer's inviting two young ladies for tea was obviously going to be kept to himself.

A middle-aged lady with a long, white apron and a bunch of jangling keys awaited them at the door and led them to a downstairs room where she said they might 'divest themselves of their outer garments'. Jackie was wearing a scarlet plaid skirt and black jersey and both colours suited her. When they emerged the housekeeper led them into a room Maud had not visited before, a sort of smoking-room with a large fire and green-topped leather tables. Two men were standing by the fire, one of them Sir Hector.

He advanced, hand outstretched. 'I'm glad you could come. And this is Miss Livesey? You're very welcome. May I introduce an artist friend of mine, James Valentine?' His companion, a small stocky thirtyish young man with a haughty expression, shook hands and seemed to Jackie to be appraising their faces rather keenly. At least she would have someone to talk to. That must have been Sir Hector's idea. And she supposed the housekeeper would also get it firmly into her head that there were *two* young ladies this time. But maybe she was imagining all this and the owner of this splendid house had but the one idea: to show it to members of the next generation whom he adjudged worthy of the honour.

There was, Sir Hector explained, a 'plain tea', to await them at half past four – the object of the visit, he seemed to imply. But Jackie saw his eyes return again and again to Maud's face and knew her first idea had not been a fantasy. This man was besotted with her friend. Maud, however, appeared as cool as cucumber, and left him to make the running.

'Jamie here is on the way to be Scotland's finest portrait painter,' said Sir Hector. 'But he also paints landscapes and interiors and has been sketching the house. It's a pity we can't go in the gardens today, but there's really too much snow – I promised you last time you came, Maud – it'll have to wait till better weather.'

He looked at Jackie as he said next 'I hear from Maud you are interested in paintings and furniture – would you like to see my pictures?'

'I'd love to,' said Jackie with fervour.

'There's one I'd like your opinion on,' said Sir Hector. 'Your friend will tell you why.' He was careful not to walk with Maud but with Jackie as they ascended the wide staircase. The painter, who had apparently once attended the university and not enjoyed himself, was asking about Maud's work there and she was answering in as few words as possible.

'I'm so glad you could come,' said Sir Hector turning to Jackie. He had seen that Maud's friend was a different sort of girl, easy to entertain as well as being easy on the eye. He wondered why they were friends, she and Maud. And all he wanted to do was look at Maud, at the girl who wasn't so easy to talk to, who wasn't socially adept and whose face he would like Jamie Valentine to paint. But that must not be broached yet. A tricky subject.

They stood and looked at Mistress Susanna, and Jackie gave the response he wanted. Hector was looking covertly at Maud again, she saw, so she said: 'Why, isn't that like Maud, Sir Hector? – it's really extraordinary!' Maud stood by with a slight smile on her face and Hector turned to the artist: 'Don't you think so?' he enquired.

Jackie supposed that he was a patron of the young man so the latter would obviously not venture a contradictory reply. But he took his time, looking from the portrait to the living face whilst Maud looked away. Not shyly or in any confusion, but passively awaiting the verdict. Finally: 'I see what you mean,' said Mr Valentine, but then said no more and they walked along the gallery which ran from one end of the house to the other. Maud had not had time to see all these pictures before, so Hector paused before the ones he thought worthy of remark and they followed him rather like pupils at a public gallery. What a marvellous collection, Jackie thought, pausing in an unaffected way before the pictures she liked.

'Do you paint?' James Valentine asked her.

'I do sometimes,' she confessed. 'Just to amuse myself – when I'm tired of words.'

'You write then?' He seized upon her own implication.

'I try.'

What a wonderful place this would be for a ball, Jackie thought. So romantic in the dusk and all the shadows from the firelight – and you could have people dancing in that enormous hall downstairs. Hector came up to her. She was looking at a snow scene with every appearance of pleasure. 'Lovely,' she breathed.

'You must see more of my treasures,' he said. 'If there's time after tea – I was glad you could accompany Maud.' Maud was some distance behind them now and had taken off her spectacles the better to examine a small watercolour of the sea apparently painted locally.

'Maud is very clever?' he said in a low voice to Jackie. 'I imagine she will want to go on with her studies after her degree?'

'Three and a half years before that happens,' said Jackie. 'Who knows?'

He looked at her sharply, but she was innocently looking at another picture before turning round and smiling at him. 'Aye – ye're both very young,' he said.

There was the sound then of a distant gong. 'Tea,' said Sir Hector and led the way down the stairs to the drawing-room where Maud had already been. On an embroidered linen cloth there was laid out a tea which only a Scot would call 'plain'. There were hot baps and butter, and fruit cake, and bread of different textures and types and currant bread and bannocks, girdle cakes and gingerbread and a shallow china dish of apple jelly the colour of mellow claret. The tea was in a large china teapot that looked as though it ought to be behind glass in some exhibition.

Mr Valentine sat down and helped himself to everything, stretching out his stumpy legs before him and looking very much at home as he munched. Jackie was asked to pour and did her best with the teapot, and Maud sat on the other side of the fire, nibbling, with Sir Hector in a chair next to her. The snow light came through the uncurtained long windows, and the firelight made Jackie think of a room long long ago where such tea parties had taken place with hidden undercurrents. It was indeed a lovely house and she felt lucky to have been invited. She supposed the host must be rather eccentric, but then if you were rich you could afford to be that.

The firelight was on Maud's cheek and gave her dark hair a tinge of red.

'I love the light from the snow,' said Jackie.

Sir Hector cleared his throat. 'I wanted James here to do me some sketches of the property,' he said. 'But James is a verra fine portrait painter. I'd like you to paint Maud,' he looked at James. 'One day you might paint Miss Livesey too,' he added, perhaps as an afterthought.

Maud looked up with a distressed look on her face, which did not escape her admirer. 'There are not many portraits of young people,' he pursued. 'It's only when you get older that people want to paint you usually – like all those worthies in the City Hall.'

'Do you do "cubist" portraits?' Jackie asked the painter mischievously.

'I might,' said James Valentine. 'But I don't think they would please a purchaser.'

'They might one day when you were famous,' said Jackie.

'He'll be famous,' said Hector.

'Was Mistress Susanna young when that portrait was painted?' asked Maud in a strangely muted voice.

'About twenty I should think,' answered James Valentine. 'I've seen a later portrait of her, in Glasgow – '

'And had she changed?' pursued Maud.

'Yes,' he replied.

68

'I suppose photographs would show change just as much,' said Jackie. Maud looked quite upset. As she said nothing more Jackie came out with – 'If the person's "inner self" is painted, does that change?'

'It may not – so it doesn't matter how old the sitter is if a real "likeness" is wanted. Think of Rembrandt,' said Sir Hector.

He doesn't want Maud to change though, guessed Jackie. And neither does she. She must be more vain than I'd thought!

'Painting the secrets of souls is not in fashion,' stated James Valentine, and they all laughed. It would never have occurred to Jackie that people dreaded their features changing. What would they all look like in thirty years? Fifty? They'd probably all be dead. She shivered.

'I thought, one day it would be amusing to have folk dress up in really old costumes and have them painted like that,' said Hector, obviously confessing a dream he had long nurtured. Maud perked up. Hector noticed.

'I have some extraordinarily beautiful old dresses – not belonging to my family – I bought them at an auction. They say that "costume museums" will be the next thing. I often wonder if dress changes people. If we had to wear breeches and jerkins, James, would we feel differently about ourselves?'

James seemed to be used to this sort of whimsy from his patron. Jackie was thinking, if he's really serious about my having *my* portrait painted too he must think I'm not bad looking either! If I'd looked like the back of a tram when I arrived with Maud today he'd never have suggested it.

Indeed, Hector – who did not miss much in the faces of women – had thought, what a perfect foil for Maud. This lassie is pretty and I'd guess sensuous. You could almost call it 'Classical and Romantic Scotland'. But Valentine might have other ideas.

James Valentine remarked just then: 'You're not Scottish, Miss Livesey, are you?' and Jackie had to confess that, no, she was only one quarter Scots.

Hector got up and reached over a silver Georgian punch bowl that was filled with shining red apples. 'Have one – it's good for the teeth after Mrs Archie's cakes,' he said. 'Being young you don't need knives.'

Maud took a rosy apple from the bowl and polished it in her

hands. James looked at his as if he might suddenly decide to paint it.

'I have to go away on business soon,' said their host. 'James – when I come back let me know what you think about my idea.'

'Aye,' said James, seemingly not at all decided about painting lassies in old silks and satins.

It was pleasant there in the firelight, but after a while Maud stood up and announced they would have to get back.

'I looked out your trains for you – Archie will take you back to the station – there's been no more snow,' said Hector, looking sad.

He was thinking – she is so far from me. When shall I see her again? I'd like to dress her in green velvet and the diamonds my mother gave Florence and which she would not wear. He sighed involuntarily, but bestirred himself to be the perfect host.

'The thing about men,' said Maud to Jackie later, 'is never to give them what they want. Though I expect I shall have to agree to be painted.'

'Yes, he's very masterful, isn't he?' said her friend. 'But – *never*, Maud – do you think that, really?'

'Withholding never hurt anyone,' said Maud.

Jackie, who wanted one day to give Calum what he wanted if he ever wanted it, was silent.

'Then they will go on adoring you,' said Maud.

'You are cynical. What if *you* want what *they* want?'

Maud looked puzzled. 'No, I'm just being realistic.'

'You were born grown up, Maud.'

Maud remained silent.

'That man – Sir Hector Heron – he's in love with you,' said Jackie.

'I know,' said Maud.

Jackie saw that Maud thought herself quite worthy of Sir Hector's admiration. She had the impression that Maud thought that both the Almighty and her Ma had fashioned her to be worth quite a lot. And Maud was clearly a receiver. Then she castigated herself for uncharitableness. Maud had done nothing

70

to receive this homage, but how in the end would she make out with this unusual, rich, adoring man?

Jackie was true to her word and said nothing to anyone about their visit to Garvits, not even to Calum, though she was very tempted to tell him. It was, she felt, the beginning of a long story, the story of Maud.

It was a dull term; Jackie made some new friends amongst the girls studying English in their second year but continued to talk most to Maud, still considering her the most intriguing woman in the place. Maud had apparently already been noticed by the new friends as being a phenomenon of scholastic achievement.

On the last day of term, just before Easter, which was late that year – so would fortunately arrive in the short vacation, – Maud found a letter waiting for her in the 'C' pigeonhole at the Hall. She had gone over to lend Jackie a book, and had not expected anything. Sir Hector was as far as she knew still away and she rarely bothered to check her mail. This, however, was not written in his flowing script with its italic curves, but in a slapdash hand, and the envelope was smeared with yellow paint. She smiled. Mr Valentine had left his signature, she thought, and was right. He was to be at Garvits the next Saturday where Hector had put a room at his disposal to start some preliminary sketches of Maud. 'The great man will be arriving that weekend and wants you to try on some old clothes for me to give his opinion of their suitability for a portrait', he wrote. The 'old clothes' amused Maud – as though she was some orphan who was to be clothed by charity. She would have to invent for Ma a vacation class, since she had already told them all at home when term ended. She hated deceiving Ma, but Maggie would worry and Maud could not have that. She wondered what 'old clothes' there would be and whether Sir Hector would choose the ones he wanted to see her in or whether she would have a say in the matter.

'H.H. wants me to go on Saturday,' she told Jackie as she handed over the book. 'Though I suppose Mr Valentine could do the portrait anywhere. It's to dress me up.'

'Is Sir Hector back now then?' Jackie asked.

'No – he'll be there on Saturday though.' Maud looked rather anxious, which was unusual for a person whose emotions did not usually show on her face.

'Aren't you *thrilled*? – it might become famous – the portrait – I'm sure Mr Valentine is gifted. Sir Hector wouldn't choose a dud.'

'It's not that,' said Maud, biting her lip. 'I'd love to try on some of those costumes, but I don't really want my portrait painted.'

'Why ever not? Are you worried about your family knowing? Artists use lots of models – anyone could have asked you – on account of your face.' Jackie spoke openly and Maud looked at her with a slightly cynical twitch to her mouth.

'Tell me honestly – would you agree if it were you?'

'Like a shot,' said Jackie. 'What fun it would be when one was old and grey to have a picture of one's youthful bloom! But I never thought Sir Hector would really want a double portrait! – '

'I don't want to change and grow older, Jackie,' said Maud, 'a portrait would only remind me of how I once looked.'

'You mean – like Dorian Gray? – you'd rather stay the same and let the picture change?'

'No – don't be daft. People change – I've a picture of Ma when she was my age – and now she's so different . . . wouldn't it be better, if you knew you were going to change not to be reminded of your good days? Women change more than men, don't they? Once I did have my photograph taken – but I was young then, and didn't think.' She looked really upset. 'I know I'm good-looking,' Maud went on slowly, looking down at her white hands – 'I used to think it was a trap – that's why Sir Hector Heron is interested in me – he wants me to stay the same for ever, I know he does – yet he knows I won't and so he wants to have my likeness to look at. It's spooky, don't you think?'

'Like primitive tribes don't want their photos taken – it gives the power to the person who has the picture?'

'Something like that. I dinna want to grow old, Jackie,' she said again. Then she added under her breath: 'My face is my fortune – Latin and Greek are what I'm good at, but men don't care about that, do they, a woman's brain? – it's her body

72

they're interested in. I'm frightened sometimes of encouraging them – '

Jackie stared at her. 'But your brains will see you through,' she said after a pause in which Maud looked unseeingly at the wall.

'Snaring a husband is not my line – I don't want to be in the power of men like most women do – but it seems men like that idea.'

'But men are in women's power too, Maud – you once said something like that to me – it's your old Puritan conscience stirring. Men and women aren't enemies.'

'Aren't they?' said Maud. 'Oh, I daresay I'll have the portrait done if that's what he wants, but he needn't think that he's somehow bought me.'

When Maud arrived at Garvits that Saturday Sir Hector was in his garden admiring the regiments of daffodils and tulips. He saw her get out of the car, this time wearing a black costume which looked like mourning clothes, for she had a black scarf round her throat and black boots. His heart contracted at the silhouette she made and when he advanced towards her pale face he thought – 'Aphrodite Urania!' – goddess of the higher, purer love, – and trembled inwardly. The term away from her had been spent doing business all over the world and trying to resolve his own stirrings of conscience. Yet one sight of her and his conscience was in ruins and his travels forgotten. He was man enough to conceal all this. It was enough that she had come for her picture to be painted. James Valentine was in the old stables where a 'studio' had been rigged up for him with an oil heater and a north light. The water colours he had done in the winter were neatly stacked there waiting to be framed. Hector had told him that he would see how his portrait of Maud turned out before deciding whether to have another done of both girls. This afternoon though there was Maud's dress to decide upon. He had had his housekeeper bring down the old trunks from the attics; his only worry was that the clothes would not fit Maud's youthful slenderness, and her lack of height might be a problem.

He shook hands with her, noted the slightly cool way she looked at him, but said: 'You go up to the dressing room –

73

Mrs Anderson will show you the costumes. Take your time. Come down to the library to show James when you're ready. You must be painted in the dress you like best yourself and feel easy wearing. Then James can think about it and perhaps begin with a few sketches before tea.' He spoke quickly and without looking at her too closely, feeling he might give himself away and betray by the tremor in his speech how glad he was to see her again.

Maud complied and prepared to enjoy herself in this part of the plan at least. There was a long pier glass in the vast dressing-room where a fire had been lit. Everything was thought of in this place: fires and teas and flowers . . . It might be rather satisfying to be rich after all.

On a moveable wardrobe there were several gowns hanging, and on the chairs several scarves, hats, gloves, and jewels. She sorted through the dresses, rapidly discarding colours that did not suit her or that she loathed. She had never seen such costumes before; some were of the eighteenth century, she was sure, the sort that might be used as props in some grand theatrical event or fancy dress party. But she wanted something worn not too long ago, not more than eighty years ago if possible, something she could imagine a great-grandmother might have worn if she had not been a humble carpenter's wife. Under a faded yellow silk Directoire dress, which would have suited Jackie, was the colour she was looking for, a pale jade green, and she drew it out. It was full-skirted, needed crinoline hoops, was of a soft crushed silk and velvet with enormous puffed sleeves and embroidery on the bodice in silver. It quite took her breath away. Please God it would not be too large for her for this was the attire she wanted. She held it out in front of her in the glass and it seemed not too long. It would need silver jewellery and she rooted in the box on the chair. There were pendant earrings of opals with a greenish tinge, but opals were unlucky. This dress needed diamonds and she would have to lift up her hair, plait it into a coronet or sweep it back. She fished out some darker green gloves and a black fan. Why on earth had he bought all this? Was it truly valuable? The jewels seemed real, and the soft fan of ostrich feathers reminded her of a picture by Winterhalter. It was an early Victorian dress, no mistake. She went closer to the fire and drew the curtains of the room, shutting out the April light. Then she held the dress up in front of her and when she looked at her face in the mirror she shivered with delight. The dress would need petticoats though, and a shawl. Maud was a perfectionist in such matters; even if her painter would not need to know what was underneath, *she* would. For the moment she slowly drew off her own skirt and blouse and took a waist-length black underskirt, which she had noticed in the pile of folded dresses. She stretched out her arms – they would need a bracelet or two. Never mind, she would do her best with what was offered and tell them what else was needed.

Maud dressed herself carefully and did not look in the glass again till she was ready to brush up her hair. She put a pair of long green glass earrings on for the present and draped a stole round her bosom and took the fan and gloves. She slipped on a ring she found at the bottom of the box, gave a final twist to her hair and pinned it up on her head. Then she drew back the curtain again, shut her eyes for a moment before regarding herself in the glass.

The picture of her great-grandmother, Preacher Gray's mother, seemed to look out at her, her cheeks faintly flushed and the earrings setting off the bones of her cheeks, though that lady would never have worn so fine a dress. Now for shoes. They would be a problem. There were none, so she put on the slippers she had brought with her to change out of the boots. Now she was almost ready. Would they approve? Pale Chinese green suited silk and velvet, and suited her. She walked down the long corridor passing by Mistress Susanna, who looked at her with some complicity. She paused for a moment at the top of the stairs. The housekeeper was in the big Hall.

'Would you tell them I am ready?' she said after clearing her throat.

Mrs Anderson looked up. 'That I will, Miss.'

Sir Hector and James Valentine came out of the library as if on cue and stood looking up at her. She swept the skirt up with one hand, holding the fan in the other and came down towards them.

Sir Hector caught his breath. She looked as though she had

75

been born to wear such a dress. He felt silly tears rise in his throat as he contemplated her.

'I shall have to borrow some better earrings,' said Maud's voice. James looked at her appraisingly.

'You really need hoops for the dress,' he said.

'Will I do?' asked Maud. 'I like this one best.'

'What do you think, James?' was all Hector dared say.

'If you want my honest opinion?' – They both looked at him earnestly – 'I think Miss Crichton would have suited a more sophisticated dress just as well – but for painting this is fine.'

'About the earrings – ' Hector cleared his throat. 'I have a pair that would just suit. This is going to be a very fine portrait indeed.'

James grimaced slightly but said: 'We'd better get on with it. Put your coat on and we'll go over to the stables. I'll make a start now on sketches.' Maud put her boots on again, both men watching her, and Hector said: 'I'll send Mrs Anderson over with the earrings.'

As they went over, Maud with her coat over the dress, she said to James: 'I expect it costs a good deal to commission a portrait?'

'Not in this case – it depends how it turns out. I've been paid for the watercolours – he's very pleased with those. I don't promise anything – it depends how it goes. He pays for my time.' Away from Sir Hector, James Valentine was more talkative. 'He wants you for his gallery,' he said. 'The picture will stay here, I expect, and if it's any good the word will get round. But I don't really enjoy portrait painting, though I didn't tell him. I have to earn my living.'

'I don't want anyone else gaping at me if the portrait succeeds,' said Maud disturbed.

'Oh, I'm sure he'll like it and you'll join Mistress Susanna for ever.'

James had a 'throne' arranged under a high window and gestured to her to sit for him. 'I don't need the dress at first, so if you're cold I'll just do a few lightning sketches of your face and neck – I can do the outline of the dress and when I start on the oils you can wear it again.'

'I feel different wearing this,' said Maud.

'It suits you,' he replied briefly. A little later, after she had watched him prowling round to draw her from all angles, he said: 'I would not have thought you'd choose Victorian. Modern girls don't like crinolines.'

'I'm not a modern girl,' replied Maud.

'No – that's true,' he said. 'Your friend is, isn't she?'

'Aye,' said Maud.

He was in control of this unusual situation.

Just then Mrs Anderson knocked at the door. 'The master wanted you to have these,' she said and handed over a small case to James. When she'd gone out he threw it at Maud. 'Catch,' he said. 'Put them on.' Maud opened the box, and drew out from their velvet surround a pair of silver earrings each with a lone diamond hanging like a frozen tear from its filigree link.

'A guid thing my ears are pierced,' she said cooly. She had had a long argument with Ma a year or two back about having her ears pierced, and had, as usual, won.

James watched and saw the expression of almost holy joy on her face. 'Women and baubles!' he said and went back to his pencil and charcoal. 'I think I shall do you full length, but seated,' he said. 'I'd like your face turned away just a little, looking in the distance.' He advanced and showed her how to hold her head. She looked so aloof and self-contained, he thought. Would the paint reveal another Maud when he began to try to convey that almost cat-like poise and the far away look in the unspectacled eyes What a fine profile she had. She ought to do this for a living. Funny that she was an academic sort of girl. Somehow it didn't assort with her face, except for that remoteness. What was she thinking about? He must draw her out if he was to know her well enough to paint more than her surface attractions.

'Can I see what you are doing?' Maud asked after another twenty minutes. She had scarcely moved, was a good subject, but he felt the line was too stiff. Not that she was not relaxed in her own way – the erect head was part of her stillness. She probably never let go her guard. A cold virgin, he thought. What Sir Hector felt about her was not his business.

'You can relax and just talk to me,' he said.

'You've finished your sketches?'

'No – I just want to see you move – I don't want a flat plane but the feeling of your life underneath the velvet and the skin. Anyone can paint a likeness, but I want more than that.'

She fingered the ring she had borrowed and stroked the velvet unconscously, then put her white hands back in her lap. 'I always keep still,' she said. 'Even when I was little I could stay still for hours. It's cold though,' she added, pulling the coat around her. 'Do you want me to take off the coat now to get the way the dress fits round?'

'I've done all I can today. You're to come to my place in the city when I start on oils. Will that be possible?'

'But won't you need lots of sittings?'

'No – once I've decided the way I'm going about it and studied my sketches all I need from you is a few sessions in the dress and then it can be left with me. Hands and faces are the distinctive things once you've got the posture right. I've already sketched your hands. I don't work like an Academy painter – do you know the work of Impressionist painters?'

'No,' said Maud hoping she was not going to be reduced to a chaotic muddle of light and shade like the chrysanthemums in the city gallery.

'Sir Hector doesn't want a conventional portrait, but he does want a likeness,' he said.

Maud felt as though all this talk was nothing to do with her. She was just a thing to be got down in paint for someone to boast about.

'Don't look so cross,' said James. 'You'll like it, I'm sure.'

Maud got down to look at what he'd been doing. He'd covered a good deal of paper with many rapid lines, and one small corner was in pencil consisting of a chin, a cheek and a hair line. She made no comment, which was a relief to the artist who was used to gush.

'We'd better have some tea,' he said. 'You'll want to change back into your ordinary togs.' He'd suddenly got an idea of how to present the girl. It was the contrast between the old dress and the knowingly 'old-fashioned' look that was the way only a girl of the present could look. 'Perhaps you really ought to have been born a hundred years ago,' he said.

'Will people think – when it's finished – that it really *is* of a last century person?' she asked.

'That's not possible, you see, because of all the things that have happened to paint since then – and to women,' he answered.

Sir Hector kept out of the way till she was down in the drawing-room again, still wearing the earrings but with her own clothes back on. He stood at the door as she warmed herself on her knees by his fire, her hands stretched out. Oh, how he wished he might give her those earrings. They suited her to perfection. She ought to have some reward for so meekly sitting for James. Had she enjoyed it? 'How did it go?' he said instead. 'The dress suited you very well – and those earrings.'

Maud put up her hands to them; she had forgotten she was wearing them. There was a silence between them.

Now, he thought, now, I must say something. Why does she think I want this portrait? Any other girl would have asked. Is she innocent, or is she completely aware of what I feel for her? Although he hardly knew her it did seem to him then that he had always known her, a knowledge that would not be made greater with the addition of details about her family, her life, her studies. Curiously he did not at present even want to know more. So long as she would go on coming to Garvits and would allow him to contemplate her, to savour her presence. He hoped it would be enough. After all, he had again stayed away three months – too long though. But it was not fair on the lassie, was it now? a little voice spoke to him. There would be young men and other friends for her, a life to plan – study, travel, work. He could not keep her immured like a princess in a tower, though that was exactly what he would have liked to do. Goddesses did not need to lead ordinary lives. Yet he was a man, not just a cold aesthete, and he was lovesick.

'They're awfu' fine,' said Maud, still thinking of the earrings which she was now taking out of her shell-like ears.

Oh, have them! have them! he wanted to say. Stay here with me in your silver perfection, wear your velvets in the evening and be like a star to a man who has forgotten what love was like.

Just then Mrs Anderson came to the door. 'Would ye no' like

a boiled egg, Sir?' she asked. 'I'm just about to serve the young lady and Mr Valentine tea.'

'Would you like a boiled egg, Maud?' repeated Sir Hector in a daze.

'No, thank you,' she said politely. 'I expect Mr Valentine would though – he's been working very hard.'

'Is he satisfied with what he's done?' asked Hector.

'I think so – he says he's got the idea now and it will be verra fine, worthy of your gallery upstairs.'

She ought to be sculpted, he thought. In marble. No, in Parian ware – that would match the purity of her forehead and bone structure. Painting was just the next best thing to sculpture.

'You know I think it is very good of you to let yourself be painted for me,' he said, knowing the tea and James Valentine would soon arrive.

'I'm flattered,' said Maud with a sly smile. When she was with him she did not worry so much about growing old and losing her looks. This man would always see her as young, she thought, because she would always be so much younger than he was. She got up and sat in the chair she had sat in when she came on her first visit. She was beginning to feel easy with him when he said softly: 'I wish I could give you the diamonds,' and she jerked her head in surprise, raised her eyebrows. 'As I ought not to do so, would you like some of the clothes? They're quite well-preserved. I'd like to think of you wearing something from Garvits.'

She gave him a long, level look. 'There was a little chemise,' she said. 'Silk – I imagine – not all that old – the sort of thing my Ma wore in the Nineties – could I have that?'

The humility of the request pleased him. 'Take it when you go, Maud,' he said. Maud was thinking, I could wear it in bed, that silk, tell Ma Jackie gave it me . . .

James Valentine came in then and handed Hector the sketches. He took them wordlessly and sat looking at them, as Mrs Anderson came in with a trolley on which reposed her usual cornucopia of scones and bannocks.

'You've got her bones,' he said, a little shyly, handing the portfolio back to James and then smiling at Maud. 'What do *you* think?'

'I'm no judge,' said Maud. 'When will I go to the studio in town then?'

'What day would be convenient?' asked Hector. 'I have to stay over here till next weekend to oversee my plans for the rose garden.'

'I shall be working Saturdays in the Public Library,' said Maud to the painter. 'But I could come round one morning if you tell me where it is.'

James explained, and Hector thought – can I let her alone with Valentine? I'm sure *he* wouldn't try to seduce her! For the sake of the *convenances* though perhaps James could ask his old aunt to sit along with them both.

'Could I take the dress with me tonight?' asked James. 'I can drape it and take some notes and do some sketches. Usually I prepare everything before I touch my paint brush.'

'You may,' said Sir Hector. 'After tea you can fetch down the little thing ye want, Maud.'

Tea made them silent, though afterwards Hector could not resist following her, standing at the threshold of the room, risky enough with all his staff around, though none would have gossiped. She turned, surprised, with the pale eau de nil silk wisp in her hands. 'Oh!'

'If you wanted you could have them all,' he said in a thick voice – 'Nobody else could wear any of them so well.'

Maud was moved, but wary. 'You don't know me, Sir Hector,' she said levelly, standing in the middle of the room.

'For God's sake, call me Hector! – Yes, I do.'

He moved away from the door as she came through it, already dressed to leave with the black coat and the bucket hat, holding the little camisole folded up, and he smelled some perfume, something flowery that seemed her very essence that came off her skin. Without a word he took her hand and brought it to his lips before motioning her through the dressing-room door and following her small figure down the great stairs.

Hector was very perturbed. That evening he sat on after she had gone, feeling at the same time sad and yet with some new vigour that could easily be unleashed unless Maud actively prevented him. What was he thinking of! He was sure she was a virgin;

81

she gave that impression. His making love to her might ruin her life. But at that very thought images arose all too readily and he felt giddy with lust. That must not be, arose only from his lonely life. If he loved Maud he must change these earthy needs into something more elevated, something more worthy of the girl. He must think about Maud as a person rather than a seductive woman.

He tried for several minutes to do this. There was a witty, acerbic side to her that he might cultivate. But what was he to her that she might want to be cultivated? He was absurd, ought to laugh at himself. Maud had what they called 'It', he thought, however incongruously that quality was allied to the rest of her. She probably mocked him in secret and he would deserve that, except that physical desire was not laughable to its possessor. He tried to imagine that he had already possessed Maud and that it was all over between them. What would he think of her then? It was still quite dark. He would go for his customary walk round his domain. There were dozens of women who would readily go to bed with him in that social world he knew best. But the ones he knew did not attract him. Never before had he loved a woman so much younger than himself. Maud came from an excessively straitlaced and joyless rank of society . . . it was wonderful that she was not like that herself.

He would have the portrait painted, and one day perhaps in the distant future when it was all over, when she was married and middle-aged and he was an old man, people would admire it and praise his patronage. Till then he would keep it for himself, to look at when she had gone away.

It was still light, for the evenings were drawing out now and he went to the garden walk behind the house. His last dog had died a year ago and he felt the need of old Rufus to whom he had talked. He ought to go to Edinburgh soon to see his children who were looked after there and would have returned from school. It was Gavin's last year. He passed the old stables and the garages where his chauffeur might be at work. But he did not want to talk to him. He vowed as he walked along slowly that he would leave Maud alone and once the picture was painted take it away, hang it, and contemplate it instead of its subject. Then he walked back to the house somehow comforted by his resolution and went to bed, but lay staring in the moonlight and feeling more in love than he ever remembered. He felt almost angry with her that she had enchanted him so, a Circe, not a Helen even.

Maud wore the little green camisole in bed that night, luxuriating in the softness of the silk. Usually she would have washed a garment before wearing it, being especially pernickety about dirt and germs, but Hector said he had had all the garments cleaned, and the material gave off a faint scent of Garvits itself and convinced her that she had not dreamed it all.

Chapter Five

Jackie had been longing to tell Calum about Garvits and Maud's admirer but had restrained herself. Instead she gave heavy hints that Maud did have 'a man' interested in her, without specifying. She was interested in the painting sessions, whose details Maud described to her when they met again on the first day of the summer term. It appeared that Maud had been to James Valentine's studios to sit again for more sketches and now he was considering how to use them before tackling the oil painting.

'Can I tell Calum someone is painting your portrait?' Jackie asked her.

'Jackie, do you tell the lad everything?' replied Maud.

'No, I haven't breathed a word about your Sir Hector – Calum would be more likely to think the *artist* was sweet on you – ' she suggested. Maud said nothing. 'Her' Sir Hector was not displeasing though.

'I'd rather you didn't say anything at all, Jackie – I've got to concentrate on my work this term for the exams in June. I just don't want to think about the picture till Mr Valentine needs me to sit for him again.'

After she had seen how Sir Hector felt for her friend, Jackie had become even more thoughtful. Not that Maud had acted in any untoward manner, but Jackie imagined she saw the seeds of the 'temptress' in Maud, the 'seductress' of the novels she read, though Maud was hardly an 'older woman'. It was her own romanticism, she knew, that led her not only to wallowing in certain novels but also to this personal fantasising, and she could not seem to resist casting Maud in the light of fiction. She knew that all these imaginings were absurd, but she could find no other way of expressing her conviction that Maud

Crichton was destined to arouse suffering in others. Hector Heron was obviously suffering already. These ideas of Maud were so fascinating to Jackie that she had already begun to incorporate them in a story whose heroine was desired in vain by several men.

Maud was spending all her time in the library when classes were finished. Ma said she was overworking and brought her a cup of tea in bed each morning before she left. 'There'll be plenty of time to relax in the summer vacation,' said Maud, but accepted the tea, which she now took milkless. Ma was to go off for a proper holiday in August with Angus, the first holiday they had taken for many years. Maud was to stay with Malcolm whilst Duncan was taken off to stay with his parents at Angus's sister's in Perth. It was not far away but would be a nice change. Aunt Agnes had room for only three people and Maud had evinced no desire to go, whilst Malcolm, who was now studying accountancy, was articled at an office in the city.

But before these gratifying absences could take place there were the exams. Maud decided once more to leave the running to Sir Hector as far as her extra-mural life was concerned. If he wanted to see her when her examinations were over he could contact her. He had apparently sent a message to James Valentine that he was prevented by pressure of work from seeing either of them at the studio sittings and she knew he was doing his best not to be tempted by her proximity. If he never saw her again – a rather large 'If', she suspected – might he cease to idolise her as he so obviously did? She supposed so, was realistic about such matters, but even if he went on with his worship in the absence of its object, that would not be much fun for her. She felt she knew him quite well after her three visits to Garvits and she did not want the worship either to cease or to turn into a more fleshly one. A long drawn-out courtship would suit her best. But her common-sense told her that such 'courtships' often led to seductions. She was not sure if she would ever be ready for those.

Concentration was the answer to most problems: keeping men interested, and getting high marks for one's work, and looking good. But Jackie rushed around in a fever of love for Calum Fyffe and gave only a sporadic attention to her work, and an even more sporadic one to her clothes which usually looked as if she had come through a hedge backwards. Maud prided herself upon her own immaculate dresses and blouses and skirts as much as on her steadily high-marked academic work. She would have been unable to go around in anything that looked less than perfect just as she would have found it impossible not to pay meticulous attention to her work. And men, if they were worth any attention at all; needed all one's powers of concentration if one hoped to exert any influence over them.

When the term was a few weeks old Maud received another letter from James Valentine telling her he would need only two or three more sittings once he started the picture proper. 'I think I may say that the champagne will be ready to be uncorked by the end of the summer', he wrote. She was to go round to the studio on Saturday afternoons. She thought she'd be able to manage that. Her work need not suffer from two or three Saturday afternoons' neglect, even if she had to give up the 'flicks' for the studio. But her respect for portrait painters, or at least this one, was rather diminished. If James Valentine could paint most of his picture out of her presence . . . Still, if Sir Hector liked the result he would pay the man handsomely, she supposed. She hoped he would like it but was not too hopeful that she would like it herself.

Back in Edinburgh Sir Hector Heron attended his board meetings and his club as usual and nobody remarked anything unusual. He forced himself to write to Switzerland and to sound as cheerful as he could, and he visited both his children at their respective schools at the first opportunity after the holiday, turning up at their Parents' Days and showing interest in them, which meant attempting to talk to Gavin and listening to Christina. There must be nothing in his life that might make him regret meeting Maud or neglect his other duties. He did not write to her but looked forward with impatience to hearing about the sittings. What if the whole idea was a mistake? The worst that could happen would be a bad picture! – it could not detract from Maud's beauty. Valentine, who also did illustrations for books, turning his hand to anything lucrative, might have turned her into a chocolate-box beauty if he had decided to get his own back on Hector's own lack of sympathy for modern art. That would be even worse than a 'blurred impressionism'. Then he heard from the painter one cool May morning. James's letter explained he was modifying his usual technique and attempting what he called an 'Academy' picture – a Victorian painting for a 'Victorian' girl. The crinoline might be Victorian, but Maud was not, thought Hector, and almost set off to see it for himself but reined himself in. There was the rest of May and June and July to get through before he might quite justifiably see her once more, by which time her examinations would be over.

He was not the only person longing for time to pass. Jackie was looking forward to the Midsummer revels in the little town by the sea. There was to be a beach party organized by Calum and some of his fellow students, and by then all the exams would be over – and her fate sealed, she thought melodramatically. If she could survive till then. There was to be a bonfire and fireworks, Calum reported on his last visit to the Library, before his own more gruelling exam began. Jackie could hardly wait. The abandoned *'The Nine of Diamonds'* lay only half-written on her desk, where she was now attempting to concentrate on her set texts. The English and French syllabuses were no problem. It was the Latin unseens that really foxed her. Many were the times when she was about to go and consult Maud, but she forced herself not to intrude on Maud's own studies and struggled on alone with a crib.

For five whole days Jackie had watched Maud writing away in the examination hall. Maud had not looked up at all, but Jackie saw that she had dispensed with her spectacles, finding it easier to write without them and bending close to the paper as if in prayer. After a time Jackie had found she could actually formulate her own thoughts quite quickly, though the dreaded unseens were no picnic. On the last day, as the last exam paper was variously answered, some people groaning aloud, some dashing away with their pens with the gestures of orchestral conductors, Jackie enjoyed herself writing an analysis of Macbeth whilst Maud finished her paper early and sat staring at it before rescrewing her pen. At the final 'Pens down. Leave your papers on the desk before you. You may go,' was intoned by the invigilator, Maud looked round and then put on her glasses.

'That wasn't too bad,' said Jackie, catching up with her on the way out. 'I didn't like the Livy though this morning – couldn't understand a word!'

Maud smiled. 'I expect you wrote well on Macbeth – I couldna find much to say,' she confessed. Everywhere around them in the hall were pushing masses of other Bejants and Bejantines saying much the same sort of thing. One girl was in tears, being comforted by a friend, and young men were shouting to each other.

'You look tired,' said Jackie. 'Come with me for a cup of tea and I'll tell you about the arrangements for Thursday.'

Maud had hurried home after each exam so this was really the first opportunity they had had to talk. Once ensconced in the tea-rooms Jackie looked round just in case Calum should appear, which was unlikely as he had his last paper the next morning. 'It's an endurance test and helps if you are a quick writer,' she said. 'Not fair to slow thinkers like Eithne Macdonald or John Wallace – and they work harder than I do, though not harder than you, I don't suppose.'

'What about the party?' asked Maud unexpectedly, sipping her tea. It was a warm afternoon and the sun was pricking through the high windows of the Rooms.

'All fixed – I had a note from Calum yesterday – you will come, won't you? They're giving permission for any-one who wants to stay on for it. Lots don't want though, he says. They want to get home the minute their exams are over.'

'Do you think if I came I could sleep in the Residence?' asked Maud. 'Just for one night – I don't want to have to rush home, do I?'

At what seemed evidence for a new attitude to 'fun' on Maud's part Jackie assured her she could have her room. 'There'll be all the medics and people from other years who are still up – Calum is hoping for a sausage breakfast at dawn, so *we* intend to sleep on the beach!'

'What time will it start then,' asked Maud, blinking slightly at Jackie's words.

'About ten o'clock, before sunset. They've got a band, and permission from the town – nothing too formal though. There are sure to be some gate-crashers.'

'I suppose one couldn't just be there at the beginning and then disappear in the "wee smalls" ' said Maud. 'I'm not used to missing my beauty sleep.'

The town was half deserted by its students on the warm, late June night chosen by Calum and his friends for their farewell party. For once there was no east wind blowing and the tide was far out. Jackie was being treated to a dinner in town by her friend and Maud had eaten a hasty cold meal. The staff at the women's Hall were grumpy. Term had ended officially that day and they wanted to get on with room cleaning and their own lives once the students had gone. There was plenty of time, thought Maud, for a walk on the beach, and she might go along the jetty. She wanted to think, away from the others and from her family, and take her mind off the results of the year's examinations which were to be posted to them all in the vacation. That morning she had had a letter from Sir Hector that had disturbed her a little. James Valentine was advancing swiftly with his brush and Sir Hector had seen the results.

'It does not yet do you justice, Maud – though I must confess he has been very quick to get on with it. He tells me two or three more sittings now will do. I only wish I could see you then, but duty calls. I hope that you will be able to come over when the whole thing is finished and celebrate in champagne. I hope too that you are going to have a holiday for you will have been very busy. Do let me know how you have fared, won't you? You may guess that I often think of you'. (Here something was scored out). Then: 'If you have a moment drop me a line to Garvits where I shall be at the end of August. But mail will be forwarded before then. Your devoted HH'.

She didn't want to think about him and the picture, wanted to be alone and her own mistress. But everything seemed flat and dull now that her first university year was over. She ought to be looking forward to the picture being finished and looking forward to her next meeting with Hector Heron, but she was not. 'I'm tired,' she thought. Yet she knew she had done well in the papers and there was plenty work for her to do before the new term in October. She would really like to snuggle down in her bed at home and have Ma bring her a plate of porridge, and forget everything – university, Hector, painting and all. Because she had felt dull and bored she had accepted to come to this beach-party and it would be even more boring, she felt. She had changed into a dress of art silk that Ma had given her the money for and she was wearing the earrings she had scrimped and saved to buy and a chiffon scarf and wool shawl.

'I am young,' thought Maud. 'I want something – but I don't know what it is.' She walked along the jetty further than she had intended and now the sun was setting over the hills behind the town. She looked instead over to the sea which lay shallowly where it met the sands in the distance. If she walked out to it and into it, who would miss her here? Jackie, she supposed. It was not her custom to go for solitary walks; she must go back. But she stood on the jetty alone and felt the warmish air on her face and shivered in spite of it.

Calum Fyffe, on his way back with some provisions that had been forgotten, saw her standing there like a figure on the prow of some ancient ship and paused for a moment, not seeing at first who it was.

Then the figure wrapped her shawl more tightly round her shoulders with a self-protective gesture and he saw it was Maud. He did not hail her but noticed that the sun, just about to die behind the western hills, was planting a golden halo over her head for a moment before it went down, and her limbs seemed diaphanous. He must hurry on, for people were beginning to go down to the sands in small groups, and the wooden platform where the band was to play was being given its final check. But he went on staring at her.

Maud looked up into the sky for a moment before turning to walk back along the jetty. She had her spectacles in her little bag, a beaded one that Ma had once had to go to parties with in the days when Maggie had been allowed an occasional treat from

90

cooking for her father, always provided she went with a group of older women to the Church social. Poor Ma, Maud thought, fingering the bag and wishing she need not wear glasses to see anything in the distance.

Calum saw her turn to look now at the sea and noted the way she stood, erect and trim, not tall enough to look stately. The small figure turned again and he looked away. The silhouette had been slim but with a pleasant curve over the waist with a shawl tucked behind her arms. He walked on wondering what Maud was really like. He had never seen her walking alone before.

On the beach little groups of students were gathering, the men apart from the women until two or three couples arrived and mingling began. A figure was coming down the pebbly road from the town, 'putting' pebbles with his walking-stick as though he were on a golf course. Professor Carmichael. Jackie detached herself from a group of girls and came up to Calum. Some other medical students were busy with a small fire and boy-scout-like were arranging sausages in pans and chucking peeled potatoes into the embers.

'When are they going to light the *big* fire?' she asked him.

'Soon – then the rockets,' said Calum. 'As soon as it's properly dark.'

'It never gets really dark in Scotland,' said Jackie. She saw he was carrying a brown paper parcel. 'The rockets?'

'Yes – that's my contribution – I promised to buy them and I hope I'll be allowed to send one up!'

'Where's the band?'

Just then a group of more medical students could be seen clambering on to the small platform which had been erected during the afternoon whilst the others were seeing to the fire, and there was the sudden sound of a saxophone and the thump of a drum The medics were to be congratulated; it had needed a lot of work to bring down tables, pile up the wood, organise a band, make the platform for the band, provide rockets – but doctors were, on the whole, practical people and this lot seemed years older than most of the other students. It must be the result of their studies that they appeared less in awe of authority, more pragmatic. A

91

few other members of the medical faculty were mingling with the students.

Now it was almost dark and there were shouts of 'Light it up! Light it up!' Calum and two others advanced with tapers and lit the underside of the wood and paper and there was a silence. Then suddenly the whole pyre was alight – not for the medics an ignominious failure of a fire. Calum stepped back to stand near Jackie and the others. About seventy people in all were gathered round looking at the 'guy' who seemed to be a woman, the ancient foundress of the place, Jackie supposed. There was a 'Hurrah!' and then the sound of music as the trombonist, the saxophonist and the drummer began to play, their notes muffled but recognisable enough, for some folk danced, arms linked and began to wind round the fire.

'Where's Maud?' Jackie asked Calum as he took her hand and joined on to the fat girl who was uttering Mohawk-like shouts.

'I saw her on the jetty an hour or so ago. She'll be somewhere around, I expect.' The band suddenly changed to a less energetic tune and the students, in groups or in couples, sat down to listen. 'Can't you play a fox-trot?' somebody shouted and a lanky medical student got up and gyrated near the fire twirling a stethoscope above his head like castanets. The party was going with a swing.

Maud saw them from the top of the path which led down from the grass to the rocky part of the strand and the beach a little further off. She had been watching the sea which was coming in slowly far away, in the distance in the half darkness. She turned towards the path. On her left were rocks and gorse bushes just below her. Suddenly she saw a curious shape standing at some distance away. It looked at first like a bundle of rags and did not move; then it seemed to turn and look at her. Then it was gone. She stood stock still, sure she had seen an old woman raise her arm before fading away into a darker part of the beach. 'Too much imagination is the work of the devil', she heard echo in her head, her grandfather's voice as plain as if he were walking next to her. She pulled herself together and walked down the path to the revellers. Someone gave her a helping hand as she jumped down behind a trestle table and someone also said: 'You came down by the wrong path – didn't we mark it clearly enough?' and handed her a glass. 'Lemonade or something stronger?' said a voice which she recognised as Professor Carmichael's.

'Something stronger, please,' she said in a small voice.

'They're going to light the rockets soon, Miss Crichton,' he said.

She was surprised to see Carmichael here, would have thought student revels held little of interest for him, and he echoed her thoughts, saying: 'I shall push off soon.'

She said nothing, held out her glass to the source of the 'something stronger'.

'The end of term for students is not the end of term for their mentors,' he added. Then he took a flask from his pocket and poured a generous dram of whisky into her glass.

'Oh, there you are, Donald,' said another voice behind Maud and a lecturer whose name she did not know stood by the professor sipping from his own glass. Maud thought she had better disappear, but it seemed rude since he had given her a drink. There was very little social contact between the students and the faculty. Carmichael had even so recognised her.

What had she seen from the cliff path? Had it been a sort of mirage? She hadn't been drinking whisky or she would have thought it a hallucination conjured up by the Preacher's 'devil in a dram'.

Someone began to sing then; it was apparently the signal for the rockets. Calum Fyffe sent up the first silver spurt of fire up over the beach. It arched and turned and fell softly over the sea as she watched.

Calum looked up after giving the matches to another medic to light the next rocket. Things were going well. Jackie was dancing from one foot to the other. Then he saw through the flames of the fire the small, composed figure of Maud, looking vulnerable all by herself on the other side of the fire. She looked like some tutelary deity, he thought, arrested for a moment by a feeling that she stood metaphorically apart and never belonged to other people's goings on. On the jetty the sunset had given her limbs a sort of fire but now she was hovering as an object seen *through* fire hovers, half-real, half-ghostly. 'There's Maud,'

93

he said turning to Jackie who began to whirl around, as the saxophonist began a vaguely South American sounding piece of dance music and another rocket was sent up. Calum walked in Maud's direction, thinking Jackie would follow. Like Nemesis or a fire spirit, he thought, she looks straight through people. 'Are you all by yourself?' he asked as he came up to her.

She did not answer at first, was watching the second rocket burst in its showers of lines and sparks overhead. 'I havena been here long,' she replied to him then. 'This whisky's gey powerful stuff!' He saw she was cupping a glass in both hands, her arms loosely held in front of her. 'I saw you on the jetty – earlier,' he said and then was silent.

She turned away again and looked at the sea. 'It's Midsummer Night,' she said after a long pause. 'They used to leap over the fire when it was low – the pagans, I mean.' She did not ask where Jackie was. He saw she was wearing a sort of ruffly silk scarf at her throat and the shawl was still round her shoulders.

'Are you cold?' he asked. 'It's warmer nearer the fire – but it won't be really cold till just before dawn.'

'Oh, I'm always a bit cold,' she said pulling her shawl round herself more tightly. She looked very seductive, even seducible, but he hastily turned his thoughts away from that and tried again: 'Come and listen to the music and have another drink.' But Maud walked a little further away, still cradling her glass. Then she turned to him again. 'Do you believe in mirages?' she asked him.

'People look funny through flames, I know,' he said.

'No – it was on the beach near the rocks – I thought I saw an old lady – but then she disappeared.'

'How strange,' he said, at a loss. 'Perhaps it was a fairy vision since it's the night you said.'

'Only Highlanders and Glaswegians believe in fairies,' she answered rather severely.

'My father came from Glasgow but he never saw a fairy,' said Calum lightly.

'I expect I'm tired – you've finished *your* exams then?'

'Aye – thank heaven.'

'Our professor was here – he gave me a drink,' said Maud. 'I think I will have another.'

'Was that Jackie's prof? – the one who tells rude stories about the gods – she told me – '

'Aye – Carmichael. I think he's clever – fancy his coming here though.'

'They have to let their hair down sometimes,' said Calum. 'Shall we find Jackie? She was here dancing a moment or two ago.'

'You go and find Jackie,' said Maud. 'I'll go for another drink if there is any – lemonade perhaps this time.' And she smiled and turned before he could offer her a drink from his own flask. Yes, he'd find Jackie, who would be wondering where he was. Maud could look after herself.

Dawn came early over the sea which had come up within a hundred yards of the rocks but there were hollows in the grass further down beyond the rocks and there Calum and Jackie had snuggled and had lain in each other's arms for the rest of the night. When Jackie woke she felt refreshed. To wake in the arms of the man you adored was, she thought, the best way to begin a new day. Calum sat up and hugged his knees and looked out over the sea at the milky light which now spread in the sky from the bright gold of another day's sun.

Jackie had never intended to return to the Hall that night in any case and Maud was, she hoped, at present peacefully sleeping in her borrowed bed. Breakfast was another matter though; kippers and porridge would be welcome.

They walked back together and waited till the first golfers' cafe opened where they consumed a large quantity of coffee and rolls before Jackie ventured into the Hall. She knew she had done the most daringly forbidden thing, but did not care. Calum was even worth being sent down for.

The town was rapidly acquiring its vacation look. The bleached grey streets looked golden today and the sky was now the pale shell blue of a song thrush egg. It was not often enough that the sun shone steadily there, or that some wind did not nip round the corner just when you thought it had gone away for the season, and May could be cold. But now at the end of June some balm seemed to have fallen on the old buildings, on the ruined cathedral and the towers, even on the rocks and the meaner streets.

She called at the porter's rooms to see that her cases were sent on to her grandmother's that morning, but was loth to follow them as long as Calum was by her side. She went up to her old room, but it was empty. Maud had already left for home, must have risen early herself. Then she saw a note on the mantelpiece addressed to her.

'Dear Jackie – Many thanks for your comfortable couch – I hope you spent as peaceful a night as I did. I'll write and let you know what I shall be doing. I shall have to go to Garvits in August if Hector and JV want to toast me (as they threaten). In the meantime, be good sweet maid'.

This was rather uncharacteristic of Maud, Jackie felt, but was amused. She'd be in the city except for August, as would Maud herself. She wondered if she might persuade Calum to accompany them to a coffee house.

Maud's study of the Ancients had taught her patience as well as much else and she was certainly a patient young woman in a way inconceivable to Jackie Livesey. The beach party had made her thoughtful but she had had no wish to stay beyond one o'clock. She was still troubled by that strange 'shape' she thought she had seen on the beach among the rocks and was half tempted to go down to the shore again and investigate. There might be some abandoned clothes there that had looked human in the trick of the dusk light. But she decided against it. Her eyes often deceived her if she did not wear her spectacles. Even Duncan had told her she looked straight through people when she had not been aware of focusing on them at all. The gods had not dealt kindly with her in this one respect she thought, giving her a myopia that did not suit her inner sharpness and was useful only in the deciphering of small print, not people. How would her eyes appear on the portrait? That was her worry at present, that they would look blank, unseeing.

'Dear Maud – Do write and tell me your results – I'm dying

96

to know how you did. I got alphas for English and scraped through the rest. I'm busy writing my stories now – before that I was in need of a rest. Calum and I went to your favourite entertainment and saw a film that was meant to be tragic but we nearly died laughing. He sends his best wishes, by the way. Is the picture finished yet and how is it going? I'd love to come to Garvits with you, but if it's August when you go it may not be possible. I'm accompanying Grandma on a tour of the Western Highlands. She says I haven't seen the "real" Scotland yet. Calum has graduated with Honours as I expected, and is at present busy delivering infants. I think he will decide for General Practice eventually. I have met his Mama who is a ravishingly beautiful woman with glossy black hair and a Patrician nose. I don't know whether she approved of me.

You must hear the records I've borrowed – singing to melt your heart, even a critical heart like yours. Calum sang for us last Sunday and his mother accompanied. He has a wonderful voice – I was surprised, though I don't know why I should have been. Tenors have always made me rave with delight, as you know. For the rest, let's meet before I go away – you could come round here if you liked or we could meet at Draffens and drink coffee with all the ladies. I've bought a new dress and hat and want your opinion if not your approval. Lots of love – Jackie'.

'Dear Jackie, Thank you for your letter. I have been rather lazy and a little tired but am getting on with my tasks for Professor C. Yes, I heard from the university and I've been offered a further scholarship. Apparently my papers overall were good enough to make me Dux, though I can't imagine why, for I only liked the classics and the history. Carmichael wrote me an amusing letter praising my Latin composition, as far as I could read his very untidy hand. Ma and the others, except for Malcolm, are away and I go twice a week to Valentine for he has decided he will change his "approach to paint" (his own words) and is to do a smoother thing altogether. He is a weird man, often in a temper with himself. I shall be glad when he's finished, for

though he says I am "Patience on a Monument" I am uneasy being stared at like a specimen on a slab. Fortunately as he paints me without my specs I can only see a blur where his face is. He thinks by the end of the month to be finished and then Sir Hector is to come and we are to go to Garvits for a ceremonial glass of champagne. I'm sorry you will not be able to accompany me there. Thank Calum for his good wishes and send him mine.
Yours Maud.

Jackie almost needed a magnifying glass to read Maud's letter for she made no attempt in their private correspondence to enlarge her microscopic hand. They arranged to meet before Jackie went off to Inverness with her grandmother accompanied by one of the cousins, who intended to fish. But Maud was quiet when they met in town for a cup of coffee and said little except that her new dress suited her friend. Jackie was dying to talk to her about Calum but could not seem to broach the subject. She was hearty in her congratulations on Maud's success and toasted her in coffee. Maud said coffee gave her a headache and confessed herself a little fearful at the outcome of James Valentine's work for he had not allowed her to look at it recently. 'I thought he ought to do you like one of the Victorian pictures,' confessed Jackie. 'I went to the gallery and saw the sort of thing.'

Maud it transpired was working in the university library when she was not needed for the sittings. Professor Carmichael had written again to her and advised her on a course of extra reading.

'Gosh,' said Jackie, 'he must want to groom you for his own job.'

Maud flushed slightly. 'It's Roman history I'd like to do,' she confessed. 'He's really a Greek specialist.'

'How much money are they giving you, if it's not a rude question?'

'They're upping my scholarship another twenty pounds.'

'That's a lot of money.'

'Yes, it is, but we need it at home till my brother qualifies. Pa is trying to establish himself in a business.' She did not invite

Jackie to her home even though they were not far away from it. 'Thank goodness ma little brother's not at home. He drives me mad with his noise,' she said.

'What about your other brother?' asked Jackie.

'Och, Malcolm's all right – but he expects me to boil eggs for him – I ask you! I hate domestic work – sometimes I wish we didn't have to bother to eat. It's an awfu' waste of energy.'

Jackie laughed. 'You must come and have dinner with us when we get back,' she said.

'Oh, I couldna do that – I couldna have you back – we don't entertain.'

'That wouldn't matter.' But she could see that Maud thought it would.

'Do you want to be a lecturer – like Prof Carmichael, I mean, be an academic?' she asked Maud suddenly. There was a pause.

Then: 'Maybe that's what I was intended for,' Maud replied warily.

'I suppose you have to start somewhere – there are not many lady professors, said Jackie. She was trying to envisage Maud lecturing to students. She could see her marking papers, or editing texts more easily. 'There's plenty of time,' she said.

'I'd like to travel,' said Maud. 'For work, I mean.'

'Oh, so would I,' said Jackie with enthusiasm. 'I want to go to Paris and Venice and Seville,' she added.

'I was thinking more, one day, of Germany,' said Maud. 'That's where all the research is taking place into the ancient world – Germany's always been the place for that.'

'Germany's in rather a mess at the moment – *everything* seems in a bit of a mess, I mean politically – '

'Oh, I'm not interested in politics,' said Maud.

The last sitting was over and James had announced he could do no more. Maud had changed into The Dress for the last two sessions in the presence of an old lady – apparently his aunt – who sat there knitting; Maud supposed she might be needed in case James saw her in her chemise and pounced. But she knew James was not likely to do that; it was for his own protection that he had brought the old woman along. She wondered if she were paid to sit and knit. As far as Maud could see, James wasn't interested at all in women and neither did he drink overmuch. He was a dedicated worker, though he must have some vices. She wondered what they might be. His studio was a bare little room with a gas fire but it had north light, and the smell of varnish and paint and turpentine pervaded it and often made her nose tickle.

'When is he going to see it?' she asked.

'He's in Edinburgh – hasn't he written to you? – he's coming on Tuesday and if he approves I shall get his chauffeur to take it to Garvits – I expect he'll be asking us round on Saturday.'

'Won't you let me look?' asked Maud once more.

'I want it to be a surprise for the both of you,' said James eyeing her from under his long, curly lashes. How would anyone paint *him*?

'I shall miss coming here,' she said abruptly. It was true. James was a person with whom she felt easy. He did not look at her the way Hector did or the way even Calum Fyffe had looked at her on the beach. She was sure she had not imagined that. On her way out she saw a young man waiting on the stairs for the artist to finish, and the penny dropped.

She tried to concentrate upon her reading of *The Iliad*; somehow she would rather read of the death of Hector than think about soon seeing his namesake. She liked reading about battles, and there were plenty of those. But her thoughts annoyed her by flying out of the window.

She was resigned now to seeing herself on the canvas. At least the dress would come out well – she had every confidence in James Valentine's ability to paint silk and velvet. Her innate pessimism came to her rescue when she decided that the artist's delineation of herself would not please his patron and so would be forgotten. The trouble was that even if nobody else ever saw the picture it would one way or another remain at Garvits to be resurrected one day if Valentine's other work was successful.

Sir Hector had not written to her again and this was a relief, gave her a breathing space. Ma and the others would soon be back, but she would have this coming Saturday afternoon clear to visit Garvits. Then she would decide what to do about it all.

100

Champagne and possible compliments were all very well, but what if things went further than stolen kisses on her wrist; what if he told her he loved her? Was there anything she could say to him so that she might extract some promise in exchange for her accepting that love? She wanted to accept it, needed to accept it, but shrank from doing anything more active than receiving homage. At the bottom of her heart she knew she had not set out initially with the intention of making a man fall in love with her who then might wish to possess her. What she wanted was for people to fall in love with her only in a certain way so that the balance of power might be shifted. She had never been "in love" herself, had never suffered for love.

Even Professor Carmichael, when she had gone to see him after the results of her exams were out, had given her one or two strange looks. In his case they were accompanied by a sort of absent-mindedness, so she was not sure whether if he knew himself that he might find her attractive. His body knew but his conscious mind had perhaps not quite caught up with the notion. It seemed to be her fate that whilst men talked to her of other things – paintings or Roman History – their gaze lingered on the parts of herself she chose to expose. Carmichael's gaze had seemed to be transfixed by a brooch she was wearing on her blouse which set off the curve of her bosom. If only she understood what she might want for herself apart from this physical empire over men. Jackie obviously wanted Calum Fyffe. But Jackie was a romantic girl, the sort who threw herself on a man who took her fancy. Perhaps Jackie felt other things than adoration too? She liked Jackie and sometimes envied her exuberance, but Jackie was rash, a quality left out of Maud's constitution.

It was therefore with some trepidation that Maud awaited Hector's verdict on the picture. Hector had never written to her at home and it was from James Valentine that she heard on the Thursday morning. The message, on a plain white postcard, was simple. 'H H delighted. Come to the studio Saturday one pm. We are both to be conveyed to Garvits plus picture.'

It was strange how her heart sank instead of rising on wings of delight. Why had Sir Hector not written to her himself?

Chapter 6

He was waiting for them when Archie deposited them both in the courtyard. Archie manoeuvred the picture out of the car where it had lain against the front seat in what James called its nightgown – a robe of canvas. Maud was nervous, James calm. Hector stood under his arches and seemed to look at her without any special feeling when she came up. Then she realised it was because he was excited. He was welcoming the picture as he might be welcoming a bride and could not welcome them both together. She gave an involuntary twitch to her shoulders to rebuke herself for being fanciful. Once in the hall though he turned and smiled a shy, kind smile.

'You must unwrap it yourself,' he said. 'And James here can place it on the window-seat to lean against the light.'

Maud saw a large silver bucket on another oak table waiting for ice and champagne bottles, but took the scissors Sir Hector offered her and cut the thread that held the sacking at the top. Then she averted her face as Hector slipped the covering down at the sides as though, she thought, he was undressing a girl. The thought made her tremble. She had her back to the portrait, but as she turned reluctantly again, he turned the picture and she glimpsed a mass of green and gold and a whitish blur in the middle. 'Excuse me,' she said faintly and took out her spectacles from her bag. The picture was, she saw now, in a heavy gilt frame and James, with Hector aiding him, placed it reverently on the window-seat. Hector switched on the electric lights that were in two large chandeliers on the hall ceiling.

'You can look now,' said Sir Hector.

She walked a little nearer to it, the two men standing near, one looking at the picture he had painted, the other looking at her, then raised her eyes and stared at the painting.

102

The paint was smooth, the strokes tiny. Against a dark green background, almost the colour of spruce, a face stared back at her, a white face on a long, white neck, hair lifted up from the brow as he had made her dress it. The woman was looking in the middle distance, her head slightly turned to the right, cheekbones emphasised by earrings following the line of the cheek. Eyebrows arched – how many painful hours she'd spent plucking them! The mouth was softly rosy, the eyelids heavy, face a perfect oval. Was that how she really looked – haughty and yet abstracted? She knew they were waiting for her to say something – she cleared her throat – 'Ye've got the dress verra well,' she said – 'and I – like the way you've used the paint.'

'He's got *you* there,' said Hector. 'In the planes of the face – though mebbe he's made you a wee bit older in your expression. I'm pleased, James – I'm very pleased – if people saw this they'd want more from you. You were right about the way you used your brush to *smooth* her into being – aye it's a great picture.'

If Hector was pleased, which he seemed to be, that was her task done. All that sitting and keeping still. She wondered how much he was paying Valentine for it. It was not her and yet it could not have been done without her – strange, that. Hector was fussing now with the ice bucket and Mrs Anderson was bringing in the bottles on a silver tray.

'Come and look,' Sir Hector said 'and fill a glass for yourself.'

'Thank you, Sir,' she said and went round with the tray taking a glass for herself before looking at the picture. 'Verra fine,' she said with a glance at the picture and a longer look at Maud who was waiting to sip her drink. 'Aye, ye've got the young lady's look there,' she said.

'A toast to all our guests, all three,' said her employer. 'Mr Valentine for his work and Miss Crichton for sitting for him and the Young Woman in Green who will now stay here in my gallery.'

Maud raised her glass and the others followed suit. The liquid was delicious, dry and cold and bubbly, better than whisky she thought, not having ever drunk champagne before.

'We'll take "the lady" into the drawing-room and sit down,' said Sir Hector. 'Bring the other bottle, Mrs Archie, will you – '

Maud thought it was odd drinking champagne at three o'clock. She must not get tipsy, not having had much luncheon. She remembered her manners and rather shyly raised her glass to James Valentine, who blinked, but said: 'Do you approve?' – of course no artist ever thinks a work is a complete success. 'Where are you going to hang it, Hector?' he asked, turning to his patron and accepting another glass of bubbly. Maud did not reply to his question but smiled.

'I'd like, if Maud agrees, to put it next to Mistress Susanna,' said Hector. 'I think each will lend interest to the other.

Now I am just a picture, thought Maud. 'Stand near the picture, Maud – ' Hector said. They placed it now against the window in the drawing-room. 'I want to see you two together.'

Obediently she stood by the frame. 'I brought the dress back,' she said, remembering the parcel she had reluctantly wrapped for its return.

'The dress only adds to the impression of seventy years or so ago – I remember my Mama in a dress a bit like that,' he continued – 'that was not so long ago of course – must have been in the eighties, when crinolines had gone out, even so – perhaps it's the hair.'

'I always wear it off ma face,' she said.

'It suits you like that,' he said. 'Never have your hair cut, Maud.' She thought, he sounds like Preacher Gray, but she was pleased.

'I've to meet someone in town,' said James Valentine. 'I'll walk to your station – it'll do me good.'

Hector looked enquiringly at Maud. Instinctively she said: 'I'd like a walk too – perhaps you could show me the gardens today – I saw your roses were still out.'

'The second flowering,' said Hector. 'That's a good idea.' He had, so far, avoided her eyes, and she had noticed. 'But first we must take the picture up to the gallery. I'll get Archie to help. You wait down here, Maud, and come when we've got it up.'

He noticed that she was wearing earrings he'd never seen before. Not the little gold ones but crystals on the end of gilt stalks, a bit like the diamonds she'd worn for him the last time she'd been there. These were fake, but set off her face. What

104

sort of character did that face reveal? He'd thought the painting would tell him, but it had not. There was still some essence of Maud that the living girl seemed to possess, an essence which a painting, however skilful – and Valentine's work was that – had not in this case brought out. But James was not in love with her, he caught himself thinking. And to cover the confusion of his own thoughts he went out to fetch Archie.

'It's a beautiful painting, Mr Valentine,' said Maud formally. 'I mean, you know – apart from me – as a picture.'

The champagne seemed to have unleashed James's tongue for he said: 'What we call beauty, Maud, is not always what makes people fall in love.' She looked at him, eyebrows raised. 'Maybe artists fall for beautiful people since they love artistic objects,' he went on, waving his glass in the air. 'But ye can love an artistic object only at a distance. Ye can admire a beautiful object, but ye canna get near it.'

'What do you mean "get near it"?' asked Maud looking at him sharply.

'I mean intimacy, Maud – not that folk get that verra often.'

'Can't you love people you admire?'

'Aye – but it isna enough. Artists have to choose.'

So the painting would have been a good thing if she didn't want Hector's 'love'? Let him be in love with a painting then. But she felt a little cheated.

'Sir Hector isna an artist,' she said after a pause.

'He's an aesthete though.'

'Are artists and "aesthetes" not human then?'

'You want to be admired,' he replied, not answering her question.

She flushed. 'How do you know what I want?'

'Och, Maud, I haven't painted you without getting to know you a bit.'

'What's "love" anyway?' she asked. The champagne was making them both bold.

'Enchantment and intoxication,' he replied quickly. 'Nothing to do with the "real" person.'

'You have to be "intoxicated" with something about them – not just anyone will do?'

'Och, anything can go to your head.'

105

'You seem to know?'

'Women like to be worshipped, I've found – but most women dinna fall in love.'

'I know women who do.'

He ignored this and said: 'Love comes unbidden – there's no knowing who you'll feel for. You don't need to do anything about it. It lasts longer if the beloved doesna completely surrender to the spell . . .' He sounded more Scots as he finished his glass. Perhaps he thought she 'Loved' Hector.

She looked at him searchingly, but he drained his glass and said: 'I must be off.'

Hector wondered what they'd been discussing, for when he came into the room Maud looked a little cross. But how beautiful she was! He'd noticed again – but it was more obvious on the picture he'd just hoisted up next to Lady Susanna – that Maud's lower jaw was a little too heavy for perfection. It was not exactly a flaw but it made him feel more tender towards her. Her portrait had paradoxically made him sure he knew her less well than he had imagined.

'You won't be going yet,' he contented himself in saying to her. If only she knew how he'd denied himself writing to her, how he had stopped himself from seeing her when he could so easily have done so, and what a struggle that had been. 'Archie or I can drive you to your train later,' he said. 'Come and see your picture hung – you can tell me whether it is really the best place for it,' – this to James, who was now looking anxious to get away. But he had had Hector's cheque the day after his patron had first viewed the masterpiece so felt he had better not appear too eager to leave. They all trooped upstairs, Maud holding the parcel which contained the dress. She'd not known how to have it cleaned, but had not dared to ask anyone to wash it.

Lady Susanna was now joined by the portrait of Maud, which was exactly the same size. 'You could be sisters,' said Sir Hector. Odd how the centuries had been bridged with the two of them. Nobody spoke for some minutes. Then – 'What shall we call you, Maud? Symphony in green? or just "Maud 1924"?'

'Let James name it,' she murmured, embarrassed.

'You'll have to give me time – it's not easy.' James shifted from one foot to the other. 'An old head on young shoulders,'

he was thinking. 'Just "Portrait of a Modern Young Woman?"'
he offered. Nicely paradoxical, that was.

When James had gone Hector took the parcel and put it in
the dressing-room. How could he keep her by him now there
was no longer the excuse of the picture which had kept a link
between the two of them for the past year? Maud was waiting
for him in the drawing-room. He was holding her summer coat
when he came in to her and said: 'Just up to the top of the
shrubberies – we need some fresh air,' and he draped the coat
over her shoulders.

She followed him up a slope behind the kitchen quarters of
the house. Great rhododendrons flanked it and at the top was a
seat looking out over another lawn behind which were the hills.
The sky was grey and it was cool. 'August is a dead month,' he
said. 'Shall we sit down for a while?'

'My parents are coming back home on Monday,' she said.

'You haven't told me how you went in your exams.'

'They gave me another Scholarship,' answered Maud flatly.
'I was Dux.'

'Oh, my dear,' he said. 'I'm so glad. You're a clever girl,
Maud!'

She said nothing so he went on. 'Do you really like the
picture?'

'It doesna seem to be me – I mean I suppose it's a pretty
good likeness but they say you can never see yourself the way
others see you.'

Hector began slowly and almost under his breath: 'I've tried
to get you out of my head you know – I've got your likeness
now so I suppose I can go and look at it, when I please. My
only criticism of the portrait, and it's not a complaint, is that
he's made you look rather remote . . . even a little cold.'

'Perhaps I am cold,' she replied, not looking at him.

'You know I love you, Maud?'

'Aye,' she said briefly. He saw a slight smile on her lips.

'I don't want to hurt you, Maud – don't want any harm to
come to you – I just wish you could be near me for always.' He
wanted to cover her with kisses, but instead took her cold hand
and turned it over between his two warm ones. 'Everything one
says sounds wrong in these circumstances,' he said. 'If I said

107

when you are away from me I think of you constantly would you believe me? – I can't believe we might not be able one day to be together, if you wanted.'

Maud swallowed. 'But you are married,' she said quietly.

'Only in name now – but that wasn't what I meant. If you allow me to write to you, to see you now and again, I'll try to be content. I know you have your own life to lead away from me – perhaps I'm being foolish.'

'They say,' said Maud, echoing James words – 'that if a man thinks a woman beautiful he prefers to worship her in the distance. Is it true I'm just a beautiful object for you, like one of your other pictures?'

'No Maud, never that – I think you are very beautiful, but it's the woman I feel for, not the beauty.'

Words, he thought. How could I tell her I lie awake thinking about her, not wanting to possess so much as to cherish and protect and serve. 'If you loved me, Maud,' he said – 'I'd sacrifice whatever you wanted me to sacrifice to have you – But why should you love me? I won't say these things again if they embarrass you.'

'They don't embarrass me,' said Maud. 'And I'm grateful. But I don't know much about – love.' He knew she meant she did not love him.

He sighed. 'I wish I could teach you – I'm only a man so it would have to be a man's way – and maybe you're not ready for that.'

'I don't want you to – to suffer anything for me,' she said. 'I do like you. I'm grateful for the painting – though I'm frightened when I think I shall change and it won't. But I've never been in love with anyone – I'd like you to write to me and perhaps I can come now and again – I like it here.' Her directness seemed to please him for he took her hand up to his lips and kissed it and she thrilled a little to this gesture. He was certainly attractive; she found him less repellent than any man she had ever known, which she knew was an odd sort of compliment, but she was wary of getting closer to him, – though she wanted to keep him, and to test her power.

'Whatever happens, Maud,' he said – 'I don't want you to

forget me. Just accept that I love you, will you – and I'll wait for you.'

'Perhaps your wife will come back – if she gets better?' she offered.

'Aye, perhaps, though it doesn't seem likely. Believe me, Maud, I'm not a rash Johnny-come-lately – I know what I feel about you is unusual – though it makes me also feel a fool.'

'No, you're not a fool,' she said, allowing her hand to remain in his. 'And I couldn't forget you either, could I? I feel quite comfortable with you,' she went on. 'But – '

'But you don't want to burn your bridges, I know.'

Maud thought, he is sincere in all he says. I wish I could commit myself to him. I want him to love me, but I can't love him back. I think he'll always love me. Though I never asked him to.

'If I can't give you the earrings, may I send you a little present to wear sometimes? – just to thank you for being alive – you know – I never expected to feel like this at my time of life.'

'You are not old,' said Maud. 'I've never fancied young men anyway.'

'You are not silly – like so many young women,' he said. 'It is I who am foolish.'

'No, you are very kind – it is that I've never wanted to be close to people – and to love, you have to be close, don't you?'

'I would go on loving you, if I were never any closer to you than I am now.'

She turned to look at him. 'I love your spectacles,' he said. 'Absurd, but they seem part of you, and they make your eyes look even bigger.' Gently he removed them and she flinched slightly as he kissed her gently on the cheek. So soft, he thought, so soft. Then he put the glasses on her nose again and said: 'I won't do that again because it makes me want you more. I shall write to you and you can come here whenever you wish and I shall send you the little present – if you will accept it.'

'I wear the wee camisole in bed,' she whispered.

'Oh, don't, don't – !' he groaned and then stood up and she stood up too feeling rather strange. She hoped she had appeared neither too reluctant to accept his feelings nor too forward and eager to have him as her adorer if not her lover. She thought she'd succeeded.

After she had gone away, he sat alone in his drawing-room before going slowly up the stairs again to contemplate on the canvas. He felt a strong conviction that one day he would have her for his own and that she would learn to call him beloved, for he always called her that in his heart. But later in the evening the conviction waned and he consoled himself by taking out the green dress from Maud's parcel and burying his nose in its folds. It was like a sickness, he thought.

There was no reason why but as the train went over the bridge Maud remembered that nasty incident four years before, which she had never told anyone but Jackie about. She was alone in the compartment as rain began to beat down upon the water beneath, and when the train suddenly stopped she wished Sir Hector was sitting there. It would be quite exciting to make love in a train. She wished she could "love" him. Convention would have it that she must play the pure virgin and would castigate Sir Hector as a wicked married man, but convention was wrong. 'True morality', the sort Jackie talked about, would prefer her either to tell him to forget her since she could not love him enough, or would allow her to give in to the desire for her which she knew he was trying to suppress. There could be love without it, and there was desire without love, she was sure. Another Sir Hector might never again present himself to her.

The pelting rain brought a clap of thunder with it and it was dark outside, a summer storm. He would write to her, had no intention of going out of her life unless she begged him to do so. It was a sort of victory for her since he was to love on her terms, but it did not truly feel like one.

She stood up and looked out of the train window. The rain was now lashing the waves below and the sky was intermittently growling. Her excitement seemed to fade and the train lights, which had gone on for a moment when it became dark, went out again as she looked out over the sea. I am alone, she thought. Tomorrow everything will be ordinary again. Ma will come back on Monday and I shall go to the library and read about other people's battles and loves. But I am alone. She suddenly remembered that 'shape' she had seen on the beach as she looked down at the bridge. She closed her eyes again to forget it, but when she opened them again some configuration behind the window seemed to take on the outline of that old ragged woman. It was like a shape in a dream or a nightmare and gave her a mental pain to contemplate. How could a shape be so menacing? I am nothing, she thought. Nothing. I might be that old woman, just a shape of no account in the world. One day I'll be old and will have forgotten Sir Hector and one day I'll be dead like Grandfather and there won't be any meaning in anything. Terror began to close in on her and she swallowed, feeling her heart thumping under her coat. She began to moan softly to herself. She was overwrought, she told herself, was not the sort of girl who went mad or was frightened of shadows. She had been dishonest to Sir Hector; if only he were here now and she could entrust herself to him and forget all the effort needed to carry on living and working and learning. I wish I knew what I really wanted, she thought, as she tried to breathe deeply and slowly to overcome the panic. She had always been frightened of madness, of losing her grip.

Then the lights came on again and the train began to move and slowly she regained her equanimity.

When Maggie returned though, on the Monday, she was a little worried when her daughter burst out crying, but could not explain why, clutched her as she had clutched her when some nameless fear had engulfed her as a toddler.

'You need a holiday, hen,' Maggie murmured. 'You work too hard.'

Maud dried her eyes and blew her nose, saying only: 'I expect you're right Ma. Perhaps I'll take a day trip in the brake to the sea when ma friend comes back.'

'You ought to invite her to take tea with us,' said Ma. 'If she's not too grand.'

Maud knew that Ma divined she was a little ashamed of her ordinary home and her father's humble occupation-for he would still come home dirty from dealing with his wholesale purchases. Maud threw her arms around her and said: 'I don't want to give you work, Ma – she could have come when you were away, but I like to keep myself to myself.'

111

She went for the promised trip to the hills with Malcolm instead, and spent the rest of the vacation in the university library or window-shopping. It was only in the last week of the holiday that a small parcel was handed to her by the lady librarian, who now knew Maud well and allowed her to wash her hands in the staff wash-room, since no other students were using the library that week. 'It was addressed care of the library,' she said.

Maud unwrapped it when she was in the train going back home. She wished he could have sent it to her home address, which she had now given him, but realised it might have been a problem. Inside the paper was a box and in the box on a bed of cotton wool, a slender hoop of a silver bracelet. There were letters encircling the inner side of the bracelet and she could read the words quite well without her glasses. In beautiful copperplate writing of the last century was the motto 'Time Will Unite Us'. In spite of herself, Maud found her eyes filling with tears.

Hector was away in Edinburgh when the new term started.

'When I miss you I go to Garvits and look at your picture', he wrote.

Jackie seemed different, both graver and more excitable by turns. She said nothing at first to Maud except that the Highlands were beautiful and she would like to live in the country.

'Alone?' asked Maud.

'Calum might be offered a rural practice – ' She was clearly envisaging a life with him one day.

'How is he?' Maud asked politely.

'Busy, as usual – he's passed all his exams – only the final report on his infirmary work now. We managed to see each other after I'd come back.'

Her face glowed with love and tenderness when she spoke of him. I wonder if she's become his lover, Maud wondered. It seemed likely. Jackie was impetuous. She would do what most educated girls would not.

Maud said nothing to her friend about Sir Hector, but wore the bracelet, putting it on under her sleeve during the journey from home and removing it on her way back.

112

Jackie noticed it one day when Maud was washing her hands and knew she had never seen it before.

'Is the picture finished? Can I see it?' she had already asked Maud.

'Yes – he's got it at Garvits – we unveiled it and hung it – he likes it, on the whole. Perhaps he'll invite us both one day if you'd like to see it.'

She sounded deliberately vague, and Jackie hardly dare ask her if she liked it herself. She very much wanted to see the result of James Valentine's inspirational labours.

'I listened a lot to music in the holiday,' she said instead. 'Caruso. Oh, he's marvellous, Maud! Opera's my favourite art form I think.'

'More than fiction?' asked Maud, amused.

'Oh, well, I suppose not – but there are feelings that only music can express.'

Later she showed Maud a notebook where she had tried to translate the words of several arias from the Italian and French. They were all highly romantic, passionate, pieces of love and loss and longing. 'Calum has this marvellous voice,' she went on. 'I think he could have become a singer – like his grandfather, you know.' Maud, who had no phonograph and whose musical taste was restricted to the better known works of Beethoven and Schubert, was silent. Hector would probably like opera too. Jackie seemed as carried away with her love for Calum Fyffe as Sir Hector was for her.

Maud had a new tutor now, though Professor Carmichael was keeping his eye on her, she was well aware, for she guessed he did see her as a future scholar in his field. The extra work she had accomplished in the vacation would stand her in good stead when she specialised in her fourth year. Apparently there were scholarships for post-graduate work. She saw many more years of study stretching ahead.

Jackie was concentrating upon English Literature, but they had both been accepted for Honours courses, and this second year was easier for them than the first. The two young women met usually only by arrangement, or at the class for French prose, which was obligatory for both of them, much to Maud's disgust, for she found French too easy. After the class Jackie would often ask Maud to take a cup of tea with her at the Women's Hall of Residence or in one of the many cafs in the town before Maud went off on her train. They both had secrets from each other now, to do with the men in their lives; they had grown a little apart. Maud had no other friends, whilst Jackie seemed to know everyone. One late afternoon they met by chance in the street and Maud consented to walk along with Jackie 'for the exercise'. Jackie had just been to a meeting of the new Dramatic Society. 'Don't you get fed up having that journey every day?' she asked her when Maud said she must go.

'No – I read in the train – I like to get by myself sometimes – '

'I wish you'd join the Drama Soc – we're reading Sheridan – '

'I couldna act for toffee. I've never wanted to. I'll come and see you though if you get that part you want.'

'Sometimes they put on Greek plays,' said Jackie, trying to tempt her. But Maud would never change, wouldn't join in.

'What about your stories then?' asked Maud as she turned to go. 'You said you were writing one when I saw you in the vacation. Or have you been too busy listening to opera with Calum?' she asked mischievously.

Jackie laughed. 'I'm sorry – I talk too much about him, don't I?'

Maud ignoring this, said: 'Did you finish The Nine of Diamonds?'

Jackie was touched that Maud should be interested. 'Just about – but I have to revise it. I really have hopes this one will be published.'

'Good luck then – can I see it sometime?'

'Well, when I've taken a carbon copy – I don't think it's your sort of thing though – '

'Let me be the judge of that,' said Maud. 'I do read novels you know – I dinna have elevated taste in these matters.'

Jackie was not hurt that Maud should think her stories might be rather less than elevated and agreed Maud could read it when it was finished.

Maud had to wait a week or two before Jackie handed her a foolscap envelope after the French prose class. 'Open it on the train. You said you might like to read it,' she ordered.

Maud looked forward to her journeys. She was up to date

114

with her work and tried to read for pleasure during her daily commuting. *The Nine of Diamonds* was carefully typed on the title page. She looked up before turning the page, trying to assemble her knowledge of the legends associated with this playing card before she saw what Jackie had done with it. Nine and five and three were mystical numbers to the Ancients, and her own private lucky number had always been three. Funny that seven wasn't of any special importance to the Greeks and Romans. Hadn't Tennyson written a story involving the Nine of Diamonds? – one of the Idylls of the King? Maud had had to read *Elaine* at the Academy, but it was not a story she had particularly liked. She was 'agin' Tennyson because he had written 'Maud', for she had suffered a good deal when young from schoolmates who found his verse amusing. "Birds in the high hall garden" were all very well, but as for:

'I kiss'd her slender hand
She took her kiss sedately;
Maud is not seventeen
But she is tall and stately'

– it had been untrue – and had a bathetic rhyme.

The Nine of Diamonds was also the Curse of Scotland, different authorities disagreeing why. She stared out of the train window.

Which legend, if any, would Jackie have used? The one about the arms of Stair associated with the Glencoe massacre? Jackie wasn't the sort to write about battles, so she discounted the story of the Duke of Cumberland scribbling 'No Quarter' on the back of the card after Culloden. Yet some folk said it was the *cross* of Scotland, not the *curse* – St Andrew's cross, that was made up of nine diamonds.

She began to read and had almost finished by the time they arrived at the city station, not even having noticed the crossing of the bridge, so engrossed had she been. Jackie really could write! She finished it off once at home, even before taking her supper, realising there was more in her friend than met the eye. Not being gifted with creative ability of any kind herself she marvelled at Jackie's imagination. The story was a mixture

of legend and modern life. Her heroine, a certain Clytie –
what a strange name – had she invented this shortening of
Clytemnestra? – was a beautiful girl descended from an 18th
century earl who lived in a lonely house on a cliff overlooking
the sea. Her mother was dead and her father was a rich man
who gambled and drank a great deal. Clytie was in love with a
young nobleman whom she had no hope of marrying unless she
could escape from her father. As she was only nineteen this was
impossible until she begame legally of age. One day in his cups
her father challenged a group of his cronies to gamble for the
hand of Clytie. Clytie persuaded her own swain to impersonate
a new neighbour who would come to play cards, for she had
found a card on the floor under her drunken father's sleeping
form. The card was the nine of diamonds and she realised that
somehow it had to do with his winning every game. She drew
a cross around the pattern of the diamonds and put it with the
other cards. The next day, when friends arrived to play, the
winning card was found in the hand of one Alexander Stuart,
her lover in disguise. (His features rather resembled Calum
Fyffe's, thought Maud). Having won the game he kept the old
man to his bargain and rode away with his bride.

It was stagey but it was stirring. She felt sure it would
be a winner, for it infected the reader with both fear and
excitement. The winning card was a nice touch too with the
cross of Scotland making the diamonds into a symbol of hope.
She liked melodramas; what were so many of her favourite
novels but melodrama after all? She wrote a short note to Jackie
and put it in with the envelope which next day she placed in her
friend's pigeon-hole.

At home her father was now determined to make a go of
his business and had taken Duncan in. Duncan was showing
surprising practical ability – everyone had thought him rather
stupid since he did not relish 'booklearning' – but now it
appeared he had a scheme for the manufacturing of fishing
floats from the cork his father was dealing in. Maggie was
delighted now that all three of her children seemed settled
in their work. She had begun to save for a larger house in a
nicer part of the city, but sometimes said: 'We'll be pushing up
daisies before we scrape together enough for it.' Maud felt a

little distanced now from home, though she was still close to the unsuspecting Maggie who had no idea of her daughter's private and secret life. After that time when Maud had sobbed in her arms in August – for no reason she had been able to discover – she had tried to give her little treats to cheer her up. But Maud's examination results reassured her and with the new term the girl seemed less agitated and Maggie relaxed.

Sometimes Maud felt that the whole business of living was only bearable because of the routine she imposed upon herself. But these times were not often and she had not had any further sight of that 'shape' that had frightened her on the beach and in the train. She decided to leave any further developments of the Garvits part of her life to fate and Sir Hector. For her part she would await whatever was in store with an assumed indifference. That her frightening feelings had been connected with water did not escape her, for she was as superstitious as only an excessively rational person could be. She was becoming known now as much for her wit and sarcasm as for her brain and aloofness. She would condescend occasionally to remark upon other people or things in general in that acerbic and salty way of hers which accorded unusually with her habitual quiet. 'Maud's quite a wag,' they said. 'When she bothers to notice anybody or anything.'

Jackie was pleased with Maud's opinion of her story and sent it off to a magazine. She was pleased too that Maud's general opinion of her abilities seemed to have grown for Maud was never one to praise overmuch, if at all. Usually she reserved her most cutting tones for other women and Jackie realised that beneath her silence, as beneath her wit, was a certain contempt.

She still did not in Jackie's opinion eat enough and was often taken by her for a bun and a cup of tea when she looked peaky. Yet she wasn't too thin.

'I had an egg for ma breakfast and ever since ma interior's been in a state of complete anarchy,' she would say. Or 'I cooked a wee piece of fish last night, can you believe it?' It was unusual enough for her to comment upon it, thought Jackie. Maud was well looked after at home and she must stop worrying about her.

*   *   *

117

She waited for Maud who was in a class in the Old Building and would come out at noon. When Maud saw her waiting, Jackie lifted up her morning post, a letter from the magazine accepting her story *The Nine of Diamonds*.

'Isna that great!' said Maud. 'I'm gey pleased for you, Jackie.' And she looked pleased, though it was never Maud's way to embrace anyone or take their arm. 'Let's celebrate with a wee dram,' she said and led Jackie to a seat on the grounds of the ruined cathedral. There she fished in her bag and brought out a flask. 'I was cold yesterday so I bought a bottle of whisky,' she said. 'And I even have a picnic cup.' She poured half into the cup and gave it to Jackie. 'To the celebrated novelist Miss Livesey.' She raised the flask and drank herself. 'How much are they going to pay you?' she enquired.

'Two guineas, isn't that good! – I expected ten shillings.'

'Will you take a pseudonym then? – you won't be wanting the university to know.'

'I think I shall use the name I wrote it under – I added it after you'd read it – "Morwenna Mackay" – what do you think?'

Maud began to laugh. 'Aye, that should guarantee a market north of the Border. Will you tell your parents? Your grandmother?'

'I'll tell father, but Granny, no – I'll wait until I have a long story accepted – there's lots I want to write. I wish I had more time – do you think I should finish my degree? – sometimes I wonder whether I'd not be better off just writing.'

Maud drained her flask and then put it with the cup back at the bottom of her bag. 'Don't go, Jackie – whom would I talk to!' Jackie was touched and Maud went on: 'You can always write, even if you are married'.

'I think I shall marry him, Maud,' she replied and looked at Maud with what Maud called her 'intense' look.

Maud thought, they must be lovers. 'Take care now,' she said.

Jackie knew perfectly well what she meant and replied 'Oh, he's a *doctor* you know', and laughed.

Maud found the idea of physical coupling more ludicrous than distasteful – but still distasteful. Many things in life she found distasteful, though well aware how often they happened. In the past, she had imagined that women needed bribes to give in to men at all and there was still something of this in her thinking. She supposed that marriage for women must be the highest bribe . . . She fingered the bracelet Hector had sent her. Was he so far removed from this sort of complicity with the physical world, this fact of life that amounted to two people, two pieces of flesh rubbing together? She supposed that desire was needed to make intimacy different and exciting, and could not seem to find that passion in herself, though she appeared to arouse it. For the first time in her life as she walked back from the ruined cathedral, Jackie having waved her goodbye, she asked herself if there was some ingredient missing from her constitution – or did most young women feel like this if they were honest, and disregarded the sentimental trappings that went with 'love'?

New Year 1925 arrived without the usual icy winds but with turbulent storms. Maud saw less of Jackie, who had permission to stay every weekend over at her grandmother's where, Maud supposed, Calum was the more easily reached. But when they did meet it was still Jackie who talked most, and mostly about the stories she was writing, giving the impression of extreme busyness, what with her academic work and Calum and her writing, for she had also appeared in the University production of *A School for Scandal* and done some reporting for the college magazine. Maud who was quite robust herself felt tired contemplating her friend's activities.

Maud sent a Christmas card to Sir Hector in which she thanked him again for the lovely bracelet, 'which I wear, and often think of you and of Mistress Susanna'. She had a reply in the New Year: she must come to Garvits when the weather improved. Not a day went by when he did not think of her, he wrote. If she would only write to him now and again he would try to be content with that. His son was now at the university in Edinburgh and both his children had been to Garvits at Christmas time and Christina had remarked upon the new portrait in the gallery and said: 'I wish I looked like that.' Maud considered her reply very carefully as the ball now appeared to be in her court. How long could a man be kept waiting? She both wanted him in her life and yet did not want to commit herself.

119

By the summer term she had still not answered his letter and he had made no attempt as far as she knew to see her. But when one afternoon Jackie told her that she was sure she had seen him in the town, and that he had recognised her but said nothing, Maud knew she had better act. She would not ask Jackie's advice – and in any case Jackie seemed preoccupied; she would have to think it out for herself. When she saw Sir Hector again she wanted the meeting to pass off on her own terms. She had just taken up her pen one morning in the library, having tried to assemble her thoughts, when a shadow fell over her writing paper. She looked up and saw Calum Fyffe.

'Have you seen Jackie?' he whispered. 'She said she'd be at Mackenzie's tea-shop at eleven, but she didn't come – I'm over here to see my professor.'

Maud was glad of any excuse to put off her letter, gathered up her books and went out with him. He seemed older, more decided, less of a joker, as he said: 'I believe you've *grown*, Maud – it must be all the walking you do!'

'No, I'm wearing ma heels,' she said complacently. 'Now where can she be? Shall I look in at the Hall for you? – she may have an essay to finish – I believe she was doing a paper on "Romance".' She looked up at him from under her heavy eyelashes with a suggestive glance.

Calum was not sure whether she was teasing him. 'Let's go to Mackenzie's then,' he suggested. 'I'll treat you to a cup of coffee.' He took her bag of books with a gallant gesture. Over the coffee, made badly with boiled milk, he offered Maud a cigarette.

'No thanks – I don't,' she said.

'Very sensible,' said Calum who did not smoke much himself. As he drank his coffee he observed her coiled hair and her alabaster cheeks and well-kept hands. She doesn't give anything away, he thought. Jackie had never told him in any detail about Maud's life, being true to her promise to Maud, but he guessed there was still someone in the background, some admirer.

Maud decided to plunge in. Naming no names of course, but as Calum was a man, he might have some idea how the minds of men worked and it also might be amusing to see how he reacted. 'May I ask you something?' she began in a low voice. 'If you were fond of a woman but you were married and the woman was not enamoured of you – though she found you attractive, would you chase her or would you let her be?'

He looked at her in surprise. 'It would depend how enamoured I was!' he replied, laughing at first but then, seeing Maud's rather troubled expression, he frowned.

'Well, let's say for the sake of argument *very* enamoured,' she said.

'I suppose it would depend on whether I thought I might get her!' he offered.

'Well, you wouldn't know that, would you? Do men follow a chimera for very long – how long do men wait?'

'You say the man is married?'

'Aye – but maybe that doesn't affect the question substantially.'

'Then it would depend on the woman, wouldn't it? – if she just was content to have a man "enamoured" of her.'

'If the man thought the woman loved him,' she said, stirring her coffee and catching her upper lip in her teeth. 'Would that make him more eager or less?'

'He would want the woman to be attracted to him,' said Calum, half a currant bun poised in the air in his hand. 'But he would not want to be too certain. I believe men like to give chase and feel they are the pursuers not the pursued. Then they can feel they made the woman succumb to their charms.'

'Does that apply to all men do you think?' she asked, thinking of Jackie.

'What a strange conversation, Maud. I am not an expert in these matters!'

She said nothing in reply to that and waited for his answer.

'You see, I think you are talking about some sort of romantic infatuation,' he said after a pause. 'Men do fall in love, poor wretches, but they are more often the victims of their rather more fleshly desires.'

'We presume women have those too,' she said uneasily.

'It doesn't seem real to me, Maud, all this talk of "Love",' he said. 'I'd have to know the circumstances.'

'As a doctor you are more interested in bodies?'

'Bodies have a good deal to do with it all.'

Maud was aware that this was dangerous sort of talk to have with a man, even with your best friend's man. Calum did not appear to be shocked at her questions, for he was looking at her with no shadow of disapproval. 'Men being, unfortunately, as they are,' he said – 'Women just have to decide what they want of them.' Just then he caught sight of Jackie weaving into the room. He waved and she saw him and came over, her arms full of books and an enormous bunch of wallflowers.

'Sorry, Calum – I had to finish my essay – did I say eleven then? – I thought I'd said twelve.'

'Maud has been entertaining me,' said Calum easily.

'But I have to go now,' said Maud. 'I have work to do waiting in the library.

Jackie did not implore her to say; she had eyes only for her beloved. The flowers were for him. Maud said 'Goodbye,' and escaped, to think over what the beloved had said. She did want to see her portrait again, kept dreaming of it in a most strange way. Dreams had never before been important to her: unlike Jackie she did not usually have very interesting ones and also, unlike Jackie, did not tell them to others. But the dream seemed to say that she wanted to go to Garvits once more. It would please Sir Hector, but she would not yet fix on a definite day, would keep him just a little in suspense.

When Calum had tried to answer Maud's questions he had felt a little at a loss. Generalities did not have much to do with his own feelings. Love, he thought, could not be rationalised and discussed as though all men had things in common. Maud was so different from Jackie for whom feeling came before all other considerations. Yet which was the typical woman? He suspected that Jackie would always be the prime mover in her relationships. Sometimes he wondered if he had accepted Jackie's love only because it went with a physical expression rarely ventured on by young women. That made him feel guilty. Maud was more circumspect; maybe it was because she felt less. Or were her feelings of a different order from that he was used to in Jackie? She was an enigma, Maud.

'Does Maud have a man?' he asked Jackie on the Saturday following his meeting with Maud in the library. 'She was asking me rather peculiar questions about men in general – I couldn't help feeling she was concerned with one in particular! It seemed unlike her.'

Jackie considered; should she tell him about Sir Hector? 'I believe there is a man who is crazy about her – she's very secretive,' was all she said in reply.

'Dear Maud – I am so happy that you want to come over here again. I could not express to you or to anyone how I have missed you. It is so long since you were here, sometimes I think it was years ago, but in fact it's only nine months.

I have managed by working myself to bits, and giving myself the treat of taking a long look at your portrait only when I feel I can't carry on any longer, will go mad with waiting just to see your real face. You see, Maud, I think now I was foolish in wanting to have you painted, thinking that somehow then I'd have a little of you here. It makes it worse that "you" in simulcrum are in my gallery and the real girl is far away. But I must not let myself begin to feel sorry for myself as you have done nothing to deserve that. I cannot heap reproaches on your head just for not being here! Can you come on Saturday June thirteenth? – If you can, I will call for you myself at the station in the car as some of the staff will be on their own holidays then.

Your devoted H H

P.S. I had to go to a tango tea dance held for my employees not long ago. They love this sort of thing and I've always adored tangos. But I was not prepared for the terrible need I had to dance that dance with you. Can you understand that, I wonder? The music seemed to speak of you, though I know you are not a melancholy person – it is I who am that.'

He wants my body and 'soul' to worship, it isna me, she thought at first when she read all this. It did excite her a little. Obscurely she knew that soon, like Jackie, she would have to meet the challenge of male desire. In what small rags of common sense or scholarship or precedent could she clothe herself to meet Sir Hector on her own ground? I need not go, I need not go, she muttered to herself in bed, but she knew she must go, that her destiny was not to avoid seeing him for ever. But how should you meet a man's desire, whether it was for your body or your soul if you did not think you felt such desire yourself?

She had seen plenty of men stare at her; heard many remarks addressed to her under their breath, and listened to more raucous praise from workmen in the streets when she passed holding her case of books, one hand clutching her high collar against the northern winds. They stared at her legs, to a larger extent than heretofore revealed by the new fashion. Silk stockings were against the Crichton sense of morality, but Maud had saved up and bought a pair and was sure her mother knew.

For her part Maggie knew her daughter for a most exceptional girl who must not be thwarted and whom she loved to cosset and pamper. Maud was too good for ordinary men. She was relieved that Maud had never spoken of any men to her, nor had appeared to take any interest in the things most girls talked about. Let her wait till an excellent marriage opportunity presented itself; there was plenty of time. Maud would first of all show them all at the university how clever she was.

Chapter 7

They were sitting together in the drawing-room at Garvits with a summer afternoon's sounds coming in through the long windows. He had fetched her from the station in his Rolls and then they had sat side by side in the garden until it became too hot. He looked across at her in her green art silk dress and her silk stockings, as she sat, head bent, hands folded neatly on her lap.

'What can I say,' he said, and she looked up at him and put one hand up to her neck in an unconsciously self-caressing gesture.

'I always wear your bracelet,' she said, and rolled up her silk sleeve at the wrist.

'Perhaps I should not have given it to you – I no longer seem to know what I should and shouldn't do,' he said.

He did not want at that moment to arouse her, even if she could be aroused, was almost fearful of upsetting her tranquillity. Yet he did want her to need him in some other way. 'You always look so – untouched,' he said, and at this she raised her head again. 'Celeste Aida', he said. After a pause she said, 'If you were not married, would you ask me to marry you, Hector?', and waited for his answer with a little smile upon her lips. It was as if this man's pouring out of his feelings for her, trying not to sound foolish, did leave her untouched, except to give her confidence in herself.

For answer he said only: 'Oh, Maud!'

'Hector, shall I dress up in the antique dress?' she asked. 'I'd like to – and then I shall look like your picture again and you will imagine me sitting here in it again when I am gone.'

'Oh, my dear – if it pleases you. I don't need, today at any rate, to go and talk to you up there in my gallery – isn't it foolish? – I sometimes go and talk to you there!'

'And what do I answer?' asked Maud, already at the door.

'You just go on looking at me when I tell you I love you and – '

'And I reply that I love you too? – Or that I do not but I will be your lover if you want?' she suggested boldly.

'No, I can never hear your reply. You listen to me and then you turn your head just a little as you do on your portrait and I can suddenly see you as I can see you now – and then you fade away and I'm by myself again.'

'I shall dress up,' said Maud, and disappeared. Hector went on sitting, looking unseeingly out of the window. What sort of future could there ever be for them? He could not, could he, make a mistress out of a girl like Maud? And as his wife – the dream was impossible. Florence had written to him only that week and he had been astonished to find that she was feeling stronger and more cheerful, and that she thanked him for having always understood her and been patient. He had found himself gritting his teeth and actually in a rage with his poor sufferer. He could not lose Maud now, he *could* not. Yet somehow he had managed without her all these long months.

When she came down again he did not hear at first, so rapt he was in his own conflicting emotions of pity for his wife and his holy joy in the recent presence of Maud. 'Hector,' she whispered softly and he looked up. There at the door she stood, young and beautiful, the green lady with hair this time over her shoulders and he gasped at its length. He was across the room before he even realised he had moved and took her in his arms and felt her long tresses and then softly pressed his mouth on hers, on the soft lips of Maud, so beautiful and so young. 'So young,' he murmured and kissed her again. Maud brushed her closed lips experimentally against his in the tiniest of movements. His eyes were shut. Like a moth's wings, he was thinking and her shoulders are under my hands, her breasts against my jacket, so soft. And her long hair all down her back. I must stop this, must not . . . He opened his eyes and saw that Maud's eyes were open also and were like dark pools of brown light, the colour of Scots burns with a little golden glimmer in them like the sun.

He raised his head. 'Let me look at you.'

Maud had expected the kiss, but was shaken. Her complicity

in the brushing of her lips against his had been half unconscious. She remained standing there holding on to the knob of the door whilst Hector, she thought, ravished her with his eyes. She was trembling a little.

'I'm sorry,' he said. 'I'm only a weak, foolish man – I should not have presumed, Maud.'

She went up to him. 'Never mind – I know you love me,' she said.

They were her first real kisses from a man. Strange that she, Maud Crichton, should never have been kissed like that before, unless you counted Uncle Dan – and she'd not allowed *him* to carry on. Just that she'd really never wanted to be kissed and even Sir Hector's kiss was strange. She supposed he could have kissed her lips ages ago if she'd given him any encouragement. Just for now though she did not want it to go further than kisses, did not want to entwine her arms around him as he had enfolded her in his.

'Sit down and let me look at you properly,' he said, feeling light-headed and unsure what she wanted him to do.

The order seemed to please her and she sat by the window and looked out on to the roses. 'I saw the picture again,' she said. 'I did want to see it.' Am I a different woman now he's kissed me? she was wondering. She twisted her hair up and back in a plait and skewered it with a tortoise-shell pin.

'The picture is of an Aphrodite Urania,' he said. 'My name for you – you must not become "Aphrodite Pandemus" or I shall lose my wits.'

Maud had no intention of becoming this for him just yet, being well aware that love could change to the carnality she sensed in others.

She would rather nurture that mystery he spoke of in her.

'You won't ever exhibit the portrait, will you?' she asked him anxiously and turned to look at him again. He was still looking at her, rather sadly, she thought, and yet she could read plainly on his face the desire he felt for her. That was admirable – not to give way to it like vulgar men did.

'No – it will stay here as long as I live,' he replied. 'But you already look a little different from the portrait.'

'Oh, no!' Maud exclaimed. 'You mean I look older already?'

'My dear – No! Only that you are growing more beautiful – each time I see you I see that.'

'I shall be twenty-one next year,' said Maud in a low voice. '*So* old!'

But he was thinking, that was why man invented art, for what can one do with beauty but worship it? If I make her mine, possess her, I lose my hold on the truth of feeling. Yet I want her as a woman and she must know that. He sighed.

'You always look sad,' said Maud. 'Did you want very much to kiss me?'

'You must know I did, and do, and can't help wanting far more than that, Maud. But, as you say, you are not yet twenty-one and I – ' He would not tell her he had heard only that week from his wife.

My God, what would he do if she ever returned?

'I can't lose you, Maud,' he said instead. 'I mean, just to have you here – in my heart where you have been ever since that first day.' He was distressed. She did not quite understand why.

Virginity and virtue are not always a protection, she thought. 'As you say, I'm very young, but whatever happens I shan't ever forget you, Hector,' she said.

'Don't even speak of it!' he cried. 'I can't hope you will ever – could ever feel for me as I do for you – but if you did – '

'I'm thirsty,' she said. 'Is there some lemonade?'

'They are all out – I shall make you some myself,' he said. 'Walk in the garden – it's a little cooler now and this side of the house will soon be in shade. You can go through the door there in the window. I like to feel you are among my roses. I'll to the kitchens to make us a drink.'

Everything in the garden spoke of summer and desire and the path to fruition –

She saw him come out into the garden with a tray which he put on a small stone table made out of the rockery wall.

'The lady in the garden,' he said and came up to her and took her hand and kissed it. It smelled of some elusive perfume that was not in the garden. 'You look so cool,' he said. 'In this weather.'

Now he looked nervous again, she thought. How strange men were.

128

They sat on the two chairs of stone that were around the little table and drank his home-made lemonade, fresh lemons and sugar and ice-cubes. 'You made it yourself?' she asked surprised.

'Of course – I can look after myself quite well, you know.'

'I wish *I* could,' she said.

He looked at her, amused. But then sadly – 'I wish I could look after *you*.' he said softly.

'Aye, I ken that.'

'I like the way you say that. I like the way you say everything. What am I to do, Maud?' He drained his glass and took her hand again, this time with such unconscious intensity that she winced; he exclaimed. 'Oh, your poor hand! Forgive me!' He kissed the white hand again.

'Life isna fair,' said Maud. 'I'm sorry.'

It was easy to make him say the things she liked to hear. The lemonade being finished and longer shadows coming upon his garden, they went in again, she thought he might take her in his arms again, but he did not. She would not have resisted him.

She pinned her hair up more tidily in the mirror and made a little murmur when he came softly up behind her and stroked her wrist. She liked that.

Then she turned and took his hand. 'I trust you,' she said. 'I will do what you wish me to.'

'I wish you loved me, Maud,' was all he said. 'I cannot claim any more of you till you can say you do.'

'Then you must give me time,' she said.

One morning in the July of nineteen twenty-five, Jackie Livesey felt sure she must be pregnant with the child of Calum Fyffe. She left her grandmother's house and went straight to him at the infirmary feeling she must see him immediately. Calum would know how to find out for certain, though *she* felt certain. Something must have gone wrong with his 'precautions'. She was not angry with Calum and felt in the midst of her dismay rather thrilled. She was only twenty, but she was strong and healthy, couldn't help feeling that Nature – and even fate – ought to be accepted. But she ought not to count on Calum seeing it that way.

He had been busy in the wards, but when he found her waiting outside guessed what had happened when he saw her face. They went into the hospital garden, and she told him.

'I'll do whatever you want,' he said. She was aware that one of Calum's friends had aborted his girlfriend's baby for her, since Calum had once mentioned it casually. But she wanted Calum to say that he wanted her to have the child. She had not even been thinking of marriage till he said after a long silence: 'Then we must marry.'

She thought, yes, I *do* want to marry him. But she said – 'You need not *marry* me, so long as you want the baby, I do not mind – I could have it without marriage. I am sorry, Calum.'

'We must marry!' he said. 'Our baby must have two parents.'

After the first shock he did not even seem surprised, or at least he did not show it. She knew Calum for an honourable young man. Maybe the residue of his mother's Roman Catholicism in him was enough for him not to consider doing away with the result of his own carelessness.

'You are not angry?' asked Jackie.

'You have more right to be angry with me,' he said. But he did not say what she wanted him to say which was – I love you, Jackie. She felt maybe he had realised he might be on the road to marriage ever since she had begun to sleep with him, but the news must be a shock.

'No – we mustn't marry just because I am pregnant,' she said in a small voice. 'Granny's not a conventional person – I don't think she'd be surprised or shocked – but I'll have to give up at the university.'

'Look, Jackie love, we'll talk later. I shall take that share of a practice they've offered me in Edinburgh in January. Yes, I will. This has made my mind up for me.

What will your Mama think – will she be angry?'

'I expect so – at first. Don't worry, Jackie – but come back at five and I can take you over to the labs. They've got a wonderful new technique for making sure!'

She might not be, he thought, as he walked away to another emergency. I wish she were not. But if she is, everyone will blame her. They never blame the man – I can't ruin her life. Dear Jackie, I'm very fond of her.

130

It was only when Jackie wrote to Maud and suggested they met in the city that she began to see how it might appear to others. As far as she was concerned they would soon get all the unpleasant things over – telling parents and grandparents – and even getting married! At some Registry Office, she supposed. Then she could give herself up to her pregnancy, to bearing Calum's child Their baby, his and hers, the product of love, the end result of all her dreams and her passion.

'I canna imagine what I'd do if it were me,' said Maud, looking really shocked and upset. In her world this was how a girl was ruined, she'd heard it often enough. It must never happen to her.

'I don't *have* to marry,' said Jackie. 'But Calum wants us to – if he didn't want the baby I suppose I'd have it alone. I do love him so, Maud.'

Maud thought, well, it's a common enough occurrence when all's said and done. 'But you canna finish your degree,' she replied in distress. 'Oh, Jackie!'

'You know I'd become in two minds about that – I shall go on with my writing. You see – I can't help feeling it was all meant to happen,' Jackie said defiantly. Maud did not seem as pleased as she'd thought she might be.

'Really?' said Maud, trying to be kind but really both angry and sorry, especially for Calum Fyffe, who was now caught in his own toils. 'Well, I suppose I can knit some bootees,' she said. 'I'm a good knitter.'

Jackie smiled weakly. She had not got round to thinking of such practicalities. 'Calum is a good man,' she said.

'Aye, I know – I hope you'll both be happy – when will you get wed?'

'Probably September when we've sorted everything out. He's accepting a job in Edinburgh he was offered. I think he would've anyway.'

'I can see you as a mother, but not a wife,' said Maud.

'People don't have to live in a conventional way even if they're married,' replied Jackie.

Maud looked sceptical. 'You will have to be very firm if you want to go on with your own work,' she said severely. 'You know what men are like once they're married.'

131

'I don't know many married men,' said Jackie, rather hurt, but not intending to be sarcastic.

Maud flushed. 'I'll miss you,' she said. 'But I suppose it is the best thing for you, really. I knew you would marry him,' she added.

'But not like this?'

'It isna your fault. Takes two,' said Maud.

'I *do* want the baby, Maud!'

'I suppose most women do want babies.'

'I feel guilty – and sorry for Calum, because he has to take the responsibility. I did want him to be free to choose . . .' She stopped.

'Well, he is responsible. The way you felt about him was obviously going to lead to what's happened, wasn't it? Wouldn't it be a miracle if women could have the love without the bairns!'

Maud was working during the vacation in the library again. She had decided to learn German, for she was sure she would need to go over there soon. One morning she went out to clear her head for twenty minutes and was on her way back from the shop where they sold the pencils she liked when she saw two familiar figures across the road who waved to her and then came over.

Calum had said to Jackie: 'There's Maud – does she ever stop working?' When they all stood together, rather awkwardly on the pavement, he went on: 'You must take a wee holiday, Maud – we're just going to the university registry.' To tell them Jackie was giving up, she supposed.

'I've just got to call in at a friend's,' said Calum. 'Meet you both at Mackenzie's,' and was off.

'What did your grandmother say?' asked Maud. She was curious to know how the rich middle classes reacted to such a piece of news. Not that Jackie's family seemed at all typical.

'She said "You'll have your hands full, but he's a handsome man. I suppose it's my fault for not taking better care of you",' said Jackie.

'You weren't scolded then?'

'Well, she did say she didn't know how my mother would react. "Anne was always a worrier. It's a good thing you've got me here and not her". Happily mother is three thousand miles away. But Gran thinks women *should* marry young!'

Calum joined them both in Mackenzie's and Maud observed him covertly, though she sensed he avoided her glance. 'You must let me know what to give you for a wedding present,' she said.

'You'll knit those baby clothes,' said Jackie. 'You promised!'

Calum looked very surprised as though he thought such things would be out of Maud's ken.

'You are lucky,' said Maud to Jackie before they parted. 'I couldna imagine what my family would come out with if I'd got myself into your sort of pickle.' To Calum she said: 'Look after her, won't you?' She collected her books and was off back to the library.

'She can be rude,' said Calum. 'More like a reproof that was, wasn't it?'

'Oh, you know Maud,' said Jackie. 'She likes to tease – and I *am* lucky – I'm happy.' She squeezed his hand. They'd make the best of it, he thought, and Jackie, who knew nothing whatever about babies, much less than he did, would learn how to manage a house and a home, he supposed.

On the very day of the new term's start in October when Maud was already well into her self-imposed study of German, Jackie Livesey and Calum Fyffe were married at a Register Office in Edinburgh. It happened also to be the day the magazine *Silver Star* accepted another of Jackie's stories. She'd borrowed the plot from *Trilby*, but had made the story her own and given it quite a different ending. Maud read the carbon copy of the typescript when she gave herself a holiday from work on the Saturday. She missed Jackie. There was nobody else among the students she cared to talk to and she had already squashed the gossip surrounding her friend's abrupt departure from the fields of learning. Hector now wrote to her regularly and she replied with news of her studies and in one letter a mention of Jackie's marriage, without mentioning the coming baby. But what had happened to Jackie frightened Maud in spite of its apparently happy outcome. It was so easy to become pregnant, and then have your whole life threatened and taken away from you. For she had no doubt that was what happened to women who were. She often used to wonder what her own mother had been like before she had children. Now she lived for them, forgot herself. I could never be like Ma, she thought. I'm too selfish – and besides babies spoil women's figures and their faces grow old and lined with worry. Maybe rich women's don't, but even Hector's wife went mad – and she had heaps of money and every attention, I'm sure.

In March of the next year, Jackie's baby was born, a boy, whom Jackie insisted upon calling Joseph Sebastian, the Joseph after Calum's maternal Spanish grandfather the tenor. 'Sebastian is after my father,' she wrote to Maud, who sent her a carefully packed parcel of three pairs of small pale green bootees, three pairs of white angora mittens and three white bonnets of varying sizes.

'You mean Maud *knitted* them?' exclaimed Calum in disbelief.

'Maud is very practical and good with her hands,' replied Jackie. 'It's very sweet of her.'

The new family had a flat in a tall building not far from the Royal Mile. Edinburgh was at first strange, but Calum's probationary year in a practice did not pay too badly. Jackie fed the infant Joseph herself with amazing ease and for about four months quite forgot about her stories, till one morning she found a cheque enclosed in a letter from the *Silver Star* who had now published her reworking of *Trilby* and wanted more like it. Jackie used five shillings of her earnings to buy Maud a twenty-first birthday present, which she had not been able to afford on Maud's actual birthday. It was a Spanish comb of tortoiseshell with a few fake diamonds and Jackie thought it was pretty and would suit her friend. With it she wrote urging Maud to come and visit.

Maud had celebrated her own important milestone in the new house which proud Maggie had bought on a mortgage, something not even the Preacher had ever done, for he had always rented his gloomy dwellings. All Maud's relations were invited to a large and splendid tea and she was toasted in non-alcoholic wine into which Uncle Hamish slipped a wee dram. *They* had not changed at all, she thought, whilst *she* had. She thought of Sir Hector's champagne and his fine wines and wondered if he would remember her birthday. She still could not write and say she loved and missed him, though she certainly missed him. But she announced shortly after Easter to Ma that now she had attained her majority she intended to live in the university town for her last year as an undergraduate. To Maggie's pleadings that she would starve, she promised to come home for some weekends.

In her pigeon-hole at the new Hall where she had been given a room she found, on the first morning of her return for the summer term, a note asking her to call at the Office for a registered parcel.

The address was typed, but she knew from whom it had come. She took it back up to her room to open, shut the door and put it on the little bed with its white coverlet and composed herself. Then she unwrapped it carefully and found a small box and inside the box, on a velvet cloth, a pair of diamond earrings. Not those she had worn for her portrait, but an even more magnificent pair with diamonds so large anyone would think they were fake. She caught her breath and tears came into her eyes as she contemplated them. Then, taking out her old ones, she put the new ones on and stared at herself in the mildewed glass which was the place's only concession to vanity.

'My mother died at Christmas', he wrote, 'and so these, which were hers, are for you. My daughter does not wear such things and my wife has plenty. Oh Maud, do you miss me as I miss you? I live to see you in the flesh again, dearest girl, and I wish you a happy birthday. But not perhaps the most happy of all for I believe and hope that one day you will spend a birthday with me, with many happy returns of that day too. Your own H H – look after yourself, my own Maud'.

She caught her breath; she would have to see him again soon. He had said he did not want to be tempted until she wanted him only because she loved him. Yet he seemed also to want to keep her as a sort of icon. Oh, if only she could want to surrender herself to him, as he so obviously wished to surrender to her. Could it be a just exchange? Why could she not love him the way he loved her? Still she felt like encouraging him a little more? She put the earrings for the time being in the purse she carried around her waist, and looked at the watch she wore on her blouse. Just time to get to her class with Carmichael. Thank goodness this year he was one of her teachers again. But wherever could she wear such jewellery?

Hector stood motionless at his library window holding an opened letter stiffly in his hand. On the green leather-covered table lay another letter, already opened and read, a letter from Maud saying she would like to see him: 'To thank you personally for the wonderful present which I have worn so far only when I have been alone in my room. The earrings are far too grand to put on with a blouse and skirt and scholar's gown'.

He had been waiting for that letter ever since he had despatched the diamonds to her, filled with foreboding that she might return them, might think he was bribing her to return his love.

But the foreboding should have related to the other letter he now held. It was from his wife Florence, and he had read it through only once. Once had been enough, since it contained the shattering news that, as she had been feeling so much better for the past six months, as he already knew, her doctors were hopeful this time of a lasting recovery. She would be allowed to try to return to normal life, to live with him, become once more his wife. 'You've been *so* patient with me . . . I do think that I've recovered my wits and much of my strength and will soon be able to put all this behind me . . .'

What a few years back would have been a matter for his most heartfelt rejoicing made his heart sink and his stomach churn.

He forced himself to glance at the letter again. Did she give a date for this proposed return to Scotland? Yes, there it was. 'They think that by the autumn or at the very latest, Christmas . . .'

And there was the letter from Maud who trusted him and whom he longed to see again, even if she would never love him, never reciprocate his love for her. He could not let Florence down now who also trusted him, though he might dread her return. He knew he was not the kind of man who could happily carry on an intrigue behind his wife's back, yet how long could he go on loving and adoring Maud in his mind alone? Maud deserved more than an 'intrigue'. How could she be heartwhole for him now; since he would be forced to tell her that Florence might return before the end of the year? And that would be the end of it all, the end of all his hopes for a passion to last him out to the end of his life, whether she became his mistress or no.

He felt upset, dislocated, angry, could not bear to sit and think, wanted some action to propel him along, wanted to go and find Maud before he replied to Florence, drive over to her straight away in his Silver Ghost, abduct her from her studies, bring her to Garvits and there confess what had happened. But what kind of confession? – that he must set a term now to his loving her? Then what might just be about to begin would never happen. No, he could not do that, must give himself time to think.

He was breathing shallowly, quickly, as though literally in fear of his life. If Florence was really well enough to return he could not stop her, and if he refused her he might be guilty of sending her back to her old state of mind. Existence without even the hope of seeing Maud occasionally, of planning a future in which she was somehow involved, would be no life. And yet it was his duty to care for Florence.

There had been no hint till last year that things might improve for her. He could not blame the doctors; little seemed to be known about her type of malady. Since her mental illness had come upon her only after the bearing of his children, he had always felt himself obscurely to blame. Puerperal psychosis they had called it and no one knew how long it might last or whether it was ever completely curable. Florence, though, would not be having any more children; and maybe her age had reversed the imbalance that had started her off on her illness.

No, he could not go and tell Maud today. She must come here. He sat down, unscrewed his gold Waterman pen and in his fine, elegant script began a letter, not to Maud, but to his wife. He would come over in July and discuss the whole matter with her doctors – who ought in any case to have written to him first. Possibly she had begged to be the first to acquaint him with the 'good' news. That would give him enough grace in which he might see Maud and – warn her? A month or two to settle three lives?

When he had finished his letter he sealed it in an envelope, stamped it and placed it on the little bronze tray for Mrs Archie to post. Then he began on his letter to Maud. Better to break the news without prevarication, tell her the truth and beg her to come over when she could. She had to know, for he sensed a softening in her last letter to him. But even if she should decide not to go on seeing him before Florence returned, she must know the truth. What a fool he was! Perhaps he ought to have respected her less, asked for more. Yet he could not imagine how she might have been seduced.

Finally: 'Dearest Maud', he wrote. 'Your sweet letter is before me as I write. I am overjoyed that you liked my little gift. Dearest girl, I have bad news for me and perhaps for you in the "good news" I have received today from my wife. She is "much better" – the last few months' improvement has been sustained with no relapse. It will depend on her doctors, but starkly this means that she may probably return here in the autumn. It will have been an absence of seven years. To me it seems more like seventy. You may guess how this might turn out for us, and yet I cannot reject her now. How can I bear to cast you out of my mind or my life, renounce all I had hoped might come to pass between us if you loved me a little? You do deserve more than a hole-and-corner love. You may say, why not carry on as before, Maud. But I have felt just recently that things were changing, that I was becoming more of a reality to you and that you might be growing to accept my love. I have, on the other hand, to warn you, for I cannot exist in a tissue of deception and half truths.

Knowing all this and knowing too how I feel about you Maud, will you come and see me soon, even if it is only to say goodbye? I never loved you more, dear little Maud, than I love you now as I sign myself – Your devoted, HH'.

Maud received the letter the next morning, read it before she went out to her classes and was angry with a cold rage. Angry at herself for not having foreseen this and angry for a time with her admirer, who seemed not to know what he wanted, but angriest of all with Florence Heron and with all weak wives who had to come first in the lives of their husbands. But she took a grip of herself, sat down by her unlit gas fire and tried to think calmly. Such wrath was alien to her.

How could she blame the poor man who was torn between duty and desire, self-sacrifice and pleasure, and too honest to play a double game? Yet there was a subtle dishonesty in his equivocations. She could not help dissecting his letter as she might dissect a rather clumsily written translation, trying to discover what he thought he meant. There was obviously still time for him to choose between the two of them. She did not want to become his wife, but she knew she could never abide second place either. If she were to become more intimate with him, 'become his mistress' in vulgar parlance, she would spend her time comforting a man for his guilt. And, to give him credit, he did not seem to want this. Did he want a clean break?

If he did, it was not very sensible to hint at further intimacies which would make that break much harder when Florence returned. His letter seemed to accept that she would eventually return.

She remembered well how he had promised he would make any sacrifice if she would love him. Was this the time? She was not 'in love' with him, had never pretended to be. She had never been dishonest with him; dishonesty was not one of her failings, she thought, with a sudden insight into herself. She might feel for him less than might some besotted, less rational girl, but that meant she ought to know how to play her cards sensibly.

Slowly she had come to understand what she wanted from men, what they might give her along with their love; a feeling of power. Hector could not make her love him; he knew that. And he needs must know too that he who loves most is the subservient one. He probably loved her too much to wrest her virginity from her by the force of his genuine desire. If she did succumb to him, where would the balance of power lie then? On the whole, in Maud's observation of the world, men took and women gave. Yet there were some men, it seemed, and Hector was one of them, who felt love was a giving, not a taking. She would have to see how far he would go in his self-sacrifice.

Jackie's pregnancy had made Maud more wary of giving

139

herself to a man. She thought of that mixture of shamefacedness and proprietorial passion on the face of Calum Fyffe when he had looked at Jackie that last morning she had seen them together before their marriage. It had not, she realised, been a look of love – not the sort of love Hector had for her anyway. Jackie was the one who was 'in love' – and look where that had got her. She herself did not aspire to the conventional virtues, though she had the necessary hardness. If Sir Hector decided he would have to go on without Maud's succumbing to the temptation he was offering her, very well, he must go on without it. But he must also continue to be tempted! He might have to do without her; could she now do without him? She had become used to the knowledge that there was always one person in the world, apart from Ma, who thought she was wonderful. If she were ever to lose her 'virtue' it might be as well with him as with anyone, and it would get him out of the clutches of the past. That to her was quite clear, even if her earlier reasoning was faulty. Once he had 'had' her she did not think he was the sort of man to despise what he had had, more a man who would be even more passionately involved.

The result of her long meditation was that she was slightly late for her lecture, which had never happened before. But it had refreshed her and stopped her from feeling sorry for herself.

During the lecture – on Greek tragedy – she was thinking again about having children. It had ruined his wife, and having a child would alter Jackie's life inexorably, making her fit for nothing but domestic battles. Becoming pregnant ruins everything, she thought, – for after that the struggle between man and woman is unequal. So long as you choose not to have children, never mind whether you marry or not, your field of manoeuvre is magically widened.

She and Hector might get together on her terms eventually, might they not? She felt her bracelet and the mark of the words on the smooth inner surface. Under her blouse she also felt the earrings which she had threaded through a strand of tough cotton round her neck. She was not going to have them loose in her room; you never knew, there were always dishonest people around. They were hers. She was not going to take second place. It was all or nothing. If Hector thought he'd have to give her up completely that would be that; she would not plead her cause.

She was there, standing again in his drawing-room, looking both anxious and, he thought, bewildered.

'But we can see each other now and again as we did before, can't we?' she had just asked in a low voice that made his heart feel like breaking just to hear it.

'I don't know what is going to happen, Maud – I had to tell you what might happen. You are so important in my life now.'

She continued to stare at him and he saw tears shining in her eyes.

'Maud – it may only be for a little time – till I can see how the wind blows – we may be able to come to some arrangement – I can't deny my wife her place, you see. I know you are a good girl or I should not love you so and you will try to be patient with me, for I can't lose you Maud, I can't . . .'

'If she comes back, Hector – I shall not be able to come here, shall I? And to see you anywhere else would be – sordid – I wasna sure before what you wanted – and I'm not sure even now.'

'Nobody but you could ever take first place in my heart, Maud,' he said simply. 'Whatever happened – even if I never saw you again it would be true.' He looked so miserable that she almost took pity on him.

'You said it on the wee bracelet – which I always wear. What difference could it make your wife coming back?' She was giving him enough rope to hang himself with, she thought.

'I know it will be all right in the end. I don't know how or where or what will have to happen for those words to be true, but we *shall* be united, Maud,' he said, turning back to her for he had been looking unseeingly out of the window as she, he thought, pleaded with him.

'We've never seen all that much of each other, Hector,' said Maud.

'No – perhaps I should have . . . and it's not just yet she's returning, – not quite yet – I told you because I felt that you might be – beginning to – feel a little for me – might be thinking of – and it would not be fair if she's coming back.'

Maud went up to him then. He had seen on her arrival that she was wearing the earrings. Her dark green dress made her look even paler against the sparkle of the stones. Some of that pallor came, however, from suppressed emotion. 'It's three years,' she said. 'And you have been so kind to me – and I havena given you anything but the one wee kiss.'

'Don't – don't, Maud!'

Conflicting emotions were fighting in him and were plainly visible on his face. She thought, he is so honest, never dissembles, not like me *now*.

'It's my fault,' he got out. 'I've never loved you more – but I must give Florence her chance to recover and if we went on seeing each other in the autumn she'd have to know – or she would find out, which would be worse – and that might set her back again. I know you understand.'

'We'd better not see each other any more then – there would be no point if there was no future?'

Maud's voice was cold but he mistook the coldness for sorrow.

'Maud – don't,' he said and went up to her, took her hand which she allowed him to do, listlessly. She was not even angry now, more aware of the alternatives, appearing resigned but wondering how to tackle the situation. He took her wrist and rolled up the sleeve of her dress and kissed the bracelet. She saw he was actually trembling.

Hector was fighting a battle with himself. Everything in him was saying, make love to her now; if there is to be no tomorrow, seal the past at least. He spoke the conclusion of his thoughts aloud. 'It would spoil everything,' he said.

'You want to let me go then?' she said. 'Not "give me up" but "let me go".'

'We must be patient, my dear dear lass.'

'I shall get a scholarship next year, and one day go abroad,' she whispered. 'I shall get away from here, but I shall have lost your love.'

'Never, never that,' he cried. He was so close to her she could see the fine hairs on his own wrist which still held hers as she looked down.

'I am going to Switzerland this summer,' he said. 'I have to go and see her.'

Maud thought perhaps she should appear reckless. 'I didna ken what I wanted – before,' she said suggestively. He went on looking at her. '*You* must not feel guilty, Hector. I've always been used to doing without.'

'Will you give me a year to . . . to see how things go?' he pleaded.

'I shall be around for another two years after ma degree,' she said. 'You mean just go on seeing each other? There's no future in it, Hector.' She knew she was contradicting her first words, but he did not notice.

'You want a future with me then, Maud?' he said, dropping her hand.

She turned her magnificent profile to the light and looked out of the window at the formal garden. He could see the swell of her breasts under the green silk. He walked up to her and as though mesmerised, he put his hand out to touch that place and felt the firm moulded flesh underneath. She gave a convulsive shiver, but looked straight into his eyes. After a moment he looked away. 'It is better to wait,' he said and swallowed, his voice sounding hoarse. But Maud was no longer the child she had been with Uncle Dan, though she still had a child's ruthlessness.

'I trust you,' she said and even to herself her voice sounded tentative, forgiving. 'I trust you,' she said again. 'If you want to see me to remember me, I can at least take off ma clothes for you!'

There was a long silence.

'I can't look at you here,' he said. 'Come upstairs.'

'I ought not to go upstairs with you,' she replied. 'But we could pretend we were going to look at my portrait, couldn't we?'

He took her hand then and together they walked, without another word, almost ceremoniously up the wide staircase and down the corridor. They stopped with one accord, first in front of Mistress Susanna and then in front of 'Portrait of a Modern Young Woman'. 'I look a wee bit older now,' said Maud in a normal voice. 'And I suppose the

143

rest of me will look older if you ever will come to me again.'

He put his arm round her shoulders and felt the curve of the top of her arms. 'In here,' commanded Maud and opened the door to the dressing-room where the bamboo trunks of clothes were.

He followed her into the room still as if she had hypnotised him. His will felt weak but he struggled to hold on to his resolve, not to think of the one thing that must not happen. Maud drew the curtains against the daylight and shut the door. There was a curved modern 'nursing chair' on a rug by the screen that was round a wash-basin, but no bed in this room.

'First I shall undress,' she whispered 'and then I shall dress up.' She took down her long hair which came almost to her knees, seemed even longer than the last time he had seen it. Then she slipped off her dress top which was fastened with plackets to its skirt. She was wearing the little camisole under that. This she unbuttoned and then slipped off a bodice and a thin, white vest and the skirt of her dress and stood in her underskirt. Then she took off her shoes and stood there in the half light looking at herself in the long glass. 'You can open your eyes now,' she said.

When Hector Heron, holding on to the wickerwork chair, opened his eyes he saw a comely woman looking at herself, not at him, a woman with long hair falling over her firm, full breasts and white arms crossed in front of her. Then the woman took her arms away and lifted the heavy hair over her shoulders and turned and looked at him. Her breasts were perfect, full and white with rosy tips and her waist was clearly defined, narrow and long.

'You can kiss them,' she whispered, but did not move towards him. He got up and walked up to her and buried his head in the white flesh of her bosom. She smelt of lemons and her other elusive scent and her skin was very smooth. Gently he pressed the tip of each breast against his lips as though he were a woman imprinting the outline of her lips on a tissue in a tender, dreamy way. He did not open his mouth to suckle the rosy nipples. His face was pale. Then he picked up the white vest and slipped it over her head and brought the heavy hair over her to the

144

front again. Maud felt excited. Was he going to murder her like Porphyria's lover in the Browning poem? But Hector, with immense patience, fumbled the rest of her clothes on to her, all except for the dress, and when she waited took her in his arms and held her in a close grip. She could feel that he was aroused, but he did not try to do anything about that, whispered: 'Put the antique dress on now, my beautiful girl, and brush your hair up and act the lady whilst I go down to mix us a drink which I think we both need.' He went out of the room then and she stood looking at herself again. When he was outside the door he took a deep breath and steadied himself on the wall of the corridor outside. It had taken superhuman willpower not to undress her then and there, not to lie with her on the rug and make passionate love. He was surprised that he had resisted and he knew there would be no other scene like this one. When he saw Maud Crichton again it would be either to say farewell to her for ever, or to enter that lovely firm, white body and make her his own, unite himself and his destiny with hers for the rest of his life.

Maud was not sure who had won the battle of wills. She had enjoyed the way his eyes had worshipped her, his warm hands on her shoulders and the tender pressure of his lips on her skin. She had felt she might have begun to know how other girls felt when they allowed the ultimate liberties. She admired him for his refusal to be seduced. He would think nevertheless that she had given him something, and probably thought her too innocent to know how she was tempting him. But she had not shrunk from challenging him, and was content.

After what had not happened they were polite with each other. It was only when Maud said she must go that Hector nearly broke down. Tears gathered in his eyes as he stood and looked at her. Then he said quietly: 'Wait for me, Maud, will you? Wait a year – it's a long time for someone as young as you, I know. I have to work something out for us all, but I will, I promise I will. Forget me for a year and get on with your work and your life. I'll come to find you if you want me then.'

She looked at him almost with pity. 'I hope you will be able to decide what is best for your own sake,' she said in a low

145

voice. 'Do that, Hector. Don't think about me overmuch. I shall manage.'

Once more in her coat and skirt and her hair coiled round her ears, she looked strangely vulnerable, even younger.

'Goodbye, Hector – look after yourself.' She wanted to say – 'If your wife comes back in her right mind and asks about that picture, what will you say? Will you say – "that is the girl I want for my lover. I love her and I am going to her again one day?"

'Goodbye, my love,' he said and kissed her hand as he had done the first time she had come to Garvits. Archie was back from shopping and was waiting with the car. 'You can write to me at the Hall,' she said. 'But only if you have found a way out.'

She does not love me, was his only clear thought as the car turned in the drive and he saw Maud's erect little figure perched on the back seat. But I can be proud of myself, a little. I did not give in and she is still almost as untouched as she was when I first saw her in that gallery with the raindrops pearling her hair. Then he went in and thought about his wife, and prayed he might at least dream of Maud Crichton that night, but that he might not go mad with desire before he saw her again.

Maud had decided to stay in the room they had offered her in the Residence for the next academic year. Her Finals were looming over her and she was determined to fulfil the promise she had made to herself and the boast she had made to Hector that she would get a scholarship to continue with her studies. Carmichael was even more attentive to her when he found her in his classes now. But the work was hard. Her only relief was still the cinema in the city which she visited on the days she went home to see her mother. Maggie was a little fearful that Maud's heavy workload would undermine her health, but Maud told her that was all nonsense and similar to the Old Wives Tale that cutting your hair was to cut off your strength, like Samson.

But by the summer of 1927 Maud had no time to visit the 'flicks.' She shut herself in the library or in her cold room at the hostel with her proses and unseens and literature texts and grammars and histories. It was indeed found to have been worth

146

her efforts when in the August she was awarded the best First in the University and a special scholarship which had never before been offered to a woman. No other woman had a First in Maud's subject and very few in any others. Most had fallen by the wayside, or achieved, at best, second class degrees which would enable them to teach in schools.

Already by September she was back in the town to start her researches into several of those Roman empresses whose lives had always fascinated her. But she knew it was a respite and that one day Hector would either claim her or cast her off. If he was going to pursue the latter course she wanted to be ready, for she had the feeling that their last meeting had been, in Duncan's parlance, a 'draw'. She had had a card on her birthday from Hector, a postcard with a picture of a church in the Bernese Oberland. Florence must now be back, but she heard nothing. In the first week of September she wrote a short note to him and sent it to Edinburgh with *Personal* on the envelope. All she said was: 'I got my scholarship and am here for another two years. I hope and trust you are well. MLG Crichton'. Then she sat back and awaited whatever fate had in store.

The day after she posted her note to Hector she was sitting in the library, a gaunt granite building, a sheaf of references before her, when the Librarian came round to whisper there was a gentleman to see her if she would care to step out. Her heart gave a dull somersault. Had Hector made his decision then? She had no time to tidy herself, prepare herself, but went out immediately.

It was not Hector, but Calum Fyffe. She had not seen him for over a year.

Chapter 8

Calum had never revisited the university town since he had married Jackie and gone to Edinburgh. It was only because he had to search out one of his old tutors for a reference and thought it politer than writing that he had decided to go there for the day and beard the lion in his den. He was also perfectly aware that Maud would be there. He was applying for a hospital post: it was now or never, for he had not decided absolutely finally that his destiny lay in General Practice. His present year with Doctor Shaw in Edinburgh he found rather depressing for there was so much poverty, such ignorance and drunken violence among his patients. One part of him knew he was needed there and was good at his job; the other felt that his destiny might be in some specialism. If he was to specialise he must keep in touch with his mentors. Jackie had been understanding. He was as fond of his wife as before and loved his 'wee laddie', but there was something missing and he did not know what it was. He looked a little older and though his fine eyes had not lost their benevolent sparkle, they were often thoughtful and serious. It had been on sudden impulse that he went to look for Maud in the library.

His first thought on seeing her, even before registering the surprise – and perhaps disappointment – on her face, was: that body was not given to her to bend over dusty old tomes in a library. His own reaction shocked him when he thought about it later, for he was a feminist, wanted women to succeed. Maud shook hands with him rather stiffly.

'What are you doing here, Calum Fyffe?' she said, regarding him rather searchingly. He explained, and she asked him how Jackie and the baby were and then they seemed lost for another topic of conversation.

'Can you come for a drink with me, Maud?' he asked her. 'Not tea, I beg you – or that awful coffee they serve here. What about a wee dram?'

'When have you to go back?' she asked, blinking slightly in the stronger light.

'I've seen my old tutor – I have the afternoon free. I suppose you will be working in the library all day?'

'I usually do – you knew I was accepted for a doctorate?'

'Aye – I had that news from Jackie – she said you hadn't written for some time though.'

'I'm not a good correspondent,' she admitted. 'Yes – I'll accompany you in a drink – better go to the hotel though – the bars are pretty horrible.'

He noticed that she had slightly softened her accent, but as it had always been strong her voice still sounded different from the refined tones of his Edinburgh colleagues.

She went off to fetch her coat and leave a note on her books so that nobody disturbed them.

Over a whisky, with soda for Maud, who said she didna really like whisky but what else was there – he told her about little Joseph.

'Has she had the time to write any more of her stories?' she asked him when he stopped for a moment.

'She's just begun on another,' he said proudly. 'She doesn't get *much* time.'

'I can understand that,' said Maud grimly. 'I don't know much about babies,' she went on. 'But I can remember when I was a child how my wee brother used to yell. I don't know how Ma put up with it.'

'Aye, they need a good deal of energy. I'm out at work all day – and sometimes at night. I thought if I took another hospital job I'd have more regular hours – still long ones though. But Jackie likes time to herself.'

'You're both happy then?' she asked, looking at him very directly. He held her gaze. There was that something about Maud that he could never quite fathom and she hadn't changed.

'What about you? Jackie said I was to find out how you were – she often talks about you.'

'Tell her I miss her – but life goes on much the same – the

academic life doesna change. At least now I'm doing what I like to do.'

Calum encouraged her to explain what it was she was researching. Maud looked slightly ill at ease. How did you begin to describe to someone who lacked your own background of knowledge the fascination of The Ancient World?

'Well, you see – there were some Roman women who had a lot of power – we don't know much about most of them. I'm trying to find out.'

'When would that be then – '

'Early part of the third century, Calum.'

'B.C or A.D?'

She looked surprised. 'A.D of course – ! during the time they always call the "decadent" period of the Empire. Like when the Emperor Severus came and conquered Scotland! You'll have heard of *him* I suppose?'

He laughed. 'But it's women who interest you, not the men?'

'I think some women are more interesting than most men, don't you?'

'Hard to generalise,' he answered, fielding her ball neatly.

'Och, well you won't want me to go into details,' she said.

'And is all this "information" here?'

'Oh, no – I'm here at present improving my languages and absorbing the background. We havena done so much on this subject as the Germans.'

'So will you go to Germany then?'

'If I can get a Fellowship.'

'You really enjoy your work, don't you?'

'Well, I wouldna be doing it if I didn't!' She looked amazed. 'I hadn't really thought of it as enjoyable – but it must be.' He laughed. 'I'm good at it you see. Like your wife and her stories.'

'Don't you ever want to marry?' he asked impulsively.

'What has that got to do with it? – No – I don't think so. Men always assume women want to get married.'

'Well, most do,' he said, draining his glass.

'I suppose if you want to found a dynasty,' she said.

He saw she was teasing him. 'Let me fetch you another drink.'

150

She demurred at first, but as he wanted another, agreed. The hard stuff didn't seem to have much effect on her. Whilst he was away finding the elusive waiter she wondered if Jackie had told him about Hector. She supposed she had. Married folk never kept anything to themselves.

He knew from experience that you could not usually tell from Maud's expression what she was thinking, but ventured on his return with the glasses refilled – 'Do you remember asking me a year or so ago – it was before I got married – whether men were fonder of women who – never – ' He stopped, thinking no, I'd better not say that –

'Who never succumbed to them?' Maud finished for him. 'Aye – it was not the usual sort of question a young woman asks of a young man, was it Calum? But you were quite helpful, if I recall aright.'

'I hope I was of some practical use,' he said.

'You can tell Jackie that the person in question's wife has returned to Scotland.'

He blushed. She had obviously guessed the direction of his thoughts. 'Oh – I see,' he said.

'So there is an additional complication of "duty",' she said.

'Not mine – I haven't any obligations.' She wondered how much Jackie had revealed.

'Don't go off with that old man,' he said in a low voice, not looking at her.

She was shocked into raising her voice. 'It isna your business,' she stated.

'Jackie told me a bit about it – about a portrait he had painted of you.'

'I did nothing to encourage that,' she said primly. 'And Hector isna old – not what I call old – '

'I'm sorry – I shouldn't pry,' he said. 'It was Jackie – she worries about you.'

'Tell her I can look after myself,' she said.

'I expect you can, Maud,' he said. He found Maud's enclosed passivity, even when telling him to mind his own business, terribly attractive. Jackie had always urged him to like Maud. Did she cultivate this enigmatic style of hers, or was it inborn? Not that it mattered, but he was intrigued in spite of himself.

151

She began to talk about her fellow research students and tutors, making him laugh with her witty and sometimes slightly cruel comments. But he could not help feeling, from the vantage point of his knowledge of at least one woman, his wife, that what Maud needed was a man – or at least a centre to her life. She certainly seemed to be able to look after her own interests in her work, though he sensed an occasional trace of anxiety about the scope of it.

How different his proximity was to Hector's, Maud was thinking as she regaled him with anecdotes and made him laugh. She did not seem over concerned about this Hector, he thought. Whoever would get the better of Maud?

'I might have to come again,' he said as they parted outside the hotel. 'McNaughten may want to see me – if he can't get away to Edinburgh before the end of term – he always says he's overworked.'

'Then I must buy you a drink if you do,' she said imperturbably.

'You must come and see us soon,' he said. 'I promised Jackie I'd ask you.'

'I'll see – when I've finished this particular research – it's taking longer than I'd imagined it would.' With that he had to be content.

He found himself thinking about her on the train. That would never do, for now he realised what his wife had so innocently meant when she had said how beautiful her friend was. Marriage and fatherhood had made Calum more aware of his feelings. He wondered now if anyone would ever have from that cold, proud young woman what he had so easily had from Jackie. And yet she was not always cold, and her pride was only a matter of his guesswork. Underneath her rather complacent exterior he sensed a certain – he searched for the word – was it, even, vulgarity? That was an odd word to use for the choosey young woman with the perfect oval face and features. She had certainly not come from the top drawer, but from a respectable artisan, or at most a petty bourgeois, family; the 'vulgarity', if that was what it was, lay in a certain directness, a lack of attention to the sort of subtlety he was used to in his young wife. Jackie had a finer sensibility. But Maud had this aura of the unknown, since she did not give anything away. He wondered about the baronet whose wife had come back. Whatever she felt about that she was keeping to herself. He told Jackie of their conversation on his return and Jackie was pleased he'd looked her up. Maud really must visit them soon. She must be lonely, thought Jackie, whose days were never lonely, rather too full of chores and obligations now.

Calum's marriage and fatherhood had, once he had accepted the situation – and he was usually of an optimistic temperament – made him paradoxically more interested in the big world outside. He felt he had done his duty by society and wanted now to expand his own interests which had been concentrated for so long on study. Jackie was easy-going and seemed contented, though she sometimes became depressed over her own writing. But she felt there was a part of her husband which she had never touched, his inner life, which must exist under the handsome face and in the midst of all his activities. She had thought she knew him through and through, but now began to find additional unsuspected charms in him. Jackie had grown up in the last two years. She would not have had it otherwise than to be joined with Calum from now on, and any vague feelings of unrest were for the moment cancelled by her happiness in the baby Joseph. Calum too adored him; he loved all children and was good at doing the things most men avoided.

Calum went back a few weeks later to see his tutor again and talk over the possibilities for his work. The tutor, Doctor McNaughten was not very encouraging.

'I've never seen you as a specialist,' McNaughten said. 'You've got more to offer folk – even if you made some progress with this influenza bug you'd still have to do another five years in the labs or at the hospital to see whether you were going to rise in the hierarchy. Stick to being a GP – you'll make a good one – that's my advice.'

Calum was discouraged but still not entirely persuaded. If he did want to change course he knew McNaughten would give him good references. The man obviously thought his heart was not in it.

He went for a walk on the beach to clear his mind. He hated

decisions; far life had made the decisions for him. Why not just settle down, as his father had done, who had been a success in his profession and contented with his family life? It must be some urging from his other inheritance that made him dissatisfied with himself. Am I really dissatisfied, he wondered, or have things come too easily for me?

He had walked a mile or two up the sands, hands in pockets, thinking, I have to decide now, then there's no going back. Maud saw him from her vantage point on the jetty where she had gone for a walk to clear her own head. She had to decide which of many leads she should follow. Carmichael, who had been at first disappointed she would not take up the option of investigation into certain of the aspects of Greek drama dear to his heart, was now persuaded she should undertake a general study of the period she was interested in and perhaps write a text eventually to introduce British students to the later Roman Empire, about which most folk knew little. But Maud was firm in her wish to write a detailed study of the Empress Julia and her court. She had another year before she had to apply for the fellowship which would get her abroad, but hated not knowing exactly where she might be going.

Since Calum had met her that day she had had ample time to reflect upon her work and upon Hector's continued silence. Heron really could not go on treating her in this way. Was he ill? Or had he fallen out of love with her? She wanted to tell him that it was over, but could not rouse herself to do it. She had taken a risk that last time – and lost. She realised that now.

She went down the steps from the jetty and walked along the beach knowing she would be bound to pass Calum. She felt empty, rather depressed.

Calum looked up as she walked, head high, on the beach path and then stopped in surprise. They stood looking at each other for a moment then: 'Why, Calum!' she exclaimed. 'What brings you here again?'

He looked almost angry, a little surly at least.

'Confounded decisions,' he said. 'I still can't make up my mind.'

This was so similar to her own state of mind that she

154

showed some sympathy. 'Did McNaughten not give you a guid reference then?'

'Oh – aye – I suppose so, but he doesn't think I'm suited to hospital research – would rather see me ministering to the poor folk who come to see the doc every day.'

'I'm sure you are a good GP,' she offered. They sat down on a flat-topped rock by common consent and she looked out at the sea. It seemed years since the beach party and their 'youth'.

'Jackie all right?' she ventured, stealing a look at his face.

'Oh, yes – she doesn't mind what I choose – she's not difficult.'

'Shall *I* make your mind up for you then?'

'What do you mean?'

'Well, it's always easier if someone else does,' she said. 'I think you ought to go on working with people. Research is only for people like me who aren't verra good with folk.'

'But you're not sorry you've chosen that path yourself?'

'Oh, no – I told you, it's what I'm good at, Calum.'

She seemed more approachable today. He ventured a: 'You don't think I'd be any good then – at research?'

'I don't know about your work – but if you'd wanted to go that way you'd have chosen it before.'

'Things were not so simple two years ago,' he said.

'I know – you had to get married – and husbands need sensible, solid jobs.'

'You blame me, Maud?'

'Not much point in blaming men for what they are, is there?'

'Jackie said you were a hard taskmistress,' he said.

'Oh, did she? I've problems with my own work too, you know. You and Jackie always gave the impression you thought I knew exactly what I wanted to do.'

'Well, didn't you?'

'I suppose so. I am a scholar – and I hope I'll be a better one one day – I enjoy learning, you see. But I don't suppose there are many jobs for women academics.'

'You could always marry,' he said cautiously.

'That's no solution, is it?'

'No,' he replied.

155

'I wish I were forty and settled in a nice little job with my own income – but there's a long furrow to plough before that.'

He looked sceptical but said: 'I suppose women are less impatient – '

'Your wife? Jackie's not all that patient!' He ignored that.

'You have to be patient for research work – it doesn't go with planning a more interesting life for yourself – *I* don't know – I "dinna ken" as you would say. You think I'd be better off going on with what I'm doing?'

'I'm not the Sphinx,' said Maud.

'Though you sometimes look like her,' he replied without much forethought.

She was amused. 'Should I be flattered to look like a big Cat?'

He did not answer that, but said: '*Do* you have problems with your own work then?'

'Oh, aye, but I never ask for advice – my professor thinks he knows what's best for me – but he does not. I know. The difficulty is sometimes persuading other people.'

'You should write about your ancestresses – women of the old world – the ones you were telling me about – I don't know much about any of that.'

'Nobody knows all that much,' she confessed. 'But there are things that don't change about women and men – even empresses. Naturally they always say life was much coarser and more ruthless then. I think *we* just cover all that up.'

'I'd have thought you were a person who believed in covering up,' he said, wondering what on earth he was talking about.

She looked quite animated – more than he had ever seen her. 'Depends what sort of cover up. Only the very rich and powerful women had any say in the manner of their existence.'

'I didn't know you were a feminist.'

'No, I'm not – not one like Jackie anyway. She is too optimistic – sees good wherever she looks because she's good herself.'

He looked surprised, even gratified. 'But Jackie is always on about the terrible things that go on – poverty, exploitation, injustices, starvation, earthquakes, Man's inhumanity to man etc., etc.'

'Because, you see, it surprises her. She thought folk were all like her and they are not. Most people are sheep,' said Maud viciously.

'You don't really mean that?'

'Aye, I do.'

'Must be that grandfather of yours who made you think like that!'

'Oh, Jackie told you about him, did she?'

'Jackie talks a lot about you.'

'Well, you go back and be a good husband to her, Calum Fyffe, and stop chasing rainbows.'

'I think I *am* a good husband,' he said.

Maud said nothing to that but turned her gaze to the sea and the cloudy sky. What sort of man would conquer Maud? he thought again. I wonder what that old chap is like.

She had clearly been thinking about something other than the landscape because after a time she said: 'I think the Ancients had a sense of doom – and that helped them to cope with life. Nothing seems to have surprised them – it was all a punishment from the gods – then later on in the period I'm doing they took strife for granted – and incest and parricide . . .'

'It must be rather depressing studying all that – I mean before Christianity.'

'No – it's not that that depresses me – that's exciting. They always knew what they wanted – power and vengeance and lots of good times.'

She turned her head away from him again and he saw the clear cut profile, like an empress on a coin herself. He suddenly wanted to touch her, touch that inscrutable face to see if the cheek was marble or warm flesh. He kept his hands firmly in his pockets. 'Aren't you interested in the way ordinary folk lived?' he asked her, to change the subject.

'We know even less about *them* – and I've never been all that interested in ordinary folk,' she replied. 'Anyway they were mostly slaves.'

She was truly implacable but he did find her physically attractive, there was no denying that. Maud was now looking at him with a meditative expression on her face. He is a pleasant man, she was thinking – but he doesn't have a sense of direction.

157

'What are you thinking about?' he asked, knowing full well he ought to go and catch his train, but somehow held there in her presence.

'Oh – I don't know – perhaps that as most folk are ordinary I've been lucky to get to know someone who was not!'

'Do you want to talk about him?' I suppose he was madly in love with you?'

Maud knew that nothing was so likely to reduce a man to an engine of lust than talk about 'love', and wisely chose not to lead him down that path. But she said frowning: 'I suppose he – the man I used to know – thought of, or rather dreamed of, a reality and then put people into it. I can't explain it very well. I expect Jackie could find the words. He created a world for himself and then put the woman he – wanted – loved – into it.' And there she was saying the forbidden word when she had not intended to.

'So anyone would do for the imaginary world?' he asked her, trying to understand. He had conversations like this with his wife, which baffled him. Maud was usually easier to understand.

'No – not just anyone – but that need not have much to do with reality.'

'Yes – sometimes the better you know people the less you seem to understand them – I can see that. Does it apply to oneself as well?'

'The better we know ourselves? Well, you know what Socrates said: "Know thyself" and "the unexamined life is not worth living".'

'I don't think I agree. Much better not to think too much, I'd have thought!'

'Well, you'll have to come to your decision then without the aid of reason. Take an "intuitive leap" and decide – General Practice or The Unknown.' She felt, my mind always cuts me off from people when I'd like to feel something for them. He must have a lot of such talk with Jackie as I well remember having had with her myself. 'The man *I* was speaking of is a Romantic,' she said. 'I am not. Jackie is – I don't know you well enough to say you are or not. On the whole I'd say not.'

'I shall stay on in the practice,' he said. 'You've made my

158

mind up! Come on – let's walk back to town – you were on your way back?' He stood up and Maud made as if to rise too. He took her hand and pulled her to her feet. 'Why, you're cold,' he said. 'We must have something to warm us up.'

'Men always tell me my hands are cold,' murmured Maud. She removed her hand from his however and they began to walk back to the town side of the beach. All the way along the pebbly beach he was aware of her close physical proximity. Intimacy with Jackie always left him perfectly happy and sated, but not moved in the curious way he felt he might be with this woman. That was a dangerous thought, so he deliberately turned their talk to the cinema and to what was going on now in politics in which Maud apparently took little interest. Odd for a woman who had said she was interested in power in the ancient world. He supposed she did not make the connection. There were things left out of her, things which more ordinary women possessed.

All the time she was talking about the latest offering at the 'flicks' – ('I didna think much of it'), Maud was aware that Calum was interested in her in quite a novel way. But she did not think he was going to try anything on with her. He must go back to the wife who loved him. Calum would never love a schemer. The ghost of Sir Hector seemed to stir in her as she now walked along the grey pavement with the young man, not realising that her very off-handedness attracted. Calum was thinking, she had done nothing, said nothing. She must be what Jackie called an *allumeuse*, lighting the blue paper, but not wanting any part in the fireworks.

But when he said he must go now to the station, he could not resist giving her a kiss, but a friendly one, to show he cared a little. She had listened to him and been helpful he thought, hypocritically justifying himself. She allowed him to squeeze her hand, but withdrew it quickly and said: 'You must go now – canna have you missing your train.'

He felt more cheerful on his return journey. He would tell Jackie he had made his mind up, though he was not quite sure how it had been made up.

Maud too felt more cheerful and returned to the library determined to work out a plan for an intensive study of one of the empresses who fascinated her. She would find out all anyone had ever known about her and perhaps things nobody had ever discovered before, every detail of her life. She knew most of the sources and her German was improving.

That night she had two dreams which for a woman who hardly ever remembered her dreams was unusual. In one of them she was walking alone along a canal with a bridge ahead over the green water. She knew in the dream that she must stop a person – who the person was she could not remember when she woke up – from jumping into the water. When she stopped and looked down into the water she saw not her own reflection but the reflection of some older woman with a long nose like a witch, and was terrified. The other dream following close upon that with an interval of wakefulness between, was much more pleasant. Yet she could not recall it in any detail when she awoke for the second time. It had been more a sensation of a shape than a person, mixed with the feeling of having climbed a high mountain towards the soft rose-coloured peaks of other mountains in the distance. It was warm, she did remember that, and she felt accepted and accepting with no effort of the will involved.

Maud was a little superstitious about such things, but gave up trying to understand these dreams, which must have had something to do, she thought, with her walk by the water and a recent talk with someone about mountains.

Florence wanted for her first Christmas back home to go as a family together to Garvits. They had been living in Edinburgh in the New Town since her return and he had hoped to put off Garvits, since it was now inextricably linked with Maud. He had promised himself not to write to Maud until he saw more clearly how the land lay with his wife. He knew that he must soon write to her, but his will was paralysed. If she had communicated with him, if only to give him a little hope that she might one day love him enough to make all his other sacrifices – and a sacrifice of Florence – worthwhile, he would have been able to write, but as she did not, he procrastinated. The visit to Garvits would bring all this to a head, he knew.

Florence, who had been a pretty young woman, was now, in

spite of her recovery, more visibly aged than Hector himself. Her initial loss of weight at the beginning of her illness had been more than made up, for she was now the plump matron in aspect, though still as careful as she had been in her young days to dress immaculately, and now she had her short hair marcel-waved and her nails manicured, her face carefully made up. Looking at her he could not believe the transformation from the wild-eyed, gaunt figure of the earlier years of her illness and that it had gone for good. She made however no claims upon him, seemed to be waiting for his first move. Even before they had parted they had slept in twin beds and she had shown no inclination to alter this situation. They were always polite to each other and Florence made it clear how glad and happy she was that she would not have to leave her home again.

Only when they arrived at Garvits did he begin to find his life intolerable. For four months he had treated Florence with kid gloves and said nothing to her about his real feelings. But he was beginning to feel that he would never see Maud again, that there was nothing he could do now, even if Maud wanted him for good. He felt more sad and empty than agitated, so much so that even Florence noticed and asked her daughter to find out if something was worrying him. Christina did this one morning after Christmas in the library at Garvits where he was sitting pretending to work.

'Mummy thinks you are perhaps not feeling well?' she began. It was so long since any discussion of his own health or state of mind had preoccupied Florence that he stared at his daughter stupidly. '*I* think she feels you are not too happy about her coming back,' she offered daringly.

Hector was immediately concerned. If all his efforts only led to his family worrying about him, what was the good? But he had to go on playing this charade now he had begun it. 'Why, Chris – *you* don't think I look ill, do you?'

Christina, who had found her mother's return a trial after so long, suspected that he did too. 'I expect it will take some time for us all to readjust,' she answered. 'Mummy is hypersensitive. It must be hard for her too.' Christina was turning out intelligent, he thought, with some surprise.

'Tell your mother I have a lot on my plate with business,'

he said. Florence should have asked him herself what might be worrying him, but that had never been her way. At least she did not take him completely for granted. And there *were* many problems at present with Heron and Company.

That evening he assumed that Christina had reassured her mother, since their dinner together, along with Gavin and his friend who was staying with them for a few days, had passed off well – and Florence had smiled at him. He had made an effort to eat the venison Mrs Archie had cooked and drank two glasses of Burgundy and was feeling, just for a moment, that somehow things might still turn out for the best, when suddenly Florence said: 'You have some new pictures, Hector – you must explain them to me – I saw a portrait up in the landing gallery which I don't think I've seen before.'

He felt his heart leap up into his throat and prayed he would not reveal himself through a blush, or a tremble in his voice. He felt as he had done when as a child he had told a lie and was about to be found out. But long experience in remaining po-faced at Board meetings stood him in good stead and he replied: 'Oh, the woman in the green dress – yes, it was painted by a young fellow I have great hopes of. It will one day be a good investment.'

Christina looked at him sharply but Florence said no more, though he noticed that she was up in the gallery the next morning examining the picture.

Why could he not come out with the truth? Maud was not even his lover and even if she had been people knew that such things went on. Florence had never been an especially censorious sort of woman, but perhaps the thought *had* entered her head in all those long years away that he might have found some consolation.

He tried to think of his love as flawed, less than perfect, a human being with no divine attributes, but the remembrance of her beauty, renewed each time he looked at her in her green dress, made him despair. He should have had the portrait removed before Florence returned; he was sure she was suspicious. He had hidden the dress up in the attics and heaped other clothes over it in its trunk. He felt like a criminal and knew himself as laughable. Maud was only a young woman, beautiful it was true, but an ordinary human being. He knew her also for a rather superstitious young woman when he tried to analyse her dispassionately, and a devoted daughter to that Ma of hers. She was a girl who would rise above her circumstances, he felt sure, and she was an exceptionally clever girl too – that he did know. He tried by these means to draw an objective picture of her in his mind. And yet he still could not write to her. He contemplated writing perhaps to that jolly friend of hers who had once accompanied her to Garvits, but Maud had told him she was married and he did not know her name. Then he bethought himself to call on Jimmy Valentine who might talk about her to him. But there was no advice to be had. He must prescribe his own medicine.

He had passed more than a year in this way after Florence's return, tormenting himself one way or another and wondering whether he would suddenly stop thinking about Maud. He remained gravely attentive to his wife, and his children noticed no difference in him, for since they had grown up and begun to notice their father as an individual he had always seemed to have secrets which they were not interested in probing.

By her second year of postgraduate studies Maud Crichton had learned better how to present herself to her own advantage. Even to her fellow students she was now less regarded as 'standoffish' than 'unusual'. She still took little part in student life, even the more rarified life of the chosen scholars, but if she did attend any of their meetings or join in any of their junketings she knew how to make an entrance and how to say so little that when she did pronounce judgment she was listened to. To some she was still 'Carmichael's pet'; to others Miss Cool-as-Cucumber. These appellations allowed Maud to do pretty well as she pleased, since nobody expected anything normal or boring or ordinary from a woman who was so far from being 'average'. They knew nothing of any inner torments she might have, guessed wrongly that she led an exotic life away from the place. She usually wore either black or various shades of green, always earrings, and tighter skirts than those of the other women, and a certain scent. As no other woman in the place did more than dab eau de Cologne

163

behind her ears on special occasions, Maud's advent was always heralded by fragrance. Some people called her eccentric, some frigid, some Puritanical, some insensitive, some vampish, some witch-like. But they could not have said how she who said so little and who was always working, had come to be regarded as extraordinary.

In truth Maud was hurt at Hector's long silence and covered up the hurt to herself by a pretence of indifference. It was her pride rather than her capacity to love that had been affected. For she had surprised herself occasionally waking up from some dream of a bliss she had certainly never experienced in real life, and remembering that she had been in the arms, not of Hector Heron, but of Calum Fyffe. She planned eventually to visit Jackie and hoped Calum would be out of the house. She wrote to her old friend finally to suggest she went over to Edinburgh one Saturday.

It was the autumn of nineteen twenty-eight when Jackie replied saying she was pregnant again. They had decided if they were to have other children that it was better not to wait too long. Calum had decided too quite definitely to stay on in general practice. His father would help him to buy himself into a practice in the city where a vacancy had appeared after the death of one of the original partners. Maud had a queer feeling that everyone else was on the move but that she was marking time. Not that she wished her life to change dramatically just yet. That would happen, she supposed, when she went abroad. Yet even Ma would sometimes give away her conviction that young women should marry, since marriage made for the good life and a 'happy' life. Maud's instincts still made her keep herself to herself. There would be no harm, she thought, now so much time had passed, in writing to Hector at his business address. She hated things left in the air and now that she had had time to organise her life to her satisfaction she thought she must see if he would reply. If she were going to write to him she would also, in this period of decision, find time to pay that visit to Jackie. She had now come almost to the end of her preparatory work and the German was going well. Every Thursday she went to an old German lady in the town, a certain Frau Meyer, the pre-war wife of an academic whom he had picked up in his travels in that

Germany of spas and art pilgrimages and musical evenings and earnest Englishwomen on their sketching and learning holidays. Frau Meyer found Maud an apt pupil and told her she had a 'German mind' far removed from sloppy British thinking.

Maud's letter to Hector was short, but to the point. 'I often think about you and wonder how you are. I assume things go well for you at home and that you have "recovered" for the time being from the malady you once described to me as being worse than malaria but, like malaria, of more than intermittent occurrence? Next year I hope all being well, to go abroad for at least two years'. She made no other reference to his feelings or hers, but added: 'I am assailed by grave doubts as to the wisdom of writing to you since you have not written to me. I hope we may continue to be friends?'

She posted this on her way to Edinburgh one Saturday afternoon and sat in the train feeling more alive than she had felt for some time. She had not been able to find out if Calum would be at home, but decided to take the risk. It was absurd that she had not visited Jackie before.

Their flat was on the first and second floor of an old house not far from Princes Street, and Maud looked round the district with interest. She had always liked Edinburgh but felt a foreigner there. It was another, more cosmopolitan world – Hector's world, she supposed. Jackie came to open the solid oaken door that stood at the top of a flight of stone stairs. The whole house was divided into flats but she had written that soon they were to move to a better one. 'I am overjoyed you are coming at last', she had also written, in a letter that looked as though coffee had been spilt over it. Jackie now characteristically flung her arms round Maud. There was a child at her skirt and this child's brother or sister was already greatly in evidence in Jackie's stout stomach. Maud allowed her cheek to be kissed and said 'Hello,' to the little boy who was now standing with his thumb in his mouth. To Maud's inexperienced eyes he seemed tall for a three-year-old. She supposed she ought to have brought him some sweeties.

'Oh, you smell good,' said Jackie. 'Joe – take your cart into your room and build us a tower. You can do it on your table'. Joe obeyed after a long look at Maud and pushed the brick-laden cart out of the hall. 'Calum is sorry, but he was called out,' said Jackie when Maud had taken off her coat and hat and gloves and deposited them on the marital bed in a pleasant room with pictures on the walls and scarves flung over chairs. 'Now sit down and let me look at you,' said Jackie. 'Then we can have some tea – Joe's had earache so he's still a bit cross – what a lovely blouse! – you look well, Maud.'

'How are you keeping then?' asked Maud rather stiffly. Jackie looked cheerful but a little tired.

'Not long now, thank goodness – I think I shall stop at two,' she replied.

Maud noticed that the room they were sitting in was not too untidy; she had expected the usual chaos attendant upon the existence of a small child.

Jackie seemed to have most things under control. She couldn't imagine her life, so full of maternal and wifely duties, so domestic. Jackie always talked enough for two, so soon there was no constraint between them and Maud felt as she had not felt for some long time, able to relax and be taken for granted.

Jackie insisted upon hearing all the latest gossip about staff and about Maud's projects. 'And what about your stories?' asked Maud.

'Oh, I'm writing – when I get an hour or two and Joe is asleep – I'm aiming at a novel now – more for my own satisfaction, I think – just to keep my hand *in* till the children are *off* my hands. I thought a really long novel might see me through!' She laughed. Maud did not envy this life of hers, but tried not to make it apparent. Jackie would know that in any case, surely?

It was not till cups of tea had been drunk and Joe had been given a picture book to look at and gone back into his bedroom with it that Jackie said: 'What about Hector then? You wrote his wife had come back.'

'Yes – I've written to him – I don't know what he wants.' Except for me to love him she thought.

'I never ever saw that picture he had painted of you!'

'I wish I could buy it,' said Maud. 'Sometimes I hate to think of it hanging there for ever . . .'

'I'm sure he must still hanker after you,' said Jackie.

Maud shrugged her shoulders. 'Oh – love – ' she said.

'He *did* love you!'

'Aye – I think he would even want to marry me – if he got a divorce.'

'But you don't want marriage?'

'I don't think I want to marry anyone.'

Jackie could not help wondering if Maud had ever succumbed physically to this man, but she could not ask her directly. She had never talked to Maud about her own earlier intimate life with Calum. There was something distasteful about talking about 'sex' with a third person, a sort of disloyalty to the absent one.

'He would have me for his mistress too,' said Maud after a pause. 'But he's not like most men, he wants love as well.' Jackie thought, the one who worships must not expect worship back. It was enough that Calum wanted me.

She said aloud, 'Men do sometimes fall in love – but women are not expected to feel desire – yet they do – and maybe call it love.'

Maud did not want to pursue the question too deeply. 'It's all *words*, isn't it, what we call "feeling",' she said. 'I think real "love" is looking after folks, being charitable.' Like Ma, she thought.

'My reserves of charity are sometimes greatly taxed,' laughed Jackie. 'That's where "love" gets you – into another sort of "love".'

Maud murmured: 'Agape and Eros,' as if that was to close the subject once the Greeks had been invoked. Jackie wanted to ask: Where does that leave romantic, unrequited love, like your Sir Hector's?, but sensed Maud would not have replied. For a fleeting moment she did ask herself: Does Maud envy me? But Maud never envied anyone. Maud was asking herself a similar question feeling that Jackie might now envy *her*. It must be a strain being charitable all the time. Poor Jackie had not much time to herself. How different they were, and how different their ideas about love. But Jackie seemed really more caught up with maternity than with her husband. Her conversation was less about Calum than formerly.

'Joseph is verra quiet?' Maud ventured, after a silence.

167

'He's probably fallen asleep,' said Jackie. 'I suppose I'd better check.'

When Jackie came back, saying that Joe was quite happy on his bed with a box of bricks and a tray, but that she supposed they'd pay for this moment's peace later when he would not want to go to bed at his usual time, Maud said – 'I'm glad you're still writing. It must be hard.'

'I get up very early sometimes – last year Joe was waking at dawn so I got used to waking myself. Now he's better about that, but I still get up and write, before the day starts to drain away my energy. I'm too physically tired at night. I don't know how I'll manage with two, but I suppose it will sort itself out. They take "bairns" early to school here.' Maud looked sceptical. 'Sometimes,' Jackie said, who appeared to be relishing an afternoon with adult conversation, 'I wonder what it's all about. They say having children makes people stop asking themselves pointless questions, and it's true one is very much needed. There isn't much time for reflection, but, you know, Maud, "alone and afraid in a world I never made" – that sort of thing.' Jackie had not lost her habit of quoting from her favourite poets.

'Well, *you* are not alone,' said Maud. 'And if you didna make the world, – why none of us did that! But you made a human being,' she added.

'Nearly made two,' said Jackie. 'But you know what I mean, Maud. 'You've read Housman, I'm sure.'

'Aye, we are all alone,' replied Maud. 'But you're not lonely, Jackie, you're certainly not that!'

Jackie thought – *she's* lonely, I dare say. But Maud, who was used to ploughing her own furrow went on: 'You were always a sociable person – not like me.'

'Living with a small child is not exactly being sociable,' said Jackie mildly.

Just then, as if on cue, a small figure appeared at the door of the sitting-room. 'I'm hungry,' it said.

'Come and talk to us,' said Jackie. 'And I'll cut you a big piece of bread and butter and honey.'

Maud thought he was rather a nice little boy, but she was not used to talking to children. When he came up and stared at her with his big brown eyes, she poked him rather inexpertly and said: 'Did you make the brick tower then?'

He did not answer, was suddenly struck with shyness and buried his face in his mother's lap. Jackie lifted her eyes to heaven. 'Come on now, Joseph lad – Maud will build your tower whilst I make you your tea.'

Maud, a reluctant accomplice, followed him into his bedroom which was littered with bricks, picture books, various toys and a Noah's ark of wooden animals. Without thinking, she arranged them in a tidy pile and stood looking at the child. This was Calum's boy and he had a wee look of him round the eyes, but was really more like his mother. He stared back at her and then took her hand. 'Build me a tower,' he commanded. Maud saw there was a little table, so took the bricks and watched by Joe erected a tall tower with a wall round it. Jackie came in then to release her from her task and smiled. 'There, Joe – Maud has made you a nice tower.'

'Thank you,' said Joe. 'But I like *my* tower best.'

'You havena built one!' said Maud.

'I knocked it down.'

'Your tea is ready,' said Jackie and bent down to pick him up.

They all went into the high-ceilinged kitchen where there was a table laid for three. 'Where's Dad? asked Joe.

'He'll be back soon, love,' said his mother. 'He's often called out at weekends,' she explained to Maud and poured her a fresh cup of strong tea. Maud was watching Joe as he ate and the child smiled at her, but he was obviously puzzled by something for he said to his mother: 'What are those things on the lady's nose?'

'He means my specs,' said Maud and took them off, much to Joe's amusement, who had never seen spectacles before. 'Do you want a girl next then?' asked Maud.

'I would like that – and so would Calum – but I wouldn't mind another one like Joe, I suppose.'

'Children need so much patience,' sighed Maud. 'I'd never have that.'

'I'm not always patient,' Jackie replied, but looking fondly at her son.

'I'll have to be going soon,' said Maud, looking at her watch.

169

Just then they heard the sound of a key in the door and Joe was straight away off his chair and running into the hall. Jackie did not say: 'Don't get down from the table till I tell you,' the sort of command Maud had been brought up on, but smiled. 'He's so fond of his father,' she said.

Calum came into the kitchen, Joe perched on his shoulders in piggy-back fashion. 'This is my Daddy,' he shouted.

'Hello, Maud,' said Calum.

'Hello, Calum.'

'We'd given you up,' said Jackie. 'Maud says she has to go soon – at least you can have another cup with us, Maud?' She got up and refilled the teapot and Calum put Joe down gently and sat down himself. They were all so easy-going, thought Maud.

'She wears those things on her nose,' said Joe, pointing at the spectacles which Maud took up again, but did not put on.

Calum thought, I've hardly ever seen her without them. How vulnerable she looks. 'Have you made any more progress with your award?' he asked. 'I was telling Jackie you'd once said you intended to go Germany. Or have you changed your mind?'

'Oh, I never asked you!' said Jackie, sitting down again. Somehow in this atmosphere Maud's work seemed remote, unreal.

'My German's getting along nicely, thank you,' replied Maud. 'And I shall go, I think, to Prussia or Silesia where all the original sources are – I'm hopeful of a National Fellowship.'

'So you'll be saying goodbye to us for good then?'

'I don't expect I shall stay for ever – but for at least two years – I have to finish the doctorate and then I'd like to travel a bit – I havena planned too far ahead.' She felt uneasy with the two of them together. Calum was a different person here in his own home with his son and his wife.

'Did you show Maud your story then?' he asked Jackie.

'No – there hasn't been time – you mean the one about the changeling?'

'She was telling me she gets up early to write and that she's going to write a long novel,' said Maud. Writing must be a life-raft to Jackie amidst all this domesticity.

Dusk was beginning to fall and they could see the darkening clouds through the high windows. 'I really will have to go – I'm off to Ma this evening,' said Maud. She wanted to get away now. Calum was looking at her when she put her glasses on again. Would he offer to see her to the station? She did not want that. She washed her hands in the tiny bathroom and put on her coat and hat. 'Thank you, Jackie,' she said. 'I hope all will go well.'

'Are you going to your Mummy?' asked Joe, who had listened to their talk. He was obviously a precocious boy.

'Aye – and you must go to bed,' said Maud severely. 'I can find my way down – don't bother, Calum – you look tired.'

Jackie kissed her cheek, and Calum shook hands and Joe said: 'I shall knock your tower down now, lady.' They all laughed and Maud waved goodbye and was never so thankful to find herself alone and quiet on the train back as it went over the Forth Bridge with the dark sea underneath. She did not regret her visit, but knew that she had been correct in thinking that her friendship with Jackie would never be the same now that their preoccupations were so different, quite apart from her handsome husband.

When she had gone Joe said: 'That lady was a pretty lady. Has she got a little boy to play with?'

'Out of the mouths of babes,' said his mother.

'No, she has not,' Calum replied to his son.

'She's more beautiful than ever,' sighed Jackie. 'Don't you think so, darling? But I think she despises me for not being free like her.'

'Come on now,' said Calum. 'Maud thinks nothing of the kind, I'm sure.'

'It's funny in a way, she's not really ambitious – not like me,' said Jackie. 'I mean for worldly success – you know – recognition.'

He was silent. He knew he could not rise to the challenge of Maud. He had quite enough on his plate for the present.

Chapter 9

Maud having decided that discretion had been the better part of valour for long enough awaited a reply from Sir Hector; things must be settled for good between them. She knew in her bones that his silence was not on account of any diminution in his love. She would not like to be Florence, however attentive she was sure he must be towards her. Occasionally it did occur to her that he might once more be sleeping with his wife, but then she dismissed the thought. Florence might have recovered but Hector would no longer desire her.

Whenever she felt a little depressed she went on a shop window gazing spree and spent time also in the insides of the best department stores. She imagined what she would buy if she had the cash. There was not a lot over for clothes at present on her scholarship. One day she must earn enough to buy what she coveted. Men might give her diamonds, but she would like to buy her own clothes as the fruit of her labours. She dreamed of a fur coat. It would be just the thing for the inclement weather on this inhospitable coast. She saw herself quite objectively in musquash with perhaps a muff of the same fur.

Hector's reply to her letter came on a late November day when the winds had roused themselves from their autumnal post-equinoctial slumbers and, rather late, decided that they would spare the place no longer. It was a Monday morning and she had returned from a weekend at home rested and ready to concentrate on her researches in the Library. The letter, in a thick white envelope, was waiting in her pigeon hole at the Hall when she went back there after her small luncheon of a bowl of Scotch broth. She took it up to her room and sat down feeling suddenly nervous.

My beloved Maud – it began –
You will not believe me but it is the truth that the day I received your letter I had begun one to you. After all this time, which has been over a year, and one of great inner turmoil for me, of great fear and guilt, I had begun to believe that I had managed to dissimulate successfully, to everyone, to my children and to my wife.

I was determined to conquer my passion for you since you could not return it and I thought until I saw your letter that it was best for us both, and certainly best for my wife. Now I know that it is only best for *you*. I had begun a letter to you to beg you to forget me. I hoped that you would one day look back upon our strange relationship as a happy one and be able to forgive me. When I read your letter I knew I had been deceiving myself and had been unkind in not communicating to you – not sensible, perhaps cruel. Will you forgive me? You see, my darling one, I know that I shall never feel other than I do for you, that never a day will pass – as it has not passed for the last sixteen months – without my wishing you were with me – but knowing that I cannot have you. I must stick out what I have now promised myself to do, must try to be an attentive, if not a sincerely loving man, to a wife who suspects nothing. If *you* will urge me also to do this I might find it easier. So much you have given me since our first meeting. You made me feel young and excited again, revivified the world for me. But it was not to be and I was greatly to be blamed that I revealed my feelings to you. The thing I do not regret and never will is your portrait. Even my wife has remarked upon it and I said – which was true – that it was painted by a young man who will one day be famous. I said nothing of the sitter. It is my solace on dark days.

It is better that we do not meet again. However cruel this may seem to you, believe me that the cliché is true – it hurts me more than it can hurt you. For if I thought you would suffer as I am suffering I would have taken you away long ago and would have disallowed my other duties. Your letters to me have always been just and wise and true and I shall never burn them, but keep them in a place known only to myself.

Dearest Maud, hate me if you will, blame me, disbelieve in me, but don't despise me. I think I am doing the right thing, for I know that your beauty will attract others who will also love you. I try not to feel jealous, but I pray one day I shall succeed in wishing you happy with whoever you choose to love. I thank God I have known you and loved you for without you my life would have been immeasurably the poorer. Sometimes I feel fatalistic and think we were not meant ever to find happiness together, for I met you when you were too young, and we were not given the time or the opportunity to learn to love each other. I try not to be self-pitying, but I know my heart is breaking. You are and always will be the light of my life. Take care of yourself, beautiful Maud. You have acted always rightly in not pretending to feel what you did not and perhaps could not. One day I hope you will love someone as I have loved and do love you. We do not know the future; that is why I have the one small consolation that you will wear the jewellery I gave you (and I wanted to give you so much more), and that Time *will* unite us. I become metaphysical in my old age, my darling. Forgive me and forgive everything. I love you for always. HH.

She sat on long after the light had begun to fade and her hands were cold. She did not light the fire but stared into the darkness, filled with a succession of conflicting feelings. Nobody would ever love her as he had and she had spoiled it all by not being able to counterfeit an emotion she did not feel. Oh, she should have done what most women would have done confronted by such a prize; swallowed her doubts, said she loved him and let herself be possessed. But why could she not fall in love? What was wrong with her that she felt neither infatuation nor desire?

Eventually she stood up stiff and weary. She would not answer this letter. She went to bed but was woken up an hour or two after falling asleep. It was the old woman shape, the black shape that had been pursuing her down the corridors of dream. She had not thought of it for a long time, and fear and dismay kept her awake again till dawn.

*   *   *

174

Professor Carmichael had approved her submission to the Carnegie Award Committee for an award to cover two years' residence abroad and all she had to do was await their verdict, about which he himself was confident. He took a good deal of trouble to write to the German authorities to get her on to an approved list of research students of a famous Privy Counsellor who was also Professor at a prestigious university and Maud went now twice a week to Frau Meyer, advancing steadily in her knowledge of both grammar and vocabulary and even conversation, when that lady condescended to speak her native language. What was there here for her now she had exhausted the Library and her teacher's knowledge? She went regularly to Carmichael with her work and he expressed approval of her tentative conclusions and helped her with a plan for further action. 'Then you must write the book,' he said. Maud felt emboldened to ask him of the prospects when she might return to her native land – though that seemed an immeasurably distant date in the future. She knew that competition for a safe job in this world of approaching slump was keen – and anyway very few women were ever appointed. 'You might take another degree later,' he said. 'Oxford degrees are always useful.'

'Surely a doctorate would be enough?' she muttered.

'Most of the scholars in your field will be Oxford men,' he said, 'even here in Scotland – though I could hazard that there is no one to beat you as far as the linguistic aspect is concerned.' She knew he still thought her historical project was somehow less worthy, even if it needed a far greater acquaintance with the originals than even a purely literary subject. She thought, I will worry about that when I've finished.

The Spring term was one in which she felt deadened and dull, but roused herself to counteract any slight depression by perfecting her 'persona' for 'abroad'. Ma was fearful of her travelling away, did not understand the need for it, but came round, as she always did, to Maud's plans. Maud spent her Saturdays now either at the cinema, or reading the sort of luxury magazines not found in libraries, which she saved up for. If she was content with her week's study she would go home and spend hours applying face packs and plucking her eyebrows, waxing her legs, polishing her nails and poring

175

over paper patterns for fashionable clothes. All this was, like the window shopping, a release from the world of thinking and studying, and seemed to point to a new Maud. Her fur coat fund was low but still in existence, and she dreamed of dressing stylishly and impressing herself, if not others. For she did not begin to do these things in order to attract others, or at least not principally, though women were perhaps more often the object of her efforts than men. She did it mostly for herself, believed that what Nature had given her she might improve upon.

Her new 'persona' was naturally remarked upon by her fellows at the university and by acquaintances. By one or two of the female staff she was regarded as 'Narcissistic', though they had no idea of her obsessive interest in clothes or aids to beauty, sensed rather that she did not think much of their own. By one or two of the younger men she was christened the 'frigid *femme fatale*' and if she knew what they called her she was not displeased. She had always thought of herself as adult – it was only Sir Hector who had considered her young and innocent, and now she felt more grown up and better informed and had begun rather to despise the place and its narrowness. The Maud both Jackie and Calum knew was unknown to her acquaintances and there was a part of her which remained most of the time unknown to herself until it arose in some momentary disquietude. That old woman, the black 'shape', something that was both oppressive and yet inexplicably terrifying, had returned only once after the night of Hector's last letter, but she had determined to deal with it, this time not to be swallowed up in panic. She did not go to Ma for comfort, instead she got up in her distress – for the vision had been once again in a half-waking nightmare – and she began to wash her hands and her arms in a sort of ritual absolvement which calmed her. It did occur to her, for she was not unaware of her own curious procedures and manias, that she might be washing away an unconscious guilt or a fear her rational mind would not countenance.

The worst anguish had seemed over by the early summer and she had adjusted to herself and was awaiting the deliberations of the award committee when the bombshell fell that almost shattered her belief in herself.

It did not come in a private letter or by word of mouth but, most cruelly, by means of a newspaper she picked up at the station one Monday morning before boarding the train for her journey across the bridge. She did not buy a paper regularly – indeed it was a pure accident that she was wearing a new skirt that day of such a pale green that she feared the cushions of the carriage railway compartment might spot it, and had bought the paper to sit upon.

She glanced at it idly as she stood in an empty carriage, before intending to lay it down on the possibly greasy upholstery. There, at the bottom of the first page, where only important "local" news ever appeared, for it was a city publication, was the sober headline: 'Sudden death of a great Scotsman'.

'Sir Hector Heron dies in his garden'.

A terrible pain attacked her loins so that she staggered and fell on the seat clutching the paper. The train had already moved. She forced herself, with an immense effort of will to read on.

'At the age of fifty-six one of our leading business men and a great connoisseur of culture, Sir Hector Heron, was yesterday afternoon found collapsed at Garvits, his beautiful home in Fife, by his wife Florence who, expecting his return to the house as they were to leave for Edinburgh at four o'clock, went in search of her husband.

Efforts at resuscitation proving hopeless the gentleman was later certified to have died of a sudden heart attack. The funeral will be at the nearby village kirk to which all relatives and friends are invited on Wednesday at noon. Turn to page five for our obituary'.

Maud came out in a cold sweat and began to moan, not at first realising that the sound was coming from her own lips. She stifled it with a handkerchief and swayed with the motion of the train, overcome with shock. The shock gave way to a grief so profound she could not at first find tears for it, but stared, dry-eyed now, at the paper whose print danced before her eyes. She took it up with trembling hands and read it through again, turning then mechanically to the obituary as though it could tell her more. Reading of his love of painting and furniture the tears began running down her face unstoppably. She realised,

177

as the train finally ran into her station, that she was clutching the bracelet which she still superstitiously wore. She stuffed the paper into her attaché case and stood to open the door, noticing as she did so that her lovely new skirt was covered in grime.

How she got out and arrived at her own room she did not know, but later remembered passing an acquaintance in the street as if he were a ghost. What should she, could she, do? Not one of his family would know of her existence; she could not even send flowers, certainly not write to his daughter. Then she thought, he is robbed of *all* his treasures now, and was seized with another attack of weeping. How could he, so full of life and passion, and so alive in his love for her, be dead?

She bathed her face in cold water and went to the library where she met no one, and stared at her neat piles of notes as though someone else had written them. He had died because of her; she was sure of it. She had brought him bad luck, had broken his heart because he loved her so and she had not been in love with him. The thought, she knew, was irrational, even as she thought it, but it would not leave her.

Later that afternoon, after she had returned to her room to think, after only picking silently at her High Tea, not hungry, two of her fellow post-graduate students whose names she did not even know, were discussing her in another room at the Hall. 'I'm sure she's been crying,' said one. 'I'd never imagined *she* could cry.'

'Only witches never shed tears,' said the other. 'Do you think she's been refused her award?'

'Oh, it might be that, I suppose,' said the first speaker. 'I can't imagine what else would make her cry, can you?'

Maud suddenly bethought herself of James Valentine in the middle of a sleepless night. But there was only the next day to contact him and he might not be at his studio in any case. Could she ask him to accompany her to the funeral? Would he even be willing to accompany her? If not, or he was away, she would have to go alone. But she must find out what was to be done about her portrait. If Hector's death had been sudden he would have made no arrangements. She continued to feel doom-laden, but the first shock was over. For the first time in her life she felt

178

what she had not felt even at the Preacher's death, that Hector's death actually diminished her, that the dead carry away a part of the living with them which will never come back.

She went back to the city early the next morning, her work forgotten. As she had feared, James was away . . . but he might himself go to the funeral in any case. And what could *he* do? Well, he might offer to buy back the portrait for her . . . But he would have spent the money – and she had none. Even her savings for the fur coat amounted only to six pounds, which had taken her a year to save. All his treasures! she thought, what will happen to them? Will his wife want to keep them? She did not know whether Florence Heron was even interested in that sort of thing. She might need the money.

After her fruitless journey to the studio, she parted with some of her savings in the purchase of a black veil which she could attach to one of her winter hats.

The evening before his burial she sat again alone in her room and tried to think of him and reread all his letters to her, which she had kept. Now in retrospect they seemed pathetic, sad. She went to bed late and tried to sleep. Usually apart from that infrequent nightmare, she was a good sleeper, but that night kept having an interminable discussion with a woman who accused her of murder. She knew it must be Florence, though the woman was heavily veiled and spoke in a foreign language in the dream. All Maud knew was that she disliked the lady who kept talking about 'over indulgence' with women of the town. Somehow Calum was there in the room too and looked reproachfully at her.

She was glad to wake and get up for the funeral. It was a lovely summer morning, but nevertheless she dressed in her dark suit, put the hat on with its veil and took the train to the little town near Garvits. No Rolls this time, and nobody to know who she was. At the station there was a whole crowd of mourners, but no James Valentine. She was in good time and walked slowly to the kirk, which was at the other end of the village.

Maud walked on alone, erect and head held high, but then crept into the back of the kirk, which was already filling up. They all looked very grand, she thought, and the service would be grander than the one she was used to at the Free Kirk. The organ was already playing and several people were praying. Who were they all? Hector had had a whole life apart from her. He had said she was the most important part of his life. Maud felt like a widowed empress whom nobody recognised whilst the chief mourners walked slowly to the front of the kirk. A plump woman, who must be Florence, and two young people, a young man who resembled his father and a weeping girl. Then there was a pause before six tall men, among whom she recognised Archie Anderson came down the aisle between the crowded pews. She had to dig her nails into her hand when she saw the coffin covered in a black pall, borne slowly to the front whilst the minister intoned the beginning of the burial service. Next to her were seated two couples who took no notice of her, but whispered to each other. She took off her gloves and stared down at her hands as the service went on. There was a short address, which she could never remember afterwards except for one phrase: 'He was greatly loved'. She wondered where he was to be buried, for the graveyard was away from the kirk. She would go another day, not with these folk. She had the vague recollection of having once passed a cemetery in the car. The coffin came back now to the back of the kirk and the widow was now weeping openly, supported by her tall son, looking neither to right or left. But when she was followed by Archie, Maud stared at him. He saw her, she was sure, for he raised his eyebrows in a curious way. People were already moving out of the pews and Maud stood sideways, waiting to follow as the servants came up from the front. Mrs Archie saw her too, but gave no greeting, only a turning away of the head. Florence looked quite healthy, thought Maud. None of this would have happened if she hadn't come back to Garvits. She was filled with a dull cynicism which almost filled the space in her head which belonged to Hector, whose body she refused to imagine in that wooden box.

She waited till the churchyard was empty and the others had gone to the cemetery for the burial and then she walked alone back to the station. She felt an outsider, a pariah; but she knew he had loved her best.

Next day she wrote to James Valentine. His reply came within a day or two. He had only been in Glasgow, he said, where he was hoping to buy a better studio. Hector's death had shocked him for he had seen him only a week or two before. 'He looked tired,' he wrote. 'I am very sorry, Maud'. She thought, he is the only person, apart from Jackie, who could say that to me. She was sure James thought she had been Hector's mistress and was not going to disabuse him. 'I'll ask about the picture, saying nothing about you', he wrote. 'I may go over in any case to Garvits for they are doing an inventory for death duties – I heard from the son this morning. They found a note for me from Hector about some pictures I was looking at for him in London – I have occasionally done this for him since I know his tastes'.

Whilst Maud waited anxiously for his further letter she decided to go to Demster to see the grave. She put the hat with the veil on once more and took the omnibus this time. A gardener directed her to the, as yet, unmarked grave in the cemetery, half a mile from the kirkyard.

Flowers had been heaped on the grave in what looked more like a field. It took the overflow of graves from the old kirk and bore the name – *Demster Cemetery – Church of Scotland*. There was no one else about and so she stood for a moment by the graveside on the freshly dug turf. Then she put a small bouquet of white roses which she had kept fresh in moss at the foot of the grave. She had considered writing on a card 'From one you loved', but had rejected the idea as tastelessly melodramatic, though it was true. All she had finally written was her initials M L G C.

She looked around her. You could almost see Garvits from here. Would Mrs Archie tell her mistress about Maud's visits? She did not really care. It had nothing to do with Hector now. Where had he gone? She closed her dry eyes, could no longer weep. His love for her had ended with him, but now she felt it in her as though his own old feelings had become hers.

James Valentine's second letter was not long in arriving and contained grim news. 'She's sending you to the Sales Rooms I'm afraid, Maud – I'm not sure which. I offered to buy you back since it was I who painted you after all and if she didn't like the picture she might have accepted a small sum in return for my removing it and trying to resell it for her. But that is not how the rich operate. Artists have no more rights once they've sold out to Mammon. I believe the Herons need to ascertain the amount of the estate for duty. Lady Heron was rather peculiar about the picture. "My daughter likes it," she said. Altogether she seemed to be in a strange frame of mind, but quite *compos mentis* and businesslike. I'd never met her before. I expect one day a rich American will buy it. I'll try to find out where it ends up – after all, I have a proprietorial interest in it! You wouldn't want it in a local gallery, would you? – so perhaps this is best. I told her the model was a friend of mine – which is, I hope, true. *Entre nous* I think she has her suspicions. Mrs Archie looked as if butter wouldn't melt in her mouth, but these old retainers know on which side their *bread* is buttered.

'I am really sorry, Maud. He was a nice man and a kind man and he had taste, which is not the same as good taste. Ever yours, James'.

His letter brought back the shock she had had when Mrs Archie turned her head away at the funeral. It had hurt her more than she would admit, even to James. Probably Mrs Archie as well as James Valentine thought she'd been Hector's mistress. What else could anyone think? And now he was gone and she felt her youth was also gone with the picture. How angry Hector would have been. He would never, never have let the portrait go out of Garvits, whatever fuss his wife had made. She put her head in her hands in a mixture of sorrow and apprehension. What could she ever do to reclaim that image of herself? If she were rich she would go and find it and buy it back, but she was not rich, and it was impossible. She wished she had never sat for it, never been persuaded against her better judgment. But he had loved it, as he had loved her. Her inability to love him had been her undoing Hector had gone, and all his love with him, all useless now . . . He had never appeared ill. How could he be dead? She wept new tears of frustrated grief and bitterness, and anger that no one might now acknowledge he had loved her. Now she would miss him truly.

In the end she wrote to Jackie, who would surely have heard of Hector's death, being an inveterate newspaper reader. There had been quite a lot about him in the papers; it seemed that his business had not been prospering. Florence will probably sell Garvits, Maud thought – or at least all the lovely things there. Her dislike of 'poor Florence' was, she knew, unreasonable, but it was strong. She said nothing of that to Jackie, naturally. Jackie was, however apart from James and the servants, the only person who had seen her and Hector together. Jackie knew it had not been a dream. But Jackie was bound to have other things to think about and could not be blamed if she was not readily available to sympathise. Jackie had another son now, Jamie, and Maud had sent her a matinée jacket, knitted this time by Ma, in pale blue.

A week or two later, after she had had a kind little note from her friend, which really offered sympathy as though Maud were the widow not a rank outsider in the dead man's life, Maud was pleased to hear that she had been awarded one of the most prestigious academic awards the country offered to its graduate students. It would enable her to spend at least two years in Germany and follow the approved course Carmichael had planned for her. When that gentleman heard the news his behaviour was quite extraordinary. Not only did he bow, but he kissed her hand – they were alone in the library at the time – making her think he must be drunk, and he also said: 'All the young men in Germany will be in love with you, Miss Crichton.' This was so unusual as accompaniment to a speech of academic congratulation that she realised that his earlier stray remarks when they had been reading Catullus together had been quite sincere. He had never attempted to touch her before. Why, he might even be rather frightened of her! Academic instruction was probably a substitute for seduction for this clever old bachelor.

She thought about her undoubted power over some men. But what good had it done her? She had liked the sensation, but had better learn how to deal with it in future. Nothing had worked out well in that part of her life. Hector and her portrait were now irretrievably the past. Any charms she had possessed had been useless ones. But she was young, only twenty-four, most of her life was before her and she should try to appear content with the accolades she received for her work. There was still the grave matter of her letters to Hector though, which made her feel most uneasy, not liking anything belonging to her to be floating around among people who might wish her ill. He had always said he'd kept them in a secret place of his own, but she felt he had meant some safe in Garvits, not at one of his places of business. Had he made a will? She did not even know, but that would come out eventually and she could go and read it at the Registry in Edinburgh. If only she could be sure that his wife had not found the letters. She promised herself to walk once more near Garvits before she left Scotland and so it happened that an August afternoon found her alighting from the local train once more. She was wearing dark sunglasses and a black scarf tied under her chin peasant fashion for the excursion. It took her only about half an hour to reach the outside walls of the domain from where the winding road led to the house. She decided to walk across the fields and if challenged say she was lost. The house came into view and she stopped to shade her eyes. The sunglasses were no good for seeing into the distance as she had to wear her ordinary spectacles to see anything beyond her nose. She saw the yew trees and the long windows and the gardens and where they had walked.

On her way back down the lane she heard the sound of a car engine and hoped it was not Archie in the Rolls. It was not. She caught a glimpse of a young man, a Panama hat on his head, in the driving seat of an open Morris, next to a young woman who turned and stared at her. But the car did not stop and Maud went on her way. It would be his children, she thought, Gavin and Christina. The journey had been fruitless; she was not sure what she had expected, but the place no longer had any charm for her, only brought back to her even more forcefully the fact that the owner of it all was gone, never to return.

On the Friday, the thirteenth of September, she sailed for Hamburg.

The young woman, Christina Heron, had noticed the small figure walking along the lane and in that one tiny glimpse had recognised the girl whose picture had hung in the gallery. She was sure it was she, for the picture had impressed her. She said nothing to anyone at that time about her conjectures. The picture of whoever it had been was now sold, along with other objects the family had no further use for. Nobody but herself had noticed Maud's white roses.

Calum Fyffe often thought of Maud Crichton whom he had not seen when she had come on a farewell visit to his wife. Apparently the man who had loved her had died; it was all a great pity, Jackie said.

'I hope we see Maud again one day,' said Calum. 'I don't pity her – I expect some interesting fate is awaiting her abroad.'

PART TWO

1929–1950

Chapter Ten

'The young lady is on the second floor – but she is out – and cannot therefore be expecting you,' said Frau Müller severely to the young man who had rung the bell of one of the tall, solid old houses on Fiedler Strasse. Frau Müller's place was a rather superior mixture of rooming house and boarding house which had once been lived in by only one family, her own, but the terrible inflation and consequent financial ruin of so many families in the last few years had forced her to find a way of carrying on. She had therefore divided her property into 'furnished flats', really bed-sitting rooms, and also organised a breakfast of coffee and black bread and raspberry conserve for her tenants in the basement every morning. The residents could either choose to eat the rest of their meals in the many restaurants of the great city on the banks of the Oder, or sample her own simpler fare at seven o'clock in the evening. Two of her tenants were 'möblierte Fräulein' – furnished ladies – and she had a contact with the university who sent her respectable tenants, both male and female.

The young man was English, of average height and with hair the colour of white gold which he wore parted at the side in the English way, hair which would gleam in the sun, but today since it was raining was covered by an English tweed cap. Except for the ears his features were not small; the mouth full and often pursed up, the chin neither sloping nor jutting out, the nose aquiline. Apart from the golden hair the eyes were the most arresting thing about him for under fair, arched eyebrows they were of a limpid bright blue. Not happy eyes though, rather yearning eyes, though nothing else in his manner would give this impression. He looked young for his age, which was only twenty-three and, indeed, had the sort of face and bearing which would look young for many years to come.

'You may leave your card,' added Frau Müller grandly, picking at a non-existent speck on her long-skirted grey woollen dress.

He said he had not brought his card case, not a lie since he did not possess one, bowed and turned away from the tall door. He looked up at the house as he left it. With its wrought-iron balconies below and triangular stone work above each of its windows it was a handsome building and could have passed muster on some Kensington square. He was beginning to walk towards the end of the street when he saw a small figure holding an opened umbrella approach from the corner. It was the young lady he had intended to visit. His face was familiar to her and as she came up closer to him she paused and turned her umbrella to quarter to the hour.

'Hello, Miss Crichton.' He did not bow, for unlike most of his fellow students she was not German, but smiled seductively.

'You will get very wet, Mr Queensbury,' said Maud. 'Were you looking for me?'

'Only to see if you would accompany me to a concert this evening – there is some Bach I thought you might enjoy – Opus thirteen Number two.' This meant little to Miss Crichton who had not 'discovered' Bach. 'There was no time to send you a note as I heard of it only this morning, and since I did not see you at the lecture in the Aula – '

'No, I had other things to do. It's very kind of you to ask me, but I have to work tonight. Prof Kornfeld wants to see me tomorrow.'

Really she did not want to bother going out again in the rain once she was back in her own room, but she had learned to be less direct in her responses. Clive Queensbury was an odd young man, she thought – so young, only recently down from Oxford – and so composed and sure of himself.

'How is your work going?' he asked.

'You will get wet,' answered Maud. 'I am afraid my work is at present a trial.'

'Come and tell me over a *Kaffee mit Schlag* then – if you have time before supper?'

190

Maud looked at her new gold watch, a present from her mother. 'Only just – very well – '

There was a coffee-house not far away which also served Russian tea, and biscuits from the Riesengebirge. Maud chose a glass of tea saying she must not spoil her appetite for Frau Müller's dumpling soup. She looked at her companion over the rim of her glass. She had realised at their first meeting some weeks ago – for he had arrived after Christmas – that he was very clever, and it was said by the students that he was the sort who would intend to cut a swathe through the female graduates. He had the air of being both needy and choosy, probably building up his own defences in preparation for the life ahead, both scholarly and amorous. Maud considered him finicky like herself, a bit 'superior', and possibly haunted by his future, perhaps waiting for something or someone. He was not the sort of man she found attractive, except when he spoke about his work, which was only rarely – but she had seen he was an unusual person. Yet she did not trust him with his 'Miss Crichtons' and his polite manners, took him with a pinch of salt, her own critical nature anticipating his criticisms, which were many – of Germany, of women in general, of the Herr Professors, of the university system. He did not appear 'solid,' and she distrusted a certain masculine arrogance which belied his sensitive features. There was no doubt however that he had charm. Fortunately his subject of research was medieval, unlike her own, but their joint Professor was not only a Roman specialist – *The Empire of Augustus* and *Alexander the Great* being among the books he had produced – but was also interested in the influence of the late Roman Empire upon the Holy Roman one, and upon the early Middle Ages.

Maud had privately christened Queensbury "Cosmo" because he had once confessed to her in an unguarded moment when he had made her the recipient of his pre-lecture chat, that his ambition was to write a history of the world. He was also knowledgeable about the convoluted politics of the country he was at present living in and spoke with much scorn of everyone but the Socialists.

Strange to say, they were not yet quite on first-name terms and Clive did not know her nickname for him, though he knew her own Christian name, had heard it from Kornfeld, who pronounced it to rhyme with 'doubt'. However this time when he had drained his cup, having first tasted the dollop of fresh cream with a long silver spoon for the purpose, he said: 'Do call me Clive – and may I now call you Maud, as I know that is your name?'

Maud put her glass down, took out a small white handkerchief and blotted her lips before replying. He noticed, not for the first time, the sensitively modelled top lip that looked soft and, he thought, kissable.

'You may call me Maud, Mr Queensbury.'

'*Do* call me Clive, won't you?'

'Clive,' she echoed. 'Verra well – '

He decided to tease her a little. 'I expect you are a glutton for work like all your fellow Scots? How *do* you get on with Kornfeld – is your thesis not coming on well?'

'He is a great scholar,' said Maud reverently, ignoring the rest of his remarks.

'An old conservative – they all are – '

'You'll have to explain all that to me one day,' she said. 'I'm no' a very political person.'

For the next quarter of an hour Clive waxed eloquent over the last ten years of gloom, crises, inflation, cabals, unemployment, capitalism, Communists, the workers, democracy and the sinister intentions of the NSDAP, the party led by the charismatic Adolf Hitler who, Clive said, would be more than a match for Brüning, the new Chancellor.

'Some folk take Hitler seriously then?' asked Maud for lack of something to say. She put her gloves on slowly.

'Hitler knows what he wants,' replied Clive, reluctantly rising from the marble-topped table. 'He has a plan – unlike the others, and he will wait, won't show his hand till he's sure of support. Not like all these last-century "liberals" and "conservatives", still wanting to get back either to old Wilhelm or Biedermeyer or the old Goethe Kultur – '

'You must tell me another time,' she cut in. Then she tried to insist upon paying for her tea but Clive said that it had been his own idea so she gave in. If they met again she would see to it that she paid for him next time. She wanted no feeling of obligation, and Clive, she was sure, had no more money than she had, being also the recipient of a scholarship, though Oxford might be even more generous than the Scottish trustees.

At least, he thought, she mentions 'another time', though I think she is too much of a blue-stocking for me. Clive liked clever women but preferred those who were intelligent but not any cleverer than he was himself.

Maud sat at her window after the copious supper. Frau Müller was a generous cook; if the quality was not quite of *haute cuisine* standard it was better than that she had been used to, except at home with Ma's plain but tasty dishes. She looked out over the city that stretched out in the distance below. Her street was almost within the boundary of the Old Town, on higher ground than the older centre. You could see the river and the ancient buildings from the top of the house through the roofs of the houses built on the main road where trams plied punctually between six a.m. and midnight.

She stayed at the window for some time as dusk fell, before taking off her spectacles and rubbing her eyes.

She moved then to the little table where her work was set out, and sat in the high-backed chair to sort, read through and transcribe the notes she had taken in the library. The Müller Haus was used to research students and each room was provided with a solid work-table and a lamp. It was rumoured that the late lamented Herr Müller had been a Herr Doktor. The table and chair, a high bed with its thick duvet, a Chinese screen round a wash-basin, a row of shelves for books and a cupboard for clothes was pretty well all the room contained, except for Maud's large trunk and a hook for her outer clothes. She was pleased with it; what furniture there was was solid.

She must begin her letter to Ma before she went to bed. So far she had not missed a week of her correspondence home. Though she had never enjoyed letter-writing it was a self-imposed duty, and she knew reading between the lines of Ma's replies that her mother missed her. At first Maud had 'edited' her letters so as not to worry Ma, for she had been unexpectedly homesick during her first five months or so away. But things had looked up once the first tiny harbinger of Spring had arrived and the winds had grown warm.

She had started to appreciate the solidity and pride of her new city, even begun to despise her earlier untravelled self. Stoicism had carried her through the initial loneliness, got her accustomed to the new sounds and the new tastes. The city itself was full of equally stoical people, she realised, who were a little cut off from the rest of their country and had suffered much industrial unrest in the previous century. Now the place exuded local pride and importance with its solid Bürger and solid Professors and solid churches and tramcars. Gradually she realised that the lost war still rankled, that financial ruin stared many of the inhabitants in the face. But at first she had thought they were all pretty sure of themselves, proud of their 'Kultur', a word so often on their lips. And the theatres! The whole population appeared to attend the *Konzertsaal* every other Tuesday and to visit exhibitions in galleries or museums.

Frau Meyer back home had been right: the Germans cared more for culture even than the Scots, who Maud thought they rather resembled once she had got to know them better. And they worked even harder.

At first she had been able to find her way only to the university, its library, and the Post and Telegraph Office further away, and had walked everywhere, fearful of getting on the wrong tram and being carried away she knew not whither. But slowly she had become more adventurous. She felt free, adult, in charge of herself, so long as she did not have to talk too much to others or be expected to get to know them intimately.

Clive Queensbury had been the one who had said more than most to her since he too was a stranger in a foreign city. She did not mind going about alone, but now after her little outing with Clive, she wondered whether he might be of some use to her, so that she would not be pursued by other men in the summer if she wanted to go on one of the steamboats for a day trip. It would be an adventure to go on a steamboat, or take the train to the nearest mountains where travellers climbed to the summit, or walk to the outer city or along the river without being bothered by men ogling her.

She was finding it hard tonight to concentrate on her work.

Perhaps she had done enough for one day. It had been a difficult day, for she had been finally confronted with the need to start writing out the first draft of her thesis which would then have to be edited and altered and typed and was obviously going to be too long. But after all, she had come here also to learn to speak another language. It had been necessary for the proper researches into her subject that she read everything written in German about it. But now she had realised that this new language, a language that was not dead like the other two she was most expert in, might in future yield a new sort of work. Recently she had begun to dream in it and they always said that was a good sign! She ought to talk to people more, now that she understood most of what was said to her. But there were few young women to talk to, except for students much younger than herself. Most of the research students were men, and most of the academic staff too. There were women clerks whom she saw scurrying to their lunches, for the city was the seat of government for the province, and there were also some women who staffed the library in lowly positions and were in evidence at the Town Hall and in the Public Reading Rooms, but how did you get to know them? The city was also the HQ (Kornfeld had told her), of two army divisions, and she often saw high-helmeted officers either marching away in the direction the tram took when she had alighted from it to walk over University Bridge, or strolling along in their leisure time in the city centre, boots gleaming. One or two had looked at her and one had murmured something unintelligible.

But if she was to be a little more adventurous when the hot weather came – and above all the vacation between the two semesters, – she had better try to earn a little extra money for herself. Her Fellowship was quite generous, but covered only travelling, academic and living expenses, and things here were very dear.

Prof Kornfeld had once mentioned the fact that one or two of the foreign students he had had previously – both Americans she gathered – had given English lessons to fellow students to earn a little extra. But the German students themselves had to be well off to pay for those. Well, she might try, even so. There might be others too who wanted to perfect their English in this

195

city of, she supposed, at least half a million inhabitants. It was much larger than any city she had known, even larger than Edinburgh, and in some ways more handsome. You felt that farms and orchards were not far away, and there were parks and gardens everywhere. She felt a little like a tightly closed bud whom warm air would eventually swell to a blossom.

She could not settle to the exploits of her latest empress so she closed the book and opened instead a guide to the city. It seemed it had a bishop too – it ought to have more than one for there were so many churches, as well as the cathedral, which she had discovered had its foundations in the thirteenth century. Most of the churches had seemed to her ignorant eyes to be what Jackie called 'Victorian Gothic' – except that they could not be 'Victorian' here and might even some of them be genuine Gothic. Certainly the Grand Town Hall and the cathedral and one or two of the other churches and even the imposing university gave her a feeling of the medieval. Hector would have been able to tell her. She had never noticed her surroundings overmuch before, had taken them for granted, with the exception of Garvits . . . She thrust away the memory of Garvits and of Hector. She had been determined to learn from that most painful lesson, but was still not sure quite what she had learned – except that love was an ambiguous emotion, and possibly best left alone.

Better think of buildings and trips up the river when she was not thinking of her work. She missed her novel-reading, for there were no English books of the lighter kind here. She had however seen a cinema, though she had not yet ventured to go into it alone. But she had heard that a 'daring' film was to be shown there with the new German 'star', Marlene Dietrich, and was waiting till it arrived before making up her mind to go. Clive Queensbury – 'Cosmo' – might take her! He might also take her, if she paid for herself, to sit in one of the cafés, for she would like to sample the liqueurs which were said to be a speciality of the region. She had noticed that women never sat there alone and students went about usually in groups, and she hated groups. Men had their uses, though she vowed she would go for a promenade alone on the fortifications overlooking the town moat one day.

196

As she undressed for bed she was making a mental plan for summer explorations – the gardens of the episcopal palace and the various squares and markets . . . She had been so immersed in her studies and in getting acclimatised, but now she must open out her wings and linger where she had previously only hurried by, above all in the largest market square which was always full of stalls holding delicious looking sweetmeats, strange sausages, smelly cheeses, lace, cloth and wool. If she had a little more cash she could buy the wool and knit Ma a jumper; she liked to knit, it was soothing.

Maud fell asleep dreaming of a large statue in a square and then of finding herself in an immense library – not the one she knew – where the books were all locked to the shelves so that she cried out in frustration.

She finished her last night's letter to Ma as she sat before her midday break in the great library whose books were not locked away but open to her as an accredited scholar. She read it through – a description of some of the statues in the city, a mention of the Museum of Fine Arts that might interest her mother. Today, on her way into the library she had purchased a picture postcard of the great gilded Baroque lecture hall where she had first come across Clive Queensbury, and slipped it into her letter home. She would be able to buy some stamps on her way back. She put down her pen after finishing a description of the Droschken, the horse cabs that clip clopped all over the town centre, and the tram stops lit up with their red lanterns at night – which had rather worried her at first. The immensity of the city and the immensity of the library were paralleled in her head, but she had the feeling this morning that she was beginning to take the measure of them. Last night she had felt depressed, but this morning she had suddenly found the conceptual key to her thesis, if not yet the words to explain the argument. Eugen Kornfeld wanted to see her that afternoon so she must have a quick lunch first. It was unusual for a professor to be available in the afternoon. Usually all the work was done in the morning, some of the staff arriving before eight o'clock.

Herr Professor Doktor Kornfeld was already an elderly man, but she did not find him at all intimidating. He looked more like a family solicitor with his gold pince nez and precise speech and he was excessively well-organised, which Maud appreciated, having sometimes become impatient with Carmichael's alternate vagueness and jocularity. Kornfeld was sitting at his table but shouted 'Herein,' when she knocked and looked up at her from under his pince-nez. This interview was the result of Maud's plucking up courage to ask his advice about the scope of her study. Her material had been mounting up and threatening to overwhelm her. Kornfeld began, with no preamble: 'Only you can decide how to use all you know. What you have unearthed – or been able to visualise,' – he allowed himself the luxury of a smile – 'from the coins and monuments is astonishing – so long as your British examiners will bear with you over your descriptions.'

Maud knew he was talking about the thirty pages she had devoted to the physical appearance of one of the empresses and the twenty or so ways of doing her coiffure. It was only a tiny part of the whole, but so far as she knew nobody else had ever managed to describe the mundane details of how exactly the 'Image' of a Roman Empress was arrived at so that those who sculpted or cast her face would be impressed.

'You have more than enough material,' he said. She had translated from the Greek into both German and English as she had done with the Latin.

'I am pleased,' he said. 'And I think now you could stop any further reading and start to write up that draft – we don't want any panic next year – so many of your colleagues leave it all too late. I congratulate you, Fräulein – and if you care to eventually transcribe all the original parts of your discoveries into German I'll see that the abstract is put in the library here whatever the outcome of your doctorate – about which I myself have no reservations at present.' Her thesis was, of course, in English for the British authorities.

Maud was very pleased. But she had another matter to raise. 'May I ask you?' she began, and he looked up and waited whilst she asked, most politely and in her best *hochdeutsch* if he knew of any present scholar who might like some private lessons in English.

'Herr Hartmann was just enquiring as a matter of fact,' he

answered her. 'I will speak to him and ask him to write to you.'

'Thank you, Herr Professor,' said Maud, wondering who Herr Hartmann might be.

On her way home that evening Maud wished she had a camera. Lots of folk had now taken up photography as a hobby but she had no machine and the ones she had seen in the shops were dear. There was the Marienkirche, she thought, as she passed it, a perfect building for a 'snap', surely the most handsome church she had seen, though she had not yet penetrated inside among its candles and incense. She rather quailed before going into a Catholic church, the guilt she knew she would feel when she did being a ridiculous legacy from Preacher Gray. She walked over the bridge and turned right by the botanical gardens whose willow trees were just beginning to show their delicate green in a filmy mist in the evening light. There was a small lake there too which would be pleasant to sit by one day. When summer came she must forsake too many churches and libraries and museums and take more healthy walks. The shops too – she hadn't dared to do more peek at the jewellers or the large department stores, for she knew that she would feel faint with envy at what was displayed.

Frau Müller had also proudly described the zoo to her – which was not far away – 'a nice trip on a steamer,' – but Maud drew the line at wild animals.

Thinking all these things Maud was almost home. It was not quite warm enough yet to sit outside, but she was just promising herself the treat of sitting soon in a small garden at the other end of the street near her lodgings, where women went with prams filled with fat, silent babies, when a young officer in full uniform crossed over from the other side of the street and looked at her shyly, but very carefully, as he passed her, without smiling. She was sure she had seen this particular officer before, though at first they had all looked the same. But this one had been by himself, not with a noisy group. The barracks was a kilometre or so away on the other side of the square that joined on to the bridge. She thought, he looks a little like Calum Fyffe – some Germans must have southern blood. The thought of Calum led on to the thought of Jackie and the necessity of replying to

Jackie's last long letter. How different their lives were now. She felt quite animated that evening over supper and talked to a middle-aged relative of Frau Müller with such amiability and wit that he said to his cousin afterwards: 'Really, some of the English can be quite intelligent!' Maud was unfolding her petals – a little.

Frau Müller's drawing-room was to be the scene of Maud's first English lesson. Maud had received a note from Herr Hartmann asking her fee and suggesting Wednesday evenings between eight and nine as a suitable time for his instruction. Her problem was where to take this first pupil. She could hardly offer lessons in her own room, which doubled as a sleeping chamber, and there was nowhere at the university, not even the corner of a 'common room', since there were no 'common' rooms even for the undergraduates. Frau Müller was unexpectedly helpful, and Maud felt it could not have been the first time one of her lodgers had had this problem. 'For a mark an hour I can offer you my salon,' she said, with a mixture of grandeur and commercial sense. She obviously needed every spare mark that came her way, but liked to give the impression she was doing her lodgers a favour. Not that Maud had ever seen anyone go into the room, not even its owner. Maud had intended to ask five marks an hour and one mark subtracted from this seemed fair enough since there would be no tram fare to and from anywhere else. Frau Müller explained that one of the tables in her salon was a folding one and there were two of her second best chairs which might be brought in for Maud and her pupil to sit upon.

The drawing-room was large and must be chilly in winter, Two gilt chandeliers were suspended from the high ceiling with upturned porcelain lamps and the windows were also high and draped with lace outer curtains and inner ones of net. There were fringed lamps on small tables covered with cloths with bobbled borders, as was the cloth on a big table where reposed a bust of some classical deity unknown to Maud, or one she did not recognise. Brackets for gas candles on the walls, two vases on a narrow sideboard and several oval-shaped frames containing silhouettes on the window wall, completed the furniture and ornaments. Everything here was solid, but faded; even the bust looked dusty, though closer inspection showed it was not. Fortunately if her lessons with this Herr Hartmann materialised they would take place early enough for natural light to filter through the curtains.

She replied to Hartmann, saying she must first ascertain the extent of his knowledge of English during their first lesson and asking him therefore, if he agreed, to visit her the next Wednesday for a preliminary discussion. He must be at number seven Fiedler Strasse at eight o'clock on the next Wednesday. In the interval Maud tried to discover what he looked like, who he was, but in vain.

'Oh, he comes now and then – an aesthetic type – he has been writing a thesis for years,' said Ilse Lau, a young woman who occasionally struck up a conversation with Maud when they came out of the library at the same time. She must be patient and wait till the Wednesday evening to discover what Ilse Lau's idea of an aesthetic type was.

She was down in the hall at five minutes to eight that Wednesday. The hall still bore the faint smell of the evening meal of onions and pork floating up from the kitchen. The drawing-room was ready, the table by the window with two chairs set out, and Maud's English grammar and her Bible (the only English books she had brought with her), on the table. Punctually, just as the hand of her watch reached eight, the bell rang and she heard Frau Müller's voice. Then the door to the drawing-room was opened wider and a tall man with a bony face and swept back, black hair, was ushered in by her landlady. 'Herr Hartmann,' she announced and withdrew. Maud advanced and shook hands and the visitor bowed. He was about thirty – she had discovered that in Germany students went on sometimes till middle age if they had the resources. She felt a little nervous, but said in German: 'Please sit down.'

'If you please,' he replied, 'Will you speak to me in English now and for the whole hour so that I might learn also the accent.'

Maud swallowed. 'If you are sure you will understand,' she replied in her native tongue. 'Cosmo' was the only other person with whom she had spoken English for six months and she disliked speaking English to people whose first language it was

201

not, finding it tiring and artificial. And anyway, she should be laying down the law, not this composed man who now waited for her to sit down and then pushed her chair into the table for her before seating himself. 'I have to know how much English *you* know before I can begin,' she said. 'How many years have you studied it?'

'Many years at school and for the *Abitur*, but I have much forgotten.' He did not smile, looked stern as though it was the fault of someone else he had forgotten.

'And do you wish to improve your written language as well as your accent?' She enquired, taking a pencil and opening her notebook.

'You have an accent which is not English, I think,' he replied, looking at her keenly. Really, she must nip this one in the bud!

'The Scots speak the clearest English of all,' she replied stiffly.

'Is that so – then I will speak Scottish!'

'Scots,' corrected Maud. 'Scottish is the adjective – in German you have the same word for both.'

It transpired that Herr Hartmann was intending, one day, to visit England – 'For business,' he said vaguely – but also needed to improve his written English.

'I think we shall begin on translation,' said Maud. 'If you are agreeable to my terms of five marks an hour?'

'That is satisfactory,' he replied. 'And also for this lesson – I insist.'

He had long hands and a long face with a certain intellectuality, she thought; his shirt was white, his cuffs starched, his nails immaculate. His eyes met hers. 'I have brought a book of German which I should like to translate,' he said putting a large volume on the table. Maud had realised that the Holy Bible would not be very helpful for his purposes.

'What is it?' she asked.

It seemed that it was a novel and she wondered whether he was wanting to test her own German if it were a book without English translation. This was absurd. She must assert her pedagogic rights.

'We may come to that,' she said severely, and then he smiled.

'If you will find me a copy we may spend part of our lesson translating it. For the present I think you must revise your grammar. As you doubtless know, English grammar is very fluid, not built on Latin as yours is, though Latin has affected our vocabulary, not yours.' She produced a passage of English and asked him to read it, which he did very creditably, but without much expression. She corrected some of his pronunciation, then gave him a dictation before saying: 'Now we can talk a little in English. Tell me, what are you studying?'

'I am writing a *these* on Aryan Kultur and the idea of the hero,' he said. 'It will be history of the epics of the Nordic races and a description of the German folk and their position within the races of Northern Europe.'

'People,' she said, 'not folk – that is Scottish or American. We say German *people*.'

He accepted the correction and as he went on to describe his *these*; she wondered how long he had been writing it.

'I think it is your colloquial English you need to practise,' she said. 'I will draw up a plan of action – conversation, dictation, translation and grammar and idiom – especially idiom.'

'Thank you,' he said, 'Miss Crichton.' She wondered if he were laughing at her, for she was unused to instructing others. There was something both attractive and yet, she groped for the word – 'sinister' about him. Now she was imagining things!

At the end of the hour she looked at her watch. 'It is time to finish, Herr Hartmann,' she said and closed the grammar. He had just said that English grammar was too easy. She would show him! – a little lecture next week on prepositional verbs would fox him.

'You may call me by my forename,' he said before he stood up and bowed.

'I do not know it,' said Maud standing up in turn.

'Wolfgang Hartmann,' he said. 'Thank you for the lesson.' He took a small bill out of his pocket book and put it on the table. 'To avoid inconvenience I shall pay every week,' he said.

Maud blushed. He seemed to look at her rather searchingly as he waited for her to go out of the door first. For a fleeting moment she felt as though he was paying for sexual services. Absurd. She must take a hold of herself. The man was both intelligent and polite. Old-fashioned though; not all younger students bowed and scraped in this way. Frau Müller came in her stately way out of the door beyond and let Herr Hartmann out of the front door and Maud escaped with a sigh of relief to her room.

Teaching was a draining business, she reflected. She did not relish it, but she was not going to allow Herr Hartmann to be critical of her methods. For the next two lessons she stuck to her guns and was very cool with him before asking him if he had found another copy of the book he wanted to read with her. He produced it with a flourish from his pig-skin case. Maud took it up to her room after he had gone. It was light now till about ten o'clock so she read a few pages before retiring, her mind not on them, thinking instead of the party some of the students were organising next week, the first week of June. 'Cosmo' had mentioned it and asked her to go with him and she was worried lest he might think she was encouraging him. Wolfgang had *not* mentioned it, so she presumed such affairs were beneath him. Should she go or not? It was easier to say no, but she knew she should occasionally appear more sociable. She decided to sleep on her decision.

Wolfgang Hartmann of the leather coat and astrakhan collar was not at the soirée which Maud did attend. She was relieved; she did not want to know him outside the confines of English lessons for there was something about him that unnerved her. She had sensed there was under his politeness a faintly mocking quality, but she thought that it might be her imagination, and tried to ignore it. She thought he looked at her sceptically because he felt she was not yet quite sure of herself as a teacher, though she was well grounded in her own language and had no self doubts on that score. If he was questioning her powers, well he was quite right to want his moneysworth of good instruction, and the extra marks made a difference to her own budgeting, paltry as they were.

But after a concentrated hour with Wolfgang she would feel quite exhausted, not a bodily exhaustion so much as one of the nerves. If one day she was to become a university lecturer herself

204

she must learn not to expend so much nervous energy. She was always relieved when the lesson was over and she could make her way rather dizzily back to her room and collapse on her bed. The exhaustion lasted only for ten minutes or so. Perhaps Wolfgang saw life as a battle of wills and this was what drained her in his company.

Clive Queensbury was at the soirée, or rather evening gathering, of research students and staff. It was all curiously formal, unlike the jollier events at home when tutors and teachers would sometimes unbend enough to sing a ballad or two or recite a Rabbie Burns poem. Whisky was not served here. They drank either beer or Rhein wine and there was coffee, which Maud noticed the few women invited seemed to prefer. She stood talking to Clive, who was now almost a friend. He seemed to have abandoned any intention of flirting with her and had been concentrating his attentions upon the niece of one of the professors.

'How is Hannelore?' she asked him mischievously.

'Oh, Hannelore is a useful smokescreen,' he replied. 'She is a nice, pretty girl, but not my type. I must introduce you to my new Russian friend!'

Maud looked round, seeing nobody who might answer to this description.

'Oh, no, she's not *here*,' he said. 'She's not in the university – she's a dancer and singer at the theatre – refugee from St Petersburg – at least her parents came here about ten years ago and stayed and now she's an orphan. I met her with her friends at the Café Hansen.' He was animated, eager to talk about this new friend. Maud hoped that Tatiana, for such was her name, would not detach Clive away completely from his old habits, for she had got used to chatting with him after they finished their work.

The door of the Festsaal opened and in came Professor Kornfeld with a young man in tow. 'Fräulein Crichton, may I present a cousin of my wife?' he said and then: 'This is Helmuth von Platen, Fräulein Crichton. Herr von Platen – Helmuth – Fräulein Crichton.' The young man clicked his heels and bowed and Maud shook hands with him as Clive looked on at this performance with a slight sneer. Eugen Kornfeld then vanished and Maud was left with the young man, who seemed nervous. Was he another candidate for her English lessons? He seemed vaguely familiar, though she thought something was missing which belonged to him.

'Are you a student, Herr von Platen?' she asked, for lack of anything else to say. Clive had disappeared and the man stood there staring at her after the initial formalities.

'No, I am a soldier,' he stated in hesitant English, but without the clipped accent of so many Germans. So that was it, he was the soldier she had often seen passing her in the Stern Strasse on her way to the tram, or walking home! The one who had seemed to look so searchingly at her. He looked smaller in mufti. She did not want to say she had seen him – why should she have noticed him anyway, except that he had seemed to cross her path more often than seemed likely?

'Where are you stationed?' she asked in German.

'Oh, you speak our language,' he said in genuine surprise. 'The city is for over a hundred years the HQ of the Sixth Corps d'Armée.'

'I am studying here under your uncle – or is it cousin?' said Maud.

'Yes, my mother is Frau Doktor Kornfeld's cousin,' he explained again.

'Do you often come to university functions then?'

A servant was hovering near with a tray of glasses of beer and wine.

'Will you have a glass?' he asked her. 'You might like to sit down? It is tiring, I think, to stand and drink, though I think it is the English custom – a cocktail party?'

Maud wanted to say that she was not accustomed to cocktail parties, but found herself saying instead: 'I am not English – Herr von Platen.' The name was noble, redolent of Prussian estates and a 'distinguished' past.

He brought a spindly-legged chair up for her and one for himself and handed her the wine. The room was filling up and several people had taken chairs to the sides of the room. 'Not English!' he said surprised. 'I thought – '

'I am Scottish,' said Maud, for what seemed the nine hundredth time. 'British if you like!'

'Onkel Kornfeld did not tell me that,' he said. He seemed upset.

Maud wondered why Kornfeld had so obviously introduced the two of them. Perhaps he thought she was lonely. Now she was indebted to him for the English lessons *and* this new young man's interest. He did seem interested. He was younger than her, she thought.

'Are you to make a career of the army?' she asked.

'I think it is my duty,' he replied simply. 'But it is good to get away from the barracks.' He did not look like Maud's idea of an army man, was of medium height, and dark with a chiselled face and moustache, and his head was not shaved like so many Germans, although it was cropped. He had nice grey eyes and a straight nose.

'My English friend, whom you must meet,' she began, 'is always telling me that political events over here are very dangerous, governments falling and the people all so restless after inflation and the slump. I suppose an army is always necessary to control things if they get out of hand.'

He looked sombre. 'Soldiers have always been necessary,' he said. 'But we are peacetime soldiers, not policemen.'

She felt suitably rebuked, but he smiled and went on in his own language, 'We could have a perfectly sensible government if the conservatives and liberals could come to some arrangement, for there are other forces around who are not so patient.'

She thought, I wonder what he would make of Wolfgang, but this man is maybe not an intellectual. Which was refreshing, for she was not sure if she really liked intellectuals.

He was looking at her very seriously. He was not exactly shy, but there was a reserve in his expression that was counteracted by his next words. He spoke in English now.

'I have to make a confession,' he said. 'When my uncle – I call him Onkel, though he is really a cousin, has asked me before to attend his parties I have not wished to come for I am always busy and it is good to get away in free time into the country, not to parties.'

She sipped her wine as there was obviously more to come. Perhaps he spoke in English, she thought, as he went on talking to her, because it was less embarrassing to say things in a foreign language.

'Onkel Eugen speaks sometimes of his students, not much, but I tell him I have seen a little lady walking alone when I am returning sometimes to my barracks and she is looking perhaps not like a German and I think she is a student, for she carries the case of papers and gets the tram in the direction of the university library. So I ask my Onkel, have you a lady student who is not German – and I describe you and say you are walking along Stern Strasse very often and he replies there is a young lady who lodges on Fiedler Strasse, for I found her the lodging. She is a student, but what is that to you, Helmuth? I say to him I should like to meet this lady to talk to her in English and so this time when he invites me to his party he will introduce me.' He stopped, out of breath.

Professor Kornfeld as a pander was a rather astonishing phenomenon.

'It is true – I wish to speak with you for I have seen you many times! Please forgive me.' He looked earnest, very young. Maud could not help feeling flattered, but replied rather coolly to this unexpected admirer.

'That was friendly of you – Herr von Platen, to want to speak to me. Now you are doing so!' She did not tell him she had often noticed him in the street.

'You do not look British,' the young man said.

Maud was not sure if this was meant as a compliment, but then, after a pause, he went on: 'I thought that perhaps you were from Greece – except the skin is not dark enough.'

'From Greece?' echoed Maud in some astonishment.

'I suppose I was thinking of statues of Old Greece,' he said with a shy smile.

'You mean Ancient Greece,' Maud corrected him, now knowing full well what he meant and feeling flattered. 'There are many dark people in my country you know. We are not so blond in general as you are over here. We are a mongrel race.'

'The Scottish are Celts?' he asked.

'Oh, yes, there are quite a lot of Celts – I suppose we all may have a little Celtic blood – but mainly in the West of Scotland. We in the Lowlands descend from Angles and Saxons

208

– what people sometimes call Aryan,' she added, remembering Wolfgang's strictures.

Helmuth's mouth expressed disapproval. 'I do not like this word. It means nothing – most Europeans are mixes. My family is old and noble – it is an important one, but we are not one of us blond and – *blau aügige* – how do you say?'

'Blue-eyed – do speak German, Herr von Platen.'

'I cannot express myself well in your language,' he said sorrowfully.

'On the contary, I understand you very well,' said Maud.

He said in his own language: 'Things are in a mess here. It is a question of values – we must stand up for them even though we lost to you last time – all was not wicked in our country you know – we are cultured.'

'Yes, I have noticed,' said Maud drily. 'But I suppose that if people had enough money and there were no problems of that sort, you could have a government like ours in Britain?'

'In Britain you have had constitutional monarchy for two hundred years at least – while we were not even one country – all our little provinces and Länder . . .'

'At least you gave us Prince Albert,' said Maud smiling.

She was trying hard to be polite. Talk of economics and politics and wars bored her. If that was what he wanted from her she had better make it clear he would be disappointed. But he went on as if to forestall her.

'I did not want to meet you to talk of these wearisome truths – but to talk to a very gracious young lady.' The way he said *gnädiges Fräulein* made her feel once more on false pretences and she smiled uneasily.

Just then 'Cosmo' came up. Evidently the Professor's niece had gone home, or preferred to talk to someone else. 'Cosmo' and Herr von Platen eyed each other, both young and personable, the one with all the ardour of an old race keen to uphold what was good in the past, the other, like Maud, somewhat of a parvenu, who had risen and was rising on account of his brains; less ardent, but equally incensed about public affairs. They skirted round each other, but after a few verbal skirmishes they seemed to get on. Clive Queensbury's German was also good, though perhaps less idiomatic than Maud's, and he used the Englishman's trick of irony and the Oxford man's love of paradox. Maud could see that von Platen was puzzled.

She broke in to say: 'Do not take all Herr Queensbury's talk seriously, Herr von Platen. Englishmen like to tease.'

They both turned to her.

'Please will you both call me Helmuth,' said the German, free to ask this since Maud was with a friend.

'You may call Mr Queensbury Clive, I'm sure,' said Maud laughing, 'but my *German* name is Matilda.'

'Mechthild,' said Helmuth. 'A good name for a warrior.'

'Exactly,' said Maud.

Cosmo/Clive, who did not yet know Maud's name for him, laughed. 'Come off it, Maud,' he said in English.

The German looked puzzled. 'Excuse me, I have to speak to a woman over there,' said Maud, inventing a necessary conversation with the only other woman she knew, Ilse, who was looking bored in a corner. She sailed away.

'She is ä great friend of yours?' asked Helmuth, looking sad.

'Oh, Maud is a fellow student. We know each other only as friends,' said Clive.

'English people are often friends, men and women together?'

'Yes – why not?'

'She is a very beautiful young lady, I think,' said Helmuth. 'There are not many young ladies at the university and none in the army.' They both laughed. Clive could see he was smitten and resolved to tease Maud about it.

The two men began to talk of the new Chancellor, Herr Brüning, who had been appointed only a month or two previously. Clive thought his policies might easily lead to the end of the Weimar government and thus to the end of democracy, since President Hindenberg had already assumed autocratic powers. Helmuth von Platen for his part was hopeful that, in spite of the economic stresses and strains, the Weimar Democratic Republic would hold fast.

'Oh, Brüning would like your Emperor back,' said Clive. 'And a nice "non-party" government with the authority to make decisions.'

'But what is wrong with that, my friend?'

'What is wrong with it is that the Social Democrats play no part in his thinking – we don't have that party in England, but we have a similar one – the Labour Party – though we are not a republic.'

'And your army – they would take orders from the – "Labour" party?'

'Our army takes orders only from the Government in Parliament, but theoretically our King stands over them all constitutionally – mind you, he is not very bright!'

Helmuth looked shocked. But then he said – 'With the American crash and the state of the world markets, what can we do? We need foreign investment'.

'Yes, that too – but you see if Brüning falls – I won't say *when* he falls if that depresses you – mark my words, if you won't make painful choices, the man with the loudest voice and the biggest promises will slip in.'

'You mean the NSDAP? They would not surely be voted in!'

'Yes, the NSDAP – they're only biding their time. Then your army will be under their thumb.'

Helmuth von Platen looked shocked once more. The idea of his noble profession taking orders from the National Socialist Workers' Party, whose leader had been a corporal in the last war, was distasteful – more than distasteful, ludicrous.

Maud came up when they had got round to a discussion of Germany's border problems and the possibility sooner rather than later of all parties but the one – that directed by the sinister Hitler – becoming fragmented, even disappearing. Men did go on and on so about politics. Maud looked from one to the other. '*I* know someone who thinks the NSDAP would be a strong and popular government,' she offered, and they both stared at her. She dropped her gaze, felt uncomfortable. 'It is only a person to whom I teach English,' she said. 'I expect he is of no account.'

Soon after this the party broke up, Helmuth extracting a promise that she would meet him for a drink at the best restaurant-cum-coffee-house on the Schweidnitzer Strasse the next Thursday evening, when he would be free from his duties.

211

He went back to barracks overjoyed, and Clive returned to his own digs to further his plan for seducing the fair Tatiana, but also one for keeping Maud interested in him too.

Chapter Eleven

Maud had to give another English lesson before she could meet Helmuth von Platen for the promised drink.

On his way to Fräulein Crichton, Wolfgang Hartmann bought a bunch of freesias from one of the flower stalls in the old Market. Flowers always pleased women and a gift always put the receiver a little in the debt of the donor. He also had a book under his arm, one regarded as rather shocking, and the origin of the film showing at present at the main *Kino*. Herr Hartmann had always been an omnivorous reader; ideas excited him, especially those of the philosopher Nietzsche, whose 'God is Dead' had been the most liberating remark he had ever heard or read. Wolfgang had had enough of ineffectual governments who promised but never delivered, and feared the masses if unemployment rose. Only a strong leader, he thought, could rescue the country from the morass of twelve post-war years. Ordinary people were fed up and there was also the Jewish 'problem'. Wolfgang Hartmann knew several of *them* in the city for they owned the largest department store and were active in banking and the professions. But 'Germany for the Germans' was his motto. These ideas, which had been festering for a long time in him and in the bosoms of many of his friends, were not the sort of thing he wished to discuss with the beautiful Scotswoman. Women had other uses, and women teachers and academics took jobs away from the men. He had been a student now for eleven years, wandering from university to university. He had had enough of this one; it was too far off the beaten track; he would go in the autumn to Berlin. But he would miss his English lessons and rather resented that Maud Crichton had impressed him as being clever. It did not suit him to be pupil rather than teacher; perhaps his resentment came from being in an inferior position vis-à-vis Maud. He found her attractive, but too self-contained. What she needed was a man. He might help her one day to find that out.

He had almost reached Fiedler Strasse. Perhaps the novel he was carrying 'for translation into English' would frighten her off him. He wished he could see her face when some of the passages were before her eyes. Hartmann was an aesthete and, rather like one of the heroes in the novels of Heinrich Mann he was taking to Maud, he worshipped beauty – and power. In this novel there was no connection between beauty and love. Worship was a thing in itself unconnected with morality, not only with the pettifogging laws of convention, but with the Moral Law itself, Kant's Law which the old thinker had found in himself. Well he, Wolfgang Hartmann, could make up his own laws. He had had a good grounding in philosophy and history, but neither was adequate for changing the world. You had to choose between freedom – which was no kind of freedom if you had no job and no money – and authority, vested in a 'strong' man with the sort of advisers who would see the people's darling did their bidding, and then get rid of him. Strange how whenever he got thinking about beauty he ended up connecting it with will to power and the salvation of the country by the little man waiting in the wings. He might recommend d'Annunzio too, to Maud – that would be more up her street. He was aware that d'Annunzio had called Hitler 'Charlie Chaplin of the Nibelungen'. That was amusing. He himself had no time for the low-born Hitler – but he would be useful.

Having now arrived at her door he rang the bell peremptorily, still in his daydream of importance. Then he recollected himself and where he was and, once he was in the house, advanced smilingly on Maud with the bunch of flowers. She recoiled slightly in surprise.

When they were both seated at the table, he gave her the novel. 'Here is the book of the film everyone is going to see this week,' he said.

'Which? – you mean *The Blue Angel*?'

'The very one – you would enjoy it, I think – about a poor little teacher who falls for a cabaret singer and is ruined by his passion.'

Clive had told her all about the film and offered to accompany her to it, but she said nothing about that to Hartmann.

'I have not read any of his novels,' she said. 'I hear that it is regarded as "decadent".'

'Oh, very decadent – but worth reading. Like d'Annunzio – you know his poems?'

'You want to translate from this book? – it seems hardly suitable,' she said, with some asperity, for she had guessed her pupil would welcome any opportunity to get on to the subject of sex and was determined they should not.

'We Germans think your island race is rather decadent,' he said to tease her. 'Your leaders are like ours, not strong enough to bring about change.'

'I'd rather not discuss politics,' said Maud.

'No – it is not a womanly subject,' he said.

That stung her. 'No – it is because I do not understand all that is happening to your republic,' she replied.

'Shall I give you a history lesson then?'

'If we have time when you have done the exercises.' She opened the grammar. 'Today we shall look at the pronominal verbs,' she announced severely. He thought, she looks marvellous when she is cross; she is a worthy opponent.

Naturally, Hartmann did not ever envisage being worsted by Maud. He did not even like getting a word wrong in her lessons, for he could not bear being at a disadvantage. When they had done the exercise and Maud had dictated a passage from Dr Johnson (she had found his complete works in the Library), her pupil handed over his homework, a short essay on *The Open Air*, a topic that bored him, though it was the passion of most of his countrymen.

'Thank you – I shall be kept busy,' said Maud.

She thought, he looks at me sometimes as though I am a specimen in a laboratory, but there is something about him . . . I don't like him and I am a little afraid of him. But he has 'charisma'.

'Your next essay subject is "Things are in the saddle and ride us",' she announced.

'How interesting,' he murmured. 'I have always been a bit of a fatalist myself.'

'You think there is nothing we can do to avert our destiny?' she asked him, looking into his eyes and then turning away her own and pretending to sort through some papers.

'Man's fate is in his blood,' said Wolfgang Hartmann. 'We are not swayed by reason but by our passions. Woman's fate too.' He looked directly at her till once more she averted her gaze.

Then she said: 'Reason is important – where should we be without our minds?'

'Oh, people think they have thought things out,' he said. 'But they justify their emotions – that is all.'

She pondered this. Her own reason told her that her pupil was a dangerous man and that he was better kept at a distance. But her 'blood' told her different.

'You must read d'Annunzio,' he said. 'I hope you will enjoy the novel I have brought you. I will bring you the Italian poems another day.'

'There is not time to translate from it today,' said Maud, rising thankfully after a look at her watch. Hartmann guessed some of her thoughts. He had never been what they called 'in love' with anyone in his life, but he had had plenty affairs with both men and women. Maud would be interesting to manipulate. They said that English women were 'easy', but he did not think Maud would be, and anyway, as she was always telling him, she was not English. There would not be time to lay siege to her once he was off to Berlin in the autumn. But he might come back. Or she might come to him. She would have to see where her destiny led *her*, he thought – he would keep in touch with her, and he felt sure she would with him.

'I am to move to Berlin in October,' he said as he took up his case of books and papers. 'You must see our capital. I will give you my address.'

'Oh – are you to attend another set of lectures then?' She felt relief mingled with disappointment.

'I shall go for four semesters to finish my thesis,' he said.

He had explained more about his thesis. It seemed less now a study of the 'Aryan' race than a study of the Hero in German literature.

'You must visit Berlin before you go back to your country,' he went on.

216

'Yes, I should like to,' she replied.

He was staring into her eyes with that piercing look he had. She turned away. – 'Thank you for the lesson,' he said, as he always did.

When he had gone she took the flowers up to her room, delicate blossoms that smelt lovely. She put them in water in her tooth mug. She wished he did not unnerve her so. She did want to go to Berlin one day, it was true. Everybody said: 'You must go to Berlin'. But there was a lot of work to do before then. Her thesis must be presented in another year and when that was done she would see about staying on for a time in Germany.

Her next little outing with Helmuth von Platen raised her spirits. He was a charming young man, so different from the brooding Wolfgang. He was also still shy – though he had not been too shy to have made her acquaintance. He seemed to have exhausted all his daring now he knew her.

'I saw you many times,' he said when the waiter had brought them two creamy cakes and two large cups of delicious coffee. 'I am so pleased you are taking coffee with me.'

'Let's talk German,' said Maud. All these young men wanted to talk to her in English, but she needed to practise their lingo.

Helmuth was taller than Calum Fyffe and not quite so dark, but he did still remind her a little of him, though his manner was very different. It was no strain to sit with him and chat and Maud was feeling light-hearted in his company, though he looked at her with such frank admiration that she knew it would not be long before he might be saying things he would one day regret. He told her about his family and his cadet school and his duties in the garrison, which did not seem very arduous.

'But you won't stay in the army for ever, will you?' she asked him.

'Probably not – when father dies I shall be needed to manage the estate at home.' This was in Prussia.

They chatted then about Kornfeld and about Maud's own interests. 'Have you seen this film they are all talking about?' she asked him. 'From the novel by Mann.'

'*The Blue Angel*? No – it sounds very depressing,' he said. He was a simple soul, she thought, having already summed him up as 'honourable'.

'I may go with "Cosmo",' she said.

'With whom?'

'Oh – I was forgetting myself! – I call Clive – you know, Mr Queensbury – you met him last week – I call him "Cosmo" as he is a man who wants to write the history of the world – I like giving nicknames to people.'

'What will you call me then, Miss Maud?'

'Do just call me Maud and I shall call you Helmuth. No! – I think I have it – you look a bit like that statue of the great general Moltke in the Square – I shall call you "Moltke" since you are a soldier!'

'There were two of them – two soldiers, uncle and nephew, and there is a grandson – I have met him,' said Helmuth. 'A very great family you know.'

It was odd how easy it was to be in 'Moltke's' company – they hardly knew each other and the young man was shy, yet for that reason she felt in control of the situation. She wondered what sort of soldier he made. Nobody would have guessed he was one, for he looked more like a gentleman farmer, which was what she supposed he would be in the end.

'Please will you make this date always with me on the Thursday now,' he said in English when it was time for him to return.

'Do you think you would be able to have a free Sunday sometime? – "Cosmo" wants to climb the Zobten – I gather it's about two hours drive away.'

'Yes, I have been in the train. On a fine day it is a nice excursion – but I have only one Sunday free in every four.'

'I'll tell him then you might accompany us – I think he has another friend who would also like to sightsee a bit.'

He told her the date of his next free Sunday and Maud promised to tell 'Cosmo'. She suspected *he* wanted to impress his little Russian friend.

It was queer how suddenly from being rather lonely in her first six months in the place she now felt almost an old inhabitant with new friends and regular meetings with them, quite apart from Herr Hartmann, who seemed to exist within another frame of reference. She would like to have introduced Hartmann to 'Moltke' and 'Cosmo' to see what they thought of him, but Wolfgang never asked her to go out with him or mix with his friends if he had any – which she sometimes doubted – and kept himself strictly to himself. As long as she was the 'teacher' she realised he would not want to see her out of that context. Between 'Moltke' and 'Cosmo', or rather Helmuth and Clive, there began a sort of friendship, though the soldier had little free time. It was arranged they would all go on that little trip to the mountain on one of Helmuth's free Sundays. Maud now met the latter once a week, each time at the expensive café, and every time he was just the same towards her. She had little to say to him, but he did not seem to mind or even realise how little they had in common until one evening he said –

'We are not friends like English people are,' They were sitting enjoying coffee on the terrace of the Garten Café.

'How do you mean? I think we are friends now, "Moltke".'

'You and Mr Queensbury, you are friends, I think? You would help each other in difficulties and yet you are man and woman. I think perhaps he is sweet on you.' He blushed deeply.

'Mr Queensbury,' she replied mockingly, 'is a friend, of course – no more. I'm sure he has *many* "lady friends".'

'But "lady friend" is not the same. I would like it that you were my lady friend too! – but *also* just friends.'

'A sort of *Brudenschaft*?'

'Yes – I like to talk and look at you, Maud – but I do not flirt, I don't think?'

Maud knew very well *he* was 'sweet' on her, but really did want him as a friend, no more. She felt bold, and so said: 'Why did you want to be introduced to me? – I am glad that you did, and it is very pleasant meeting and chatting and eating these delicious cream cakes but, it is a little odd . . .'

'Maybe I should not have asked to be introduced to you – I have nothing to offer a young English lady but cream cakes,' he said mournfully – 'But I think you are a very lovely person. *Du bist schön*. How do you say in English – handsome? pretty?'

Maud did not reply to this, but went on sucking the cream from her coffee spoon.

219

'Beautiful,' said Helmuth finally and then reverted to German. *'Du bist so raffiniert – wie eine Göttin, wirklich.'* He took out a white handkerchief to wipe his brow. Oh dear, this could spoil everything thought Maud.

'Please – let us just be friends. I shall not charge you for looking at me,' she said and smiled.

Helmuth had needed to pluck up a good deal of courage to say what he had and he did truly feel that there was something unusual about this young woman.

'We *are* friends,' said Maud again. There was something trustworthy about him, though he obviously had a lot to learn. But she did not feel at all romantic about him, no more than she did about Clive who was back to flirting with her when he could, as a matter of course.

Clive was, in fact, amused by the soldier's adoration of his little compatriot and not in the least put out. He took Maud to see the film everyone had been talking about when it returned to another cinema in the city. When they came out of the cinema, Clive, who had sat very properly by her side in the darkness, said: 'Would you come with me to the mountain *before* that Sunday we arranged with von Platen? We could stay in a little inn there – what about it?' She knew that he would have made the offer to any personable woman and would not be insulted if she refused, but was amused that he had felt compelled to ask her.

'I am very popular all of a sudden,' she said. 'There is Mr von Platen telling me I look like a goddess and you are inviting me to assignations in mountain huts – no, thank you, Cosmo – nice of you to offer, but let's stay friends, shall we?'

Clive made the same offer to the Russian girl, Maud discovered afterwards, but this time struck lucky. She saw him the day after he returned from his illicit weekend strolling along the main street with Tatiana and looking very pleased with himself. She was a handsome girl – Helmuth's adjective would have fitted this time, for she had rich, creamy Slav skin and the mien and carriage of a dancer. She wondered how long their affair would last. Clive might appear offhand and promiscuous, but she sensed that he had high standards, so she hoped the girl was as bright as her face was pretty.

The four of them did eventually go on the promised day trip to the Zobten, leaving on the train early one Saturday morning in July. Helmuth surpassed himself in attentions to Maud, picking flowers for her, and giving her a helping hand when they climbed their little mountain, a favourite tourist spot. Tatiana taught them all some Russian on the way back and Helmuth repeated that Onkel Kornfeld had told him Maud was a genuine scholar, which gratified her more than his own attentions.

Maud relaxed her working hours a little, but continued to work regularly in the library. The thesis seemed now to have sorted itself out in her head, though there would be a lot of work to have it finished in the next two semesters. She panicked occasionally when she thought of all the footnotes and references she would have to write up and check – and how on earth was she going to get it all typed in English? But she put those thoughts away for the summer and found time to read the books Wolfgang proffered her. She had now read the book of the film *The Blue Angel* and told him her opinion of it and of other pessimistic offerings – or at least a modified opinion, for she found much German writing mystical and mysterious or plainly incomprehensible when it was not being sadistic. She also read the German translation of the Italian poems which Wolfgang had mentioned.

This happy summer life found her doing the things she never seemed to have had time for in Scotland.

The warm sun aided her feeling of acceptance. She had not felt so calm for years, chatting with Cosmo-Clive, who now knew her nickname for him, sitting on the ramparts to eat bread and wurst, or going for a decorous evening stroll with Helmuth. The four of them went for another trip one Sunday on a steamer and the two men sang the Lorelei whilst Tatiana Semyonova sunned herself and Maud gazed into the water. Even listening to Wolfgang Hartmann expounding the latest move in the political situation to her in his best English was tolerable. The end of the semester would come soon enough. Then Helmuth would eventually receive a posting elsewhere, Clive would go back to England and Wolfgang would go off to Berlin. She would have to look for another pupil. By the end of the term she still felt suspended in a kind of amber, as though

221

time would have to stop, though she knew that was impossible. Already Ma was writing to ask her to come home for Christmas if she had to stay in Germany over to the next summer.

And now the real end of term came, the last week, the last lesson with Herr Hartmann and then the long vacation before her to fill up with work. Clive was going home only for a month – he had not apparently finished his researches and his parents had sent him the fare. Helmuth was still to be in the city but with more arduous duties, so that their meetings would be fewer. He had progressed to holding her hand as they took a walk by the river and one day, in a roundabout way, he even mentioned marriage. It was absurd, she could see that he was meeting with infatuation for the first time. But he was far too shy and idealistic to say anything more directly or attempt to do more than kiss her hand. He suited her very well.

Eventually though she thought she might have another admirer, one far less easy to disabuse or deflect – Wolfgang Hartmann. Unlike sweet little Helmuth, he did not go in for hand-holding or soulful looks. In fact he said nothing whatever to her on their last lesson that she could have construed as even faintly lover-like. He was off to Berlin within a day or two to find digs, he said. He reiterated that she must come to Berlin and he would look forward to showing her round. 'It is an order,' he said. Then he expressed his thanks for the lessons and gave her his new address. His unexpected letter arrived a few days later and it was written in English.

'Dear Miss Crichton – or may I call you Maud for that is, I believe, your name? I could not intrude upon your last lesson with me the thoughts which I now express here. You must have realised that I find you very seductive, though I have been at pains to be nothing but an apt learner at the shrine of your language. However, now I am no longer *in statu pupillari*, I wish to tell you that I shall look forward to seeing you in Berlin when your time in Silesia is up, should you ever wish to receive homage. There are great things to be done in my country, things which will push to one side adventures of a more "personal" nature, but one day, beautiful lady, you might wish to discover more

222

of life. Till that day I sign myself yours in waiting – Wolfgang Hartmann.'

This letter made her feel quite dizzy, casting all her pleasantly contented days into shadow. But there was no need for her to accept such a proposal, she told herself, whatever sort of proposal it might be. But she thought she knew what sort it was. Beside this gloomy, clever man, Helmuth and even Clive were, she thought, infants. Her lessons with him had been a mixture of an affliction and an excitement, for she had recognised the strange stirrings of desire in herself and immediately repressed them. She was aroused by her intuitive knowledge of the way "homage" would be offered and both shrank from it and was excited by it. He seemed sure he would see her again. But she would not answer his letter just yet.

During Maud's second and final year in Silesia, she did often think of Wolfgang Hartmann. Clive, when he did have time, was usually to be found with the delectable Tatiana, who it was rumoured was going to join a cabaret act in the capital. Helmuth was transferred to Saxony for six months, but wrote Maud long, romantic letters. Maud, was again much alone. She was now twenty-six, with her feet firmly planted on the ground. Sometimes though, when she had been working late and especially when she had been translating from the Greek, which was hard on the eyes, she would wonder whether the city and the parks and the trams and the people were 'real'. Her *work* felt real; books seemed more solid than people when people were not the objects she spent her day with. Wolfgang, however, never lost in her mind an essential 'reality'. Finally she had replied to him without referring to his personal remarks, but saying that she would try to find work in a school if it were possible to extend her stay over another term. That was if her thesis was accepted. If it were not, she did not know what she would do. Drown herself most likely.

His reply to this letter jerked her into watchfulness and made her take an interest in what was actually happening in Germany. Whilst she, if she had an hour free, might wander on 'Sand Island' or watch the sun set over the river, hearing the cries

223

of animals in the distant zoo, or watch children with shaven heads playing in the parks; there were apparently great events taking place in which Wolfgang Hartmann wanted to play a part. She must come to Berlin, he wrote back, and she might see a revolution!

In September 1931 there were elections in the whole of Germany, in which the National Socialist party achieved astonishing success. Maud had been right in her feeling about Wolfgang's politics, for she had had another rapturous letter from him in which he told her he had joined the Party – it was 'the only hope' for Germany. At the same time Helmuth, in his army fastness in Saxony, also wrote to her in great distress. He was always much more profound in his letters than in his conversations. 'The Nihilists have joined the savages', he wrote. 'There are many joining the Nazi party from the ranks of the army – many of my own friends even. Bad things will happen. When will you return to your home? I wish I could see you, but we are being sent on manoeuvres now in Thuringia – everyone is jittery, since nobody can tell exactly what will happen. Please, Maud, do not forget one who will not forget *you*'.

She showed part of this letter to Clive, who had earlier come back depressed from his holiday in England where there was still a Great Depression – and unemployment as bad as in Germany. It amused him that Helmuth von Platen was so clearly besotted with Maud. The man was shy and adoring. Maud could do much worse than accept his overtures. He said as much to her. Maud looked amazed and then rather angry. 'Just because I went for walks with him and ate ice cream, and we talked, do you imagine I would consider marrying him? That *is* what you mean, isn't it?'

Clive laughed. 'All women want to marry – why should you be the exception?'

'Don't be ridiculous – I suppose your Tatiana wants to marry *you* too?'

Tatiana did, in fact, want to marry Clive Queensbury, more for her own security than from any overpowering love, and he was finding it harder and harder to wriggle out of the affair.

'Well Helmuth is a damned sight nicer than your old pupil

224

Wolfgang,' he said, hoping that she would take the implied warning even if she did not begin to take her 'Moltke' seriously. 'I'm sure he didn't lend you Fascist novels.'

She replied in anodyne fashion in her letter to Helmuth, whom she rather missed, but whom she had surely never encouraged to be 'serious' about her.

But Maud kept Wolfgang Hartmann's address in her pocket book, hardly asking herself why, for it was a relief as well as a deprivation no longer to have his sacred Wednesdays marked out on her calendar, no longer to have that slight churning feeling in her stomach when the time approached. Whatever there was between them was not finished, but she resolved to forget him until her work was, though she did intend a little time in Berlin before returning home. But home too seemed a distant and not very attractive prospect.

In the months before that success of Herr Hitler's, she had been working fourteen hours a day on the final version of her thesis. In spite of Kornfeld's urging her to select and select again, she was temperamentally incapable of 'wasting' work. She thereby gave herself unnecessary headaches, but knew that, even if she did not use all her material, she had enough should she wish to pursue the subject post-doctorally and perhaps write a book. She had put the finishing touches to her *magnum opus* before scouring the city for a typist who knew English. She had almost left it too late, made two false starts with a woman whose claim to knowledge of English was not substantiated and then with an elderly man who could not read her handwriting. She was forced to read it aloud to him for days on end, a costly business and very nervously taxing. Clive was aghast – he did all his own typing so that if he made mistakes there was no one else to blame. It was with great trepidation that she finally posted the bound volume to Scotland. She would have to be back home at the latest early in the New Year for her *viva*, but now intended to squeeze two or three months' teaching in Berlin before that. She would be sorry to leave Silesia, but must see the country's capital city before she returned home. As yet she had no idea and no plans for what would happen then. Carmichael had not yet written with any news of possible vacancies for assistant lecturers.

She knew she ought to feel pleased with the result of her labours. She had kept steadily in front of her, in spite of all distractions, the eventual possibility of financial independence arising from all the years of her academic work and it had kept her going when she was disheartened. Why could she not feel tender towards nice men who would relieve her of all future work and financial worries if she gave in to their pleas? Helmuth was rich and she was clever enough for him to pose no threat to her freedom, but she had no desire whatever to be committed to him. She had more in common with Clive, but Clive was more dangerous and she was glad he had decided to live with Tatiana. Herr Hartmann she did not compare with either of them. How he had known her birthday she did not know, but a card from him had arrived in the spring when she was up to the neck in work and beginning to panic a little. The card was a reproduction of a statue of Diotima and bore only the legend – 'von W Hartmann in Berlin' with his address, which was different from the previous one. She kept that too.

She had written her last words about 'her' empress feeling that lady had perhaps had similar problems to herself. She did not think there had been romantic love in the Ancient World, though there had been sexual attraction and a good deal of sexual activity. The Empress Julia had managed a salon of clever men and been admired for her beauty and brains, but as far as Maud could ascertain had never fallen in love, though she had married – and married well. How had such women accepted the habits of marriage, even unChristian marriage? Familiarity must have led to contempt. Julia's fate had at last caught up with her and she had starved herself to death after the death of her husband and the plots and machinations of her sons. Maud could not express her feelings about this in an academic thesis, for that was not what such writing could encompass, though she did make a few jokes about the empress's vanity. Professor Kornfeld approved; 'Most original,' he would murmur.

English sometimes seemed to her now almost a foreign language. She found herself when writing it dropping in German words and spellings and not even noticing till a second reading. A remark made about her by a German *Lektor* and reported to her by Clive, had faintly disturbed her.

'*Fräulein Maud? Eine kleine Göttin mit Ichor anstalt Blutes*'.
They were partly the words used of her by Helmuth von Platen
– but she knew that real human blood did course in her veins,
even if only because the perverse Wolfgang Hartmann made
that blood course more swiftly.

The day she posted her thesis to Professor Carmichael she
chanced to pick up a leaflet dropped in the street. Looking at
it casually she found it spoke of 'Jewish atrocities'. Clive was
not comforting when he took her for a drink of peach liqueur
– 'to cheer her up' he said – for she looked pale and tired.
'It's disgusting,' he said. 'The Jews here are more at home than
they've ever felt in England – and Tati's mother is Jewish.'

Maud bit her lip.

'You need a holiday,' he went on. 'Aren't you going home
yet?'

'No – Kornfeld's found me a school in Berlin – I think I'll go
there for a month or two – see how it is anyway – if I go home
I feel I'll never get away again.' She added, 'I havena seen a
film for three months, Cosmo – and my wardrobe's threadbare
– I need to earn some cash – '

He smiled. She was very feminine, he thought, in spite of her
erudition. He looked at her closely. She plucks her eyebrows
usually, he thought, but she's neglected them recently – she
must be very busy to forget that! There was also a slight cast
– almost imperceptible, but there all the same – in one eye
which he had never noticed before. She was parting her hair
in the centre too, whilst before she had always parted it at the
side. It looked too severe and he almost told her so.

Prof Kornfeld said – 'Look after yourself, Fräulein Maud,
won't you? These are curious days in Germany.'

'Politics is my blind spot,' she said to him in English and then
tried to translate – 'My weak side,' she said in German.

He had found her a small boys' private school in a Berlin
suburb and the address of a private hotel. With the salary
she would just have enough left to live on for another few
months. Her heart sank when she thought of returning home
in the New Year.

After the nerve-wracking weeks finishing her thesis she knew
she did need a holiday. There would be ten days before the term

began in the Quellstrasse Schule; she would sightsee in Berlin once she had moved herself there.

Clive was sombre and taciturn when he called to say Goodbye. He would be back in London for good himself at Christmas – along with Tati!

The last thing Maud did before shaking hands with Frau Müller, who looked sorry to see her go, was to post a letter to Wolfgang Hartmann with her Berlin address.

Chapter Twelve

An October sun mellowed the broad sweep of Unter den Linden, and the Prussian eagle was glittering on the Brandenburger Tor when Maud saw it for the first time. She had no English teaching until the following week and so was spending a few days sightseeing. Berlin was such a vast, sprawling city and in her opinion not very beautiful with its dark stone and overabundance of nineteenth-century monuments. Not that she had been inside many of its buildings, its hotels, stores and cafés. Her own hotel room was a little way out in the suburbs, reached at the end of an interminable tram ride, not smart, but handy for the work she was to do. She felt lonely, which was only natural, though she would never have admitted it to anyone. In Silesia she had begun to feel she had the measure of the country, but all her new-found confidence evaporated in the seething crowds. But she plucked up her courage one afternoon and spent some of the marks she had saved on a pale green silk pyjama suit as worn by Anna May Wong in a film she had enjoyed. She tried it on as soon as she returned to her room. Seeing herself in the long, rather spotty mirror, she thought she looked rather exotic. She unpinned her hair and brushed it briskly. The weather was not yet cold and the pyjamas were meant for lounging in, not sleeping, so she kept them on and slipped her feet into a pair of embroidered mules she had picked up in the market. Then from her small jewel case, always kept under lock and key with the key on a chain round her neck, she extracted Hector's diamond earrings, which she allowed herself to look at occasionally but had not worn for two years. This evening she put them tenderly through her ears. They did not go with the pyjama suit, but then they did not go with any of her other clothes either, which were all what Ma called 'serviceable' except for her one black silk, 'best' dress.

A deep, involuntary sigh escaped her; perhaps she had been wrong to come here alone, should have gone straight home once her thesis was finished. Yet she thought she was owed a bit of fun, for she had worked hard. A capital city needed men friends though, and money, if you were going to make the most of it. Not that she minded being alone for she was used to it, but there were some places you could not investigate alone if you were a woman and she liked walking around.

Maud anointed her face with the almond oil which was said to prevent wrinkles in future, then pressed her fingers to the gardenia scent bottle, before patting the skin behind her ears and on her wrists. The bottle was nearly empty now, but the fragrance brought back far-away 'Moltke' who had bought it for her. She sighed. She might as well go to bed.

As she performed her nightly ritual of thorough scrubbing and nail-buffing, she found she was thinking again about Garvits, thinking of it now as The Past, no longer there, now that its master had gone. It had promised so much and she had been too inexperienced to take advantage of it. Never the time the place and the right person together it would seem. She kept telling herself now that she had had over two years to recover from the shock of his death – that it was all over and done with. He was dead; life had changed; she had achieved her ambition of writing a doctoral thesis – and that was surely something? But Hector had been a bigger catch than anyone she had met since, and a better man. Neither 'Cosmo' nor her 'Moltke' matched up to the Master of Garvits. Wolfgang Hartmann was the only man who had matched his intensity and he was a dangerous unknown quantity. Obscurely she felt that if once in her life she dared to challenge such a man she might be the more ready to deal with the better men who would surely follow. But it would be a personal risk.

It is because I have worked so hard and my work is finished that it seems insubstantial and I feel occasionally insubstantial myself, she thought. I want to be recognised as a person in my own right, but I also need adventures, not just academic accolades, or even, just yet, the offer of work. I need a change.

I *will* see Hartmann again even if it leads only to his taking me out and about.

There were scores of night clubs and cabarets in Berlin, places where the rich and the young – and the perverted – spent their nights, secret places, sinister rendezvous, and she wanted to explore that side of life just a little, a side she had resolutely refused to consider up till now. She would leave her options open, but the prospect of returning home knowing she had not taken up the ultimate challenge from a man was dreary. Life owed her pleasure and beautiful things and a happiness that had so far eluded her.

Two or three weeks later Maud was returning one afternoon from her teaching duties. The thirty small male pupils were exhausting, though they were good little workers and she had established her *modus vivendi*. Also she now had a very respectable knowledge of German and could make jokes in the language and lard it with slang expressions. To her own surprise she felt quite affectionate towards the little lads whom she teased and prodded into mental activity. Her days were busy and her nights spent alone. She had been out only once in the evening – to a film of Greta Garbo's, made in Germany where it was set. Garbo was wonderful – aloof, quietly elusive. Garbo's film renewed her sense of dissatisfaction with her own life. Before, the 'flicks' had been an escape; now she wondered why she could not have some of the sort of life the cinema evoked, if she wanted it, a life far from her real scholar's life, a life that would satisfy that other part of her nature so long dormant. Not that there was anything of the actress in Maud, only that of the dreamer and schemer who wanted a homage that was as safe as it was imaginary.

'Two letters for you, Fräulein,' said the peroxide blonde receptionist in the hall of the small hotel, and jerked her head to the wall where visitors' mail could be seen behind a complicated sort of lattice-work.

'Thank you,' said Maud. She took the letters up to her room on the top floor and put the gas fire on before sitting down to open the letters with her little silver paper-knife. One was the regular missive from her 'Moltke', the other was addressed in that spiky writing she knew well after correcting so many exercises in it. She read Wolfgang's first.

'Dear Crichton,
You are invited to my apartments – Heiligenstrasse 24 no 3a at 6pm on Thursday to meet some friends. Telephone please if this is not possible. You kept me waiting a long time so I daresay you can wait a few more days! We shall take you "on the town". Grüsse – Hartmann.

What a strange letter! Gruff, even rude. She wondered what kind of apartment he lived in, having never previously seen him anywhere but at Frau Müller's and the university. Now she would find out what he was really like under the forbidding exterior.

On the Thursday she dressed carefully after her day's work and was off on the tram to the city centre, through the great broad streets all now lit up for the night's pleasure, to find Hartmann's flat.

Wolfgang greeted her in the warm, well-lit vestibule of a very modern block. He had put on a little weight, but looked trimmer and with his hair cut shorter. He took her up by lift to the first floor and she started a little at the evidence of wealth, or perhaps what passed for wealth, in the large, light apartment with floor to ceiling curtains over plate-glass windows, steel chairs, leather easy chairs, a Lalique mirror and Art Deco lights on the walls.

'You like my little place?' he asked her in German as he busied himself at a glass-topped drinks trolley with syphons of soda and a bucket of ice.

'It is very spacious,' she answered also in German. She was glad she had put the diamonds in her ears and dressed in her black silk.

He gave her a drink of whisky and soda, explaining it was imported from Scotland. She had not tasted Scotch since leaving home and it was strong, even with the ice cubes.

'Now we will drink to you,' he said.

The aesthetic pose, if it had been a pose, seemed to have left him for the time being, but she noticed shelves full of books on the wall facing her.

232

'So – tell me what you think of Berlin, Crichton.' This new affectation of calling her by her surname did not displease her and, strange to say, she did not feel nervous of him.

She told him, cutting down reference to her teaching day.

'I have often thought of you, Crichton – Fräulein Maud,' he said. 'So you have finished your researches? I hope you are now enjoying life!'

Maud looked at him levelly as she sipped the golden, fiery stuff, tasting it on her tongue and rolling it around. There was nothing left in him as far as she could see, of the 'apt pupil'.

'You have been around? Our public transport system is good – ninety-two tramlines, you know, and you can go anywhere you want for only twenty pfennig. That should appeal to a woman from Scotland, *nicht wahr*? You are going to meet my friend Franz and a mutual friend of ours tonight. I had thought of taking you to a little *Kneipe* off the Kurfürstendam – you won't have been to such a place I do not think.'

'To dance?' Maud said quickly. He had taken charge of the evening; all she had to do was be gracious and submit to his plans, she supposed.

'Yes – we may dance – and eat, drink and be merry. Do they dance tangos in Scotland?'

'Some people do – I have never done so. You'll have to teach me. I was never a dancer, I fear.'

Wolfgang lit a cigarette, Maud having refused one.

'Have you been to the Royal Palace? – have you been on the U-Bahn? – have you eaten our famous goose with fruit dumplings?'

Maud said Yes to the U-Bahn, No to most of the rest.

When she ate in small Berlin restaurants she had found the food very different to what she had become used to in Silesia. There was yellow pea soup, pig hocks, meatballs, lots of herrings and smoked food, salted pork, eels – Northern food for cold winters. She told Wolfgang Hartmann that she had not felt very hungry in Berlin. Wolfgang replied that she must learn to enjoy Berlin food. The whisky seemed to be taking any slight wariness away. It would be good to be looked after for a bit. She was a little tired of always fending for herself.

Whilst they waited for his friends Wolfgang began a conversation about her reading. She had just finished *Berlin, Alexanderplatz*. Would that be the kind of book Wolfgang Hartmann might enjoy? She was not the sort of woman who liked holding intellectual conversations with men, so she usually hesitated before mentioning this sort of thing, apart from her official lessons. She had no idea what Wolfgang's feelings were about her – he seemed to withhold himself and at the same time to judge her. She remarked that the novel's hero was very stupid, then remembered that the hero had flirted with the Nazis, and that Hartmann was now a member of the NSDAP; she pushed the thought away.

'Have you lived in Berlin before?' she asked him instead.

'I came originally from Berlin,' Hartmann replied. That surprised her. This then might be his own apartment, not a rented one?

He went on: 'My parents are dead.'

'I'm sorry – '

'A long time ago.' He paused. 'Have another drink. No?'

She walked to the window and looked out.

'You are looking remarkably beautiful – but of course you always look very beautiful,' he said quietly.

She turned round and saw that he was pouring himself another Scotch.

'Berliners are a cynical lot,' he added. 'And very boastful – but we are getting somewhere at last, I feel.' She waited, not sure to what he was referring. 'I told you about the Party and that I'm a member now!'

'The Nazi party?' said Maud, resigned to a political discussion but determined to say little.

'None other – you will have heard what happened in the recent elections, Crichton? – more votes for us than for any other single party! *Democratic* elections! What do the English say? – if you cannot beat them you must join them? – but it is not only for that reason. Believe me there is no other way.'

Maud held her peace, amused again that he called her by her surname and wondering whether this was a "Nazi" custom. Now was not the time for arguments – and she had heard so many

contradictory ones. Instead: 'I read *d'Annunzio*,' she offered.
'You recommended him to me.'

He sat down in a leather armchair opposite her, when she
moved back to the smaller chair. The sun was setting behind him
in the plate glass. From below there was the faint rumble and
squeak of trams and cars. 'He is a friend of Benito Mussolini,'
he said. 'Can you remember some lines, quote them?' he asked
peremptorily.

'I don't speak Italian – in German it isn't so good,' she replied
with more honesty than tact. Nor in English, she thought.

'Pupille ardenti – O voi senza ritorno
Stelle tristi spegnetevi incorrotte,'
he quoted in perfect Italian. 'The old fellow may be a friend of
Il Duce, but Italians! – you can't trust them an inch – not like
your Romans.'

'The Italian words sound good, but I'm not always sure of his
real meaning.

' "The dawn is born from my own blood" – good that!'

A new dawn, she thought – the blood of the people – they
were always talking like this. But just then there was a ring at
the electric bell.

'Our friends,' said Wolfgang, and rose. Maud heard their
voices in the vestibule, a woman's with a strong Berlin accent
and a deeper male voice.

Maud rose from her chair when Wolfgang brought them in.

'Franz Immerman – Mitzi Sachs,' he said. 'This is my British
friend – Maud Crichton,' he seemed to stress the *British* – 'She
is as admirable as her namesake.'

Really, thought Maud, he is quite skittish. Immerman was a
very handsome man in his early thirties, sunburnt, green-eyed,
solid. His friend Mitzi was a plump, giggly woman who appeared
to prefer talking to Wolfgang Hartmann for she paid no further
attention to Franz Immerman for the rest of the evening.

Immerman smiled at Maud and began to talk to her quite
informally. He had not met many of her compatriots. From
America, yes, but from Great Britain, no. All the time he was
addressing her she had the impression of a simple, strong man
who exuded health and well-being. He did not appear to be
interested in politics, was not an intellectual; his main interests,

he said, being dancing and sport – and then cinema. Maud found him refreshing.

At eight o'clock they all piled into this Franz's sports car and he drove them across Potzdamer Platz and then down some narrower streets where they parked. Franz took the lead and she followed him, and the other two made up the rear of the party. Wolfgang seemed amused by Mitzi's idiotic conversation, which she continued when they were before a neon-lit door. Down some steps to a cellar underneath a restaurant, and then they were ushered to a table in semi-darkness. Franz explained that the cabaret was in an adjoining room and there was also a dance floor. Their orders were dealt with promptly – eel in sauce with boiled potatoes, and frankfurters and sauerkraut, and then Leipziger Allerlei, a dish of tiny vegetables that Maud found delicious. She had quite an appetite by now and ate with relish, washing down the food with lager. Afterwards she followed Mitzi to a powder-room that had mirrors all down one side of the wall.

'Your friend is very pleasant,' she ventured to her as they tidied their hair and washed their hands.

'Franz is a honey,' said that lady. 'But Wolfgang – *ach* he is so *deep*.'

It was ten o'clock now and they followed the men to another large room with a stage, and tables round it it in a circle. At the other end of the room was a raised dance floor and several couples were swaying to a saxophone. The place was full. Maud had seen that it was not a cheap dive. Then a 'cabaret' came on, consisting of two tall women arguing in a strong dialect, provoking much laughter and clapping and cheering from the tables. Maud could not follow it at all until the women began to take their drab clothes off. Underneath they were dressed in short skirts with spangles and sequins and silver brassières, and she saw they were men. Everyone fell silent when the couple began to dance to a reedy trombone. Then the darker of the two opened his mouth near a microphone and sang falsetto another ditty, once again in Berliner dialect.

Franz was laughing. 'You have this in England?'

'I don't know.' Maud tried to imagine such goings on at home, but failed. 'In London, I suppose,' she replied.

236

Wolfgang ordered more drinks and then Franz rose and said to her: 'Will you dance with me?'

She thought Wolfgang was looking at her in an amused way. Would he mind if she went off with his friend? Mitzi certainly did not seem to mind and Wolfgang patted her plump hand from time to time. Yet he did not look really attracted to the woman. Maud could not be bothered to work it all out and felt reckless and also rather happy. She had not drunk very much, so it could not be that. Franz, who was a very straightforward type, took her hand and led her to the small, circular floor where now a tango band was playing a sad tune she recognized from a film she had seen years ago.

'Just follow me,' he said and she found herself in his arms, swaying and turning and bending to his will. Dancing with this man was quite easy and the rhythm was very seductive.

Franz concentrated on the music, not on her, but when they played *La Paloma* he smiled down at her for one moment and said: 'You are dancing well.' When it ended he took her to sit near the band and said again: 'You did well.' She felt she had just been given a *cum laude* mark.

'Thank you. It was thanks to you, I mean – it seemed quite easy.' She had never danced with Hector. Once or twice she had danced decorously with 'Moltke', though it had not been like this.

'You must practise,' he said. 'Practice makes perfect.'

Then he seemed struck by something about her and began a sentence that she could not understand, that tailed off as he looked at her with his calm, level gaze. 'Wolfgang,' he said and then cleared his throat. 'Wolfgang – *Der Wolfgang hat mir gesagt und es ist wahr.*'

She looked at him interrogatively, her eyebrows raised, and he went on in a low voice: '*Du bist schön, Fräulein Maud.*'

Maud was emboldened to say: 'Your Mitzi is a pretty girl.'

He roared with laughter, put his head on one side. 'Mitzi and I – we are friends – but she is not my girl.'

'She likes talking to your friend, I think,' replied Maud.

'Oh, he does not like women very much, but he likes *her.*'

Maud was surprised – if he meant what she thought he meant. It might explain rather a lot. But in that case, why lead her on

237

to think he was interested in her, for he *had* done that. She was not perturbed. It was kind of Wolfgang to introduce her to someone who did like women, she thought in a muddled way. Her thought processes were sluggish; all she knew was that she found this Franz extremely attractive, a pleasant and cheerful companion, and very restful. Surely he could not be a Nazi sympathiser too? He seemed not at all interested in politics. For a fleeting moment she wondered if Hartmann too found Franz Immerman attractive.

These thoughts were going through her head as Franz was sipping his beer, the music having changed into a slow fox-trot, when he said suddenly with no preamble and took her hand: 'I should so like to sleep with you.'

She could not believe her ears at first, but kept her composure, for he was looking at her with an honest, above-board look.

'Let us dance again,' she said.

The music was so slow the dancers hardly moved, locked in each other's arms. She felt the man's body hard against her silk dress – closer even than Hector had ever been. *This* man would not wait six years for her! But I need never see him again, she thought. I don't know him. She was sure he was experienced.

When the music finished he held her close against him. 'So nice,' he said, before piloting her back to their original table where they found Wolfgang and Mitzi telling each other jokes. But Wolfgang looked up at them and said: 'I have to get up early tomorrow – and Mitzi says she has a headache. I will take her home as she lives nearer to me and needs fresh air.'

Mitzi did not look surprised.

'I can take Fräulein Maud back in my car,' said Franz. 'Mitzi has been drinking all afternoon, I think.'

'Oh, but – ' Maud realised she did not know Franz's address – or anything about him except that he exuded sexual self-confidence and was nice and uncomplicated and she wanted to burn her boats.

'I have to work tomorrow too,' she said. 'I have to go back to my hotel.' She explained where it was, not looking at Franz.

'Then Franz can take us all back and drop you first, if you insist,' said Wolfgang with a look at Franz.

238

'Yes, please,' said Maud, feeling virtuous.

But when she was dropped off at Siegsmundstrasse Franz accompanied her to her door and took a card out of his breast pocket. 'Please – telephone me and come to see me,' he murmured. 'Tomorrow evening? – I *must* see you again!'

She took the card and he kissed her hand. These Germans, they were all *so* polite.

All next day as she laboured with her classes she wondered what on earth had possessed her. But when she got back to the hotel she telephoned the number on the card as though something not herself had decided her.

'Franz Immerman,' said the voice.

'Hello,' said Maud.

'Hello, Maud – what about meeting this evening,' he suggested immediately.

'If you want.'

'I shall come for you in the car – seven o'clock, yes? I was frightened that you would not telephone, my tango dancer.'

She put the phone back on its hook in a daze, went back to her room and dressed in the pyjama suit – no jewellery except her bracelet, and a comb in her hair, and no make-up, but the gardenia scent at her wrists and behind her ears and in the crook of her elbow. When he came for her she was demure, passive and he looked at her searchingly, a little baffled, but said nothing and Maud did not try to start a conversation either. He drove them to a high apartment near the Tiergarten, a comfortable place, very unlike Hartmann's, with furniture more appropriate to the last century than anything fashionable. There was a divan though, with a yellow linen cover and a table set for two in an alcove. The curtains were half-drawn.

'You see – I can cook!' he said.

She said nothing, just stood there feeling abandoning and abandoned.

He took off her coat and stood just looking at her. 'I like the green clothes,' he said finally. 'Wolfgang said you were a learned lady and a beautiful woman, but not how beautiful.' He took her in his arms and Maud Crichton did not raise a finger to stop Franz Immerman with infinite patience, a little

239

passion and a good deal of energy, relieving her eventually of her long-preserved virginity.

For once, she had abandoned control, hypnotically impelled by some need in herself, not truly desire for the smilingly simple Franz. But he looked quite satisfied and brought her an omelette and peaches on a tray with a glass of wine. 'Now we shall dance the tango better,' he said.

Maud was happy to be waited on. It had been a little painful, but Franz seemed to have enjoyed himself hugely. She tried not to think of anything, too sluggish to delve down deeply into his assumption that she had certainly welcomed his love-making. All she had had to do was lie back and let him get on with it – it did not seem to have been a matter of moral choice. He had remarked upon the pyjamas as he slid them off – *ach*! silk, and remarked upon the flesh they had hidden with a murmur of pleasure.

He did not appear to want to talk about it after his remark about the tango. She did know she was not going to allow it as a matter of course in future. But perhaps there would be no future? She sighed, and he came over to her with another glass.

'No thank you, Franz – I must get up and dress. There is work for me to do tomorrow.'

He began methodically to clear the table and soon had everything shipshape. Whilst he was in the kitchen she dressed hurriedly, noticing a few spots of blood on the yellow cover. Only little spots. Evidence, she supposed. Would *he* know she had been a virgin before that night?

When he returned she was sitting in the armchair putting up her hair.

'Such lovely hair,' he said. 'Not so many foreign girls have this hair. Our German girls, yes – ' He sat down opposite her and lit a cigarette. 'I would like to buy you a present,' he said. 'What do you like? The scent you are wearing it is good – tell me what you would like.'

Maud thought rather long before coming out with: 'There is nothing, Franz – the scent is Gardenia by Leichner,' she added.

'Then I shall always be able to remember you by it,' he said.
'You are going back to your country soon?'

'Yes – in the New Year I must. I have to see about work.'

'What will you do? You are too pretty – beautiful – to be a Professor!'

'That is nonsense,' said Maud rather enjoying herself. 'In a university I hope – not in a "gymnasium", not a school 'professor'. We don't call teachers that back home.'

'You should be a film diva – you have the looks,' he said.

Maud appreciated this evidence of his admiration. 'I cannot act – but I admire your Dietrich – and Garbo – ' she said.

'Ach, Dietrich has gone to Hollywood. But Garbo – you know they are making a film at this very moment here in Berlin? It is about our great hotel – she will be the star. I have done a little film-making myself, you know.'

'You have?'

'Yes – I do the riding and the swimming when the actors cannot – it is only to earn a few more marks for myself.'

'Is Mitzi an actress?' Maud found herself suddenly asking.

'Mitzi! Good gracious no – she is, between you and me, a bit of a whore, the Mitzi!'

Maud's stunned look made him change tack. 'You know she is like many girls fond of furs and jewels – so she sleeps with rich men sometimes to get them – many do it, especially since the inflation and the lack of work.'

'Is Wolfgang a rich man then?'

'No, no I did not mean that – and I told you Wolfie is not interested really in the ladies. But he knows all sorts of people – did he tell you he had joined the Party?'

'Yes,' Maud replied briefly. She wanted to anchor her stockings on her suspender belt, but could not do that with Franz looking on. There were some things which you did not do in front of people even if they had just explored even more inaccessible parts of your anatomy.

'He says it is a return of national pride,' said Franz eagerly. 'We must have people with loyalty and courage – ready to make sacrifices.' He sounded as though he were parroting Wolfgang's words and suddenly Maud felt rather annoyed.

241

'Strength through joy,' she murmured. Then, 'Do you think Herr Hitler would approve of Mitzi?' she asked him.

Franz giggled. She could see that he was no real follower of the Brownshirts. Then what was he doing being a friend of Wolfgang?

'How did you come to know Herr Hartmann,' she asked and Franz looked for once a little shifty.

'You ask him,' he answered. He went up to her in the chair. 'Your hands are so soft and smooth,' he said taking one of them and kissing it. 'And your mouth too – '

In spite of his words Maud felt obscurely at a disadvantage. But there was a sort of mindless pleasure in listening to him. She had come up to the expectations of one ordinary man at last!

Franz was looking at her now rather wistfully. Was he about to make another assault upon her virtue? She stood up. 'I must go back,' she said firmly.

'Tomorrow evening I will take you for drinks in the Kempi,' said Franz. 'I will come for you.'

When they arrived back at Maud's hotel Franz kissed her hand. He was really rather a nice man, she thought.

Next evening he called for her wearing a leather coat of great style. She thought, I'd like one like that. He handed her into his little car and then gave her a small packet. 'The scent,' he said.

He had not forgotten. She was touched. Scent she could accept; she wondered from whom Mitzi had received her furs and jewels.

In the café he said: 'You know Hitler does not like Berlin.'

'Why is that?' she asked, sipping a strong liqueur, that warmed her throat tired from talking all day. School had seemed strange after her adventure of the night, but nobody had remarked any change in herself. And she had no urgent desire to repeat that adventure, though Franz was looking at her with frank lust in his clear eyes.

'Oh, he is a low-class Austrian, you know – does not know about High Life.'

'Why does Wolfgang Hartmann admire him? – surely Hitler is too much of a barbarian for him,' she asked.

'Wolfgang is a strange type – he despises everybody, I think,' replied Franz, then went on: 'Last year it was exciting with the big torchlight procession through the Brandenburger Tor into the Wilhelmstrasse with all the shouting – but there was violence.'

Maud remembered Clive telling her something about that night. What had they shouted? *'Deutschland erwecke, Juda verrecke!'* something like that. 'Why do the Nazis hate the Jews so much?' she asked Franz boldly.

He lowered his voice in reply. 'Because they envy their wealth – it is the same in Britain, isn't it?'

Maud had never known any Jewish people but knew their theology from Preacher Gray who had preferred the Old Testament. She changed the subject. 'Will you see Herr Hartmann again soon? – I want to thank him for the party – '

Franz looked suddenly shifty again. 'Oh, yes – I shall see him on Saturday,' he replied.

'Tell him thank you then, from me – I do not think he wants to be bothered with me, you know,' said Maud surprising herself by uttering this truth. She had decided she disliked Hartmann.

'Tomorrow I can take you to another little *Kneipe* on the Kurfürstendamm,' said Franz.

'I'm not used to going out every evening,' said Maud. 'But it is good for my German.'

'I can teach you more words of love,' said Franz. Maud looked away. 'Wolfgang said you were cynical – a little,' he added.

She was surprised. 'Herr Hartmann knows me only as a teacher,' she said rather stiffly.

'And *I* am *your* teacher,' he answered gaily.

'I am not really your type,' said Maud. 'Confess it – '

But he stopped her mouth with his fingers. 'We Berliners are also cynical,' he said. 'But we are tolerant – and sentimental too – we have had to live through terrible times, you know.'

'But you are not so poor, Franz,' said Maud. 'Was not that your parents' apartment where we went yesterday?'

'No – no – I rent it since I do the film work. My parents are poor – they live beyond the Alexanderplatz. Let us not speak of them.'

'Why not? I am not rich either. I have had to live off my brains – I expect you have too.'

243

'Ah – certainly. But you *are* like a Berliner, Maud. You are witty.'

Maud wondered what she had said to make him think this.

'You know we have over one hundred and fifty newspapers here,' he offered after a pause.

'Really. Who buys them all?'

'The rich and the students – '

How they liked offering you precise numbers of things! Like Wolfgang and his tram routes.

'Wolfgang Hartmann used to write for the papers,' said Franz. 'By the way, he does want to see you again. He asked me to tell you.'

'He telephoned you, did he? Or did you meet him?'

'Oh, we keep in touch – he may like to see you on Friday next week. I go to see my parents on that day. Can he call for you?'

'I suppose so,' she answered without much enthusiasm.

'*He* thinks you are very beautiful,' Franz went on. 'I do too – your face is like marble – I hope you will have many children, Maud – so your face will be carried on.'

Maud's face went pale. 'I hope not,' she said, wondering if he could be referring to their lovemaking.

'Wolfgang thinks a beautiful couple should make a beautiful child,' said Franz rather artlessly.

'Children do not always turn out like their parents,' said Maud.

'You know I would like to do again with you what we did before. I think I love you, Maud.'

'No – no Franz – you don't – I am to return home very soon – I am pleased you like me – but you have a saying I think – ships that pass in the night?'

'Oh, do not say that, Maud,' he cried looking quite upset. She could not make him out. What did he really want from her?

'Can I tell Wolfie you will see him next week?'

'I will drink a cup of coffee with him,' said Maud. 'But only if he comes to fetch me – I am rather tired after a day of work.'

'Yes, yes, I know – you must be. I will take you back soon.' He took her hand and raised it to his lips. 'That scent that I

244

bought for you. It is a little secret between us! Will you put some on now?'

Maud realised that he did not want Hartmann to know he had been buying her presents. 'All right – a little secret,' she said. He sniffed the delicious sharply-sweet odour on her wrist when she had anointed it.

'Will you not come back with me again – not because I give you the perfume – but because you like me?' he said.

'I do like you, but I am tired – and in Scotland men do not bribe girls with presents.' What a lie, she thought. Whatever else did Hector do? You could not find any two people more different than this rather sweet, good-looking, but unsophisticated man and her old 'lover'.

Franz took her back to his flat another evening that week. Maud lay passively and calmly in his arms on that occasion, allowing him to do to her what he so obviously enjoyed doing. He was never violent and she allowed her thoughts to roam whilst he stroked her and fondled her. It was not unpleasant but it actually moved her very little. What excited her was seeing the effect she had on him. She became a *voyeuse* as he enacted his desires. 'Ach, Maud,' he would say – 'I desire your hands,' (kissing them), 'your arms,' (walking little butterfly kisses up her elbow), 'your armpits,' (burrowing into them with his fists), and 'your terribly attractive bosom,' (which he proceeded to treat as though he were a baby).

Then for a few days Franz had to go away for some mysterious 'work' and on the Friday evening of the following week she found herself, as arranged, sitting with Wolfgang in a *Kaffeehaus* near her hotel.

Wolfgang seemed mightily pleased about something, in high good humour. She hoped that he would not want to discuss politics or books, for she always had the feeling of being sneered at or at best teased when these were the subjects of their conversation.

'Let's go for a walk on the Kurfürstendam,' he said. She had been surprised when he had consented to meet her near her humble hotel, but she had no wish to be one of the crowds on the smart shopping area with him. But she was intrigued about the relationship between him and Franz since they seemed to have so little in common. How should she go about asking him?

'I'd rather sit here and talk to you,' she replied. 'I have to get up early for school – they begin at eight and I need my beauty sleep.'

'Oh, very well,' he said, but looked rather cross. Maud poured herself a glass of water. 'And how do you find my friend Franz?' he asked finally, after draining his cup and ordering another.

Maud found herself blushing, but she composed her face and answered coolly: 'He is very sweet, isn't he? How do you come to know him?'

'Yes, Franz, unlike myself, is not a disinherited intellectual,' he replied, not answering her question.

'I should imagine he is a member of the proletariat?' she said.

'I believe his parents are workers,' said Wolfgang vaguely. 'Of course the boy is very gifted – he's a good athlete, you know – just the sort of person the Party will be looking for to revitalise our tired old country.'

She let this pass, not wishing to get him on the subject of the Party, but Wolfgang continued. 'We need loyal Germans and brave ones.'

'I'm sure Franz is both,' replied Maud after a pause.

'I expect he found you very enticing,' said Wolfgang Hartmann then, looking her full in the face. She did not drop her eyes, tried not to recall the dominion he had had over her when she was teaching him, it seemed oh so long ago.

'Of course,' Wolfgang went on. 'You *are* enticing – '

'*He* is also a very good-looking man,' she got out.

'You find him so? – is there not something a little too obvious about his looks?'

Was he jealous, she wondered? But he had introduced them – and then taken no further interest in her that evening at the *Kneipe*. She decided to indulge him in a little philosophical debate.

'I believe you once told me that in your opinion there were no absolute values. What is good-looking for one will not be for another,' she said.

'Yet most would agree, I think, that old Franz is handsome

– though, as I say, not in a very subtle way. It is true there are no absolutes – and where does philosophy lead us? The race is won by the most daring or the most powerful – in beauty, as in politics or morality.'

'You are a Nihilist!'

'No longer. You see, nihilists take what is given as well as anyone and what is given at the moment in our country is chaos and a lost will. A leader is needed to *lead*, not *follow* the people as in democracies. Power is fascinating,' he went on as though she were not there. 'It has always fascinated me. Ask your little Franz?'

'What should I ask him – ?'

'Ask him how to use the power placed in one's hands.'

Did he mean that Franz had power over her or that she had over him? 'I wish you would stop talking in riddles,' she said rather severely.

'Oh, Fräulein Crichton,' he answered mockingly. 'You are back in the pedagogic mode – I thought Franz would release you from that for good. It is I who should have bitten the softness from your mouth. I might be a worthy opponent.'

'What do you mean?'

'Women are all the same underneath – they need a strong master – you would be better off learning to cook and bringing up decent children than spending your youth poring over old manuscripts.'

'I have no wish to cook or bring up children,' said Maud. She remembered what Franz had said about beautiful people having beautiful children.

'Oh, having children – that is not always in one's power to avoid,' he said and he looked at her from under his eyes with a half-reproving smile.

Maud hastily brushed away any thought of the consequences of her time with Franz. What might Wolfgang know about her? 'That is a personal private matter,' she said.

'Youth fades,' said Herr Hartmann.

'If you brought me here to talk platitudes,' said Maud, 'I think I have better things to do.' She still feared any reference to losing her looks.

'Don't be angry – I speak in truisms because I think you are the sort of person who never thinks what happens to others will happen to her. We are alike, you and I, Maud. We both find violence and terror fascinating.'

'That is not true,' she replied and changed the subject. 'Franz was telling me about the demonstration last year in the Potzdamer Platz,' she offered. 'He says you actually know Hitler.'

'I have met him, yes – you ought to go and listen to him yourself.'

'And yet I think you are not a "joiner", as I am not,' said Maud. 'Don't you think they are all a bunch of second-raters?' She was quoting Clive.

'What else is on offer?' he burst out. 'He will be elected "democratically" – your country and America will not be able to complain – oh, no, and once he is selected – which he will be – then he will be able to begin to transform Germany. Next year there will be even more seats for us – and the year after that – it is easy to predict. It is always easy to predict if you know human nature. As I suggested to Franz – about you – '

Maud felt an icy hand lie on her spine.

'What did you suggest about me?'

'Oh, more than *suggest*, my dear! Ask him! Do. Nature will always take revenge upon the proud! Perhaps you are like that Estella in the story, but you must take care not to become a Miss Havisham!'

She would like to have asked him if it were true that he preferred men, but dared not. 'I really must go,' she said. 'It is always a tonic to talk to a thinker.' She meant it ironically, but he took it seriously. But what had he 'more than suggested'?

'I expect you will be returning home soon?'

'After Christmas, or even before – when the term ends.'

She was not even sure when she would return, though she knew she must. She was suddenly filled with an overpowering need for Ma. What was she doing here talking to this unpleasant man?

He clicked his heels when he said goodbye to her and she was relieved of his overbearing presence. There was, always an implicit threat hanging in the air near him. Was that why she was disturbed by him? Yet he had introduced her to Franz, she had

248

not had to spend her free time alone, wandering about the city when she was not earning her living. There was a fascination in the decadent Wolfgang. She arranged to see Franz the next evening and promised herself she would not submit again to his embraces. But why should that matter? A sort of revolution had been effected in her by the love-making, but it had not yet turned her ideas over. She was surprised by the abandon of his embrace once she crossed the threshold of his apartment. For a moment she could not remember what Wolfgang had said she had to ask him. Something about power or violence? She patted his hand saying: 'Oh, I'm exhausted – can I just sit down for a minute?'

He looked at her affectionately and went to pour them both a drink.

'Wolfgang talked a lot about Hitler,' she began. He grimaced.

'Wolfie is clever so I always try to believe him,' he said.

'I think he wants a revolution,' said Maud, thinking suddenly of Clive's words to her once about Wolfgang's 'hero'. 'Everyone with a grievance is turned into a hero when the fanatic speaks to him'. 'Does Wolfgang have some sort of "grievance" against life?' she went on.

Franz looked surprised.

'I mean, if six million people are unemployed. But why does Wolfgang bother? He's enough money, it seems, even though he may be unemployable.'

Franz looked shocked. 'I expect he will be a professor when he's finished his *these*,' he said.

'Don't you believe it – ! He'll be a politician. If you're still trying to finish your *thesa* after eleven years I don't think you can be very serious. I finished mine in four you know,' she said proudly.

'Ah, but Maud, you are always working – Wolfie told me – "I want you to meet a British lady who is always working", he said to me.'

'What else did he say about me?' asked Maud. 'I'm curious. He said he had predicted something to you about me. Said I was to ask you.'

'Wolfgang asked you to ask me?' Franz looked embarrassed,

249

but then smiled and said: 'Oh, I expect it was that he said I would find you very beautiful – and that you might like me!'

Maud did not think for a moment that Franz was telling the whole truth and she felt that little chill laid on her neck and back and recoiled from it.

Franz came up to her. 'I do find you very beautiful,' he said. 'And now you are here I want you again, Maud . . . all the time now.'

He went down on his knees and nuzzled her lap, at the same time beginning to undo the buttons of her blouse. She felt again that desire to lose control, to give herself over to another's lust. 'I *love* you, Maud. Nice Maud,' he said and stroked one of her breasts, which he had released from its bust bodice. It lay, a shapely globe, creamy under his hand.

'Don't say you love me, Franz – don't fall in love with me – just have your – little "fun".'

'But I do love you, Maud,' he said. 'Love can come quickly – I love you because I want you. At first I did not, but now, yes, I do.'

'I was taught it was the other way round,' said Maud after a pause in which Franz looked away though he went on mechanically stroking her. He said nothing to her observation; she could see that all he wanted was for her to stop talking and let him get on with it. But she put her hand over his and he risked a glance at her.

Maud tried to gather her thoughts together. 'Franz – wait – tell me first – what did Wolfgang "more than suggest" about me? I want to know. Did he say I was cold and heartless?'

Franz buried his head in her lap. 'No, not heartless – he did not know you anyway, did he? He said you were proud, though.'

'"Nature will take its revenge upon the proud" – that's what he said to me – did he tell *you* that?'

Franz said: 'Oh, Maud, stop talking about Wolfie – let's go to bed.'

But Maud was determined to get an answer to her question. 'Tell me exactly. I could not understand last week when he invited me to go round to him – he had once hinted he was a little, or even quite a lot – interested in me, Franz, but he

250

introduced me to you and went off with Mitzi.' There was a silence. 'It was arranged?' she said wonderingly in a small voice. 'But you had never *met* me! How did you know you would like me and that I would let you – unless you would have done it with anyone?'

Franz looked up with such a miserable face she almost relented. Then he sat on the arm of the chair and took her hand. 'I did *not* know. But when we got on well I began to desire you,' he said, not altogether convincingly.

'Franz – tell me – whatever you say you feel now – I'm not in the habit of going to bed with strangers. Tell me – was I set up?'

'What do you mean "set up"?'

'Did Wolfgang tell you to make up to me? Come, tell me the truth.'

Franz looked down at the carpet. 'Wolfie said to me – "I have a friend from out east I want you to meet. But she is not the sort of girl to sleep with a man or allow him liberties. See if you can melt her heart."'

'A command?' asked Maud, and went pale.

'Please, please, Maud – he said that – but that is nothing to me now. I *do* like you, Maud. I *love* you, Maud. Wolfie has nothing to do with it now.'

'He put you up to it then! – Even if I had looked like the back of a tram it would have amused Mr Hartmann to have me seduced – Is that what you are saying?' She amazed herself as she said all this in his language.

'Maud! Maud – no! no! I said to him, "Yes I will entertain your friend if you have no wish to yourself." You see – I told you he is not fond of ladies – in his bed – '

'But he likes to take his pleasures vicariously?' said Maud in cold tones. 'Do I suppose that after Tuesday he telephoned you to see how things had gone, and you were able to inform him that you had successfully assaulted the ramparts of my virtue?'

'What do you mean "vicarious"? I am not an educated man, Maud – yes he did telephone me and I told him I thought you were a very nice lady and I found you very attractive.'

'But did you not tell him to go to hell and leave you alone? You doubtless also reported on all the details?'

251

Franz was silent.

'What has he got on you, Franz? To make you do what he wants?'

'No! It is not like that.' But she saw that it was.

Suddenly she felt sick, disgusted with herself rather than with him. She saw clearly what Hartmann had planned. But why should he want to do such a thing? If it was a revenge, a revenge for what?

There was worse to come from the simple Franz. 'If I tell you, will you please believe, Maud, that I like you now and want you for my friend – and to go to bed – nothing to do with that man?' Franz said in desperation. She had buttoned up her blouse and sat – like a statue.

'Please, Maud – be nice to me – '

'What *did* he say to you then?' She was determined to discover the truth. She had not quite bargained for any of this with her initial curiosity.

'He took me for drinks in the Kempi – oh, it was before you came to Berlin and he said, "I have met a very beautiful woman, but she is not German and she thinks she is more clever than I am. She is fascinated by me" – yes he said that – 'but I have no interest in 'love'.' He knew I liked women – it is true, I do – and many women have liked *me* – but, says Wolfgang, "She will not go with just anybody. She is proud and likes to think highly of herself. If she comes to Berlin you must take her out. We must show her round," he says, "I think many men may have fallen in love with her, but she is cold. You might give her a nice time – if she wants." But she will not want, I said to him – it will be you she is interested in – for he had told me about his lessons with you. I think he had a small tenderness for you – but because you are not easy – ' Maud was listening to him like a snake enchanted by the music from a pipe. He took her attitude for the usual intense interest evinced by women when the talk is of themselves, and continued. ' "I shall be interested to see if you can succeed with her", Wolfgang said. He said "Can a statue come to life?" '

'And when did you stop your act?' Maud asked coldly.

'Right from the beginning when Mitzi and I were introduced. I said to myself – she is a good, serious lady – true, she is beautiful, but she will not be interested in a poor man. Yet I will be nice to her. I was surprised that you did like me and that you, that you liked it . . . when we danced . . .'

'And surprised I did not resist you later?'

'Yes, I was surprised because I thought you would refuse me. But you did not, so I saw that you liked me – it was not because of him.'

'How do I know? Mr Hartmann likes power – he told me so – many times – I supposed it amused him to think what you were doing to me – ' She had a sudden graphic picture of Hartmann undressing her in his mind and watching Franz make love to her. 'I am surprised he did not ask for a ringside seat,' she said. Then another thought occurred to her as Franz got up and pretended to fuss around the glasses on the table. Very softly she said: 'Was it a *bet*, Franz? Tell me.'

'A bet?'

'Yes, on whether my virtue would remain intact. But how would he know in any case? You could always lie to him – And what was to happen next? What usually happens next? – I don't suppose I am the first woman he has tried to sell to you?' She spoke rapidly, breathlessly. 'What a fool I was! He wanted only to humiliate me – he doesn't care about you.'

'No, I know he does not care about me,' said Franz, 'but I have to do as he tells me – a long time ago I was involved in a bad thing – I cannot tell you exactly, but it was to do with when our money became worthless – he knows he could tell the authorities of me – and one day he will be perhaps the boss himself – it is hard not to do the things he wants. I am sincere when I make love – I did not hurt you – you liked it. You will like it again, you are not like the others, Maud! I have thought, he can have a big surprise if we get married – then he can leave us alone!'

'Married!' Franz must be mad. Telling her how he had plotted to humiliate her – probably giving his 'friend' a blow by blow account of her in bed – and, she supposed, pleasing him even further by advancing his theories of the beautiful couple by producing children for the future Reich. Either he was mad or she was. She could not believe all this was happening.

'Why did he want me to ask you about it all unless to humiliate

253

me? He hoped I would "fall in love" with you and then realise I had been duped. Has it not happened like that before? Tell me the truth.'

'Yes – but only with Mitzi a long time ago.'

'With Mitzi!'

'Yes – she was very pretty and he knows her through friends and she will do anything for men, anything. Hartmann tells me to make her fall in love with me so she will have nobody else and then we can both be his servants when he buys his house in Berlin. But he never buys his house, and goes away, and I am not in love with poor Mitzi, though Mitzi thinks she is in love with me. Then she turns the tables on him because she knows something we do not about Wolfgang and this keeps him quiet. So now she is just our friend – though she has changed and has taken drugs . . . but with you, Maud, it is *not* like that – '

'I am going,' said Maud, rising up.

'Please, Maud – he wanted to spoil it for me – I see now for him pleasure is a wasteland, he wanted you to know about the bet and then I would lose you. He guessed I had fallen for you.' He looked terribly upset. Perhaps he really did care for her?

Maud hesitated, but the feeling of shame was growing in her. She who could have had a great man or a good soldier as a lover, she who had denied herself – to fall for a common little confidence trickster. She wondered how much he had been paid and who had won the bet. And where did Hartmann get his money from? It was all too sordid, beyond her comprehension, except that now Franz was standing by her side as she was putting on her coat and he was begging her . . . She took a deep breath. 'Franz – I accept that you do care a little bit for me – but it must stop now – tell Mr Hartmann I shall be back home by Christmas – don't touch me.'

'Maud – I am sorry. You are right to be angry, but I am very excited by you – believe me you are my ideal lady, let me see you again when you have thought about it! I will not tell him, I promise – it can be a secret between us. Please think it over and let me write to you.'

Maud was reluctant to accept that her first sexual experience should end in a fiasco and one part of her still wanted to stay, to say damn Hartmann, let's just enjoy ourselves, forget about anything else. But the other, stronger, part was adamant. However Franz had wangled himself into her affections he was a weak man with a past. Not as blameworthy as Hartmann – but she did not want a weak man for a lover.

'I can't stop you writing to me,' she said. 'But I am not what you think. Nobody could forgive what you have done to someone who stayed in good faith.' Her lip trembled.

'Yes, Maud – and you were before a virgin – is it not true? I had your maidenhead?'

'And did you tell your friend Wolfgang that?' she choked out.

'No, I swear I did not.' He fell on his knees at her feet. 'I did not have to tell you. It is because I am an honest man!' he cried.

She looked at him sadly now. Any anger was for herself. She fastened the belt of her coat and was about to turn to go out when he came up to her, took her wrists and sniffed them. 'It is my perfume,' he said. 'Remember me, Maud, when you wear it. I shall not forget you. I shall say nothing to him. And I will write to you if you will forgive me one day.' He even had tears in his green eyes. He could easily have overpowered her, but some chivalrous instinct must have been working in him.

'I never want to see Hartmann again. I have nobody to blame but myself,' she said, believing it. She went quietly down the stairs and into the street. He stood watching her as she went and sat for a long time in the chair she had vacated, smoking, drinking some whisky and cursing Hartmann. But there was no way he could escape him as long as he remained in Germany. And Wolfgang would ask him what had happened, and he would have to tell him.

The next morning she received a letter from Clive Queensbury. He was going to marry his Tatiana. She wondered why. Perhaps he just did not have the strength to break free. And Franz Immerman had actually asked her to *marry* him! Had he meant it seriously? Had anything he said been serious? Did people just go around saying things like 'Will you marry me', for a joke? He could not possibly be in love with her – and yet he had looked upset . . .

She had allowed him to make love to her. How could she? She did not love him, did not love anyone – and hated Wolfgang Hartmann. She must not see *him* again. Yet how to avoid him if he came to the hotel? There was another month of her contract at the school to run and she was not one to shirk responsibilities and let people down; she could not leave yet.

That evening, coming out of the school in a daze, she passed the tram stop before she realised. It was getting dark. She would walk on to the next one. She crossed a canal bridge and stood for a moment looking down into the murky depths lit up by a street lamp. Her pride was wounded and she felt utterly ashamed. The conductor of the next tram looked at her curiously, for she seemed to be in a dream. But he was used to people who sleep-walked in Berlin.

Not only Maud's pride was wounded, but her belief in her own judgment. As though her humiliation had not been enough, the period she expected that week did not come and she faced the fact that she might be pregnant from her encounter with Franz. The old woman in black re-entered her dreams then and terrified her. She felt she was falling into an abyss, and longed for Ma to pull her out of it. But now she was grown up and had to pull herself out. She went over and over the conversation with Franz and it grew ever more shameful. Franz telephoned once or twice, but she told the receptionist to say she was not in unless the call was from Scotland. It had been a trick so beautifully tailored for her, she thought. Maud, whose reactions were always rather slow but deep, was caught in a terrible self pity, kept remembering things Franz had said, and worse, things she imagined Wolfgang saying. Was he clinically insane? Then she wondered whether she was pregnant and what on earth she could do about it. The fear of pregnancy was not the worst of her fears. The old woman in black was the most frightening warning, but what sort of warning?

Did she still have a little bit of sentiment left for poor Franz?

She had a letter from her little Prussian, who wrote telling her how his friends were beginning to quote Herr Hitler with his talk of loyalty and courage and sacrifice. 'If he gets the petty bourgeois *and* the students *and* half the army, I fear the old

Germany will be lost. If there were not so many unemployed though, there would not be so many votes for him. I am sorry to talk of such things to you, for I would rather just sit and talk of nicer things and watch you lick the cream from your coffee spoon. Oh, Maud! I wish we could be together, but I fear it will never be'.

Maud could not bear to think of herself as a fool; she might have lacked judgment and taken a wrong turning, but she was not stupid. Unconsciously she began to turn matters around in her head.

Whilst she was in the east she had read in a newspaper the strange story of "Die Seiner Unbekannte," the unknown woman drowned in the Seine. Now, with her photographic mind, she remembered every detail of it. It had been, she recalled, on the 27th of February 1919 that the body of a young woman had been found floating in the river Seine in Paris by the Quai du Louvre. She was a small young woman of about twenty-five or twenty-six – maybe that had attracted her to the story in the beginning. The woman had no outdoor clothes and was wearing no jewellery, and her dress, a new one, had no distinguishing features. The body was taken to the morgue and various people asked to view it, including some prostitutes and pimps. But nobody recognised it. The verdict was 'death by drowning' and after the statutory three months the body was buried anonymously. So the matter might have rested except that the whole time it lay in the morgue on the Ile de la Cité the face of the unknown woman seemed to observers to be smiling. The expression was variously described as happy, joyful, radiant, mysterious. So intrigued were the people who came to stare at the body that they took photographs, and an artist was asked by an unknown person to make a death mask. Everyone who saw the face felt that the woman had a secret, but nobody could guess what that secret was. Maud had thought a good deal about what such a secret might be. The story attracted countless journalists who wrote it up, and it was thus that she was baptised *L'Inconnue de la Seine* and joined European folklore.

In France poets had versified on her account; other writers wrote articles about her and all these things were published at

257

first to great public interest. Maud had made it her business to find all this out, for she felt an obscure connection, linked her 'vision' of the old woman on the beach long ago with the drowned Unknown. Did her old woman, then, symbolise death?

One evening, when it was dark by five o'clock, she went out again after her return from work, driven by some restlessness. She had not eaten all day and felt light-headed. She walked along the pavement in some obscure suburb; it could have been anywhere or nowhere she thought, featureless, dull; the sky grey-black. The canal gleamed below a little bridge and she stood looking at the water. Who would miss her if she jumped like the girl in Paris? Only Ma, she thought, and Ma was far away. She found tears scalding her cheeks, no longer tears of rage, but tears of loneliness. She had been used for purposes she could not understand. Her conscious mind, which she always heard speak quite clearly to her, said: 'You have no wish to die, though you have been badly treated. It was not your fault. If you are pregnant you will have to look for a woman to abort you; if not you will, I hope, learn by your mistakes. One day all this will seem trivial. A little melodrama. You will not make the same sort of mistake again.'

But underneath, some other voice seemed to be murmuring about fate and destiny and shutting the heart to love. She leaned over the parapet and it was as if she could hear both voices at once. But when she shut her eyes weary of the clashing voices she was filled with a sudden nausea and somehow inside the nausea was another voice thundering.

'Sin! Sin! Sin!' it intoned, 'the vices of the body, O! shameful for a woman to act like a brute beast, to have no shame, only to be left with eternal shame. The wages of sin is death. You shall be punished as a harlot and for ever excluded from the company of the Elect. You drew all this upon yourself, wanting to be like other women who cast themselves out from the circle of the saved into outer darkness for ever and ever. You will rot in hell.' She cringed. Stop it! Stop! she tried to shout, but only a whisper came out from her cold lips.

But then a woman's voice could be heard faintly in her head, a cracked old voice, saying 'Leave the lass alone, leave her alone,

258

you don't want her to end up like me – she's grown up now and can choose for herself.'

'Throw yourself in the water' thundered the first voice. 'End it all. The quicker you repent, the swifter will be your punishment and God may then be merciful when you have suffered the whips of scorpions and the burning fires of Hell!'

'Punishment on earth or in Heaven?' she muttered aloud and found she was gripping the railing that ran along the canal bridge so tightly that her fingers were numb. She shut her eyes.

Then she seemed to see her mother's face as it had been in her childhood. Ma would always love her. She need not love anyone but 'Ma. You don't have to die yet,' said the voice. 'I don't want to live on to be an old woman,' she cried back. She thought I want to stay with Ma as a child, with Ma who spoiled me and washed my clothes and my hair and cooked for me and saw to everything. Ma, who wanted to be and do all the things she was denied because of the thundering voice of that Preacher.

Then she found herself thinking about 'her' Empress. 'Nobody could have dared to play such a trick on *you*, Julia. What would you have done if they had?' 'Oh, Maud,' said the Empress, 'I was shamefully treated – not least by members of my own family.'

Maud opened her eyes and the voices stopped and she thought, Julia would have had her revenge in the end, quite forgetting that the Empress had starved herself to death.

She swallowed, her mouth was dry, and she was shivering uncontrollably. Then suddenly something seemed to change in her, and she smiled – Julia and herself, tragic heroines of a drama confected by men, not victims, but exceptional people, always courted, desired, inviolate . . . All her horror and shame over the loss of her self esteem, all the fear that she might be with child, left her, and turned into an icy self-regard. Maud, in the few moments after those aural hallucinations, pulled herself together and drew a protective cloak, a beautiful, shimmering cloak of romance and glamour, a cloak of self-centredness, over the empty kernel of her heart. Nobody is going to get the better of me, was her only rational thought as she left the dark water and with it the memories of other waters, of the Seine, of Lethe and the Tiber and the Oder and the Tay and walked back to her hotel. She would go home for Christmas. She would one day return to Germany though; there was always her Moltke who would be so glad to see her. And even Franz might be useful.

That night she slept long and soundly and woke refreshed.

Before she embarked on the long journey home, she wrote to Clive Queensbury, soon to be married to his Tati, and to Helmuth von Platen and also a short note to Franz Immerman. To Franz she wrote only '*Auf Wiedersehen*. I forgive you. It was not your fault. Good Luck.' This she felt was a magnanimous and Christian gesture. To Wolfgang Hartmann she did not write and expunged him so completely from her memory that for many years she was not to remember what he had done, but knew as clearly as though she could foretell the future that he would one day perish by his own hand.

She wrote home to Ma, and then packed carefully, gave her last lesson and then wrote to Carmichael to enquire about her viva and about any possible vacancy in the department. Then she bought a dark green leather coat with the rest of her savings, feeling she deserved it. The furs and jewels could wait. They would come.

The day before she left she learned that her thesis had been accepted *magna cum laude* without need for a viva. There was a vacancy in the department, for which Carmichael, on the verge of retirement, asked her to apply.

On the morning of her return journey, when everything was ready and she was about to order a taxi to the station, she found that she was not pregnant. The blood arrived in a great flood and was to soak her for three days as if she had really miscarried a human child.

Chapter Thirteen

It was in the late June of 1932 that Calum told Jackie Maud was back from Germany. He'd seen her walking down Princes Street on the other side of the road one afternoon, had run across and caught her up. There was something 'different' about her, he said – but it might just have been that she was thinner. Jackie said: 'Well, I wish *I* were thinner,' and he replied, as he always did, 'You're fine as you are.' Jackie wasn't truly fat, but a combination of having children and Scots baking had not been conducive to sylphlike proportions.

But Maud had been a bit odd, he said.

'Didn't you ask her whether she'd heard yet about the lectureship?' Jackie had received a letter from Maud before she left Germany in which she said that Carmichael was about to retire and there would be a general shuffling around of the faculty with a sure vacancy for a junior lectureship for which her old professor wanted her to apply.

'She said she was about to study for a teaching certificate,' said Calum, adding – 'She looked embarrassed.'

'Good Lord!' said Jackie. 'No wonder – she can't have got the job then! What a shame – I was sure she'd get it – it's what she's been looking forward to for years.' Jackie was really upset. 'I hope you were not tactless enough to bombard her with questions about it?' she went on, but realised he would have had more sense. He had taken Maud to a coffee shop and it had all come out. She'd been back for over six months and reiterated that she was going to teach in a secondary school when she was trained. He'd muttered something about it being a very worthwhile career and then she'd looked up and said: 'They didna want me at the university.'

'Who did they appoint to Carmichael's post?' he'd asked,

261

thinking that was a tactful way round if he wanted to find out the truth.

'A man from Oxford,' she replied.

'And I don't suppose there were any other vacancies then?'

'Yes there were – you don't think I was applying to be a professor, Calum?'

'I believe Jackie told me Carmichael wanted you to fill a lecture post?' he ventured.

'Oh, he did – but he was overruled. They've never had a woman in that department, except years ago when there was a special category of teacher for the women students. But this time there was a man of my age from Edinburgh,' she went on in a flat voice. 'They asked me if I intended to marry. I didna think it was any of their business, but I couldna say that. I said, no – and then they asked me about my research and so on. The upshot was that this other individual and I were the two strongest contenders – and he got it.'

Calum had had the idea of asking her about her doctorate.

'Aye,' she said. 'I got it, *magna cum laude*.'

'Isn't it a shame?' said Jackie to her husband on hearing all this. 'It's pure prejudice – Maud is as well qualified as anyone. If she were a man she'd have got it.'

Calum said, 'I'd have thought she'd have been angry – like you are about it all – but she was more sort of flat and resigned. She even said "They probably want a more sociable person than me". But I think it's really hit her hard.'

'Surely she can apply elsewhere? – there are other universities, you know!'

'No, I think she must have set her heart on this one. She looked very pale.'

'Did you ask her to come round to see us – ?'

'I did indeed – do write to her – she must be feeling pretty dismal.'

Jackie wrote to Maud saying she was really angry that they hadn't given Maud the job, especially as Carmichael had practically begged her to apply for it. She was longing to see her again and congratulated Maud on her doctorate which was indeed an achievement, for there were not many post-graduates with such a degree, and very few women among them. 'What will you teach?' wrote Jackie. 'Do come and see us.'

Maud didn't reply for about three weeks but when she did it was only to say: 'It seems they wanted a man. You can't blame them really,' which aroused Jackie's dormant feminism. In what spare time *she* had she read and wrote, had indeed never stopped writing her little stories which she wrote to sell. Women's magazines did not want to hear anything remotely subversive, so Jackie got round the problem by setting her tales in bygone days with brave heroines. She had still not written her novel.

Perhaps it was what Maud had said, they just wanted a more 'sociable' person, one who would fit in with the male atmosphere and not ruffle the feathers of what few women there were in the place? Probably they wanted a good teacher for junior lecturer rather than a research minded person like Maud.

'But she'll end up teaching children!' cried Jackie to Calum, and went on, 'I must say I can't imagine that. Maud doesn't even *like* children!'

In her letter Maud said she'd come to see them, so Jackie replied, offering three dates, for she was longing to see her. Maud still fascinated her because she was so different from herself, the sort of person Jackie had used to think that medieval poets might have written about.

When a reply came agreeing to come one evening in late July before the Fyffes went off for their family holiday, Jackie was delighted, but also a wee bit apprehensive.

The Fyffes were living in a much nicer house by this time, an omnibus ride away from the centre of Edinburgh. Jackie wasn't too sure she really liked it better for she'd enjoyed being so near everything that was going on, but there was a garden for the boys, so she resigned herself to a rather genteel middle-class life, though she knew she didn't fit into it and was liable to say and do the wrong things.

Jackie was always to remember her first sight of Maud that evening. It was three years since they'd met and here was Maud now on her front doorstep wearing a smart dark green leather coat and looking quite foreign. That was the first word that came into Jackie's head as they embraced, Maud rather stiffly consenting. Jackie began to burble, as she always did if she was nervous, but took her into the sitting-room and offered her a drink of sherry. Maud was quiet at first and Jackie saw she *was* thinner, and paler – and even more beautiful. Jackie, knowing nothing of Maud's traumatic experience with Franz Immerman nor how her friend having once dared to go against the strictures of Preacher Gray had eventually been filled with self-disgust, thought the pallor made her interesting. She put it down to the shock of her rejection by the university – which must have been a greater blow to Maud than any deviousness of Man.

They talked, and did not at first mention Maud's disappointment – it was almost as if she had been jilted in love, Jackie thought. They talked of Germany, though Maud seemed reluctant to pronounce on its politics, but alluded to several people as 'friends of mine' in a mysterious way, with hints about a part of her life her friend could no longer share.

'*You* look well,' said Maud politely.

Jackie looked more closely at Maud whose mouth still looked soft, whose hands were still white, the nails polished in a way housewives never could find time for. She looked like a woman with a past, not a woman with a disappointing future, and Jackie could not help asking herself if that was the impression Maud was trying, quite consciously, to convey.

It was not till Jackie finally did dare to say how deeply she was upset that Maud had been passed over for the job she wanted that a little crack appeared in Maud's smooth carapace. She had been occasionally larding her talk with German, probably not on purpose to impress Jackie, but because she was still thinking in that language. 'Ach,' she said, and looked away.

'Do you *want* to teach school?' asked Jackie with her old lack of tact.

'I can earn a good living teaching Latin,' Maud replied, looking at Jackie now over the brim of her glass, an old crystal goblet whose beauty she had remarked on.

'And Greek?'

'I suppose so – but I'd rather teach German, ye ken – not so many can.'

'Will you stay in Scotland?'

'I don't expect so.'

'I wish I'd trained for something less risky than a combination of motherhood and journalism,' said Jackie.

'You don't need to, Jackie – you have Calum,' said Maud.

Now was Jackie's opportunity to ask her about men and love and her real self, but she felt annoyed that Maud assumed that a man was a meal ticket. Jackie did her share in earning a little money as well as in the upbringing of their children. Maud had never been the sort of woman for confidences. But now she looked up when Jackie said something about a husband better not being regarded as an eternal provider, and said: 'Marriage is what most women want, isn't it? Well, I don't.'

'You want love though, don't you?'

'I'm not sure what that means any more,' said Maud. 'I know what desire means and lust, Jackie, but love – I don't think I feel it.' Then she walked to the window before turning back to face her. 'I expect I am doomed, Jackie,' she said, but not in a histrionic way, as though she really believed herself exceptionally chosen for tragedy.

'Don't be ridiculous, you're only twenty-seven,' Jackie almost replied, but Maud looked so stony and closed in on herself that she did not. Instead she said lightly: 'Like one of my romantic heroines? – but *they* all want a man!'

She was thinking, Maud does look like a *femme fatale* when she has that blank, creepy face on her. She'd never been an actressy sort of woman but had she already chosen to play a sort of role? Or had it chosen her?

But Maud revived suddenly and began to talk of some of the other people she'd met abroad, though she wouldn't be drawn on anything to do with politics. She could be very witty when she chose. She had been saying something uncomplimentary about the wives of one of the lecturers being no 'chicken', for she had always been hard on womankind – and Jackie thought: the *femme fatale* bit might be the desired end, but it would not have duped any woman with experience, though it might have impressed men.

'You'll be teaching German then?' Jackie said. 'I ought to learn it myself – ' and mentioned some German writer whose novel she'd been reading. Maud did not appear interested, but said: 'Oh, he's Jewish – he's a psychiatrist in a poor quarter of Berlin.'

'I liked the bit where nature took her revenge,' said Jackie. 'What is it *really* like in Germany? Calum is very suspicious of the Nazi party.'

'I get letters from several men over there,' said Maud after a pause 'One of them wants to marry me – an officer in the Army – *he's* against the Nazis. Other people I knew were members of the Party, one in particular – but I shall never see *him* again.'

'Did you meet any British people?'

'A man from Oxford, Clive Queensbury – I called him "Cosmo" – you would have liked him, I think – he was a socialist. A historian. He's married to a Russian girl. A dancer – *she's* half Jewish. I don't expect I shall ever see *them* again, either. We did a bit of sightseeing together.'

'Will you go back?'

'Of course! – I like it out there you know. Not this summer because I have to start my new course and I havena enough cash. But once I'm earning I shall spend all my holidays there, I expect.' She began to talk of her job teaching little boys in Berlin, which she had apparently quite enjoyed.

Jackie thought if Maud had to earn her living she might just as well do it abroad, but Maud said: 'I couldna leave Ma for good – I've been too long away in her opinion in any case.'

Soon after that Calum came home and Jackie served them both soup and a simple salad and some fruit and bread and cheese.

Maud began to speak of the torchlight procession in Berlin whilst they were eating the supper. Calum asked her about Hitler worshippers in the army – he knew what questions to ask. Maud said she'd had a letter saying there were now a lot of Nazis in the junior ranks of the army. Jackie wondered if it was from the man Maud said wanted to marry her.

Calum then tried to get on to the subject of the Jews, said he'd read a report in a newspaper about the way they were being blamed for all the ills suffered by the Germans and Maud looked uncomfortable.

'There *are* a lot of rich ones over there,' she said.

'Bankers?' asked Jackie.

266

Maud shrugged her shoulders.

Calum said: 'I don't like the sound of it at all. Why do you want to go back, Maud?'

'I like speaking German. And it's more civilised than here.'

After supper they sat and talked and Maud was shown round the house. The little boys did not wake up, though Maud stood a moment looking at them.

'He has changed,' she said of Joe.

All the time Jackie felt there was something Maud wasn't saying. She had the impression Maud would like to have been a divine diva, like Garbo, But she knew Maud had been born with a Calvinist temperament in a Calvinist country and her idea of glamour was always second-hand.

Calum tried to draw her out on the subject of her thesis, but Man would not be drawn. It was a sensitive subject. She said she had no plans for writing a book.

When she'd gone Jackie exclaimed: 'Oh, I never asked her about the portrait and what had happened to it!' Perhaps she would tell her when they met again.

Letters from Maud were a rarity; Jackie kept the few she had from Maud with the idea one day of writing about her as a fictional mysterious woman. 'She's rather unhappy,' Jackie later remarked to Calum.

'Old friends always see through each other,' said Calum. Jackie had a strong impression that he had desired Maud at one time.

There was never any unpleasant tension between Calum and his wife. They had both been sexually passionate at first – and got on well most of the time, having many interests in common. All in all Jackie was glad she'd married him, but often felt that her becoming pregnant had cheated them both of some of the fun of their youth. If he ever committed adultery, even in his heart, as the Bible said, Jackie thought it would be with a completely different sort of woman. But she didn't want it to be with Maud Crichton. About whom he finally pronounced: 'She is decidedly odd, you know,' so that Jackie knew the danger, if it had ever existed, must be past.

The Fyffes spent a wonderful holiday that summer in the Western Isles. When Jackie returned she saw Maud only once when they had coffee in the best store in Edinburgh, whose branch they had used to frequent as students. Maud had passed her teaching diploma but was going to have a semester away in Germany before taking up a permanent post, as yet she knew not where. She was not going to Berlin though but to the city where she'd done her graduate work. 'Oh, do take care, Maud!' said Jackie. 'Horrible things are happening everywhere in Germany.' But Maud just smiled.

When Maud said goodbye – it was September with its leafy-mouldy smell in the air, even in the city – Jackie wondered when they would see each other again.

'Do keep in touch,' she said. 'Let me know where you go to teach, won't you? Maud just smiled and looked mysterious and Jackie gave her a peck on her alabaster cheek. Then Maud walked away and never once looked back.

Jackie had decided that if Maud really wanted to go on being friends she would write to her certainly at the New Year, when Scots wrote their thank-you letters and their keeping-up-with-Auntie-Agnes ones. She sent Maud a letter with a card at Christmas but had no reply.

She was hurt when Maud continued not to get in touch.

She missed Maud more than she had when Maud was away studying in Germany, had an idea that something strange had happened to her. But apart from the obvious things that might happen to young women of twenty-seven – though Puritanical society pretended it never did – Jackie could not think what. She felt sad that Maud had not been offered what she deserved.

One day, a year or two after Maud's disappearance, Jackie went to read her thesis, which was now in the University Library. It was a real work of scholarship. Of course they had realised that and given her her doctorate. If Maud had ever wanted to write a book all the material was there. But apart from academic ambition Maud had never wanted to write. If she were vain about anything it was her sexual attraction. Would her failure to be appointed sour her life for ever? A teacher in a secondary school was, in Jackie's eyes, an unfitting end rather than a beginning of a new life.

It was just after the visit to the University Library that the idea came to Jackie to write a story about an aesthete like Sir Hector who loved a young woman and had her picture painted. Ten years had passed since then and Jackie thought this was long enough not to worry about anyone's thinking she had taken the story from real events. She wrote of a girl whose face actually became *more beautiful* because of her experience of life and who ended more lovely in later age than in her youth. It was published in a national magazine and brought Jackie in a tidy little sum of money towards the fees for Joe at George Watson's Academy. There was no word from Maud, so Jackie assumed she had not read *A Picture From Life*. One day however, when the boys had gone off to school, Jackie was sorting through the post with a cup of coffee and a cigarette prior to shutting herself up to write till lunchtime, when she found a blue envelope addressed in a hand she did not know. She loved getting letters and since most of her mail was bills at that time, she slit it open with feelings of anticipation. She looked at the signature, a rounded 'arcaded' sort of hand, pleasant, obviously a woman – Christina Squiggle – Hellan? – no *Heron* – ! Jackie's heart missed a beat. She read the letter quickly and poured another cup of coffee as she re-read it. The woman had read the story and was fascinated because it reminded her of something in real life and wanted to know where the writer had come across it or had she invented it? If not – 'I would very much like to meet you', it ended. Jackie supposed her description of the picture must have been a little too lifelike; she ought to have been more careful.

Jackie wanted to meet Sir Hector's daughter; more than anything she wanted to know how much the family knew about his passion for Maud. Christina Heron might think it was Maud who was writing about her own past. Jackie knew she had no right to poke about in Maud's life, and to salve her conscience finally wrote to Mrs Crichton to ask for Maud's address in England. But as the weeks went on and she didn't hear from Maud she thought, blow it, I'm going to meet this Heron woman. The story was my responsibility and I want to know what happened to the real picture.

She must have been in her mid-twenties, the tall young woman who came to meet her in the Caledonian Hotel lounge that June morning. She seemed nervous, but Jackie was nervous too, with vague ideas of being prosecuted for libel. But Hector was dead, she kept telling herself. She had not explained who she was in her letters; just said she'd go into details at their meeting. But she liked the young woman straight away. There was a directness about her. She had lovely long hands and a shy sort of coltish look about her face – with its long nose and spatters of freckless. A face like her dead father's, as Jackie remembered it.

She ordered coffee – Jackie was her guest, and then she said: 'Did *you* know Daddy then? You're not the girl of the picture, are you?'

'No – she was my friend. I did meet your father though, about twelve years ago.' Twelve years that seemed an eternity to Jackie. She saw the woman was wearing a wedding ring – why had she called herself Heron?

'The initials on the card she put with the flowers were M L G C,' she said.

'I didn't know about the flowers – ' said Jackie. She must mean at the graveyard where he was buried. 'But her first name was Maud.'

'Maud,' repeated the young woman. 'Did he love her then? It was before Mummy came back. He must have done!'

'He had the portrait painted because he loved her,' replied Jackie and was visited with a lump in her throat – it all seemed such a waste. Should she have kept the name from Christina?

'Where is she now, your friend?' asked the young woman, and fiddled with her coffee spoon.

'I don't know for certain – she's a teacher, probably across the Border.'

'A teacher – Good Lord! She doesn't look like a teacher!'

How had the girl guessed her father had loved Maud? He might have just liked the look of her and commissioned a portrait by an artist in whom he had faith.

'My mother didn't like the portrait,' said Christina. 'She sent it to the Sales Rooms. I thought it was a lovely painting. But I found out who had painted it – it was a man called James Valentine.'

'Yes, I know,' said Jackie.

270

'Did you both come regularly to Garvits then at my father's invitation?'

Jackie told her she'd been there only once, but went on to ask: 'Did you ask Valentine to buy it back?' The girl looked intelligent and practical. When she'd spoken of her father her face had softened.

'By the time I'd tracked him down again he was in London and he said he hadn't had the money to buy it. I hadn't either. I didn't come into my money until I was twenty-one. I couldn't find out where Mother sold it – she said it went with other pictures . . . Was she *very* beautiful? She looks beautiful! Father never mentioned her – but I'm sure he must have loved her like he did in your story. I think he was a romantic sort of man.'

'Is your mother still alive?' asked Jackie.

'Flourishing,' she said. There was no love lost there. Jackie supposed there had been no recurrence of Mrs H's nervous trouble.

'After the funeral your friend went to the grave,' said Christina. 'I found the white flowers she'd left. She *must* have loved him.'

'She was very young. If your father had lived and if – ' Jackie stopped.

'You mean if my mother hadn't come back? Yes – I thought of that – he'd have married her, wouldn't he?'

Jackie chose her words carefully. 'Christina – may I call you that? – don't build too much out of all this – my friend *was* the object of your father's love, that's true, but I never knew how she really felt about him – she was still at university – I think it was all a little too much for her.'

'I just wanted to know her name – I promise I won't tell anyone else. My brother takes no interest in Father's pictures or his life. I just want to get that picture back one day because Father loved it. I'm sure he loved *her* too. But mightn't *she* perhaps like to have it? After all, she provided the reason for the painting!'

'I think she did not really want to be painted,' said Jackie. 'You see – she thought that when she got older she would see that the portrait would never change and she would.'

'So she was beautiful? It must be hard to be like that when

271

you're young – like being photographed and then everyone expecting you to be the same years later – I hadn't thought of that.'

'If you do find it – do tell me,' said Jackie. "I haven't the money to buy it back, even if it's still in Britain, but you never know – if Jamie Valentine doesn't "make" it, his pictures won't be so expensive in future!'

'And you won't tell me her full name. Just "Maud"? May I keep in touch with *you*, though, Miss Livesey?'

'It's Mrs Fyffe really,' said Jackie. 'Livesey was my maiden name and I write under it. I'm married with two little boys. My husband's a doctor.'

'Is "Maud" married then?' she asked.

'Not as far as I know – Maud's not the marrying sort,' replied Jackie and thought Christina looked rather pleased. Like her father, she was probably a romantic.

'If we ever find the picture I think it should go back to my friend Maud, don't you?'

'Yes. We've rented out Garvits as a convalescent home, you know – if it can't go back there it had much better be with her. But I wish I could meet her,' she said wistfully – 'I'm beginning to feel I never really knew my father. I suppose I've changed since he died – I feel there's a lot I'd like to say to him now.'

'He was an awfully nice man. You have a look of him.'

'If I do have any luck tracking it down,' she said, 'I'll let you know – and then you can tell *her*.'

'I've a feeling that if James Valentine did come across it one day when he had money, he'd buy it – it was one of the best things he ever painted. I believe *he* thought so too, though it wasn't his usual style – he was the sort of painter who could paint in different ways to please different people. He thought Maud ought to be painted in the old high Victorian style.'

'She was an old-fashioned sort of girl then?' asked Christina tentatively.

'I suppose she was – is. If you really want to know her name it will be on her thesis at the university. I won't tell it to you – I suppose then my conscience will be clear,' said Jackie.

'M L G C,' said the young woman. 'I took her card away from the grave in case mother saw it. I think she suspected something.

Your friend looked so lonely when I saw her walking away down the road, but I recognised her as the girl in the portrait – wasn't that strange, I was just sure, you know – the way she held her head in the picture – so upright – and the way she was walking then. I tried to pump Mrs Anderson, our old housekeeper, but I could get nothing out of her. I asked Archie – her husband – if the girl in the portrait we sold visited a lot at Garvits, but he pretended he knew nothing about it. I'm sure they were both holding back.'

They were both silent for a moment. Jackie felt curiously that it was Maud who had died, not her admirer. Then Christina said: 'It was kind of you to see me and tell me about her. I wish you luck with your writing, Mrs Fyffe. Here's my card – I'd love to keep in touch.' Jackie saw her married name was Gordon. She stood up and held out her hand and Jackie shook it. Her tall, tweeded figure walked away.

It was to be many years before Hector's daughter was to see the portrait again.

About a year after the meeting with Christina Gordon, Calum saw the announcement of Maud's father's death in the *Tayside Gazette*. Maud would be sure to have come home for that, Jackie thought, so wrote to her at the old address with a large 'PLEASE FORWARD IF NECESSARY' on the envelope. About three weeks later a reply from Malcolm Crichton arrived:

'Mrs and Miss Crichton and Malcolm and Duncan Crichton and all the family thank you for your kind letter on the demise of their husband and father Angus. Miss and Mrs Crichton's address is 65 Market Street, Redport, Co Durham'.

So Maud had her mother with her now! What scope would there be for her in a small seaside town in the North East of England, Jackie wondered. How could she ever be happy in such a place? Perhaps she had been there ever since she had begun to teach?

Only some months later was there a reply from her old friend. It was an odd letter, half stilted, half the old Maud. Ma was now 'looking after her' and she had a temporary post teaching

Classics and German. She spent all her holidays abroad where she had friends. 'In case you worry, Jackie, I am not a Nazi – but I feel in some ways more at home over there. The daily grind is worthwhile if I know I can escape during the holidays'.

In her reply to this Jackie told her that Sir Hector's daughter had been wanting to trace her father's old friend and was keen to locate the portrait and buy it back. Maud's reply was quicker this time. Jackie was not to tell Mrs Gordon of her whereabouts. All that was over long ago. If she had known where the picture was she'd have bought it herself as soon as she had saved up – but only to destroy it. The knowledge that her likeness was somewhere with some unknown person gave her an uncomfortable feeling.

Jackie did not write to Maud again for there seemed nothing to say. Her old friend had receded for the time being beyond the horizon. Would she ever see her again? Calum said it was up to Maud to reply to letters, you could not go on posting letters into a void. But Jackie felt obscurely guilty. It was pride that kept Maud from writing to her, she knew. But Jackie had her own pride, and anyway she was busy. There were times though as the Thirties went on, engulfing them all finally in war, when she would wake from some dream of Maud, imagine she was crying out for help.

Life was to take Jackie and Calum by the scruff of their necks and shake them till their teeth rattled. Good old life that pushed you here and there, willy nilly.

That Joe and Jamie would grow up was inevitable, that there should be another war was also seen as inevitable by some, including Calum. But that Calum should have gone in 1937 to visit his beleaguered relatives in Catalonia, should have witnessed the murder of his own cousin there; that Calum should have also whilst he was in Barcelona have fallen in love with a pretty nurse on the Republican side and confessed his whirlwind affair later to his wife was less predictable. Nothing came of it; Jackie did not think it was her business to make a to-do about 'forgiving' him, especially as he was miserable. They carried on together, though neither forgot what had happened.

The war was a different matter. Jackie took war work in a

Ministry that had moved to Edinburgh, but Calum, who did not need to join up, decided he would, with a division of the Royal Army Medical Corps.

Calum was with the 51st Highlanders, in North Africa helping with the injured, when the plans to attack were secretly changed at the beginning of October 1943. The result was a resounding victory for Montgomery, though the British lost between seven and eight thousand men. One of them was Calum Fyffe.

Before her husband died Jackie had heard one of his Spanish cousins, who had escaped to London from France, sing in a concert at the National Gallery. This was Carlos Vallés, a man twelve years younger than herself. She had been carried away by the magic of his voice that seemed to speak of long-forgotten feelings far away from the nitty gritty of marriage or war. It was only three years after Calum's untimely death, when she had already begun to write the historical novels for which she was to become well-known, that Jackie took herself and her tall sons on an impulse for a holiday to that city where Calum had stayed ten years before. And it was a quirk of fate that ordered that Carlos Vallés should also be back there in his native city, already making a name for himself, and that he should remember her from that crowded concert in the war. That she should fall in love with him and he with her was less fate than a glorious accident. Love and death and war were all mixed up for Jackie, but she accepted Carlos as she had been forced to accept Calum's death. At a time when many thought she should be preparing for a tranquil middle-age she sold up the Edinburgh house, moved to London, and bought a flat in Pimlico where her sons could stay in their university vacations. Then she waited for the visits of her Carlos with all the ardour of a much younger woman.

During their first Christmas in London before Carlos came to sing at Covent Garden in the following February, Jackie was unpacking various cases and boxes with Joe and his brother, exclaiming over old snaps of their childhood. Her sons approved of their mother's new love for only they knew how sincerely she

275

had mourned their father and they were glad that she should be striking out for herself and, with the egoism of youth, relieved that they were not to be called upon to fill the void where their father had used to stand when they were children. Jackie was going through her photograph album dating from her university years and they were peering at the sepia prints. One photograph was the official one taken of all Jackie's year and on it she was looking rather untidy with a strand of hair escaping over her forehead and her habitual rather soulful expression.

'You haven't changed,' said Jamie kindly. 'Who's that?' he asked, pointing to Maud Crichton who was sitting not far away from her friend with a butter-won't-melt-in-my-mouth look, staring straight ahead, her hair tidily parted, the classical features almost expressionless.

'That was my best friend,' replied Jackie. 'You met her, Joe, when you were very small – remember?'

'Yes! I remember she built me a tower of bricks, but she wore black spectacles – I can't see any here.'

'No, she took them off for the photo, I expect.'

'She's very good-looking,' said Jamie. 'What does she do now? Is she an actress?'

'An actress!' echoed Jackie – 'No – I believe she teaches girls somewhere – she was exceptionally clever – got a Double First and then a doctorate . . .'

'She looks as though she ought to have been a classical actress,' said Jackie's younger son. Most things at that time gave Jamie ideas to do with drama, and he was later to become a producer of it himself.

'More like a Romantic Heroine,' said Jackie. She had not thought about Maud for ages, but suddenly the photograph set her thinking how she might try to put someone like her in a book, her next book, the sequel to her first successful historical novel.

'She had an older man for an admirer,' said Jackie and found herself telling them about Sir Hector Heron. 'I wonder what did happen to her portrait,' she mused. 'His daughter said it was sold somewhere.' Now she was in London she would have a look round.

She searched everywhere in dusty little galleries in Chelsea and in more imposing, more fashionable ones in Cork Street, but drew a blank. To find Maud herself might be just as hard. Out of curiosity she wrote to the Durham address, but drew a blank there too. Maud had vanished into thin air.

A year or two later she was at a party at her publishers where she met a man who had known Maud Crichton. Carlos was away singing in Vienna and there were rumours of a film to be made of a little known Mozart opera, not the sort of thing he usually sang. It was a June evening and Jackie was wishing she was in the country. She enjoyed her Pimlico flat, but longed more and more to wake up to birdsong rather than traffic or the sound of next door's prostitutes returning from their night's work.

She was 'circulating' and got talking to a man who had written a history book which had won his publishers a prize. It was not on any subject that especially interested Jackie, but as it was a German theme she tried to say something intelligent about Germany and asked the fellow how well he knew that country. He was a small man with a *dégagé* air about him and he seemed to be enjoying the rather warm white wine which was offered.

'I've never been,' she said and added for lack of something to say – 'I had a friend who worked out there just before Hitler – I was always telling her to publish her researches. I expect it was before your time.'

'Where was she?' he asked. Jackie told him and he exclaimed: 'Was she called Maud?' Jackie looked so amazed he burst out laughing. 'Oh, yes, you may not believe it but I've been writing about my subject for over twenty years,' he said, assuming Jackie must have thought him younger than that. 'Maud Crichton was a friend of mine.'

Jackie had forgotten his name. As usual at these parties she had not caught it the first time round. 'Clive Queensbury,' he said. 'I knew your friend quite well. What is she doing now?'

'I have no idea. She wasn't given the job she wanted – pure prejudice against women,' said Jackie. 'So she decided to teach in a school, and I lost touch with her. It's years since I last saw her.'

277

'She *was* a strange girl,' he went on, apparently glad of a gossip. 'Did you know her well yourself?'

Jackie explained they'd been at university together and that she'd known her as well as anyone did.

'A case of arrested development,' he pronounced magisterially. 'A very good-looking girl – but cold, very cold.' She must have rejected his advances for it was Jackie's experience that men only say this sort of thing about women who have. 'She was a typical blue-stocking,' he went on, frowning.

Jackie decided to plunge. 'I believe she did mention you. You were going to write a history of the world, weren't you? She called you "Cosmo".'

He gaped. 'I'd forgotten that,' he said rather huffily. 'She went around with a nice chap though – a soldier – from the barracks there – an office. He was sweet on her – I do remember she called him "Moltke"!'

'I remember her mentioning a soldier,' said Jackie. 'Was he a friend of yours then too?'

'Oh, yes, we were quite friendly. Strangely enough I did hear about him from other friends after the war. Poor chap, he was killed at Alamein.'

Jackie swallowed. The word had been said so suddenly that she felt quite strange. 'So was my husband,' she said.

'Oh dear, I am sorry – how dreadful!' and he began to talk of something else. She gathered he had never written his history of the world. Hadn't Maud once told her that 'Cosmo' had married a Russian girl of his own age, a dancer? The woman who came up then could not be she; he must have remarried.

When she got home she sat down, feeling rather shaky. Was 'Moltke' the man Maud said wanted to marry her? She tried to remember. If so, she and Maud had both lost men in the same battle. It didn't bear thinking about. That night she dreamed that Calum was back and that he was telling her Maud had killed him. She tried to remonstrate with him, but 'No, Jackie! Maud killed me,' he said quite soberly and she woke up crying, but determined to find Maud Crichton's portrait one day and lay that ghost at least.

* * *

278

It must have been shortly after that in 1950 when Carlos Vallés came back from Vienna and they were down in Sussex buying a little cottage that Jackie became pregnant with his child at the age of forty-five.

INTERLUDE

1944–1952

Chapter Fourteen

MILLY HARGREAVES: THIS DIARY IS PRIVATE

I have nearly finished my diary for 1944 and there has not really been anything very interesting in it up to now, except my descriptions of Morecambe Bay, but this afternoon something really wonderful happened. Dorothy and I were staying late at school for the Literary and Dramatic Society and Miss Crichton was there too – I don't think she's been before. It was very odd because it suddenly came to me how very beautiful she was. I mean, Dorothy and I have always found her good-looking, as well as a bit eccentric, but today I couldn't help thinking how lonely she looked, and just as I was thinking this and also how beautiful she was, before they started the speeches, she looked up at me across the room and for a moment she really stared at me. She's always been nice to me since I had my tonsils out in May when she kept asking me if I really felt better when I got back to school, but today I suddenly felt interested in her in a strange sort of way. I think she is fascinating, different from anyone else at school. The meeting was rather boring. I have not yet spoken at one, but I shall when it's a more interesting debate than the British Empire, which was the one today. Most of the girls never open their mouths and let the boys drone on. Miss Crichton looked bored too. She sat there as it went on with her hands tucked in the sleeves of her gown looking stonily ahead. She always looks cold. In class I've noticed she sits as near the radiators as possible. Now that I'm writing about her I find all sorts of other little things I've noticed about her. But I haven't yet written about what happened after the meeting.

I decided to see if I could walk to the bus-stop with her – she comes on our bus sometimes as she lives near Sheila – I've often seen her on it. She always walks through the park with that big old Gladstone bag of hers, so I followed her to the bus-stop, having dashed out of school as quickly as poss. I waylaid her just as she started across the park. I said: 'May I carry your bag?' She turned round and she said: 'You've got a heavy satchel yourself, Milly.' It was true, I had, because since September there's that whopping German dictionary I had to buy for her lessons, but I said: 'Oh, do let me,' and she smiled – 'Perhaps another time,' she said. She was wearing one of those strange hats of hers perched on her coronet of plaits. 'You go on my bus, don't you?' she said as we walked down the hill. She seemed quite pleased for me to walk by her side – anyway she didn't mind, for I asked her, I said 'May I walk with you?' and she replied. 'If you care to.' In the Woolsford bus I sat next to her, on the inside next to the window as she had to get out before me

'Do you like living in this town?' I asked her.

She always talks with this wonderful Scots accent, and she replied: 'I dinna ken how long I'll be here. When the war's over the gardener will want the Lodge back.' So then she told me that she lives in the lodge to Sir Francis Brown's big house – just rents it – and it's 'verra cold'.

After she'd got off the bus I watched her cross the road. She always walks very uprightly and is never in a hurry. I thought about what she'd told me. She is a strangely exciting person, *I* think.

Nov 23rd Thursday

Horrible school dinner with lumpy potatoes and sponge pudding with (also lumpy) custard. Miss Crichton always drinks a cup of hot water after the meal. She boils it in a kettle by the sink. I think she must suffer from indigestion Last night in bed I was thinking about the time last winter when we were having a Latin lesson with her and it was interrupted by a knock at the door and the Senior Mistress came sidling in and went up to Miss Crichton who was sitting at her desk in the front. I remember we were doing accusatives and were on *Julia amat militem* or

Miles amat Juliam, but then Miss Lorimer whispered something to Miss Crichton and put an arm round her shoulders and they both went out. We were all stunned into silence. Miss Lorimer is a very nice woman, and I love History – nearly as much as languages. We found out later that Miss Crichton's mother had died that day. I do remember it was a Friday. Well, on the bus this evening I was again with Miss Crichton and I thought as I was talking to her that she must be lonely because her mother had died.

Sunday 26 November

Did my homework – ten hard sentences for Latin and then some German vocab to learn. I am lucky that Miss C teaches them both. I think about her all the time even when I am doing other things. Sunday School this afternoon – I don't believe any more in Jesus, though I still do in God, I think. I am growing up fast. I shall be fourteen in a few days – can't believe it, but roll on sixteen, and then twenty-one! – it seems so far ahead I can't believe I'll ever get there and be grown up.

Description of M L G Crichton

She is not a lot taller than I am yet. She wears medium heels and her shoes are usually black leather, or mixed suede and leather with high laces. Everybody talks about her stockings – they are pale, almost beige, with designs up them. Jessie says they are 'clocked'. I'm sure you can't buy them here. She wears her hair plaited into a coronet on the top of her head parted in the middle – I have never seen this sort of style before except in old books. She always wears her black-rimmed glasses, and usually wears earrings, very often green ones. Her leather coat is almost black, but really a *very* dark green, with a tight belt. She has a very good figure – I do not usually notice such things, but Kathleen said that one day to me and I agreed. I don't know how she gets her hats to perch on her head as she does. I wish she would not wear such hats. They embarrass me rather, though I would never confess it. They are like small black vultures! She looks 'foreign'. I was always interested in her, I now realise, but I realise I have fallen in love with her (I love her even more than I did Miss Dundas when I was eleven) I believe she likes

285

me. She wrote some very nice things on my last report and I am determined to stay top in her subjects. Dorothy partly agrees with me about her. Dorothy is always sympathetic to me; she is a much nicer person than I am and will always be my best friend. She said: 'I feel sorry for her. She must be lonely.' That is just what I feel too, but *more* than Dorothy does. We have had Miss C now for nearly four terms.

Dec 8th

I have been so busy with school work and swotting for the exams and then choir practice that I haven't been able to write this diary. I am looking for a special Christmas card for MC and wondering what I might dare to write in it. I've never enjoyed school more, though much of it is wearisome. I love German, nearly as much as Latin. Sometimes I wish Miss C taught my favourite subject of all, English, but you canna have everything, as she often says. I manage to get on to the same bus most nights. We break up on Friday – however shall I endure the days when I cannot see her?

Saturday

I had a very good report – top in everything but biology and maths, and first position in the form. Miss C wrote 'an exceptional pupil'. HM says I am to be an 'open scholarship candidate' in the near future. I wish I could paint Miss C – I think her more and more beautiful, and mysterious. I can't explain these feelings but they are very strong.

For my birthday I got amongst other presents a lovely new exercise book with stiff backs. I shall use it when this diary is finished. I have found a beautiful old Christmas card that I can put a new middle in, all blue with a little church in silver, and I shall write 'With love from'. I wish I could write 'With all my love'.

Dec 26th

I shall go during the holidays on the bus to Moor Top just to see if I can catch a glimpse of her. Christmas was lovely. On Christmas night Anne and I undressed by the gas fire and I gloated over all my presents. I've begun a long story in a big leather book I was given, perfect for stories. Whenever I start to write I keep thinking of Her. Everything I look at seems to connect with her. When it snowed, I was beside myself with the beauty and I imagined she was there in the snow like the Snow Queen. It is as if she has touched me with a magic wand, like the one with a star on the end we used to have in the acting box. My feelings quite overcome me and even make my throat ache. She adds to everything in my life – so that I feel more alive because she exists. Everything is so exciting, even the holidays when she is not here, although less so than term time when I can see her.

Jan 4th
I did go over to Moor Top but she was not there in the lodge. The knowledge that she did live there was enough though, and I felt really happy and excited, imagining her there.

Jan 10th 1945
Strange to write another year. The last year has been so marvellous. I don't know how I could bear it if she left.

Jan 16th
She has given me a special name – she often gives nicknames to people. Now she calls me 'Hero'! Nobody knows *her* Christian name – she has never breathed it even to me and I dare not ask. I think she ought to be called something like Marguerite, but she doesn't like French people, so that won't do. 'Matilda' would be right if it were not so old-fashioned. I love names. They are as magical as people.

Feb 8th
She was away from school and I was so worried when I did not see her in Assembly. But then up came Sheila with a note for me! Her father often gives MC a lift in his car from the Top in the morning. It is the first note I've ever had from her and it said she was ill with stomach pains and would I go to the shop where I'd accompanied her last week and ask about her wireless which had gone wrong and was being repaired. It was such a sweet, funny note. I'm sure she does not eat enough so I shall

bake her a cake when she is better and can eat it. Walter from the farm brought us some duck eggs yesterday and I suppose they would do better than dried egg. Anyway, I felt so anxious at break that I plucked up my courage and went to HM and *actually asked him* if I could go in the dinner hour to see if she were all right – I could have easily slipped there on the bus and been back for afternoon school. He glared at me. 'Certainly not! Nobody leaves this school during the dinner hour. What was I thinking of?' etc., etc. Next time I shall just go without permission. I went to the shops after school and did what she asked me. I do hope she'll be better tomorrow. I have kissed the note and put it under my pillow.

Feb 15th

The days are getting a bit longer. On the bus this afternoon she said with a really pathetic look: 'Sometimes I think Ma sent you.' I did not know what to think. I was overjoyed for I feel she has accepted my love. But I do not believe in an after life. I stared and didn't say anything. I would like to have squeezed her hand. When she got off the bus I looked at her as she crossed the road to her lonely lodgings. I just ached to help her, comfort her. I want to serve her and sacrifice for her, and protect her. I feel so strongly that I want to protect her and yet I am only young and I feel so frustrated sometimes, especially when I am treated like a child by others.

March 3rd

Today being Saturday I went to her lodge with a cake I'd baked and found her sitting darning her stockings, listening to her wireless. She was touched I'd baked it for her. She was sitting on a little buffet stool with one bar of an electric fire on. She was surprised to see me, I think, but I did not overstay my welcome as everybody thought I was at the Sunday School concert. The lodge is very dark and chilly.

March 17 1945

Such a scene there was today! I was at the same time ecstatic but also almost terrified. I had accompanied Miss C on her shopping yesterday after school as usual – some facial unguent at the chemists and then we went to see about her electric blanket which had gone wrong. But today after dinner I was in the Library as it was raining, and she came in. There was nobody else there. 'I wanted to see you, Hero,' she said, and I waited. She was looking out of the window and she began in a quiet voice to me. 'You must not follow me round the way you do.' I was horrified and upset and I was trembling and my throat went absolutely dry. I wondered though if this was HM's doing. She was silhouetted against the long window and her voice was very low as though she had rehearsed it. It did not sound convincing to me. I burst out with – 'But I *love* you!' I have never dared to say it to her before. She looked at me, and she said, 'I know you do,' in quite an ordinary voice. I was suddenly filled with the bliss of being recognised and a name given to my feelings which I *knew* she had accepted. 'You can't stop me loving you – even if I did as you ask,' I said. I was just burning with a mixture of adoration and apprehension and I had to hold the table to keep steady. When I looked up at her again after a silence she said: 'You have your parents – all your family – you don't need me as well!'

But her words did not fool me. What had my family to do with it?

'I bring bad luck to people who love me,' she said. I saw that there were tears, actual *tears*, in her eyes. My throat was still parched and she turned back to the window. I burst out with: 'Do *you* want me to leave you?'

She turned round and said: 'I shan't ask you again.' I did not know what to make of that. I was excited and amazed and delighted for I knew she had accepted me. I felt HM was at the bottom of it all. Miss C was actually acknowledging my love for her.

'I do love you so,' I said again, and she just said: 'Yes – '. I felt very strange. 'How could I "promise" to stop loving you?' I went on. 'Even if I said it, it would not be true. I can't help it. It's something bigger than me,' I said. I know it sounded corny, but it was true. I spoke at random trying to convince her and what I wanted to do was to take her in my arms and kiss her and look after her for ever. Then she said: 'Well, I've *asked* you.' She did not say *she* wanted me to stop. She knew it would ring false! So I said 'Then you will let me go on loving you – you won't stop me?'

She just looked at me again, saying nothing, and then the bell went for afternoon school. I ran back upstairs to our classroom. I have never before been part of a 'scene' like that. It it is only four months since I fell in love. She had asked me in a sort of mechanical way to stop, but she had not forbidden me to love her. I was still shaking with emotion until half way through the afternoon and by degrees my heart stopped thumping. I had promised nothing and now she was certain I loved her, so the 'victory' was mine, wasn't it?

I know that word love will now lie between us whatever happens. I know I am selfish for I often think it is only I who can make her happy, whereas if I truly loved her I'd be glad others did too. It is a puzzle. Sometimes when I think about her before I go to sleep, I imagine all sorts of ways of 'saving' her, I even imagine her ill so I can tend her. Yet I know that They wouldn't let me. I am not a child though. I'm as grown up as I'll ever be and these feelings are the strongest I've ever had. All I want is to be accepted.

March 31 Saturday

Holidays have begun. On Tuesday I spoke in the debate "Away with Convention" and HM looked furious. Miss C was not there. She has asked me just to call her 'C', wouldn't tell me her Christian name. But Linda Johnson was in HM's study on Wednesday and saw her signature and her name is Maud! – Maud Livingstone Gray Crichton. I will not let her know I know, as I do not like the name Maud, and I'm sure she does not either. She always calls me Hero now.

15th April

Yesterday was the best day of my life so far. I had a letter from her on Thursday asking if I would like to go to the cinema in Woolsford with her. She told me to tell my parents where I was going. Fortunately they raised no objection, though I've heard them muttering about my 'unsuitable' feelings when they have not thought I could hear them. I don't blame them really – or HM – for I know that by the standards of 'The World' I have very 'unsuitable' feelings. But *I* know that my feelings are good ones, not wicked ones, and I also know that *I* started all this, whatever they think.

It was so exciting to meet her in her fur coat and to go into the Odeon. School seemed far away and there were just the two of us in the darkness. After a bit she took off her gloves – I was not wearing gloves. Then she took my hand. I could hardly believe it. My hand lay in hers all the time and I leaned my cheek against her fur coat. She took her spectacles off too and so I could just catch a glimpse of her face without them – most intriguing. She is even more beautiful without them, though I received only a sideways view. The film, was from a du Maurier novel, not the sort of thing I like – the women are always so soppy! But *she* seemed to enjoy it. I was too moved and excited to take much of it in.

When we came out of the cinema, which she calls the 'flicks', I wished I could hold her hand again, but I am always very careful not to do anything unless she asks me or does it first.

School on Monday once more. They say the war will soon be over. Perhaps she will be able to go back to Germany then. She gives the impression she was happy there. John W calls her 'The Beautiful Spy'.

22 April

Went to Woolsford with Father. It hardly seems the same place as the city I went to with Miss C, whom I am now going to call Helena. I think it suits her, and Helen was the most beautiful woman in the world. We went buying books. Next to love, I think spending time browsing in bookshops is my favourite thing in the world! Coming back in the train we went through all the awful, smelly part near the iron works. Shall I ever get away to live in a beautiful place? In the evening Mother had arranged for me to go to the dressmaker's to be fitted for a blue dress. I'm not very interested in clothes – Helena is, though. She takes such care of her things. At the dressmaker's I thought about writing a story about fat Mrs Wilson who makes our dresses. She has quite a pleasant smell about her – well-scrubbed, but she is so fat she has to lever herself down on the floor to pin the hems. She keeps the pins in her mouth and is always breathless. I dare not talk to her in case she swallows the pins. When she does speak her voice is gruff.

Helena knits a lot, I've discovered. I know such a lot about her now, more than anyone else at school does, I'm sure, even other teachers.

HELENA'S SAYINGS

'If you listen you might learn a thing or two.'
'Great ideas are always simple.'
'You're still wet behind the ears.'
'What a crop of howlers!'
'Pearls of wisdom.'
'She's bone from the neck up.'
'As my grandfather used to say.'
'Put your thinking cap on.'
'You canna make a silk purse out of a sow's ear.'
'Put your skates on.'
'The cat's Pyjamas.'
'Possess your soul in patience.'

When I wrote to her in the holiday I told her that I had got a book from the library called *Brush Up Your German* and she said: 'Don't get your morals corrupted brushing it up!' when she wrote back to me. I love everything she says to me. I have put the two letters I've so far had from her in a special box.

I copied out the passage from the Book of Ruth tonight and learned it by heart: 'Intreat me not to leave thee'. I shall say it to her when I have a chance.

21st April 1945

I'm sure her birthday is about now because once when we asked her, she would not deny it was April and when we asked certain dates she would not answer around this week's dates. I've noticed she likes men more than women, on the whole, but disdains the wives of male members of staff.

We walked together to the bus-stop today in the sunshine, it was blissful. I wish time would stop when I am with her.

In the lesson today she had been talking about 'When we shall all be pushing up daisies.' I thought of her dead and hoped it would not be for many, many years. I remember she told us last term that she had always thought she would die young. I hope she is wrong. Yet death seems both sad and thrilling when I think of it.

May 8th

After school we were practising long jump in the field for Sports Day when the news came that the war was really over. I dashed down to the bus-stop as I'd seen her leaving the school. I caught her up and I gasped it out. I wanted to be the person who told her, for won't she remember one day in the distant future that it was I who told her? 'Now you'll be able to go back to Germany,' I said. 'Not my part – it's full of Russians,' she replied. We had a grand fire in the village elementary school field tonight to celebrate. It was like Guy Fawkes, which I haven't seen for over six years. I was a child in 1938 and now I am not.

Tue May 27

Back in school after half term. I am enjoying Conrad's *Youth* and the poetry we have in English, and the American history from Miss Lorimer. I hope to come first in everything but Geography and Geometry this term but I only really care about English and Art and languages.

Helena is so lonely and I love her so much and we are so often parted.

Mother has arranged for us all to go to the North Sea coast this summer and I shall buy Helena some jet earrings. I long to give her presents as much as do things for her. The way I feel does not get less but more, yet as I get to know her it is different. She drops hints now and again about her past life. I imagine she has had 'lovers', the way people here do not. She says she never wanted to marry and that 'babies spoil a woman's figure'. I'm not keen on babies, but I think they might be worth losing your waistline for. I said that and she looked at me quizzically.

She says I'm one of the best pupils she's ever had. I don't think I'm swollen-headed about my school work because I know it isn't really difficult. I wrote several poems to Helena in the holidays and I gave her some of them. She liked the one about the moon 'shrouded in cream-coloured veils'. I ended it saying 'Never say Goodbye', and I think she liked that.

Today she said she once had a friend of whom I reminded her. 'She ruined her life for love,' she said. She loves giving nicknames to people. She had another man friend she called 'Moltke', she told me, and said I should look the name up. I gather he was a soldier.

June 13th 1945

I am very busy again for we have exams in all nine subjects. I was so glad that I won my heat at Sports Day for she was there waiting near the tape. I'd like to have thrown myself into her arms. I did it only for her.

I know a lot now about Helena. She said something mysterious the other day about women who don't understand their husbands' needs. I wondered what she meant. She also has mentioned, with a sort of secret smile, a jeweller in Woolsford – I wonder if he gave her those new silver earrings? I am not jealous of men. She can be very mysterious though. I love that silver bangle she wears, and the little green ring.

July 27th

Term has ended. How shall I bear the days without her? But I shall write to her and I hope she will reply.

August 20th

I had the most wonderful letter from her today, the longest she's ever written to me. In it she said she had dreamed of me, which she said was unusual for she does not dream very often. I was doing something to her that shocked her so much she woke up! I wonder what it was? She says I am a young 'baggage', which is not very complimentary, I suppose. But now I seem to have known her for years even if it's mostly walking down from school with her, and carrying her bags for her at the end of every lesson, and the occasional times we are together in the holidays, or if I visit the Lodge. I think she is quite fond of me. She is a very passive sort of person, I think, not at all like me, *au fond*, as the French say. She dislikes French.

294

Helena is very 'canny', a word she uses a lot, and a critical sort of woman, not like me. But she does listen to me and does not tease me too much. She is mad about Greta Garbo so I got a book from the library with pictures of that film star. I think she looks a bit like her, especially the lips.

Shelley is my favourite poet. He was quoted in the best novel I've ever read, Charles Morgan's *The Fountain*: 'He has outsoared the shadow of our night'. I urged Helena to read it and she lent me some of the novels she gets from her Book Club for the holidays.

She is inscrutable, I think – which makes me even more anxious to understand her. I have learned the Greek word 'Pothos' from her. She said it was the same word for Suffering as for Love. Her favourite name is Clodia.

August 27th

Only two weeks now to the end of the holidays. I've enjoyed the time at the sea. I shall be fifteen at the end of the year and School Certificate work will take up much of my time when I'd much rather be reading. Dorothy came for tea and we talked about our ambitions. We get on very well and we both want to go to university. Mother said I might invite 'that teacher of yours' for tea but I don't think Helena will accept.

NEW JOURNAL

Dec 25th 1945

I wrote a lot of my new story tonight. I have finished my old journal and started this new one. Every school day something interesting will happen, I know, but I may not have time to write it all down.

So many things make me feel angry. Pictures of 'High Life' in glossy magazines, for example. And the attitude to marriage. I am a feminist, but I also believe in Romantic Love – *not* the domestic sort. I hate conventions.

I had my 15th birthday earlier this month and then the exams began. I have done well. We gave a pantomime at school and had a Christmas Party and Carol Service. The party and carol service were lovely and Helena came to the first in a long black skirt and silver earrings and *short* sleeves. I had never before seen her arms as she always wear those long-sleeved wool jumpers. Eileen is giving a party on the 28th and then I am going to London for a week, my first visit, to stay with Mother's friend. May Helena have a Happy New Year.

May 1946

I have had no time to keep up my journal, except for short entries about the books I read, and yet so much has happened since I last wrote. I seem to change and feel different and new, all the time. I shall be awfully glad in September when at last I'm in the sixth form. I have loved Helena now for eighteen months. I hope I have grown up a bit, for I was so naïve when I fell in love. I've discovered that the lovely scent she wears is Gardenia. I think whenever I smell it in my future life it will bring her back. I wish she would give me a photograph of herself. She says she's never liked having her photo taken.

She has had little things wrong with her – her ears had to be syringed, and drops put in her eyes, and then she had an infection on her finger that went all green. And she often has this indigestion. She hates cooking, she says, and the only thing she likes to eat is fish which she steams in milk. This last winter she knitted what she called her 'winter sock trousseau' in angora wool. When I went to the lodge in September I did not know it would be the last time before she was turfed out by the man she calls The Returning Warrior, Sir Francis's gardener whose home it is. I often tidied the garden and left apples on her doorstep last year and I shall miss going there. She is temporarily in a horrible Gothicky house near the town station.

She writes to me only in German now so nobody else can read her letters. I suppose it's good for my language, though it is sometimes hard to understand.

Helena added to her Words of Wisdom when she said about Miss Dundas (when she came back to visit the staff) that you 'could cut her accent with a knife'. I was amused, though I did not tell her, because *she* has an accent too, though I can recognise the difference between Glaswegian and Helena's. She goes on calling the Germans 'Jerry' and she's been reading

296

a lot of German novels recently. She says – 'Only a certain sort of Jerry can think up these things', when she finds them unpleasant. They have very weird plots, I must say. Sometimes she describes them to me. She is very clever, but not truly a 'literary' person.

The other day I was waiting for her to go downstairs with her bag at the end of the day and she said something about how she could teach me so much. 'You could begin where I left off,' she said. 'What a pity it is that people can't learn from the experience of others.' And I wondered, where did she 'leave off'? And what suddenly made her say that? Was it about love? She's contemptuous of other people's opinions and says '*Dicunt. Quid dicunt? Dicant*,' which I've copied into my commonplace book.

I had to read in Assembly last week. It was *Ode to Autumn* and she said, when she came into the classroom for the first lesson, 'I couldna have read it better myself,' which was, I realised, the highest praise.

Sometimes I wonder how *she* sees *me*. We are very different kinds of people. I'd never be so well-turned out as Helena (or as beautiful) or so sure about my own opinions (even if I sound it). I still get very angry about the way women are treated by men – all the injustices, – but I don't think that she does. I was told by Mr Dixon that he once read aloud in the Master's Room my essay last year 'If only I were a boy' and they all had a good laugh! Then the other day I was going through the swing doors from the quad and a young master came behind me and said 'I don't suppose *you'll* allow me to open the door for you since you are a Feminist?' I don't see what being a feminist has to do with opening doors for people, for if he had been carrying a pile of books as I was I'd have held the door open for him.

I must get on with my exercise on the sequence of tenses for Latin composition. When shall I be able to address my journal again in all this busyness and work?

May 30th 1946

Another 'scene', this time with HM. I cannot really blame him. But I felt embarrassed because I know I've read more about 'adolescent psychology' than he has! Even if all these psychologists said I was wicked and immoral or it was 'just a crush', I know it is not. The Church is worse about love between people of the same sex, and all the books I can find say that this kind of love is 'immoral'. It is not.

Friday May 31st 1946

It has not been a good week for me. Today I had the bombshell from Helena that if I persisted in going to France with the party arranged by Miss Smith, that would be the end of our relationship. I don't understand why she is so against France, but I know that Miss S hates her and I'm sure that she was behind HM's nasty words to me yesterday. He told me to 'behave myself' and to stop being 'too friendly' with a member of staff. I wonder whether Helena knows about it? I don't expect he's told her, and I shan't. Meanwhile I shall have to give up a holiday in France to keep H. I was really looking forward to going abroad for the first time. If only I were twenty one and free. I don't want school to contact my parents – which HM threatened to do if I did not 'mend my ways'. I could not tell HM I *loved* Helena – he would think that was disgusting. So long as I can keep a gulf between home and school and let it simmer down . . . It makes me feel so alone to have to fight Authority, because I know I am not 'wicked'. But even if it were wicked in the eyes of the world, I would not stop. For relief I go to Shakespeare's sonnets. I am also very busy with School Cert as I want to do well in everything. I'm sure that HM does not want to lose me as he thinks I shall bring the school academic glory. My love for Helena is above all this pettiness.

June 3rd Monday

I was thinking today as we were supposed to be revising biology, that I have discovered that falling in love, means that the quality of your attention changes in the presence of only one particular person. I did not 'decide' to have that special quality of attention for Helena, but I did realise very soon that it was called 'falling in love'. Everything connected with her was magical and so I was able also to attend specially to the things she taught as well. When I look back at the beginning of learning German and remember that day we were reading *'Ich weiss nicht was soll es bedeuten*' and she asked me to translate it, I feel that the words and even the shape of the Gothic letters, are magic, glamorous. I wish I could feel this about all my subjects. I am able to concentrate especially on the things she teaches because they seem part of her. I wish I could express myself better. I know I am very ignorant in spite of being good at school work. I am sure there are thousands of people who are a lot cleverer than I am, which is a sort of comfort.

Helena once said to me that I 'did not want to miss anything', and it's true. I just want to feel and experience *everything*, but I have to be very determined to go against School authority, and perhaps hurt other people close to me – will do it if necessary because I love her. I know at the bottom of my heart that she should not have asked me to give up France, but a sacrifice is worth it if I continue to be the person she most relies on. I try sometimes to see her as apart from the person I love and can manage it only occasionally. She makes all the class laugh sometimes – not that many are left for Latin, and fewer for German. It must be so boring to have to teach idiots. No wonder she is often sad and tired, as she said to me in her letter at Easter. It was the letter she described her feelings about the sea after I had gone on about Whitby. 'It is cruel as the grave,' she wrote, 'but I was brought up beside it.'

She says she is going to Switzerland in the summer holidays. I wonder whether she is going to see that German she told me about who wrote to her in January, – 'Molte' – who said he had never forgotten her. I remember I asked her if he was married and she said he was, and stupidly I said, 'Oh, you must not let him love you if he is married,' and she laughed and said, 'What a good girl you are, Hero!'

15 June
Lovely weather. Dorothy and I walked back from the swimming baths together. She said to me 'You love Miss Crichton the way a man loves a woman, don't you?' I said 'Yes,' and she did not say any more. But she is perceptive and does not judge me.

16 June
I talked a bit about Thackeray to Helena after school today

when I helped her shop, now that she is in the new digs and does not go on my bus any more. She said her favourite novel was *Vanity Fair*. Curious, because I've never been able to get into it. She says Becky Sharp is her favourite character in fiction. I prefer Jane Eyre. I wonder what would happen if Becky and Jane met, especially as Becky is a generation older than Jane. If Helena is my Mr Rochester, am I *her* Rawdon Crawley? I've never felt I belonged in a melodrama, though I think Helena does. I feel sometimes I've strayed into one. I think I belong to tragi-comedy, like a Tchekov play! I had the idea that Becky and Jane would meet in a Tchekovian play in a 'pistol-shot of love'. Helena does not really influence me in my *mind*. It is only in my feelings. I have modelled myself on her, I know, though my handwriting could never be so tiny and tidy. I am interested in things she is not truly interested in, like Virginia Woolf and Romantic poetry. I wish I had a platonic friend, perhaps a man, to whom I could talk about thoughts rather than feelings. Especially about ideas. Someone much wiser than me. I wouldn't want him to love me, just have the same sort of *mind*.

July 6th
Exams are over, thank goodness, and now I can read to my heart's content. As I am not going abroad I shall make the most of the holiday. He is preparing passports and things to go to Switzerland.

July 7th
Helena reported a conversation she had had with Miss Smith today. Apparently Miss S said to her 'Milly Hargreaves is just the sort of girl to have a crush on a mistress.' Helena looked at me ironically as she said this. I said after a moment, 'Well, I suppose I am!' But it is still not a 'crush', even if it may have been at first. It is a *grande passion*. I don't know why Helena thought it worthwhile to report this. They must have been having some argument. Thank God Miss S is to leave at the end of term. She must be about eighty. Miss Lorimer would have understood me, I think. Perhaps Miss S meant to hurt Helena, implying it didn't matter who the person *was*, a

person like me would just pick on anybody to fall in love with. But I know that Helena is not an ordinary woman and that is why I don't love her in an 'ordinary' way. I *am* the sort of person to fall in love 'unsuitably', but it matters that it is with Helena that I am in love. I often wonder what would have happened if she had never accepted my adoration. Would I have fallen in love with someone else? I can't believe that.

18th July

What a strange thing I was asked today by Helena! I can scarcely believe it. I know that she is now trying for another job; she is often alone writing in her form room, away from the others. I knew that she had been away for an interview after half term and must also have gone somewhere last weekend. She returned by train, she said, in the evening. Then she said in a roundabout way that she was left alone with a business man before he got out at Calderbrigg. I waited, unsure what she was driving at. Then she said, would I go to Calderbrigg this afternoon after school – she told me how to get there – and put an advertisement in their local newspaper to the effect that she wanted the gentleman who had met The Lady in Black that night to communicate with a box number as she had something to ask him.

'What have you to ask him?' I demanded.

She paused for a moment, then raised her eyes. 'He has an item of ma clothing,' she said finally. I must have gaped at her, for she laughed. 'Can't you guess what?' she asked me.

I knew what she wanted me to say but my mind refused to contemplate it. And in any case the whole thing seemed to me to be out of character. Was it a test of my devotion? How could Helena, who still refuses to dance with anyone because she 'can't bear to be touched', divest herself of intimate items of underwear for a stranger? Apparently the man lives in Calderbrigg. I thought the mission ridiculous. They do not put personal announcements in their paper and Ladies in Black are, I am sure, not welcome in their columns.

But I did as I was asked, as I always do, tramped to the road at the top of the moor where a bus to Calderbrigg stops, and entered the newspaper office with my absurd message. The woman at the counter looked at me suspiciously as I described

301

the 'friend' who wanted to get in touch with a man she had met on a train. I had not, of course, to give Helena's name and address, but my own! The woman read the Lady in Black bit with a sour face. She looked up at me again. I did not look like a practical joker, I'm sure, in my sober school uniform with two long plaits and a worried expression. Perhaps she thought I was doing it for a dare. In any case the notice was refused, though I proffered Helena's money to pay for it. 'We don't print anonymous messages,' she said. 'Tell whoever it is to put her proper name and then we might consider it.'

'I think she lost her . . . handbag,' I extemporised.

'Well in that case she won't be getting it back.'

I left the office thankfully: at least I have *tried*. What am I to make of all this?

July 19th

I rather crossly reported the outcome to Helena. She is such a mystery. I could not confess to anyone but my diary that I cannot always approve of her, but it is fascinating to imagine what happened, though incredible.

20th July

I am so angry and indignant still about the position of women in our society. But I think I am also a Platonist (as far as I have read) and how can you be both a Platonist and a Feminist? It is a problem.

Helena said recently that her favourite quotation from the Bible was *Vanitas Vanitatum* (Ecclesiastes). I think sometimes about her lovers – I feel sure she had some. Everybody is still singing *Lili Marlene* and I managed to get the German words. The '*verliebter Mund*' is hers.

I remember last year, before the war finished, she was very sardonic about the factory workers who pushed on to the bus screaming 'Workers First'. 'What do they think *I* do?' she said. Yet she is not a middle class sort of person, in a funny way. When she wants to talk about a man and a woman being intimate she calls them being 'matey'.

But how can you understand someone who sent me on that errand to Calderbrigg and also used to let the boys see her

302

underwear when she sat on the desk (she favours silk underwear, she told me), but who will not (she says) knit on a Sunday? I no longer go to church and I don't think she does either. She reads *Vogue* every month, just loves clothes and is at present knitting some mauve socks which she spells sox.

July 26th

The last day of term. I decided to say 'Goodbye' to Miss Smith, to sort of say 'Bygones will be Bygones'. I wish I had not, for she said, 'I hope you will mend your ways – you know to what I am referring,' and I just could not speak, I was so embarrassed. I shook hands and fled. I hope Helena does not know I tried to be polite to Miss S, but I fear Miss S will tell her and hint I am 'repentant'. I was stupid to say Goodbye. Helena will not tell me if she has yet got another post, but cannot have, for we went down to the stockroom yesterday for the new texts for next term's study and she has given us for the Sixth Form a German story called *Tonio Kröger* by Thomas Mann which looks very difficult. I have decided to do English Literature, French (!) German and Latin for the Public Exam in two years' time.

I wanted to walk H to her lodgings but she refused, saying she was busy. So now I have six weeks not knowing if she is cross with me or why. I will write to her to ask if she would like some more earrings from Whitby. Why should she be angry when she knows I gave up my own holiday? It must be because I foolishly shook hands with Miss Smith, her deadly enemy.

Aug 7th

She wrote to me in German, posted in London on her way to Basel saying she did not want any more earrings.

She called me Sie instead of Du. I still have the other letters, one of which she started 'Hero, *mein Liebling*'. I hope when she returns that she will be nicer to me for I never stop loving her in spite of everything. I remember how humble she sounded when I said she ought to be teaching in a university and asked her why she was not. 'There was only the one post when I qualified,' she said. 'It was also open to men and a man got it. I didna mind that.' I thought she should have minded. I would have done. I tried to find out about her doctorate and what it was about, but she clammed up. I suppose he just gave up trying, having been rejected once.

I know *so much* about her – and yet *so little*. I just could not ask her more personal things like, was she ever in love? She always says, when talking of love, that love is what she had from her mother and she quoted that piece from *The Song of Solomon* which I've put in my commonplace book, that begins 'Love is as strong as death . . .' I think she is *still* mourning her mother. She once said to me: 'I thought Ma had sent you.' I do not think Helena is a complicated person if you could only find the key to unlock her. She is a bit cynical and pessimistic and I think rather superstitious, but that only makes her more dear to me.

Even a girl in the Upper Sixth, whom I did not know, said to me last Christmas that she had a marvellous figure. I hoard things other people say about her. I know that some of my feelings for her are also mixed up with physical desire. But love is more important than sex. Sometimes I have this feeling that Helena has cut herself off from the sort of thing D H Lawrence would call 'nurturing roots', that the sap stopped flowing upwards; that is why she needs someone to look after her, and I want that person to be myself.

August 27th
Back from Whitby. I had a marvellous time wandering about with Anne and we got up and saw the fishing boats come in at dawn from the jetty. Anne sketched them. I thought a lot about Helena. How I wished she were there with me, especially at sunset with the riders on the sands and the smell of the sea and that music from the pier. When I think of my life so far I see it as BH and AH – before and after Helena. Yet I have been having a lot of other thoughts too about Life. I wrote several poems recently.

28th August
I walked down Blackholme Road this afternoon by No. 62 just to see if she were back, though I did not ring at the door. There was no sign so I went to the Library where I read the fulminations of Dean Inge on 'Homosexuals'. How many times have I waited

304

for her since March on that road further up near the school! Just waiting for her to appear has always been an ever-present joy. Perhaps if she comes round next term she will let me see her new rooms. Thank goodness she's now left that awful Gothicky house with pointed turrets.

Dorothy is back from France and just *full* of it. I envy her, yet I have had a very good summer, for I've read and thought a lot. There seemed to be so much time – I suppose because I could not see Helena.

August 31st

I read in some book of French sayings that 'It would be impossible to love anyone or anything one knew completely'. If that is true, it means you can't go on being 'in love' with a person you know well?

September 9th

I did not put my School Cert results here before as they seem rather irrelevant. Thank goodness I can now drop geography, maths and biology.

Helena is back! She looks tired and not all that well, but there she was in the classroom when I came in for my first Sixth Form Latin lesson. I had forgotten how beautiful she is. Afterwards I asked her 'How was Switzerland?' but she did not reply. I think she is still cross about something, but I hope to win her round. They are thinking of putting on a school play, the first since the war, as there are so many good actors in the Sixth Form. I hope I shall be chosen.

In the choir we are singing *My Love Dwelt in a Northern Land*. I imagine the moors behind the coast where we were in August and that I meet Helena there and we walk on that northern shore in the twilight. How exciting and yet how mournful these thoughts are!

Languages are now much harder work and I shall be busy. I watched her as we started *Tonio Kröger*, which I read in English in the holidays and absolutely adored. It could have been written for me! I don't think Helena really likes it. The relationship between Tonio and his friend Hans is like the one between us, except for the ages and the sex of the characters.

305

Her eyes are heavy-lidded now and her face is a bit thinner,
I think. But her skin is still white, her neck long and the
shape of the mouth is perfect. I wonder if anyone has kissed
it this summer. Her ears are like rosy shells and she has some
new earrings. I was sad she did not want any more jet ones
from me.

30th September

A year or two ago Miss Derwent confiscated my picture of the
four daughters of the Tsar which I cut out of an old annual
of my mother's. Where is that picture now? They were so
beautiful and doomed. Like Helena is, I still think, beautiful,
and maybe doomed. I was thinking last week when I went down
to Woolsford to the big library and browsed in the bookshop to
see what I wanted for my school prizes, that when I first fell in
love it was like a tune played on one line by a recorder that
suddenly broke out into arpeggios and chords and then a full
orchestra playing.

I think Helena is coming round, as she accepted my help with
the shopping on Thursday. I told her my feelings about Free
Love, and she smiled. I feel all this fuss about 'pre-marital sex'
is misplaced. Boys are so unromantic. It *is* what the Frenchman
says – one can love a mystery, an enigma, a beautiful person
who is just a bit remote. Yet I still want to know Helena better
– shall I ever?

October 5th: Description of a Latin lesson with MC

We were attempting to translate from the fourth book of the
Aeneid, without much success. I found it hard going. I'd read an
English crib last week but honour insisted I made no reference
to it and in any case knowing the story helps only a little. He
makes no *drama* out of it and seems to take little pleasure
in the process of rendering into English what to her must be
elementary stuff. If I were teaching it I'd read the Latin aloud
with 'expression' to make us guess the meaning. What is the use
of treating Virgil – or Vergil, as Miss Crichton prefers to spell it
– as though he wrote in order to persecute schoolchildren with
linguistic conundrums?

'Translate, Hero,' Miss Crichton ordered me.

'Accept then this spirit of mine and dissolve my cares,' I began –

'Where do you find "then" there?' Helena enquired sharply.

'I thought it sounded better,' I replied. But a literal translation is what she always wants.

'I have lived and I have come to the end of my earthly course – which fate has given me – ' I went on.

'Parse it.' I quailed before her intellect. I did my best, and the lesson went on, and Dido having tried, as I know from Shakespeare, to waft her love to come again to Carthage, was now preparing to immolate herself for his sake. The bell rang before we could get to the funeral pyre. Bells are a dratted nuisance always interrupting you just when you've got into a lesson and are making some progress.

I went up to Helena. She was dropping her text books and the class homework exercises into her big bag, and I waited until this was done, and then stooped to carry the bag out and away to the mistresses' staff-room for her as usual, walking behind my love, who sailed along, head high, her gown giving her the grace and dignity of a small galleon. No words were exchanged between us, it was enough that she consented to receive my help. When I handed the bag over, my hand brushed lightly against her polished nails and smooth palm. She looked me full in the face as she turned into the room. The look said: 'I accept your service, Hero, but a conversation will depend on my mood.' I went away. No more lessons with her now till Monday; a desert of longing stretches ahead till we are inevitably together once more. I think I'll write a poem about Dido and put into it all my longing and love.

October 10

I shall be sixteen in two months and so much has happened to me since I was fourteen. I know that Helena is still trying to find another post. I think I am in favour again. Indeed, I know I am. But yesterday, when I was going off to my bus – we had been shopping together and she was going to walk back to No. 62 – she said: 'You'll forget me, Hero – you'll go to Oxford and you'll forget me!' 'How could I forget you?' I cried. 'I know I never shall.' But she looked at me a bit sadly and cynically and

307

I said again: 'Whatever happens to me I shall never forget you, Miss Crichton.' I wish I could call her Helena – she still does not know I call her that to myself. It was windy and cold and soon we would be parted again, but I felt that I would remember that remark of hers.

Saturday Nov 23rd 1946

It has happened. At last it has happened. I have loved her for two whole years and at last have had the courage to kiss her. It was our school winter party, all lit up everywhere, the Assembly Hall transformed into a dance floor. Tables were laid down the corridors, and the Hall and corridors decorated. A Christmas tree stood, as it did last year, at the far end of the hall, and the music of Veletas, Military Two Steps, Foxtrots and Quick-steps whipped up our senses. Supper was laid all the length of the top corridor. The principal excitement was in seeing the staff emerge in their finery as human beings.

The girls were allowed a Ladies' Choice, and all of us a last valse when lights were dimmed. No strong drink of course, or cigarettes. The younger men and women staff danced together; the older ones took a few stately turns round the floor and then sat down to talk. All was most decorous. Helena would never dance, I knew, even with me. I asked her last Christmas and she refused. She always comes late, to make an entrance.

A little knot of pupils formed round her when she came in and I waited until she was alone. She was wearing a little coatee of white angora, leaving her arms bare from below the elbow, only the second time I had seen them thus. New silver earrings swung from her lobes and her skirt was long and black. No concession over the hair – still swept up, scraped back. She had put on her gardenia scent and I think she had applied lip salve. I could not see her shoes. I edged near her when the next dance began and she had once more refused the importunities of a Sixth Form boy. I tried once again:

'Will you dance with *me* then?'

'You know, Hero, I never dance.'

She seemed remote. I stayed by her side even so. The girls' party dresses swept by and the lights were low. I thought, it is enough that she has come; she is here and I am near her again.

308

I wanted just to stay by her side and smell that scent of gardenia and look at her arms. We talked a little until I was swept off unwillingly by Trevor and did my best to follow the steps. I hoped she was watching me as I attempted to give a slight dramatisation of the indifference I felt. I know HM was.

When the lights were dimmed for the last valse, I saw her disappear through the big oak doors and took my chance. Even HM was dancing. Fortunately no one asked me for this one, the romantic one. I knew that I must follow her, thought even that she would guess I might. Though she had not seen me looking at her as she disappeared, she knows that I am always aware of her every movement.

I slid out of the doors a few moments later and no one noticed me. I walked along the familiar corridor with its parquet floor and turned up the girls' stairs. Everything now was dark except for a faint glow when I rounded the stairs near the Mistresses' Room at the top. I could hear the slow music from the hall. I knew she would be there, and she was; hovering in the dark doorway as I came up and round towards her. She said nothing as I approached and without a word I took her in my arms. Of course she had known I would come . . . of course. Now I am almost the same height as her and it felt like a recognition of a likeness and equality as she allowed me to kiss her. I shut my eyes as I did. Her lips were so soft, like moth's wings, and she faintly brushed them to and fro against mine until I finally opened my eyes. Hers were already open. Somehow I had not noticed that she had taken off her glasses.

'I love you so,' I said, my heart thudding against hers. Her little angora jacket was soft too. We drew apart and she looked at me. I was thinking, this is it – this is what I have wanted to do for over two years now, and at last I have dared. My arms were still around her. 'I would like to drink you in,' I said. I think there was the ghost of a smile on her lips.

'Satisfied?' she asked.

'Oh, I do love you,' was all I could repeat. Did I now want her to say that she loved me? I don't think so.

'Hero,' she said, 'they'll be coming back soon.'

'I knew you'd be waiting,' I said.

She smiled again in the dim light from the half closed door.

There was no one else about. What a strange place for my first kiss, the very first kiss of love I have ever given anyone! I was profoundly moved and excited. I wanted to go home with her and yet I also wanted to be alone, to savour the event, to remember her lips and the feel of them against mine – and to look forward to another. Later I saw her walk alone out of the school down the road to her new digs. I felt light-headed.

Dec 1st

Everything has been different since the dance.

I do wish that it had all happened earlier though I would not have dared when I was younger. It feels like a sort of responsibility. I feel our relationship will change. Before the term ends at Christmas I must kiss her again. I do wish I were older. I know that I am utterly responsible for what happened between us, whatever anyone else says about that, but also that I am very impetuous and rash. But there is nobody to ask and I have a whole secret life as well as the other life of thinking and reading and sometimes despairing over my lack of talent.

Dec 24th

Now it is Christmas Eve and I wonder where she will be – perhaps with the brother she told me about. Last week I kissed her again – in the stock cupboard, a snatched kiss. I felt guilty and excited and just grabbed at her and she did not resist. We were supposed to be sorting books and there was the danger of interruption. I feel more and more angry at the way people write about 'homosexuals'. I believe romantic love can happen between people of the same sex. When I am with my family I seem to be a different person.

Next week in the holidays we are to have first rehearsals for the school play and I have been asked to take one of the main parts. It is very cold and I helped Father shovel coal from the bunker into the coalplace near the door. It began to snow a bit too. Apparently there is a fuel crisis.

February 21st 1947

I enjoyed dressing up for the first scene of the play in black shoes with heels and long earrings and my hair piled up on top of my head. I suppose I did look rather like Helena, but hadn't really thought about it like that. I kissed her for the third time after the play. It happened like this: The dress rehearsal was performed in front of the school in the afternoon and when it was over I ran all the way from our dressing-room to find her. We were to give another performance in the evening; the afternoon audience had dispersed. I found her in one of the downstairs classrooms. In the doorway in the full light of the afternoon I flung myself at her, careless this time as to whoever might see, full of the intoxication of the stage. I had done it for *her* – not the dressing up, but the rôle, even the boring love scenes with my 'lover'. I wanted her to see me 'grown up', in charge of myself and of the part, the success of the play depending partly on the zest I could put into it. It was then she said: 'Well, they say that imitation is the sincerest form of flattery.'

Out of the corner of my eye I saw the producer, Mr Cooper, at the end of the corridor, staring at us for a moment. He made no gesture, turned away after a moment, and disappeared.

'Was I all right?' I asked Helena, still glowing from my prowess. She said nothing, only smiled once more.

March 11th 1947

I have now visited Helena's digs. She has some of her mother's furniture there and has two rooms on the first floor and a staircase leading from the landing to a space where she stores books and magazines. The first time, I sat in the sitting-room by the gas-fire on a pouffe and she sat near me in an armchair and we talked and then I stroked her hands, or just held them in mine. The second time she offered me a glass of wine from Morocco. I have never drunk wine before.

Monday 21st April 1947 – now back at school.

On Saturday I went to the town to look for her. She had asked me if I would like to visit Harrogate with her on Thursday but it was only at a day's notice and I could not because I had promised to go to tea with Mother's boring friends. So on Saturday I went looking for her in the shops. Finally I caught up with her as she was returning home past the Public Baths, a region of cobbled

311

grey streets, with the sound of a train hissing steam below us in the narrow gully where the town station is. It was bitterly cold and she was wearing her musquash coat.

'Let me come with you. Let me carry your things.'

'No. Go home, Hero. I'm tired. I don't want to talk to you.'

'Oh, please let me stay with you! Please. I've been so miserable.'

'If so, you know why.' I supposed it was because I did not accompany her last Thursday.

I was walking by her side as this was going on; I was not going to give up. I had done nothing wrong and I so missed her when there was no school.

We stood outside her door. I stopped begging. 'If you don't want to let me come in with you, I'll go. But I want to kiss you first. I *love* you – whatever I've done.' She looked at me coldly. I was angry and bold. No one seemed to be around. The house was as usual dark and quiet. I pounced on her, seized hold of her, of her deep scented furs, and flung myself around her neck, planting a long kiss on her cold mouth. She did not push me away, but neither did she return my kiss. I forced more kisses upon her and finally she put down her basket and said in a low voice: 'You must go now.' But she did not look angry, shaken rather. I was both triumphant and ashamed. I could not have believed I should ever act like that.

May 6th

I was allowed back to the house yesterday and she was really nice, though today she is angry again – I do not know why. Last week I bought my first pair of heels and wore lisle stockings. I was allowed by Mother to buy some suede brown lace-ups. Mother went with me in case I bought something "unsuitable". They are size five and I took them to school yesterday and when Helena said I could call in on my way home she said: 'Let me look at you.'

I stood by the window of her sitting-room near the table with the 'studio' portrait of her that she said was 'Ma's' and after a pause she said: 'Your legs are not bad – the shoes suit you.' This was high praise, I thought. Yet she did not say it as though she was a person whom I loved, but more as one woman to another.

312

There is, I am sure, just a quarter of a century between us. But I feel more like a mother to her.

June 24th

I have not been able to write in this journal for weeks and so much has happened. But I want to write about all this because I think it has been the most important thing in my life so far. A day or two after I wrote the above she was upset about something, though she had let me kiss her goodbye on May 5th. Then she said on the Wednesday, 'You know I am going away next term?' I was very surprised as she had not said anything about that for ages. But I said 'Why must you go?' And she said 'Why should I stay?' I could not answer that. The day after, I was out of favour again – maybe she feels that I am slipping away from her in some ways because my interests are not always hers – I don't know. Anyway it was during one of her cold moods when we returned to school on May 12th after the weekend. I hoped to find her friendlier, for her coldness made me wretched. In spite of all my other activities and interests, Helena still dominates my life.

'Didn't you know?' said Trevor who lives in the same road as her 'landlord' and whose parents know her as a neighbour. 'Didn't you know – she was taken ill yesterday night, rushed to hospital! They say she'll have to be operated on.' *Operated on*! I froze, went away quickly from the form room, dismayed and terrified. At break I sought Trevor out again.

'Which hospital? How do I get a visiting card?'

I should have known these things. What if she died and wished she had not been angry with me and I never saw her again? She should have called on *me*. It hurt me that I had not known. But I live three or four miles away so could not have known. Trevor gave me the details and added that her landlady would have information about visits. Alone in a hospital room, in pain, perhaps frightened, and no one familiar with her . . .

At dinner time I made a swift illegal sortie to her house, where the 'landlady' produced a visiting card, not seeming surprised to see me.

'There are two,' she said. 'Visiting only Wednesdays and Saturdays.'

'When will they operate?' I asked.

'Well, she went in yesterday and they'll do it today, I expect, if it hasn't been done already.'

'Oh,' I said, clutching the card.

'I must say she was in a bad way,' she added before shutting the door.

I tried not to let my imagination run riot. She was very ill. I would go to the Infirmary straight away, although it was Monday, not a Visitor's day. No one would stop me because I should tell no one except Dorothy. That afternoon there was to be an interminable 'rehearsal' for Sports Day next Saturday and fortunately I would not be missed. My running days are over! Now that I weigh over seven and a half stone I can't dart ahead of everybody in the hundred yards sprint.

I decided I would slip out, play truant after the register and go to the Infirmary in Woolsford. I did not stop to think, just disappeared at two o'clock. I had enough money with me to get there and return home afterwards – if I ever returned home. I wanted to burst out crying, but pulled myself together, took the bus and managed to arrive in Woolsford an hour later. I was not sure of the way, had to ask directions, all the time sure I would be late and she would be dead; I would never see her again.

It was a hot afternoon and the low walls around the hospital, and the flowers planted in beds behind them, blinded me with their glaring whites and oranges. Doors, entrances, notices were confusing, but I found my way to Enquiries. I felt I was in a waking nightmare.

'No visitors today unless it's an emergency,' said the woman behind the grille.

'Yes, it's an emergency – my friend is in for an operation. I have a visitor's card. They told me on the telephone I could come and check she was all right,' I lied quickly.

'Well – I suppose it wouldn't do any harm if you just went across to Women's Surgical – they could tell you, though you couldn't go on the ward,' she said, taking pity on me. 'What did you say the name was?'

I told her. She checked a list, looked up and went on, 'Just ask at the lobby on the left of Ward 10.'

If Helena was still on a list, she was alive. I ran down polished, quiet corridors that smelt of antiseptic and ether.

There were giant swing doors with circular 'portholes' when I finally reached Ward 10. I peered through them, could see only rows of beds with humped figures. I waited. Somebody must come soon whom I could ask. 'Oh, please God, don't let her die. Let me see her again.' My prayers were answered in a curious way.

I had waited several minutes when there was the squeak of wheels and round the corner there arrived several orderlies wheeling a trolley. On the trolley was a scarlet blanket. I shrank back against the wall and the trolley came slowly past me. One of the orderlies opened the door to let it through and I looked down at the blanket.

Under the blanket there was a woman, only the head visible. The eyes were closed, hair was streaming out across the low pillow; the face was flushed, unconscious.

Before I could even realise it, the trolley had gone through and as it disappeared I knew it had been her. I had arrived just in time to see her emerge from the operating theatre. Yes, I was sure that it had been her in the few seconds I had seen the figure – who else had long hair like that? Another part of my mind was too amazed to be sure. It seemed impossible that I had seen her as she had never seen herself, as though she were dead. But they would not wheel a dead person back into the ward.

A nursing sister went into the lobby and then came out again to me, asking 'What do you want?'

'I came to see Miss Crichton. She's in for an appendix operation.' I didn't say that I had just seen her; some reserve prevented me.

The sister did not refer to it either, but said: 'Well, you can leave a message. I believe she went down today. Are you her daughter?'

How odd, since I had said 'Miss'. I was not going to say she was my teacher either, but replied: 'No – she is a friend of mine. They gave me a visiting card.' I waved the talisman again. 'Will you please tell her when she comes back (I wanted to say "wakes up") that Milly has been and will come again next Visitors' Day – unless I can come before that?'

'Visitors' Days are Wednesday and Friday but if she's having her op today, Wednesday might be early.' She looked at me

315

incuriously, for which I was grateful. I was in my hated school uniform, untidy, still breathless with shock. 'Well, Friday then. Please tell her I came and that I'll come again on Friday.'

'All right, I will. What did you say your name was?'

'Milly,' I replied again. I could not say 'Hero'. Here in the hospital it sounded outlandish. I wanted to appear ordinary. Just a concerned visitor. What would they say? – 'A schoolgirl came to see you?'

'Well, you'd better go now. Visitors aren't allowed on Mondays, you know.' She smiled.

'Thank you – oh, thank you,' I blurted. I was loth to go when Helena was on the other side of that door, bandaged and bleeding, even far away in her own mind. Yet I had to leave. I cast one more look at the ward through the window and saw screens drawn round a bed in the middle. I felt choked with worry and misery, with love. Why could *I* not tend her? I felt they had taken away my love from me. I ran out of the hospital. If she were dying I did not care to live, I thought. I was almost run over as I reached the road – a car bonnet caught me lightly on the back and brought me to my senses.

When I arrived home I was not hungry. It was hot and flowery in the garden, peonies and lilac in bloom. I kept thinking of the blood-red blanket, but told no one about that.

Our garden was full of late lilac. I gathered great swags of it and took books too in a basket and went alone on the Friday evening to Woolsford. I did not know how I should be received. Would my message have been relayed to her? I did not write her a letter. I felt that to plead my case needed my presence. She had been cold and distant with me the days *before* she was taken ill. How would she receive me in a hospital bed?

I looked for her as I shifted the lilac from one arm to the other. She was in that bed in the centre where the screens had been on the Monday – It was a large ward and there were women on each side of her. One of them smiled at me as though she knew I would be coming.

Miss Crichton lay pale, propped up only a little, her arms outside the coverlet, palms downwards. I hesitated a moment, put the lilac on a table at the bottom of the bed, then advanced. Would she be angry? I stood there and I said, 'I had to come.'

She looked at me and said, quite softly, 'You should not have come.' Then she looked at me for a long time.

'I had to,' I said. 'I came before.'

'Yes – they told me. Sit down, Hero.'

She put out her hand and I leaned towards her and took it in my own. She crooked her little finger in mine so that we were linked through a small part of each. It was almost a defeated, certainly tender gesture. I looked at her and there were tears in her eyes.

After a silence I said, 'How are you?'

'I'll be glad to get out of here,' she said in a weak voice.

'When will you?'

'In another week. I was really ill, you know.'

'I brought you a book – and the flowers.'

She was silent, just lay looking at me. Then she turned her head towards the woman in the next bed, a middle-aged, fair-haired woman who was looking over at us with interest.

'You've got your friend here now, then, love,' shouted the woman.

Helena smiled. 'That's right.' She must have mentioned me to her!

'Has anyone else been to see you yet?'

'My brother. Other people may come on the other card my landlady has, you know.'

'Yes. I suppose so.' I looked at her again.

'*You* can fetch me back next week, Hero. I think they'll send me in an ambulance on the Saturday.'

I was moved, overjoyed, felt like crying myself. I loved her so much, in spite of everything. But I never told her I had seen her lying unconscious under the red blanket. It would have made her feel too vulnerable, as though I had an advantage. When I had to go, she said, 'Kiss me, Hero.' I was never so happy. I kissed her on the forehead and there were tears again in her eyes. Of weakness? Of sorrow? That kiss of all my kisses has meant the most to me.

My third visit to the Infirmary was on Saturday the 24th of May. I wrote instead of visiting her on the Wednesday, having an instinct to leave her alone to recover herself.

Helena was waiting, ready and dressed. She looked thinner, paler, and it was a visible effort for her to climb into the ambulance, refusing a stretcher or offers of help. We sat beside each other and, once underway, she said: 'I'm glad to be quit of that place.'

'You'll feel better once you're home.'

I had the whole afternoon and evening in front of me. I suppose it was the longest time we have ever spent together without the presence of a third party. I helped her out of the ambulance and I walked slowly up the path with her. The horse-chestnut trees were out and freshly green and there was a lightness and a scent of summer in the air. We took the stairs to her first floor slowly. I put her small case down and she sat down to rest.

Then, 'The first thing I shall do is have a bath and wash my hair. Get that hospital smell out of it,' she stated. 'You can help me.'

I ran a bath under the ancient geyser while she undressed in the bedroom.

'First the bath, then the hair,' she said and came into the bathroom dressed in a pale green cotton housecoat. She was carrying *Vogue*. She tested the water. 'Now you can sit on that stool and read this and be there in case I feel faint,' she said. 'You must promise not to look at me!'

I took the magazine and buried myself behind it, not taking in a word of it. I heard: 'That's better. Oh, how I needed this?' and calm, splashy sounds. I never looked up once from that accursed magazine. Though I turned the pages I could not read it. There she was a few feet away from me, naked, and I did not so much as glance at her, was careful to hide my face behind the magazine as though, if by accident I had glimpsed her, something would have been broken, some trust been ruined for ever. I knew she trusted me. But was it too a test? What would she have done if I had looked at her naked body in the water? She could have done nothing. She just knew that I would not. I am always to be trusted.

The towel had been laid neatly on a chair. I heard her step out of the bath and wrap herself in it.

'I shall get dry in my bedroom. Then you can help me wash my hair. I canna lift my arms very well – still weak.'

I put *Vogue* down when she had gone and ran a jug of warm water for her hair. She soon came in again, once more in the pale eau-de-Nil wrap. She looked younger, smaller somehow. Her hair was down her back. She took her spectacles off once again and put them on the window-sill. 'I feel much better for a bath,' she said. 'Now I'll bend my head over like this and here's the shampoo – wet my hair for me.'

She bent her white neck over the basin and I began to wet her long, brown hair. There were a few streaks of grey in it, but not too many. I did my best. I had never washed anyone's hair before. I was enjoying being a handmaiden. At least I could be of some use to her, I thought.

After she had dried her hair with my help, I ate a sandwich which I had brought with me and H boiled a kettle for tea, which we drank in her sitting-room.

'Will you now give me a photograph?' I asked – 'Like the one you have here on the table. It's lovely. *Please.*'

'I don't like giving photos away to people, Hero – but I might make an exception in your case,' she replied, looking at me over the rim of her cup. She gave me one, not identical with the one in the room, but very like it. I have put it in my treasure chest.

Afterwards, she weak, I strong, we sat together. I held her hand and we talked quietly for a long time. Her hair was drying down her back and she still wore the pale green cotton wrap which suited her so well and made her look like a person of my age.

'You can stay the night if you want,' she said.

More than anything in the world I wanted to stay with her that night, to hold her gently in my arms, nurse her, feel I could help her, feel at last grown up, accepted. But how could I? I had promised my father I'd be back at eight o'clock, I explained, ashamed.

'Can't you ring him up and ask to stay?'

'He wouldn't let me. They don't like my being with you.'

She was weak, tired, ill, and needed company. I should have asked her to speak to him, but it did not occur to me. What harm could come to a sixteen-year-old staying overnight with an invalid? Any embraces that night would have been in the nature only of tender loving care – they would not have been passionate. I had not even seen her naked in the bath, had not *wanted* to. But I would have been able at last to learn all I wished about her. I would have sat up with her or stayed by her bedside as she slept and stroked her forehead and held her hand if she were afraid or had bad dreams. I felt so close to her and I was not thinking about myself but about her. She had chosen me out of all her relations and friends and neighbours and pupils to take her home and look after her and I was about to desert her because I wanted no trouble at home, didn't want to upset my parents. I have never felt so strongly the indignity of being under age.

'You are sixteen, Hero. They can't do anything to you.'

'You don't understand. It's that I don't want to do anything to them.'

But there was still time together.

She told me many things about herself that afternoon and evening, treating me in fact as my parents do not, as the adult I most surely am by now. Young perhaps, but capable enough and loyal. I felt privileged too, liked her better than I had for a long time – and loved her even more with a sort of ache, a tenderness far removed from rapture.

'I bled like a pig before the op,' she said. '*You* know – I hadn't had it much recently, my age and all. But it came all of a sudden when I got to hospital. They didn't know what to do.'

I felt, we are both women. Do I wish I were not one?

Her confidence touched me, though I know she had not said it to touch me. She had tacitly accepted that I too had these problems, would know about them, though we had never mentioned such things before. As we talked, I was thinking – I have braved HM and Miss Smith and public opinion and a hospital hierarchy and hidden my feelings from my parents, but now for some reason I cannot insist to my father that I stay.

He telephoned me at half past eight. 'Where are you?' he asked (unnecessarily). 'We told you to be home by eight.'

'I'm coming soon. I'll be home by ten. There were things to do,' I replied.

When I put the receiver down and turned to see her standing

320

on the landing in her little green cotton housecoat, her hair still damp and down her back, I felt my heart would break with love. She came up to me and clung to me gently.

'Don't go. Don't go, Hero!' she begged.

'I have to go – I promised.'

We put our arms round each other. Her body was soft and light through the thin cotton, and warm. We stayed a long time like that.

'Oh, don't go, don't go,' she said again.

I stroked her hair, but I was sick at heart.

'You'll be all right now. I'll come on Monday. Please don't be cross. I'm torn between you and home. You know I love you.'

I knew that she thinking that if I truly loved her I would brave parental wrath. But I had a vision of my father coming to fetch me back, and an ignominious exit with him. That I could not have borne.

Even so, I should have stayed.

My last memory of that summer day – which was still not quite over, for the dusk came late and it was still light when I left – was of her face turned towards me, her hands dropped at her sides, defeated. I had failed her. I should have kept my arms round her, round the pale cotton wrap, and held and held her and watched over her for as long as I was needed.

Now we have only a month of term left and only a month of Helena being with us here. She is now back at work, though I don't think she is really better. Never after July shall I walk down that chestnut-fringed road with her or wait for her to appear in the distance or find her alone and cover her hands with kisses. Since she has returned to school she has been cold towards me and tried to either ignore me or criticise my work in class. I am holding back from her, the first time I have ever done this, because I know that I am not only being punished for not having had the courage to stay with her at the last moment that night, but also for her actual dependence on me. She is playing out some drama and there is nothing I can do about it. She will go away and I know that I have only to say the word and I could go with her. After three years this is what it has come to. She has made me feel paradoxically that I am the stronger of the two of us in the end. I have decided that I *shall* go to Paris on a course and that I shall also go to visit one of my French pen friends. She knows I shall go to Paris. She will have to pack up, move away, finish her convalescence, and start a new job before September. She needs a holiday. Will she go to Basel again? I'm sure she met a man there, but I have the feeling that she will not go to see him again.

July 23rd

I have glimpsed her in these last few days going in and out of school and I have not gone up to her or asked to help. I too have my pride. She can ask me if she needs me. Trevor and the others wanted to take a snapshot of her today and I would have liked to have them take her and me together, but there would have been something false about it.

I'm going to have to work for money this holiday and entertain Cécile – all this before I go abroad. There's a lot I want to read too. I have decided to sit the Oxford Entrance exam and have begun, now the silly exams are over – to read some Flaubert and Stendhal. I intend to try for Oxford before the Public Examination next summer.

I am so busy but I must write of what I feel at the moment for Miss Crichton, my Helena. Yesterday was the last day of term *and I did not go and say Goodbye to her*. It would have been ridiculous. I am leaving it to her for once. She has a lot to do and when she has settled herself in and I am back from France I shall see how I feel about it all and how she feels too. After all, she has chosen to leave. If she loved me as much as I do her – or as much as I did love her? – she would not have chosen to go away, would she? Yet I too want to stretch my wings. I know it is not "over" – whatever happens she will affect me for the rest of my life. She will write to me, I think, in autumn. I have all summer to think it over and also to see how I manage away from the family and school. I go to Paris on August 17th.

September 17th

Back from France today – see all my diary from Paris and Burgundy. I have grown up in other ways this summer, have travelled alone and spoken another language and eaten strange

322

things and drunk lots of wine and begun to smoke and actually been chased by (rather horrible) men. Last term seems a hundred years ago, but I still feel guilty about Helena, from whom I have not yet heard. I went for a walking holiday at the end of July with Anne and Cécile – we went youth-hostelling in York and on the coast and then I did my two weeks of slavery in the office in Woolsford. Now I am teaching a young Swiss Au Pair English and am back at school, busy reading French literature. I *loved* France! Though some of the students at that vast *Cité Universitaire* campus were horrible. Winnie, who shared my room in Paris, hated it and came back home after two weeks. But now I am quite fluent in French. It needed only a month to understand most of what they said to me. It was a marvellously hot summer after that terribly cold winter – the *vendange* will be the best ever, they say. Helena is now in the Midlands. I have written her a note to say I am back and to hope she is feeling better and wondering if she is wearing the 'New Look'. One part of me feels numb and another part feels treacherous, but the best part feels as though I too am convalescing. I know I have changed. I feel emancipated, and school means little to me. It is true there is no more magic or grief there, but I know it will come back one day, elsewhere, when I am 'properly' grown up. All I want is for Helena to be happy. I think often of all she said to me, of all the hints she gave about her life, about the man who loved her who wanted her portrait painted (she would not say if it ever was), of the German she saw again in Basel, and the man in the train. I find her still an enigma, but also I think that perhaps one day when I know more of the world, I might come to understand her better.

October 13th 1947

I had a letter from H today. She says she is offering me a 'last chance' to go and live with her! Perhaps she is surprised that I have not written more often to her? She says she '*always* wears a "new look"'! – what am I thinking of?' She never mentions France or my studies. But if I don't want to go and live with her there is someone else who would jump at the chance, she says, a teacher, I think – who has fallen in love with her. She

323

replied to what I had said in my letter about wanting her to be happy, even if I were not there, by saying 'If you were by my side you would feel differently', which is possibly true, but I am not, and the reason I am not is partly because she chose to go away. Her words fill me with a sort of apprehension, mixed with guilt. I feel for the first time that I have the 'upper hand' and it makes me sad. I am being offered a home when I know my home will not be with her – or even with my parents for very long – but away from everyone here, with people like myself. I feel unkind, but what can I say to her? I want to be 'free'. I am not proud of myself or even happy about feeling independent and I am not rejecting her, just rejecting certain possibilities in myself. I do not believe I shall ever be able to love anyone ever the way I loved her, but without the experience of loving her I should be a different woman.

Nov 1st
I take the College Scholarship and Entrance Exam in ten days. I had another letter today from Miss Crichton with a veiled reference to my being 'looked after' financially if I went to live with her [I must have said something about needing a scholarship]. She never even mentioned my parents. I know I have not been very open with them, but I have to consider them too. Her letter has shocked me, for she must be desperate. I know I am no longer a child, but I am not yet quite free to go away 'forsaking all others'. How I would have wished to do that even at this time last year! She still wants *me*, rather than this other woman, I can feel that. It disturbs me though that she is quite obviously wanting to make me feel jealous, which I no longer do. Is it because I have fallen out of love? I still 'love' her, but I am not 'in love' with her – I don't know why. Maybe because now I feel more of a woman myself so a woman cannot be a mystery to me as she used to be. It was not worthy of her, but it must have cost her something to write.

I have let her down, the first time ever, except for the times I could not go to her on account of the family. It is all too late. Yet I long to see her, so I can show her my new self. I also want to know that she is all right, for she is very vulnerable and cannot look after herself properly. I don't mean in things like work or money or clothing herself or keeping sane, but in things like being lonely and not eating enough. But I want now to be free to follow my other inclinations; I have to harden my heart and be a less nice person. I have lost *her* in order to find *myself!* Perhaps one day when I have found myself I shall find her still in me and make sense of it all. So much to remember: the overpowering smell of the chypre in her furs I could smell even through her bedroom window at the side of the Lodge that first year, all those stories about her grandfather, all her little phrases, all the times she had tears in her eyes when she talked of her mother, – the sight of her in the road walking so firmly along, head held high, with her big bag; her self-containedness, her jumpers, hand-knitted in jade wool, the strange, half-equal, half-unequal relationship, the feeling I always had, especially as I got to know her better, that she had created a self to get her through life but that underneath was a real little self telling jokes or darning or feeling lonely . . . her laughing at me when I said that the only worthwhile things in life were Nature, Love and Art, her pretended amazement at my boldness, but her acceptance of it too. Her cleverness; the way she lay propped up in that bed in the Infirmary, so brave and lonely; the tiny stitches she sewed on her stockings when she sat darning. She once said to me: 'You are clever, Hero, and good-looking,' and, knowing it was high praise from her, I replied, 'But *you* are beautiful and brilliant.' I felt she had shut up her heart to feeling, but opened up just a little chink to me.

I still do not know how I could have acted differently, feeling as I did. I feel that I did not take anything away from her life but added to it. I would like to have talked about love with her in an impersonal way. How she sometimes made me suffer!

I sometimes feel that if I could be free for a few years, and then go back to her if I found that I really could not love men, I would do it. Shall I never, never see her again? I cannot believe that. I am also sometimes frightened of what I unleashed in myself. Maybe there won't be anything else in my life like Helena – whom I shall never forget, who let me – I now see – play with her heart at an age when I was too young to realise her real needs as I was so self-centred three years ago. I would not like her to think that she was just a part of my growing up and it consoles me to think that if it were that, at least she hardly ever let her guard down, for I am beginning to think that life is very hard, especially for women alone, even if they are alone through choice. One thing though I do know and that is that I shall never forget the feeling of being made to feel wicked, that my best feelings were dirty and wrong. The way people feel – conventional people I mean – about this sort of love, and about other things to do with sex, is horrible. I shall never renege on that, whatever happens to me.

Oxford May 1952

I had a letter from 'Helena' Crichton today. She says she wants me and Trevor to show her round the place. It made me feel very strange. It is almost five years since I saw her and over three years since she last wrote to me, (five years on the 24th since I took her back home from the hospital). I have always felt that something was not 'finished' there and I was right. I shall write back saying I'd be pleased to show her Oxford.

May 20th

She wrote to say she would not come if it rained. It did rain and she did not come. Sometimes I still dream of her, though I have been 'in love' since, more than once, – and not with a woman – and I feel guilty. But I console myself that I *did* love her, truly love her. I try to see her objectively, but that is still impossible for me. I see her silhouette, beautiful and terrifying, weird and sad, her hat an arcane helmet, her hair a coroneted Medusa, yet her lips then soft against mine – the source of the most thrilling desire in these dreams. When I wake up I try to discount this lost paradise that is locked inside me and know that I had a life 'after Helena'. But I don't forget my first feelings, though I no longer speak of them very much. She was a sort of religion to me, separated from another part of myself that went forward and looked for truths elsewhere. I pressed hungry kisses on her willing lips and enfolded her in passionate embraces and then I woke up – (and wake up) – and found that when the fever was over there was still some firm ground under my feet and that I was young and had a future even if I had betrayed the mystery of love.

326

PART THREE

1965–1989

Chapter Fifteen

Milly Eden's daughter Lucy was having her second birthday party the very same week that Maud Crichton retired from teaching and Jackie Vallés celebrated the third anniversary of her return to live in Scotland.

Maud's mind was far from thoughts of her long ago friend Jackie, or past pupils, or birthday parties, for she was busy that evening packing up for her usual summer vacation in Zürich where she was planning to enjoy spending some of her savings. There was a reasonable pension waiting for her, one she thought she richly deserved, and she owned her own house in a market town near the Lincolnshire coast, not far from Scalby where she had taught for ten years. The idea of an earlier retirement had often occurred to her, but she had been loth to let go of the pension, although having spent four years working for her doctorate, she would not have worked the requisite forty years for the full amount. Not many women worked even for thirty years. Most women teachers married and left when they had a baby, even if they came back later. She was of the last generation to remain unmarried with no break in service.

In her opinion things were going from bad to worse in education, but as she had always preferred to be a large fish in a small pond (as Jackie Fyffe had once opined), she had gritted her teeth and stayed put, teaching whatever she was asked. She had even filled in teaching English when women staff had babies. People seemed to want German on the syllabus too, though not many pupils passed their 'O' levels in it. Greek had been out of the question for years except in some Public Schools, and even Latin was now useful only for the few who might wish to go to the older universities. Not many did from that sleepy part of the country, but there were occasional private coaching jobs for doctors' or solicitors' offspring. Maud had shut her eyes to changes and carried on. If the Grammar schools ever disappeared in this rather conservative area she would not need to know about it once she was retired. Scalby houses were built solidly and were not so expensive as in the bigger towns and she had bought one on a mortgage, and stayed.

As she had grown older Maud paid even less attention to the opinions of others. Many folk asked her why she did not return to Scotland, where education was said to be taken more seriously, but that was something she did not ever propose to do. At the bottom of her mind rejection still rankled. Also, it was even colder up there.

By degrees she had become a licensed eccentric in Scalby, nobody remotely resembling her ever having lived in the place, unless you counted the local landowner, Sir Harry Spack, who was also eccentric and lived with his housekeeper and several dogs in a large turreted house in the middle of fields by lanes that led to the sea.

Maud had planned her trip abroad with her usual care. Everyone went abroad nowadays, even the riff-raff. After two vacations in the Federal Republic after the war she had stopped going to Germany, would rather visit Switzerland which was so clean and had no memories. The language spoken by the West Germans dismayed and annoyed her, unless it was that of refugees from the East. It was quite another Germany from the country she had once known, even though she admitted it still had a few good points: older women still wore hats, and some well-brought up children curtsied to adults. She had never stayed again in Basel either, not since just after the war when she had gone to meet Franz Immerman that terrible summer when she had had so much pain. Franz had been starting up some business or other and had actually proposed she live with him. He had written to Prof Kornfeld who had moved to Munich after the war and it had been a fluke that Kornfeld had her new address, Maud having written to enquire what had happened in the war to his old department. Franz was now in the building trade and said he intended to make money.

They could live in a little house in some mountain village, he said, somewhere in the Oberland, but she had been amazed, not at all flattered by his proposal and he had been disappointed by her curt refusal.

'But Maud – we parted friends – you liked me still,' he said.

She had had to forgive him his duplicity because the man who had penetrated Maud Crichton's defences had to be special and he had been useful to her in 1937 when she had met him quite by accident in Berlin. In Basel he had told her that Wolfgang Hartmann had killed himself in 1945. 'A wicked man,' he said virtuously. She was glad about Hartmann but thought more of little 'Moltke' of whose death in North Africa Professor Kornfeld had apprised her when he wrote to ask if he might use some of her research in a book. Her old professor had been in Munich when he died a year or two later. They were all dead now, her old acquaintances, and she had heard nothing of Franz for years, who would have prospered, she was sure. He had long ago stopped writing to her.

Now she was sixty, and sat alone in her sitting-room which she had had fitted with central heating. It was a great extravagance, but well worth it. She checked her money, her passport and her tickets. This time she was flying from Heathrow – less dirty and less tiring than the sea crossing and the trains. Her passport photograph looked back at her unblinkingly. She thought she had not changed since it was taken some years before. She tried not to think of her age, and managed most of the time to convince herself she was on the right side of forty-five. For this trip though she had asked her brother Malcolm if he would like to accompany her. Carrying luggage, of which she always took a large amount, was tiring, and porters not always to be found in this new world of Do-it-Yourself. Malcolm would have been useful for that. He lived in Birmingham and was successful, but she did not see him very often, as she did not get on with his wife and now grown-up children. Malcolm though had refused to accompany her, saying he was too busy. Duncan had emigrated to Canada, at first to stay with Ma's sister's family, and then he had remained there, and she had not seen him for years. 'You never change,' Malcolm had said to her the last time he had visited. Well, why should she change? What merit was there in changing yourself and your way of life when you were perfectly

331

happy with the way you were? Malcolm was only fifty-eight, but he looked an old man!

'You'll miss your work when you retire,' he had warned her. Maud was aware that a regular job kept you on the alert, but she had never enjoyed her work except when an occasional pupil had seemed to make it worthwhile for a time.

None of them came back to see her – not that she expected or even wanted them to do so. The world had changed, not she. Britain had changed and was still changing; pupils were no longer as bearable as they had used to be, and people no longer cared to do a good job of work for good money. There was sloppiness and "couldn't care less" everywhere. You'd never have imagined that we'd actually beaten the Jerries!

Even the novels she got from the Book Clubs were changing, and the films at the cinema. No good stories any more with beginnings, middles and ends; and as for any decent music on the wireless, it was just shouting and squawking – jungle music.

She got up and went upstairs to wash her hands – you never knew, after handling all that foreign money. She'd have an early night with her electric blanket – there was no central heating upstairs – too wasteful. Even at this time of the year the wind came over from the North Sea and chilled you. By the bathroom mirror she took off her glasses and rubbed her eyes. They were being tiresome again, although a few years ago the short-sight seemed to have improved. She had washed and coloured her hair the day before in preparation for the holiday. Always set off on a journey with everything clean, Ma had always said. You are not sixty, Maud, it is impossible, she thought.

In Edinburgh, 'Georgina Henderson', previously known as 'Morwenna Mackay', was singing her granddaughter to sleep. Isobel was pushing through her back molars so was at present rather fretful. Joe and his wife Stella were out at a Medical Ball and she had been happy to have Isobel and little Calum, who was three years old, to stay with her, though it looked as if she might be having an exhausting evening and perhaps night. What grandchildren did for you, she was thinking, as she held the small hand of her granddaughter, was to make you profoundly thankful you were no longer 'in charge', at the same time as occasionally being pleased to look after babies. It made you feel useful without being used. She was especially fond of Isobel, had been so as soon as she saw the small red-skinned, black-haired creature. Privately she thought the baby looked rather like her. Isobel's brother, young Calum, was already, she thought, a small version of his dead grandfather. But she might be deluding herself; it might be another of Nature's wily ways to get a response from an older generation. Stella had parents too, who probably thought their grandchildren looked just like *them*. She smiled, and the baby, quiet for a moment, suddenly smiled back before shutting her eyes and falling asleep. For how long was doubtful, but Jackie crept thankfully downstairs and poured herself a large Scotch. Charlie Vallés, her youngest son, was going to be back late – his school had bought one of these new computer affairs and there was an Open Evening for parents to be told about its wonders, an evening Charlie had earnestly urged her to avoid. It seemed ages since Charlie had been a baby. However had she coped, with Carlos always away on some tour? Her face softened A portrait of Carlos in one of his roles hung on the wall, looking at her out of those wonderful dark eyes, eyes which his son had inherited. Though her second husband had been dead now for ten years she thought of him every day. Death was nothing to be frightened of if someone you loved had experienced it before you.

She must write to Jamie tonight. His letter was on her table. Since emigrating to direct plays in the States seven years before, Jamie had always written every month. He knew his mother did not like telephone conversations and she suspected he enjoyed writing, as she did. She had kept all his written accounts, for she was sure that he wanted her to, and might one day write a book himself about his work out there. It was a pity that her own parents were dead, though he had seen his grandmother before she died in Toronto.

She had had a letter from Christina Gordon only the other day. Christina was still after all these years on the track of that portrait her father had once owned which Jackie had had no luck in tracking down in London. This time Christina hinted she might try again one day to contact Maud Crichton, having failed years ago.

Jackie sipped her whisky, her ear alert either for the door being opened by Charlie or some wail or murmur from above where the baby lay.

How many years ago would it be since Valentine painted that picture of her friend? It must be exactly forty, for Joe was thirty-nine. What *had* happened to Maud? I wish I could see her, she thought; I really would like to see her. She could not help asking herself if Maud read her books. She ought to like them, she thought. I write for people like Maud. Then – what nonsense, I write for younger people too!

She got up, and her cat Silas came into the room mewing. Poor Silas, neglected on account of Isobel. Jackie got up to feed him. That was all they wanted – food and a few caresses. Cats and flowers, she thought, I remember saying to Maud that I liked cats and flowers and scents and colours and Maud said 'What kind of cat? Which flower? Which scent? Which colour?' in that rather maddening way she had, thinking her too indiscriminate in her enthusiasms. Had there been tragedies in Maud's life, as there had been in her own?

But if that portrait were ever found, *then* she would try to find Maud.

Lucy's mother was exhausted. Children's parties were more tiring than anything on earth. But she had done her best to make them happy and they all seemed to have enjoyed it and had gone home with their mothers or fathers, clutching balloons and small gifts of jelly babies. Lucy was not indulged too often, but what was a party for? George would be home soon and she would tidy up before he arrived. He was busy enough with his important new job at the Ministry without having to clear up when he got back. Lucy was in bed now, having had a specially long time in the bath with her new plastic boat. She was such a loving little thing and already talking in sentences. It was all worth it when you saw a happy child. She went to the sink after picking up various toys and burst balloons and bricks, and emptying the beakers of those who had not finished their orange juice. She washed up in a trice, put on some lipstick, shoved a dinner for two in the oven – you didn't want to tire a man out with evidence of a child's party but he needn't expect cordon bleu! He would have had lunch with some of his staff today so would not want a big meal. *She* was hungry, so she buttered some bread and smoothed honey on it, ate it, lit a cigarette and sank down on the sofa with the latest library book and a glass of sherry. When George returned she was still sipping it. She wouldn't bother to hoover. Mrs Kelly was coming tomorrow to clean whilst she escaped to the library to do her translation from the French, a small commission but one for which she was grateful. Translating was more soothing than copy-writing.

Throughout her childhood Lucy Eden was always used to see her mother sitting at a table, writing, writing . . .

Maud looked disbelievingly at the letter she held in her hand. She did not receive many letters and was suspicious of any that arrived. The school must have sent it on to her. She peered at the envelope which had been addressed several times for there were labels underneath, sent on from Scotland to various schools in the Midlands and thence to Scalby Grammar. What trouble someone had taken to find her. You'd think that people could be left in peace. The travels of the envelope had taken some time, for the letter had a date three months ago.

7 July 1975

Dear Dr Crichton,

I apologise for troubling you, but I hope you will be able to help me. Many years ago I contemplated writing to you but decided against it. Now that almost fifty years have passed since my father's death I am still hoping you might help me, or rather the person who has been commissioned to write of the work of the recently deceased James Valentine RA. I contacted an old friend of yours whom I first met many years ago but she was ignorant of your whereabouts.

I gather that you knew my father Sir Hector Heron in the early Nineteen Twenties and that he commissioned a portrait of you. Indeed I remember seeing this portrait at Garvits, but after my father's death it was sold. The present biographer is Gervaise Brook, a young man highly regarded in the field

335

of art criticism. He is anxious to trace all the work of his subject, and also to discuss the development of Valentine as a portraitist. If you have any memories which might be of use to him he would be grateful to hear from you. I have told him all I know – that your portrait was commissioned by Father and offered for sale by my mother after his death. I do not know who bought it for I found no mention of it when perusing my dead mother's papers and it has been lost since its sale. This portrait is of great interest to Mr Brook as it marks a turning point in Valentine's work.

Even if there is nothing you can do to help Mr Brook, perhaps you might still communicate with him?

There is another more personal side to all this. Some years ago I discovered in a false back to a desk my father had kept in his office (not at Garvits) a bundle of letters marked "From Maud". I have not read these letters and I should like to know if you would like me to send them back to you. I could easily have burned them, but I felt that for them to have been preserved after so long was perhaps a message to me that my father valued them highly and that they should by rights now be yours. If anyone ever wanted to write about my father as a collector or industrialist, these letters would not, I promise, come to light, unless you consented.

I am sure you will be as anxious as I am myself to trace the portrait. We can only hope that it has not gone to the States as so much of James Valentine's work has done.

Once more I apologise for troubling you. If you would like the letters, please let me know. My father clearly had a very high regard for you.

I hope you are well and that you will forgive my intruding upon your time.

Yours sincerely

Christina Gordon née Heron.

Maud was trembling so much that she had to sit down. But it was from anger rather than excitement. The thought of letters she had written still there for anyone to read made her burn with shame. Then she pulled herself together – why should she be ashamed? She was getting foolish. But she did not believe that the daughter had not read the letters. Most people were curious. She sat on unseeingly at her kitchen table and then re-read the letter. That devilish portrait – if only it had never been painted! But fancy James being dead! They were all dying off like flies. Hector had kept her letters though. What had she written in them? Nothing very revealing, she imagined: she had been young and overimpressed at the time. Had she kept *his* letters? A vague memory came to her of putting something in an old briefcase when she moved. Where had she put that? Why could she not remember things she had done in the last few years when her sessions with James Valentine and the sight of Hector Heron were still as clear as day in her brain? She detested people prying into her affairs, people forcing her to acknowledge things she had forgotten. Except she had not forgotten them. She would deny everything, though she still had his bracelet, and the diamond earrings. What if they found that picture and tried to trace its sitter? She pushed the thought away. Nothing would upset her more than evidence of how she had looked in the past.

The next morning she got up with the intention of writing a reply to the Heron girl. Thoughts of the past had tormented her all night – as though she had done something wrong, when she had not. People should mind their own business.

Finally, after a cup of tea and having taken off the telephone, which often annoyed her with folk ringing up to try to sell her new windows, she sat down with her old pen and a writing pad she found in the spare room. She tried to think clearly, then could not find the letter she'd received the day before. She started her letter: 'Dear Madam' – and then sat staring into space. How would she know where to send her reply if she could not find the letter? She spent the rest of the morning trying to find it and finally unearthed it under a pile of newspapers. She had not put it there, she was certain. 'Dear Miss Heron', she started on a fresh sheet of paper. 'Your letter disturbed me. I have no idea where this portrait is, which you say is of me. I'm afraid your biographer will have to do without personal details which are of no interest to the development of James Valentine as a painter. (She was rather pleased with this turn of phrase).

As for the letters, which you say were written by me, I have no recollection of them, but would ask you to burn them as your father should have done.

Yours faithfully, Maud Crichton.'

Then she thought, why should I reply? Why not let her think I never received this letter of hers – it went to so many places. It was all too muddling. But the letters nagged at her. If they thought she was dead they would read them and then unknown people would know something about her that was not their business. Why, even Malcolm might discover them quoted in a book if this biographer was unscrupulous!

So she rewrote the letter, but could not seem to get it right. Either she admitted nothing or she admitted everything. It was a problem, and her logical mind did not help her. She recopied her first letter and then thought again, why should I bother? But she put it in an envelope for further consideration. She hated indecision and recently she could not seem to make her mind up about anything.

She could not remember later if she had posted the letter and would wake up in the night feeling she was being pursued by Christina Heron. As time went on and she never received a reply she assumed she had not posted it. Only the letters went on worrying her; she saw them lying on that woman's table with blue ribbon round them and someone untying the bow and reading them aloud.

She grew increasingly stern with herself as time went on. The council sent her Home Helps who did nothing in Maud's opinion to help but insisted on trying to chat to her.

She was obsessive about personal cleanliness but neglected certain things, always having been used to her old daily cleaner going behind the gas oven and cleaning its inside. There was dust under the bed too, which the new helps did nothing about, though they enjoyed squirting lavender polish on her furniture. 'Walls need a lick of paint,' they said. 'Why don't you have it done this summer?' They saw that Maud was not poverty-stricken. Maud could not bring herself to get painters

338

in; it was an unjustifiable extravagance. Disorder was different. She spent weeks 'tidying' her clothes and books and throwing away old notes, but still felt somehow things were not right. When she went out to the shops on the bus she imagined people were talking about her and was sure that children were giggling rudely, though why they should she had no idea. Men still stared at her, she knew. In her coat and best hat and with her hair newly dyed she thought she looked pretty well, and she polished her shoes every night.

The *femme fatale* that was Maud in her old age was taken for granted by those who had seen her all their lives, though some children in the neighbourhood claimed she was a witch. Whilst she still went by bus into the town women moved away from the smell of naphthaline she carried round with her. But her visits became increasingly rarer, and at home she no longer noticed the disorder piling up. She told the last home help to go as she was doing nothing useful. The help reported this to her employer, but the wheels of the Town Hall Social Services were slow to turn and it was only when the Meals on Wheels people also reported that the door was shut against them that things began to happen to save Maud Crichton from herself and to bring a virtual recluse into the daylight.

The gods could not have loved Maud. The ministrations of the 'carers' having been spurned, and the Meals on Wheels having been refused entrance, she who had never bothered to cook, she with her lady's hands still unsullied, but with no immediate family to care for her, neglected to eat. The woman in the house next door had used to drop in to see her sometimes with a gift of a hot meal. Then that lady moved house. Before bureaucracy caught up with Maud and registered that she refused 'charity', she had lost a good deal of weight. Her niece, the now dead Malcolm's daughter Janet, came over from Birmingham to investigate and was so shocked at the deterioration in her aunt that she took a specialist's advice. By this time the Town Hall had caught up with the 'problem' and both they and Janet and the doctor judged Maud was in need of 'care'. Maud said little, sat staring fixedly ahead. Maud's solicitor was approached, and

339

Maud's bank. She was found to have a sizeable amount of money, for she had spent very little of her savings, and her pension was still coming in, index-linked, and when her house and furniture were sold this sum would be enough for her to spend the rest of her days in a good Nursing Home. Her solicitor approached her doctor.

Her mind was not always wandering and she 'woke up' sufficiently to tell him it was about time someone was paid to look after her properly. Eventually she consented to be driven away in an ambulance with two large trunks of clothes and other oddments. Janet went thankfully back to Birmingham when she had settled her in and put Maud's house on the market, arranging for the Post office to be apprised of her whereabouts.

Maud ate what was put in front of her at Dedlock Grange and soon regained some weight; she had never been a gourmet. But she required value for money – *her* money – and this included devoted service. For many months at home she had not been able to wash her crowning glory but once it was expertly washed by the Nursing Home hairdresser, who called constantly to keep up the spirits of the old ladies, all the old-fashioned black dye came out, revealing hair of a greyish white

She refused point blank to have it cut – who did they think they were? She was not in prison, was she? But either from weakness or vaguenes, she could no longer properly confect the elaborate coronet, so it was left in plaits down her back or tied back with a ribbon on the days the nurses were too busy.

'It makes her look like a little girl,' said Sister Farmiloe to litte Nurse Wood.

'You can tell she was once good-looking,' said Nurse Wood.

'She gets these ideas into her head,' said Farmiloe, 'as though we've nothing else to do but look after her ladyship.'

Maud had her 'good days' when she would remember bits of her past and begin to dictate letters, and if her doctor or solicitor visited her she had many questions and commands for them.

'She is a law unto herself,' said Sister Farmiloe who suffered from Maud's sudden whims when she would be peremptorily asked to undertake some errand or other. Nurse Wood did not mind running these little extra errands and went shopping for face wax or hunted for rye bread.

There came one day when Maud decided she was no longer to be known as Dr Crichton. She sent for her solicitor, who now held power of attorney for her, and required him to perform a statutory declaration that she was now to be known as 'Dr Gray'. The solicitor told her quite truthfully that this was not necessary and a waste of good money. She could be called what she wanted – and Gray *was* one of her names. But Maud insisted on her new name and appeared quite *compos mentis* and determined.

'It will be a trouble with the bank and the pension people,' he murmured.

'Not if it is done legally. See to it please,' she replied.

The next few weeks, until she heard it was done, she spent uttering short commands to all and sundry, having one of her 'difficult' periods. Once he had done as he was asked she relaxed and began to talk in a more friendly fashion to her attendants.

Nurse Wood was sorry for her, but was planning to leave the Home soon and marry and live elsewhere. She worried what old 'Doc Gray' would do without her ministrations. They were always short-staffed, though the Home was an expensive one and the staff paid more than market rates. On bad days Maud would whisper to her: 'I dinna want to see anyone, so mind if they call to send them away.' Nurse Wood knew that nobody but the solicitor and the doctor ever came, but promised faithfully that she would. A letter came from Birmingham every month which Maud scarcely bothered to read.

When she had lived in London Jackie had enjoyed going to auctions and sale-rooms, antique shops and junk shops, and even the secondhand furniture shops of large department stores which did brisk business at a time when new furniture was 'Utility'; decent, but rather unimaginative. On her return to Scotland she had continued her bargain-hunting, not now so much for furniture as for small pieces of china or glass, jewellery and secondhand books.

As though she didn't already have enough books! thought

her son Joe, who was not a bookworm. But Isobel, Joe's daughter, who had loved accompanying her grandmother as a child on what the former called her 'scavenging' expeditions, still enjoyed going with her to pick up a bargain.

Isobel was now grown up and studying veterinary science at the university, renting rooms not far from where Joe, her father, had lived as a boy just before the war with his parents. Grandma Jackie was in the New Town in an old house, having made quite a lot of money from her books. Eventually Isobel got herself a secondhand car for which Jackie paid the petrol and maintenance – 'the least I can do with all my ill-gotten gains,' – and they scoured the countryside to the south and east for 'bargains'.

One Saturday in summer she was taking her grandmother to see a Victorian work basket which she thought might do for Stella, her mother's, birthday as a present from Jackie, since Stella was a great embroiderer. Having crossed the Forth bridge they followed the railway for a time in the Kirkcaldy direction and then Isobel switched to several minor roads, ending up, after an hour or so, in a small village, not much more than a cluster of buildings around a crossroads, but set in beautiful countryside on the way to the coast.

'I expect they catch the American market, on the way to the Golf Links. I can't imagine locals spend much time in these little shops,' said Isobel.

She parked outside a shop which had a mixture of 'new' junk inside, with boxes of books piled up by the door. 'Inside,' she stated, piloting Jackie once she was out of the car. They entered, and found the shop lit by a pretty little chandelier. In its light, many cases of jewels sparkled on velvet. The sewing box was still there by the counter at the far end, behind which a young man was sitting reading. Behind the counter too was a half-open door leading into a stone-flagged corridor. Having agreed with her granddaughter that the box was indeed pretty, and signed a cheque for Isobel to fill in, Jackie peered round this door. A quick glance had told her that the books outside the shop were not her sort. The young man had put his own book face down on the counter, and was enthusing with Isobel over the sewing box.

'I'm here to help out,' he was explaining to her. 'My grand-dad's ill – he's the collector – used to visit all the auctions round here – have you seen his collection of Pacific shells?' Then, to Jackie, 'Aye, there are a few oddments in the back room – you're welcome to have a look.'

Jackie wandered off down the corridor and went in through a door on the right where the first thing she saw was a gilded bird-cage with no occupant. She ducked round that and saw piles of boxes which stretched almost to the ceiling of the dark room. Straightening up her stiff old back she accidentally knocked back the boxes behind her. How clumsy she still was! She'd better enlist the young man's help. The boxes had been obscuring more boxes and several more pictures stacked against the wall. In the half-light she suddenly caught a glimpse of a green dress on a canvas framed in dirty brown gilt. She began to pull out the boxes that obscured it. It could not be? Surely not, not here in the depths of the country in some forgotten village. She managed to move the rest of the boxes from the wall by shoving at them with her feet, and stood panting, grimy from dust, and looking at the face of Maud Crichton which stared back at her in the gloom.

Jackie bent to look at the signature – yes, it was a curly 'JV'. In her excitement she knocked over a candlestick perched on an upended trunk. Ignoring that for the present, she went straight back into the shop where the young man was covering the work-box in brown paper 'against knocks.'

Jackie cleared her throat. Her excitement was almost choking her and her heart was beating wildly. After all these years! . . . it was like seeing Maud herself . . . ! 'Excuse me,' she said in a croak. 'You have a picture in the back room. I'd like to know its price.'

'With you in a moment,' said the young man. Isobel raised her eyebrows at her grandmother.

Jackie returned to the back room and waited for him there, and Isobel followed her in. 'It's a Valentine – a James Valentine,' whispered Jackie. 'I met him once – tell you about it in a minute.'

'Don't look too excited or he'll put up the price,' said her canny granddaughter.

'No – all right.' But her heart was still thumping away. Isobel looked at her and then studied the picture, an old-fashioned sort of picture with a young woman, rather a good-looking young woman, in a green crinoline, looking out in three-quarter profile at the observer, or at something in the distance, for there was a far-away look in the eyes, she thought.

'What date is it? How could you have known him? – The girl's wearing a crinoline!'

'Yes – I'll tell you about that.'

'Her hair too . . . yet I suppose it doesn't look all *that* old – the colours are still bright.'

'It can't be anything but 1924,' said Jackie.

'Sixty years ago! – same generation as you?'

'Yes,' said Jackie, holding on to the trunk.

The young man sidled in and Jackie apologised for the boxes, and said, 'I was wondering – that old picture over there – is it for sale?' She tried to sound casual.

'Oh, everything's for sale – been here for ages, I expect. But I wouldn't know what to ask for it. Granddad puts a lot of junk in here – not the books – he hides his guide-books! – they're more valuable than the other stuff sometimes, but he hasn't had time to sort them recently. Do you want the picture? Victorian, isn't it? Go nicely with your new sewing box.' They waited whilst he picked his teeth. Then he said: 'Say twenty-five quid – the frame's not marvellous, but worth almost that if you clean it up, I'd say.'

Jackie was thinking – I'll not push my luck – but he seems more interested in frames than pictures. She tried to look hesitating, to gain Isobel's approval.

'I wonder where it came from?' she asked innocently.

'He gets job lots. Like it then, do you?'

'Er – yes – I'll give you twenty-four pounds,' said Jackie nervously. She must not appear too eager, Isobel was right. He might ring up his granddad? A genuine James Valentine! Perhaps the old man did not know its value. As if to answer her unspoken question the young man said: 'Granddad is an expert on silver and bric-a-brac – and books. He's not so interested in paintings. OK. Twenty-four then – I'll get it out for you.'

'Will it fit in the boot?' murmured Jackie to Isobel.

344

'Should do – put some paper round it – there's no spare tyre in the boot, so – '

The picture was pulled out from behind the boxes and the young man produced a duster and took it into the shop where they followed him. 'Nice looking girl,' he said. 'Victorian paintings coming back now too – ' he added encouragingly.

It was not too heavy for Isobel to carry, seemed to have been reframed, for there was a space between the canvas and the bottom of the frame. Evidently someone else had thought the original frame more valuable than the picture! Jackie paid and then followed Isobel out, and the young man laid the sewing box on the back seat of the car. He'd done well that afternoon – two objects sold. When they had gone he went back to his science fiction.

In the car Isobel negotiated the crossroads. A soft rain was now pittering at the car windows. Once back on the main road she said: 'Tell me then – What is it? Who is it? You look as though you've swallowed a pot of gold.'

'He almost painted me,' Jackie said and then she told her the rest of the tale, ending with: 'And, apart from the subject, it's a Valentine. Ten years ago they were selling very well, I do know. I saw the retrospective when he died.'

'Maybe he's out of fashion again?' suggested Isobel, keeping her eyes on the road. 'But how did it get there?' murmured Jackie.

'You said – "Garvits"?' asked Isobel after a silence.

'Yes – Garvits.'

'Just up the road,' said Isobel. 'Not far anyway – east of where we were.'

Jackie was silent then. Excitement had been replaced by an almost superstitious fear that the young man would have telephoned his Granddad and even now would be on their trail to get the picture back.

'Don't worry,' said Isobel, who could read her grandmother like a book. 'You've paid for it – now it's yours.'

Back at home Jackie leaned the portrait against her dining-room wall and sat looking at it. To think this was the first time she had ever seen it! Now she owned it, but was it hers by moral right?

345

Valentine was dead; Christina had wanted it; and its progenitor, Maud, might want it too. Maud, whom she had not actually seen for almost fifty years, Maud who would now be an old woman like herself, probably suffering from arthritis and all the multiple ills of age, if she were still alive. I shall write to Christina Gordon, she decided. It's only fair. Her father would never have sold that picture.

She sat on in the summer dusk with Maud's young eyes upon her, Maud, who had been superstitious about being painted – and who was to say she had been wrong? Yet it was unbelievable that it should have been herself who had rescued it. It was like one of her own stories, with life as its raw material. If Maud were still superstitious she would doubtless find some dramatic irony in the story. Maud's gaze seemed, when she looked at it from all angles, to mean different things.

She rang for her cook-housekeeper. There were some consolations to being fairly well-off. She'd get to bed and look at it again in the morning, and on the Monday she'd call in a picture framer. Maud must have the best. She smiled to herself. Maud, or rather this facsimile of Maud, should hang for the present here in her dining-room, where Christina could come to see it.

But if only she might now find Maud. That seemed impossible. And even if by a stroke of luck she did find her, Maud might not be pleased. If Maud had wanted to keep up their friendship she could perfectly well have done so for she had only to write to 'Morwenna Mackay's' publishers. Except that she didn't call herself that any more, and the books were out of print.

'I could not trace her – she never replied to my letter – It's several years now since I started trying again,' said Christina Gordon née Heron, now a trim old lady herself in Donegal tweeds, her hair whiter than her father's had ever been.

She accepted a dry sherry and then sat down by Jackie's fireplace. The picture was hanging now in the dining-room where Jackie occasionally entertained.

'Hamish would love to see it too,' Christina said. Hamish was her son. Jackie had already offered the portrait to Christina,

346

hoping she would not accept, it must be said. 'No – you bought it – you must keep it. I shall always know where to come to see it!' Jackie did not insist for the time being.

When they were sitting in the other room, Christina said: 'I remember it so well – it does bring me back my father, you know. Sometimes he'd go up to the Gallery at Garvits when Mother was out, or in the gardens – and he'd just stand there looking at it.'

'I thought Maud ought to know about it,' Jackie said again now. 'But if she's got any interest in her past she's certainly not letting it show. She was always strange about the portrait, quite upset. She said that people changed and pictures didn't. I think when she was very young the idea of growing old – of changing – just appalled her.'

'It does a lot of people,' said Christina comfortably. 'And it must be harder if you're very beautiful when you're young. Easier for people like me who never were! But most people stop being frightened of age, don't they? Perhaps Maud has too? She must have known she was beautiful.'

'Yes, she certainly knew. He captured that "look" of hers on the picture – as though she was looking past you – or doesn't see you – I always thought it was short sight actually. But she knew she was beautiful all right.'

'It was clever of you to find it,' Christina said. 'Let me know if you do find her, won't you?'

Jackie promised. 'The only way will be if another piece of luck turns up – we can hardly advertise, can we? Maybe *she* wasn't meant to see it again.'

'Or us her,' added Christina.

Later that year, in the early summer, Isobel invited her friend Lucy from university to stay with her in her little flat. On the second evening of Lucy's holiday they were both round at Isobel's grandmother's for dinner.

This evening there were four for Jackie's dinner – Jackie herself, Isobel, Charles, Jackie's youngest son, and Lucy. Jackie had heard a lot about Lucy who had just achieved a First in Psychology and was now wondering whether she might read medicine too.

Lucy knew that Isobel's grandmother was a writer. Some of her novels had been filmed or televised. 'She still writes,' Isobel had said.

'Do you think your father might find me a job in some hospital through his medical contacts?' Lucy had asked her friend. 'I want some more experience with children and old people. I still haven't made up my mind yet what to do. The degree was so theoretical.'

'I'll ask him,' Isobel had promised. 'He won't be here tonight though, he and Mother are on holiday abroad.'

They had tidied themselves up for the visit to Isobel's grandmother. Isobel said the food there was delicious and there were all sorts of interesting things to look at – first editions and old theatre prints.

'Is she formidable?' Lucy asked. 'Tell me what to talk about with her.' She was rather nervous.

In the drawing-room Lucy was introduced to a tall, dark man called Charlie who then went out to 'see to the wine' before the old lady came in.

Lucy thought she had never seen anyone so powerfully attractive in her life, but was not sure who he was.

'That's not your uncle?' she enquired in a whisper. He could not be; he was surely younger than that. Isa's own father was in his late fifties.

'Yes, that's my uncle Charlie,' replied Isobel, laughing.

'Your *uncle* – but he's only in his thirties? I thought you said your uncle was a film director in America?'

'He is. This is my *other* uncle. My grandmother had three sons – Charlie is the youngest one – my father's half-brother, you see. He's twenty-five years younger than Dad.'

So "Georgina Henderson" had been married more than once? Further explanations were not possible, for Isobel's grandmother arrived, a tall woman in a dark red dress with hair still a silvery brown, and a rather deep voice. Lucy found her very easy to talk to. Over their drinks she found herself telling the lady all about herself and her family. She did seem to be interested. Isobel was looking at her approvingly.

Charles came in again and said dinner was ready and the claret was warming up. Lucy hoped she would be able to say something intelligent to this Charles and was pleased when he turned to her and said: 'I hope you like oysters – I got them this morning from the fish market – Just a squeeze of lemon and there is some nice brown bread.'

She looked round the room. There were lovely paintings on the walls – a landscape of a forest glade with sun filtering through branches and one of a little boy in a red cap and a larger picture in a gold frame of a young woman in green with a haughty look.

'You like my pictures?' asked the old lady. 'Tell me – what is your impression of the lady in green?'

Lucy looked again and said: 'I think she looks rather haughty – but beautiful.'

'Aha!' said Charles. 'The mysterious lady.'

'She was my grandmother's best friend aeons ago,' said Isobel, tucking into the next course which appeared as if by magic – *paupiettes de veau*. 'This is delicious – though I can't bear it when I think of the poor calf. We ought to be vegetarians.'

'It's fashionable once again' said Jackie. 'I remember in the Thirties many of our friends became vegetarians – then in the war we ate just what we could get hold of. I did have a neighbour who went on being one though – she was very *pale*.'

'There aren't many Spanish vegetarians,' said Charles. 'Not surprising when you know what they do to bulls.'

'Your father was very much against bull fights,' said Jackie. 'Got into a lot of trouble from his fans over there – when he wouldn't sing at a corrida.'

Lucy was trying to piece this bit of information into what she already knew of Charles when he turned to her and smiled. 'Have you been to Spain?' he asked her.

'No – only Mallorca when I was little – we stayed in a lovely little village miles away from other tourists – Mother wanted to see where George Sand and Chopin had lived. I can remember the orange trees though – it was my very first trip abroad.'

'Do you like living in London, Lucy?' asked their hostess. 'I lived there for almost twenty years, but people tell me it's no longer safe to walk about at night by yourself.'

'Oh, Gran! – nobody takes any notice. If you're going to be mugged what can you do about it?' said Isobel.

'People worry about burglars,' said Lucy truthfully.

'And drugs – here in Edinburgh there's a lot of that – where can you go that has not changed?'

'Even Spain,' said Charles. 'But when I was working in Africa there was hardly any crime – only in the cities.'

So he had worked in Africa. Lucy wondered what he had been doing there. After dessert and coffee they moved into the drawing room, where Charles handed her a tiny glass of greenish liqueur which he said matched her eyes, which observation threw her into such confusion she only just managed to get up when Jackie stated she was off to bed.

'I have to get up the same time every day,' she said. 'Or I don't get down to my work properly. So if you'll excuse me – you stay and listen to some music.'

Soon after this Isobel said she thought they must be going – she had to get up early too. Charles shook hands with Lucy in a friendly fashion and said she must come over again. 'It keeps my mother young,' he said, 'to have young people round her.'

Lucy thought, well he's not so old himself, and asked Isobel, when they were walking to where she had parked her car exactly how old he was.

'Charlie? About thirty-five, I think – he's nice, isn't he?'

'Your grandmother married twice then?' Lucy asked.

'Yes – she was quite old – Charles's father was the tenor Carlos Vallés – he died when Charlie was small – it was the second tragedy in Grandma's life. My Dad's father was killed in the war.'

Lucy thought, yes, Charles does look foreign. Then – 'You mean *the* Carlos Vallés? Mother's always listening to the records he made when she was young! – I ought to have looked among the discs – '

'It was before I was born,' said Isobel. 'But actually Charlie's father was also a sort of cousin of *my* grandfather – Gran's first husband was half Spanish too. Charlie isn't musical though – isn't that a shame? – he's an agricultural scientist – does good in the Third World.'

'You've an awfully interesting family, Isobel – mine seem rather dull – '

'Well your father got his K, didn't he?'

350

'Who wants to swank about the Civil Service – very stuffy!'

Isobel laughed. She could see that Lucy had found her uncle Charles extremely to her taste.

The wheels turned slowly but they did turn, and the year after her visit to Scotland found Lucy Eden working first in a Children's Home and then in a Nursing Home. It was Maud's third summer at Dedlock Grange. Nurse Wood had departed and the nursing staff had changed its composition many times when Matron interviewed the young woman who said she wanted experience of geriatric problems 'at the grass roots'. Doctor Atkinson had recommended her and the Nursing Home was chronically short of staff. 'She's got a degree in something or other, but says she's prepared to muck in with the least pleasant jobs,' Atkinson had said. Matron detailed her at first to go round and talk to the patients. This she thought would make a good impression in case the girl was a 'spy'. You never knew. Her Home was well-run, but there were always shock reports in the media about places that were not. She did not make an enormous profit, as Atkinson well knew, even considering the fees, and she had nothing to hide. But she knew the value of Public Relations. And the girl had contacts.

It was in this way that Lucy met 'Dr Gray', whom nobody knew as Maud, for Christian names were not used unless the patients specifically asked to be called by them, the Matron being old-fashioned.

When she came for the first time into Dr Gray's room, the patient was sitting quite still in her armchair, eyes shut and hands folded. Occasionally though, as Lucy watched, the lips would move and the muscle round her mouth twitched as though she were holding a conversation that amused her.

Lucy stood quiet as a mouse observing her. People did not pay enough attention to the psychological problems of the old she was firmly convinced, so busy were they in hospitals and homes, clearing up, feeding, bathing and occasionally bellowing some cheerful message into a possibly deaf ear. She had told the doctor friend of Dr Fyffe that she would accept just board and pocket money if she could be of any use. This would allow her to

351

feel freer if she wanted one day to "use" the experience to write an article – not an exposé, just an article for the psychological or even the weekly press. The old, as far as she had seen, were treated either as little children or as lunatics. But most of them had not lost all their faculties. They must have all been young, some of them pretty, some lithe and active. Mostly now, families were encouraged to keep their old with them. It was usually those without a family whom one was more likely to find in such places as Dedlock Grange. What a name! – had nobody read Dickens? Lucy could not decide whether death was preferable to some of the deaths-in-life she had seen in the larger geriatric wards of hospitals, especially for those whose minds had gone before their bodies decayed. Matron had said that this Dr Gray was an intelligent woman, but had clearly always been eccentric.

'People just get "more so",' Matron had stated. 'If they can afford to be here they pay to have their whims pampered.'

Lucy reserved her judgment on Matron, knowing full well how difficult some old people could be, though not usually the defeated ones she had seen on the public wards.

She was still looking at Dr Gray when the latter suddenly opened her eyes, stared at Lucy, who was standing in a beam of sunlight from the window and said in a clear voice – 'Xanthe.'

'Sorry?' she said. 'I'm Nurse Lucy – helping out for the summer so the staff can take holidays. Shall I fetch you your tea?'

'Nurse Xanthe,' said the woman. 'With your golden hair.'

'No Lucy – Lucy Eden. Would you like your tea now?'

'I don't want any tea,' said Dr Gray fretfully. 'I want my hair brushed.'

'OK. I'll brush your hair,' said Lucy cheerfully. 'Where do you keep your brush and comb?'

The private room was small, but had its own bathroom, where Lucy found the hairbrush. 'Have they been in yet for your physiotherapy?' she enquired as she gently unwound the ribbon holding back the long hair.

'Physio-fiddlesticks – I don't need that,' said Maud. 'I wouldna have come here if I'd known how neglected I'd be. Plenty of time to pull you about, no time to do a bit of shopping for you. Mark my words. Nurse Wood used to fetch me my charcoal biscuits, but she went away. I asked the young man today – but he never came back from the shops.'

'Perhaps you were asleep,' suggested Lucy, seeing an unopened packet of biscuits on the dressing-table. She brushed the hair, plaited it, found she had a rubber band in her pocket, fixed the braid with it and then handed Maud the packet. 'Is this what you want? I'll fetch you a plate and tell them you don't want any tea.'

'Oh, I might have just the one cup with a wee biscuit – but no sugar and milk.'

Lucy smiled and went out into the corridor where a trolley was stationed. Ambulant invalids were helping themselves. Dr Gray looked as though she could walk if she wanted. She'd been told there was nothing wrong with this patient physically except old age, though she might have had a slight stroke that had left no visible effects.

Lucy found a plate and tray, measured out some of the strong tea, added hot water as it looked so poisonous, and returned to Dr Gray.

'Xanthe,' said the latter, 'I thought you were never coming back. You've brought me my tea?' Lucy extracted a biscuit and put it on the plate and then placed the tray over Maud's knees.

Maud sipped. 'It's less strong than usual,' she admitted. Then, after a pause, 'You have yellow hair – that's why I call you Xanthe. Greek for yellow,' she added.

'Yes?' said Lucy, intrigued, thinking, there is nothing wrong with her brain. 'Then call me Xanthe, Dr Gray,' she said.

'You are very good looking,' Maud went on. 'Beauty is a great burden.'

Lucy thought, being old is a great burden. This old lady seems different from the others I've seen here. An edge of command in her voice.

'Did you teach Greek then?' she ventured, sitting down on the only other chair in the room.

The woman put her cup back on its saucer and said: 'Oh, no – *never*!' as though she were disavowing some sin. Lucy waited, feeling she had better get to know the woman better before she asked personal questions.

'I'm tired,' said Maud. 'I forget some things – though don't tell Doc. But I never taught Greek.'

'Would you like another biscuit or shall I help you lie down for a bit if you are tired?'

'No, one is enough – and I get my sleep at nights with those pills. It is not that sort of tiredness I meant.'

Sister Farmiloe had said the woman was 'proud' and 'difficult', that she had arrived in a condition bordering on anorexia, but Lucy was thinking she did not look too thin now, so some of the chunky Nursing Home bread and butter must have been swallowed occasionally. Neither did the woman at present give any evidence of being too 'difficult,' though Lucy could imagine she might well be proud. They could hear the television blaring away in the next room. Lucy closed the door. 'She has it on all the time,' said Maud. 'I'd have one if there were any decent films, but there never are – not the ones I like.'

'Which are those?'

'Oh,' Maud looked suddenly sly. 'Foreign ones – ' she said and pursed up her mouth.

When Lucy rose to go she said: 'Will you come again, Xanthe?'

'Yes, certainly. Do you want the radio on? Do you like music?'

'Only sometimes,' said Maud. 'Their heads are all filled with TV rubbish, you know! You can give me my handkerchief – and take the tray away,' she added, rather peevishly. Lucy found a clean lace-edged hankie in a drawer and took the tray from her knees, noticing that the woman was wearing a long, black skirt.

'I might show you my jewels one day,' said Dr Gray as Lucy turned to go. 'They are locked up you know – there are thieves everywhere.'

'That would be nice,' said Lucy/Xanthe. 'Sure there's nothing else now?'

'No.' She turned her head away and shut her eyes again. But as Lucy was going out of the door she murmured: 'You might buy me some *Kölnisch Wasser* – I am running out of the stuff Nurse Wood bought me.' But she said it so softly that she did not appear to expect a reply. Lucy walked away thoughtfully.

The next time she was in Scalby she went to the chemists and bought a small bottle of cologne.

She was puzzled by the old woman who seemed to be an odd mixture of the ordinary and the extraordinary. There was something unusual about her – maybe something not even very 'nice', but a quality that held your interest. And she had immediately given Lucy a name – almost a pet name, because of her golden hair. Lucy had to admit that had touched her. When she took her the cologne she would try discreetly to find out more about her. What was she a doctor *in* to start with? Was it just a fancied honorary title? In her mind's eye she saw the old woman sitting there, her head half turned away. If she had turned it back to say goodbye, Lucy felt herself imagining, there would have almost have been, something *familiar* about her. Yet she was sure she had never seen her before. Enquiring a few days later out of sheer curiosity about Dr Gray's jewels, Lucy discovered they were mostly deposited in the bank.

Lucy had intended to spend six months at the Nursing Home but had at first wondered if she could stand six days. She had not bargained for the depressing effect upon her of the helpless old, and the only true end to their helplessness. Doctor Gray was not a problem in this way, being not completely helpless if not averse to service, and Dr Gray always amused her or left her feeling intrigued after one of their conversations. You felt that this woman had always been more than her physical embodiment, had reserves of strength.

She wore spectacles – 'I've worn them since I was a child,' she said. 'Not for reading – I can still read without them – but to recognise people.' But if she could read she never seemed to want to do so, and this puzzled Lucy. Also, Dr Gray was not always so lucid. This remark had been made on one of her 'good' days. She spent little time out of her room and took all her meals in it. This was allowed – the patients were given the choice. Most, being more convivial than Dr Gray, spent as much time as possible with others.

Since Lucy had no 'side', Matron was quite pleasant towards her, though the young woman was aware that if she overstepped the mark, was too 'familiar' with the doctors for example, or did not do her share of the 'dirty work', the pleasantness would soon end in criticism. But 'You've really cheered up our old doc,' she said at the end of her first fortnight. She meant Doctor Gray. Another nurse, Nurse Williams, said they were grateful for a bit of peace from 'the old doc's' grumbled orders. Lucy was glad she had helped, but feel frustrated; not having any medical qualifications she was unsure what, if anything, was wrong with most of the patients, especially "the old doc".

As time went on, Nurse Williams, a widow who seemed to have taken Lucy under her wing, confided that losing their long term patients was as bad as losing relatives or friends. 'You get used to folk. It's hard work, but leaves you better tempered than if you were coping at home with elderly parents. I know – I did,' she added.

'It must be hard for *them* too, if nurses go,' suggested Lucy. 'Like a child losing its nanny.' Then she could have bitten her tongue off, for she was falling into the trap of seeing the old as children. She was half afraid to get too close to some of the patients, especially Doctor Gray, since she knew she would worry what they would do when she too departed. But you could not remain uninvolved.

One afternoon she went to see if Doctor Gray wanted anything and found her sitting with a darning mushroom in her hand, bent like Penelope over her stitches. Occasionally she would put down the work to flex her hand with its green ring on the little finger of her right hand, and would look up at the clock on her dressing-table, which she had brought with her and which had, she said, belonged to her mother. Where had she found the stocking and the darning needle? It must have been in the drawers which contained things they had brought with them. Another nurse must have sorted it all out for her.

'What tiny stitches!' said Lucy. Whatever the woman had lost she could still darn! Yet she could not put up her own hair. Odd. Then she saw that there was no thread in the needle and that the woman was pretending to sew over where there were already darns. It shook her. Maybe Doctor Gray was less *compos* than she had imagined.

The woman looked up, laid down the stocking and said 'Xanthe – will you fetch me my cologne.' The morning Lucy

356

had brought the *Kölnisch Wasser* into the sleeping woman's room had been a Red Letter Day apparently; Doctor Gray had been surprised to find the bottle on her dressing-table, having forgotten, it seemed that she had ever mentioned such a thing. 'It was you who brought it, wasn't it?' she had enquired when Lucy appeared. 'Yes – you mentioned it – I hope it's the right sort?' She had paid for it herself and no payment was offered. 'What a good present – in my experience females are usually stupid,' she said. 'They just do not see what to do. I'm not looked after properly here, you know.'

'Oh, why is that?' asked Lucy, and then listened to a detailed account of the wrong sort of bread, the wrong way to wash hairbrushes, the 'neglect' of her bed which was not made the way she liked it. All these items were perfectly justifiable grievances if one were staying in a hotel, Lucy thought. Perhaps the woman thought it *was* an hotel. She ended with 'It's very expensive, you know.' Lucy knew it was expensive, but that complaints like these were not taken much notice of.

Doctor Gray was not however immune to flattery – Lucy had seen that immediately – but she could look cynically at you if you overdid it. She got a kick out of 'service' and Lucy did not mind that. It must be terrible to find yourself no longer in charge of yourself. She saw that the woman might very well once have been quite 'difficult', for it was on her good days that she could be most awkward. On the bad days she refused to speak or eat.

Most days however, were 'good', and if this involved a certain amount of raised voices, that was what they had come to expect from this patient.

'Physically, once she's being looked after, she's fine,' Matron said in answer to Lucy's enquiry as to Doctor Gray's mental state. 'But it's hard to draw the line between their physical and mental decay sometimes when you've not known the person when she was normal.'

'I think she ought to walk around a bit more, Lucy suggested tentatively.

Matron was a rather intelligent woman, she had decided, and one who at least talked rationally. 'You're welcome to try!' she replied.

357

Sometimes after supper, Lucy would help the nurses on duty with the drugs, handing them the correct bottles from the wheeled dispensary. 'Cross between a loony bin and a Brownie camp,' one of the nurses said one evening, a day or two after the 'darning' incident, as they both went into Doctor Gray's room with her cornucopia.

'How did you sleep last night?' she asked the woman who had now been put to bed.

'I always sleep well – except when I dream,' said she in a rational tone of voice and was given her two pills which Lucy helped her to swallow with a glass of water.

'Not what I've been told,' muttered the nurse to Lucy when they were out of earshot and ready for the next room. 'Sometimes that bell goes all night – she's had a nightmare, she wants to go to the toilet, she wants this and that – she's been a bit better recently though, they tell me.'

How awful to wake with a nightmare when your living days were possibly another kind of nightmare, Lucy thought.

The next day she was busy helping in the kitchens as one of the washers-up was off sick. After finishing this job she was free for the afternoon, but thought she might drop in on one or two patients to see if there was anything they wanted in town. One of the men wanted her to register a racing tip for him, which with some amusement she agreed to do. He was a spry old thing who had once been a jockey (he said). In any case, he must have made some money somewhere along the line. Then she tapped on Doctor Gray's door. She still kept thinking of the doors as cell doors – it was absurd.

'Do you need anything? – I'm going into Scalby,' she said.

Doctor Gray did not reply at first. Then – 'I need quite a lot of things, Xanthe, but they are unobtainable,' she replied. Lucy waited by the door. 'I need something for my – ' she searched for the word.

'Hands?' suggested Lucy. She was well known for the many bottles of hand lotion she got through, sometimes spending hours smoothing in the lotion. A head was shaken. 'Cleaning fluid for your glasses?'

'I had a nightmare last night,' she said. 'I think I needed an umbrella, Xanthe, to protect myself from the water – or the old woman would have drowned me.' Lucy waited, trying to make head or tail of this. 'Yes, *I* often have weird dreams too,' she replied. 'Everybody does – but you are safe here.'

'That's what *you* think. Nobody is "safe" anywhere, Xanthe.'

'Can I get you something to read? I imagine you are a great reader?'

'Aye – but there is nothing worth reading, you see.'

'I'm sorry – why not read something you read before then? – The large print books at the Library have a lot of titles – books you might once have read.' Lucy, who was an omnivorous reader, had even read some of these herself. '*I* couldn't manage without a book,' she confessed.

The woman stared into the middle distance. Today she was wearing her cotton gloves. 'Well, if there's nothing I can get you, I'll go,' she said. The woman's mind must have been wandering more than usual for she said as Lucy was about to shut the door – '*You* are looking after me now, Xanthe – not that other woman.'

'We all look after you,' Lucy said, holding the door knob and wondering what was coming next.

'If you look after me properly I shall give you my bracelet, Xanthe.'

'No, you must keep your bracelet, Doctor Gray – and all your jewels – I am here only for a few months – you can give the other nurses little presents perhaps, but not me.'

'You have never seen my bracelet – I will show it to you tomorrow.'

'Thank you – I'll remind you,' said Lucy and made her departure. It was difficult to know what to say sometimes. The bracelet was usually on the woman's wrist and carried with her when she went to the bathroom for her bath, where it was placed round the tap of the basin. Lucy had seen it. At night it was put under her pillow.

How dreadful it was to grow old. Which was the worst? To lose your mind or the use of your body first? If you lost your mind you would not know, whereas if your mind was normal and your body refused to do the things for you it had done for years and years and years, you must get very angry. Doctors kept some people alive who were nothing but empty shells.

Her growing depression at the fate of the old, her uncomfortable feeling that death-in-life was not preferable to dying, made her thoughtful. Yet there *were* old men and women who were interesting, and some cast themselves as the heroes or heroines of their own lives. She knew that Dr Gray was one of these when she was having a 'good' day. On other days, maybe it was the contrast between her memories and her present predicament that made her withdraw or be awkward. Old people were proud, and none prouder than those who half-realised they were incapable of conducting their lives as once they had done.

Lucy would sometimes wake in the night, thinking, the next generation takes over in life just as a writer writes a new book about a new young woman when the previous one has stopped being a heroine on her marriage. That was the problem – in books the heroine ceased to be that when she was no longer of the youngest generation – her fictional daughter took over in the next book! But in the life she saw around her here, those women who had no offspring, no daughters to carry on for them in the big world, stayed stuck in some time warp of their own youth. It was sad. Books told lies, she decided. She must try to see it all as part of Nature's Plan – one lot succeeding the other as flowers died and became seeds. She often thought of the childhoods of her old ladies and what they had been like.

To Dr Gray one day she said: 'Have you photographs of yourself when you were a child?' They often told you in lectures on Psychology how important it was for old people to talk about their pasts, and handle old familiar things – to keep a grip on their lives and therefore on their present world by seeing them as a whole.

But Dr Gray replied curtly: 'I never keep photographs.' Lucy dared not ask her why. Did they make her sad to think that she had ended up here? Then, after a pause, the old woman said: 'There are letters in one of my trunks I brought here. I don't want to see them. I should have thrown them away. One day, will you destroy them for me?'

'Why not have a look at them and then destroy them yourself if you don't want to keep them?' Lucy replied without thinking.

'I dinna want to read them – I want them burned.'

Lucy wondered if they were love letters. Doctor Gray was very lucid today and went on: 'They are in a leather wallet inside a brief case.'

'Have you no photographs at all then? Or do you wish me to destroy them too?'

'I told you – I never keep photographs – promise me you will get rid of those other things.'

Lucy could not promise. She knew the woman meant when she was dead, and she might live on for years after she herself had left the place.

'I am here only for a few months,' she said gently. 'Why not put it in your will – if you don't want to look in the trunks yourself?'

'I have made no will,' said the woman, and closed her eyes.

'Perhaps you had better mention it to another member of the nursing staff,' Lucy suggested.

'They are all fools.' She opened her eyes and now looked agitated.

'Did you bring nothing else you might like to look at then?' This question was ignored. Lucy hoped that she had not upset her. It was difficult sometimes to know what to say.

'What shall I do without you? You can't go away,' said Dr Gray peevishly. This troubled Lucy. One ought not to become indispensable to people. As she had said to the nurse it would be just like a child losing its Nanny on whom it depended. Not that she spent an inordinate length of time with this patient, but she sensed that she was appreciated by her even when the woman was cross or wandering, which she was the day after this conversation. She would have to talk to her less in future.

But whenever Dr Gray wanted something and rang her bell, which on some days was often, she always complained if it were not Lucy who came to her.

'What will she do when you go?' asked one of the nurses. Lucy began to feel worried.

The week after this she had to go into Dr Gray in the night. Nobody else had, and it was not her turn on night duty. It was a moonlit night and the curtains had been left undrawn so that the first thing she saw was the old woman's profile in the silvery, shadowy light. Her eyes were closed – perhaps she

361

had forgotten why she had rung? She lay on the high mattress like an effigy, except that her hands were not neatly folded like the stone effigies Lucy had seen, but lay on the coverlet palms up. They always loosed her hair for her at night and it was humped round her ears where she had probably twisted it herself. Lucy stood looking at her. The face, though the mouth was sunk, looked handsome, even beautiful, like the profile of a Mohawk Indian with its salient cheekbones. In spite of her tiredness and annoyance at the call she felt sorry for her in a more personal way than she felt for the other old ladies. The moonlight streamed in and Lucy continued to stand there as though by a catafalque. Then the catafalque seemed to stir and a long shiver went through it from head to toe like the surface movement on the sea which evinces only a slight ripple when the depths have undergone a seismic upheaval. Then Dr Gray shouted in her sleep and woke herself up. Should Lucy switch on the light? No, it would be cruel.

She could not make out the words, they were more a low moaning and she went up to the bed. By degrees the voice faded and then the eyes were open and Lucy took the hand that had twitched on the coverlet.

'Were you having a bad dream?' she asked sympathetically.

Dr Gray opened her eyes. 'Go away, old woman!' she said clearly.

'It's only me. It's Xanthe,' said Lucy, holding on to the hand. 'You rang for a nurse.'

'Where are you, Ma? Ma! Ma!' screamed the old voice. She did not seem to see Lucy, who decided she might sit on the bed – it was rather tiring standing there. But she held on to the hand and by degrees the woman quietened down and went back to sleep.

Lucy crept back to her own room. In the morning it seemed like a dream she had had herself. She did not see Dr Gray till the afternoon when she went in with a cup of tea.

After Lucy had tidied her dressing-table for her, the woman watching from the armchair where they usually put her in the morning for her lunch she said: 'Xanthe, I am still beautiful?'

It would be cruel to take her the mirror from the dressing-table and Lucy thought, yes, I suppose she still has something in her face that hasn't crumbled. At least the bones are not overlaid by layers of fat or a double chin or wattles or harsh wrinkles.

'Of course,' she said and the woman smiled. Lucy remembered how she had looked in the moonlight before she began to tremble.

'If you call me Xanthe, I shall call you Cleopatra,' she said jokingly, hoping nobody was passing to hear her.

Dr Gray looked at her quite seriously and replied: 'If you wish – Now will you clean my spectacles for me please? I can hardly see through them they are so smeared – nobody ever sees to me properly.'

Lucy cleaned the glasses and looked up at the face, which was hardly ever without its protective shield. In the moonlight she'd had a look of an Indian squaw. Perhaps she would tell her her first name. Matron knew it, but her instructions had been not to reveal it. But this was not to be an afternoon for taking liberties, rather one for a shopping list. New hair pins and hand lotion were required. As the hair pins were never used, Lucy wondered whether she should bother to buy them. There was a perfectly good unused pack on the dressing-table. But it was the woman's money to spend as she wished.

Later in the Nurses' sitting-room that evening, where for a few moments several of the night nurses congregated before going on their drug round, Nurse Dodds asked: 'Did I hear you go down in the night? There was a bell, but it wasn't one of my patients.'

'Yes, I got up for Doctor Gray – but she'd fallen asleep again. Then she had a nightmare so I stayed with her for a bit.'

'Oh, that one – she's taken a fancy to you, hasn't she? A law unto herself, Doctor Gray. Has she got you to do her shopping for her?'

'Yes – I do a bit occasionally. I'm sure she could get up if she wanted. But you can't force people to walk, can you?'

'If *she* doesn't want to do something, nobody can persuade her. Full of silly ideas she is. We had an awful fuss last year when a nurse gave her a mirror. She took one look and began to scream – you've never heard such a hullabaloo. Since then she's refused to have one in her room.'

363

'But there's one on her dressing-table,' said Lucy – 'I nearly gave it to her myself!'

'Then one of the orderlies must have put it back in the wrong room when she cleaned it – better take it away and give it to Matron.'

Lucy thought, but she asked me if she were still beautiful! Dare she not look for herself?

'She's calmed down a bit recently,' said another nurse. 'She was always ticking us off when she first came – when she was "with us", so to speak.'

The next day, after a peaceful night, Lucy went in with the hand lotion and the hairpins. 'Here's your hand cream,' she said cheerfully.

'Hand lotion,' corrected her patient. Once a teacher, always one, thought Lucy. Dr Gray could be very pedantic. She saw that the mirror had been taken away. Nurse Dodds was efficient. Let her think she was still beautiful though if it helped her. But if you had been intelligent, surely your looks were not the thing you worried about most? What was the difference between illusions and delusions?

She cleaned the spectacles again and said: 'Would you like a newspaper?'

'I never read newspapers, they only tell lies – '

Lucy gave her back her glasses and helped her put them back on. 'Fetch me my bracelet, please – it's under my pillow,' said Dr Gray. They did not put it on for me this morning.'

Lucy found the silver bracelet and, as she put it round the woman's wrist, remarked how pretty it was. Dr Gray put her hand over Lucy's. 'Shall we have a secret, Xanthe?' she said. Lucy waited, allowing her to keep holding her hand. It was unusual to say the least to have Dr Gray initiating anything so personal as hand-holding or mentioning of secrets. She must be extra specially alert today. Maybe it was a good sign. 'Inside this bracelet, Xanthe, is a message,' she said in a low voice. 'I think Ma gave it to me – I'm not sure, but I know there is a special message. One day *you* can have it – you must sign a paper saying you will take it. Will you?'

She was now becoming more agitated. Lucy thought, it will look odd, but if it pleases her. 'Yes, Doctor Gray, if you would

364

like that,' she replied. 'But I don't deserve it. Haven't you got a niece?'

'You will know what to do with it, you see, when my mother comes for me,' said Dr Gray. She released the girl's hand and lay back in her chair, shutting her eyes. Lucy crept out, rather disturbed.

During the next two or three weeks, Dr Gray's mental condition went up and down from one day to another. One afternoon, when Lucy popped in to see her, the doctor had been and she was sitting in her chair wearing a lacy bed jacket. It had evidently not been her own choice, for as soon as Lucy looked round the door and said, 'Hello,' there was a reaction.

'Please take this ridiculous thing off – I hate pink. It is na mine. I told them, *you* are looking after me now and I don't need that doctor coming in. He makes that woman think she owns me.' 'That woman' in Dr Gray's parlance was Matron. She never acted rudely to her in her actual presence, but to others was always full of her inadequacies.

'I expect she thought you would like it,' said Lucy, sliding the old arms out of the pink armholes and putting on the buttoned-up black jacket that was her favourite garment.

'*You* are looking after me now,' said Dr Gray again, as though one might say to a recalcitrant receptionist: 'I have changed to Doctor Hopkins, please note'.

'We are all looking after you,' Lucy replied tactfully. She must not put Matron's back up.

That afternoon, however, there was to be no more talk of Ma or of mirrors, only of Matron.

'Thinks she's the cat's pyjamas,' she grumbled. 'I don't suppose she has a professional qualification, has she?'

Lucy said nothing to this, not being sure herself. 'I suppose you can be a good nurse without a degree,' she murmured instead. 'I'm not a trained nurse, Doctor Gray,' she ventured to say. 'But I have a degree in psychology.'

'I suppose you need that to wash my hair,' was the reply.

'No – but even hairdressers have professional qualifications.'

'Professional rubbish – !'

Lucy tried another tack. 'What was your degree in, Doctor Gray?'

The woman looked up with an expression that Lucy found hard to decipher. Astonishment, yes – but also a little sliver of what she took to be fear. 'That is nobody's business but mine,' she answered.

'No – of course not. I only wondered.'

Was Dr Gray quite sane? She did wonder sometimes when an innocuous question would elicit such a strange response, as though she had been struck off some roll of honour and was ashamed about it. Yet she could also be sardonic and amusing and seemingly perfectly *compos mentis* quite a lot of the time. Lucy decided to investigate further.

'I would have thought your work was once very important to you?' she ventured. Should she not have said 'once'? Did Dr Gray think she was still employed? She must be in her early eighties, must have retired years ago.

'My work was my salvation,' was the surprising answer, though she still did not say what the work had been. She added, after a glance at Lucy, 'It was not sufficiently honoured, so I gave it up.' She was so quirky and uncompromising. But she did like occasionally to talk about herself, though you had to guess the links between the remarks. Lucy had heard her speak of a person called, she thought, Frank, and one called Hector. Once there had also occurred a rambling monologue about a girl Dr Gray said she once knew.

Now she said, 'I wasted my life, Xanthe,' and Lucy knew she must be back in favour, though she was obviously not going to learn anything about the woman's studies.

'I'm sure you have not wasted your life,' Lucy said consolingly now.

After a long pause the woman said: 'Now I'm widowed, even my sons won't speak to me.'

Perhaps she *had* been married then? It might be something that did not appear on the admissions portfolio. You never knew. No good asking her who her husband was; that was the sort of question which made her close up like a clam. 'It was in Rome,' said Dr Gray. 'Not Scotland, you know, but Rome. I'm not sure if I had any daughters,' she went on. 'I think I did, but I've forgotten.' She was 'rambling' again. What a pity. For something to say, Lucy changed the subject.

'I think my grandma must be about the same age as you. She was a teacher too.'

'I am *not* a teacher,' replied Dr Gray.

'No, not now, of course not.' Perhaps she did not like to be reminded of it? She must think of something less agitating. 'If it's fine tomorrow and not too cold, would you like me to wheel you out into the garden?' she asked.

The question did not seem to have been registered, for all Dr Gray said was: 'I am going to have a nap when I have drunk the tea.' She pointed to the tea on the table and Lucy brought it to her and placed it on the moveable table she put across the armchair. 'You can go now, Xanthe,' she said.

It was obvious that she was never going to penetrate the woman's defences. She had no right to, of course, but she felt intuitively that the woman *needed* to talk, would have been happier to talk, but could not get herself on to the right track. Lucy went out, shutting the door quietly behind her. She was a failure as a psychologist, that was clear.

She was to remain puzzled and cross with herself for perhaps being too nosy for a few days after this. Dr Gray retired into her shell and said little, so Lucy concentrated on doing a few other jobs for Matron, including the updating of files in the office. As she began one Wednesday to take out the cards for patients who had died or been transferred to hospitals, whilst the typist did Matron's correspondence, she realised that here might be the clue to Dr Gray's career. But it would be snooping if she peeped at it. She resolved not to look for it specially, but if it came under her nose to allow herself a quick glimpse. But she did not find anything, though she thought she had seen all the cross-indexing. No Gray anyway.

Maud's screams brought Lucy quickly to her room one night in the following week. There had been no bell pressed, Matron was away for the night and none of the other nurses seemed to have heard. Lucy did not switch on the light, but went up to the woman saying: 'Hush, hush – it's all right. I am here,' and tried to grasp Maud's hands, which were flailing around weakly in front of her face. Was she asleep or not? Suddenly the screaming stopped and the silence was more frightening. But she lifted her up on the pillow and knew she had not died, but was awake. She kept turning her head from side to side as if she was trying to escape some terror that enfolded her. Lucy held on to the hands and decided some light might now restore normality. There was a small lamp by the bedside that was not so glaring and when she had felt behind her for the switch and turned it on, she saw the woman's eyes were still closed. 'Wake up Dr Gray – you are all right. I am here. It's Xanthe.' She stroked the hand, remembering how when she was a little girl her mother had come in and done the same for her whenever she had had bad dreams. Looking down at the old face she felt a sudden access of tenderness and pity. Then Dr Gray opened her eyes and swallowed.

'Why are you here? – what is the matter?' she muttered.

'You cried out – and I woke up.'

Then Dr Gray seemed to remember whatever had been troubling her for she said in a surprisingly firm voice – 'Don't let that old woman dressed in black get me – she waits for me every night.'

Lucy was thinking, some of the nurses are no more than children themselves, how do they cope with this? 'Nobody is here but you and I,' she said reassuringly. The screams had been frightful, you would not have thought she would have had the strength to utter such bloodcurdling sounds. Some of the other patients must have heard them, but they tended to worry only about their own nightmares, not being interested in or responsible for those of others.

'Would you like a drink of water?' What did the books say about recurring dreams? Maybe the medication was at fault – but they only gave her tranquillisers as far as Lucy knew.

Dr Gray accepted a few sips of water and lay back. Now she looked quite peaceful. Lucy wiped her face with a flannel soaked in the *Kölnisch Wasser* she had bought for her and as she did so had once more that strange feeling that she had seen this face before. Not here in the Home. She could not place it. Perhaps she had just seen her in a train or in London – but Dr Gray had

368

not lived in London for she had asked her and she herself had never visited this part of the country before. Matron had told her they had taken her away from her house in Scalby, hadn't she? It was something about the eyes . . .

The next day she seemed to have recovered. Whatever worried her only came at night or in the dark it seemed: everybody had nightmares at some time, she supposed, some people more than others. But Dr Gray had also said to her, and seemed quite decided as she said it: 'I never dream – or hardly ever.' Should she try to reassure her about it. No, she would not bring the subject up unless her patient did.

'What a noise there was coming from the old doc's room,' said Mary Hill, the lady who had the next room, when Lucy went in to change her water jug. 'Sounded as though someone was being tortured – I took another of my pills – these rooms should be soundproof.'

Lucy checked what sort of sleeping pills were prescribed for Dr Gray. They were the usual ones that gave three or four hours if you took one, twice that time if you took two. She remembered that some medical authority had stated that sleeping pills reduced the time for dreaming. What time had it been when she had been awakened? Four o'clock – the worst hour of the night. It must have been that the first pill had worn off and then she'd fallen asleep again naturally and then been woken by the nightmare.

All that week Dr Gray muttered a good deal to herself, but was no trouble. 'Trouble' meant something that medicine was not able to control. The patient might not be remotely troubled herself that her mutterings made no sense. Occasionally Lucy heard a phrase or two in a foreign language. It was certainly not French, – might it be Russian? Or German? Languages had never been Lucy's strong point.

Chapter Sixteen

Lucy was looking forward to her weekend leave. She was going for two nights to Scotland – a great extravagance, but Isobel had suggested it, and her own parents were away on a cruise and would not be back for two more weeks. Since her father's retirement he had been nipped by the travel bug and her mother went along to keep him company, though Lucy was sure that she'd have preferred to stay put. Her brother Giles said it was good for them both and might cure Dad of his workaholic tendencies.

Lucy caught the train, managed to sleep on it and arrived in the early hours in Edinburgh where Isobel was waiting with her car. The wind as they walked up from the station was keen and crisp. How lovely it was to have escaped for a bit. She half expected that everyone in the street would be ill or old, and told Isobel this. 'I know – when I was a student I was a postman one Christmas and I thought of letters all the time and seemed to miss carrying my heavy bag when I was off duty.'

In the afternoon they were to go for a trip in the car into the country and Lucy sighed at the luxury of it all. Normality *was* luxury after all those weeks. 'I've to call in at Grandma's later for a book she wants,' said Isobel.

The morning was spent in chat and in eating food prepared by Isobel who was a good hostess, if not yet an inspired cook.

'She'll be having her nap – then we'll take the high road.'

When they arrived at the old, tall house they found Charlie Vallés there too, but on his way out. Lucy was very pleased to see him again. Though she would not have confessed it to a soul, the thought of such a nice man, and most particularly the remembrance of those eyes of his, had sometimes come into her mind in the last few weeks when she had been feeling depressed. He remembered her immediately, which was also nice, and, what was more, asked her how long she was staying in Scotland. Lucy explained.

'What about my taking you to our National Gallery?' he suggested. 'It's open, though not for long, on a Sunday – you haven't been, have you?'

Lucy had to confess that she had not and would just have time on Sunday morning. She was travelling back once more in the evening. At this rate she would get used to nights of only four hours sleep, she thought.

'Tomorrow then – I'll meet you at Isobel's and we can have a little healthy walk.'

She laughed. Then he was off, his expression rather preoccupied. He must be a busy man, but how exciting he wanted to see her again! She hoped it was not just 'hospitality' that had made him ask her. Isobel said nothing, but went off to see her Grandma upstairs. Lucy was left downstairs and wandered into the drawing-room where there was a small fire in the grate. The connecting door to the dining-room was half open and she peered in, remembering the dinner-party. Opposite her was the painting of the girl in the green dress and the landscape of mountains underneath it. She caught her breath, walked right into the room, stood by the picture and knew then where she had seen old Dr Gray's face before. It *must* be – it was unmistakeable. No wonder she had imagined she 'knew' her, though she had not been conscious of concentrating specially on the portrait on her visit here, being more interested in Charlie Vallés. She must have registered the eyes and their curious blind and yet watchful look. She stared at it for a long time to imprint it on her inner eye. What a beautiful dress it was. But why was it here? Did Isobel's grandmother know Dr Gray? When Isobel came down again saying: 'Gran's just having a rest – she sends her regards,' Lucy said – 'Do you think you could ask her something for me before we go? I think I've met the woman in that portrait your Grandmother has here in the dining-room! Ask her if she was called Gray, will you?'

'Come up yourself and ask her – I think she'd be very interested,' said Isobel. 'She lost sight of this woman, you see – she was her best friend. I was the one who was actually the reason for her finding the picture – we found it in a little antique shop in Fife – '

Lucy followed her friend up to Jackie's room. This was another sitting-room with a large fire and a chair drawn up before it. Mrs Vallés was sitting with a board on her knee, obviously deep in the throes of composition. Lucy suspected that a 'rest' was often the excuse for a nice quiet session with the book she was writing. The housekeeper, Mrs Thomson, always looked after the domestic side of things.

'It's Lucy, Gran – she thinks she's met your Green Lady,' said Isobel. 'I'm just going down for a word with Mrs T and then I'll wait in the car.'

Jackie had looked up, startled at her granddaughter's words. 'You've met *Maud*!' she said. 'Where?'

'Well, I'm not sure – it's just that we have an old lady in the Nursing Home who looks like the lady in your picture. I saw it last time I came, but I never made the connection till just now when I peeped inside your dining-room. I'm sorry – it was rude of me.'

'My dear, you can't imagine how exciting this is – but are you *sure*. Is she called Crichton?'

'They call her Doctor Gray,' replied Lucy. 'But she won't tell us her Christian name – I expect Matron knows it.'

'Did she marry then? Her name wasn't Gray – it was Crichton.'

'I don't think she's ever married – of course we don't know everything about our patients.'

'Let me think. What was the name of that mad grandfather of hers? You know, I'm sure it was Gray – it's a long time ago, but Maud had several initials and one of them *was* G after her preacher grandpa – I do remember her telling me that. I haven't remembered it for years! Tell me, what she is like and why is she being looked after in a Home?'

'She's – er – well – old – ' Lucy got out, hoping Mrs Vallés would not mind this reference to her own age.

Jackie laughed. 'Yes – she must be if it's Maud – but what else? Is she ill?'

'I believe it got so that she could not look after herself,' said Lucy. 'Matron doesn't tell us much about the patients, but she

372

did say that Doctor Gray had not been eating and was sometimes getting rather wandery – you know. She needed to be looked after, I expect. And she's often not completely lucid – I don't think there's really anything *much* wrong with her physically. But – Maud she was called? Do you think I could ask her her name? She probably would not tell me. She is rather secretive about some things – '

'Ask her if she remembers Jackie Livesey – or Fyffe – I expect she thinks of me as Fyffe if she thinks of me at all. If it *is* Maud, well, I *would* like to see her. Does she have many visitors?'

'None – expect a niece now and again. Why does she call herself "Doctor" if it is the woman you used to know?'

'Maud had a doctorate,' replied Jackie. 'You know, I haven't seen her for nigh on fifty years. Unbelievable! We lost touch before the war when she went away – to teach – Do find out, Lucy. I hope it *is* Maud. What a strange coincidence though. Like one of my own stories – truth stranger than fiction.' She was excited.

'I'll try to discover who she is – she hasn't any photographs – I did ask her – she said she never kept them.'

'Just like the old Maud,' murmured Jackie.

'I must go – Isobel will be waiting. I hope it *is* your friend,' said Lucy.

'Take another look at the portrait as you go – and have a nice afternoon and let me know when you get back to England.'

Lucy did not mention the fact that the old lady's son was taking her out on the morrow. One shock was enough in one day for an old lady she thought. After she had gone, Jackie put down her work and rubbed her eyes and found she could not concentrate any more that afternoon on the proofs for *Mistress of Muirside*. She had begun to write of Scotland again.

Lucy and Charles Vallés had spent a very satisfactory morning in the Gallery. He was an enthusiast, but not an overbearing one and she found him both stimulating and restful by turns. He stopped by the picture of a young girl sitting on a moor with a sunset behind her. 'Isn't it lovely? So Victorian – and yet not an ordinary girl.' Underneath one of the pictures he pointed out a copper plaque. 'That's a family Mother knew,' he said. 'The father had this picture and his widow bequeathed quite a few to the Gallery when she died.' 'Lady Florence Heron bequest', it said. 'Mother told me last night on the 'phone how she believes you've tracked down her old friend. She was *so* excited – when she found the picture she was the same. Both you and Isobel – magic girls – to find the picture, then the lady!'

'It's a lovely picture your mother has, isn't it? Who painted it?' 'James Valentine, I think there's one of his here,' said Charles. 'He painted my mother's friend when they were at university – nearly painted mother too, she *says*, but his patron only wanted the famous Maud. Then the patron died, but his daughter sought my ma out years later. She wanted the picture you saw in the dining-room at New Square. Nobody could find it till that day Isa went to a little shop in the country – you've heard all the story from Isa, I expect.'

It was raining outside and Lucy could have listened to that pleasant deep voice forever. They went for a drink afterwards now that Scottish licensing laws were even more liberal on Sundays than south of the border.

'It used to be terrible – even the Festival people couldn't get a drink, you know, except at special clubs. But now they've caught up England in this respect.'

She noticed he didn't say 'we', but 'they', supposed he was not Scottish in any case. Lucy was aware of the symptoms of extreme romantic excitement in herself as they sat drinking their sherry. It was so long since she had had them that at first she wondered if she were going to faint. She'd been burned before and a sensible burnt child fears the fire. But he looked at her so penetratingly and yet with what appeared to be a quite genuine interest . . . he would be an ideal friend if nothing else.

Reluctantly it seemed on both sides, their morning together came to an end. 'You must come to Scotland – soon,' he said when they parted. She felt quite delirious with happiness. She said nothing to Isobel but 'I can see you've enjoyed yourself,' Isobel said.

When she get back nothing much had changed at Dedlock Grange. She did not see Dr Gray until the day after her return for a nurse had gone down with a bad cold and the nurses were not encouraged to tend their patients in such cases; if the patients caught the cold their relatives complained. So she did Nurse Carter's rounds as well as her own and it was not till the Tuesday afternoon that she knocked at Dr Gray's door. She must be careful, not frighten her, or she would clam up again.

'Xanthe – ' said the old lady and Lucy was struck how different this old lady was from the one in Scotland who exuded mental vitality even if her physical energy flagged. Dr Gray looked pinched and lethargic, she though, even more than she had in the last week. If only she could make some excuse to see the files on her which must be somewhere in the office. Yet she hesitated now it had come to the point. It was not her business. It might wake up Dr Gray though, might give her a new lease of life, someone who remembered her?

'You weren't here,' said Dr Gray. 'Why did you go away?'

'You remember – I had a long weekend leave. I went to Scotland,' Lucy said and sat down opposite the armchair. 'Shall I polish your nails?' she asked.

'They need to be cut – and my glasses are dirty.'

Lucy got up again and busied herself with these small tasks. Dr Gray's hand lay inertly in her own. How could she begin? Well, since her patient never spoke to anybody else about anything, she might risk a direct approach.

'I met a very nice man in Scotland,' she began. 'He is a scientist at the university. He is half Spanish, but his mother is English. She writes novels under the name Georgina Henderson.' There was no flicker of interest on the woman's face. 'Of course, that is not her real name,' she went on. 'Her real name is Jackie Vallés.' Dr Gray was silent. 'She is also the grandmother of a great friend of mine whom I met at university – that is Isobel. Isobel Fyffe,' she said with a clear emphasis on the name. No flicker yet. 'Mrs Vallés used to be called Mrs *Fyffe*, Jackie Fyffe,' she went on. 'Her first husband died in the war.' Dr Gray was now watching her with what might be a slight interest. 'You may have read the Georgina Henderson books?' No answer. Why put it off?

'She thought she might have known *you* once,' she said boldly, looking up from the hand whose nails she was buffing.

'Who did?'

'Jackie Fyffe – the lady I met.'

Dr Gray was still silent, but when Lucy looked up the

375

woman was looking at her searchingly. There was another long pause.

'Her first husband died,' Lucy went on. 'He was called Calum, I think.'

'Calum Fyffe,' said Dr Gray. Lucy held her breath.

'He was in love with me,' said Dr Gray complacently.

'So you knew Mrs Fyffe – Jackie?'

'She had a wee baby,' said the old woman.

'She had three sons – the oldest is my friend's father. He's called Joe.'

'Calum Fyffe,' said Dr Gray once more.

– 'And Jackie.' But there was no reply to this. Why couldn't she just say 'Were you called Maud Crichton?' But she dared not. She decided to try a negative approach. 'You didn't know a Jackie Fyffe then?' Dare she mention the picture? Better not today. 'She'd like to see you,' she went on.

This was registered. 'I don't see anybody – and *she* is always busy with her bairns.' Dr Gray was plunged back, Lucy saw. If she had known Jackie, time had stopped for her in that relationship.

She tried once more 'She remarried,' she said.

Dr Gray looked blank. She would try again another day. But Calum Fyffe to have been in love with her! Was it true? Did Mrs Vallés know about that?

'I'll fetch you some tea,' she said and went out. When she came back Dr Gray was still seated as she had been, but there was one large tear trickling down her cheek.

Lucy wanted to be sure, and then she would write to Mrs Vallés. Even if Dr Gray refused to see her, she could give her news of her. Accordingly she asked the secretary where the other files were. 'The other ones? – you saw them the other day, didn't you? Was it for a letter or something?'

'No, I just wondered if you had a file on my patient, Dr Gray – I wanted to tell Matron she isn't sleeping very well again. I thought she might ask the doctor about another sort of pill. I believe the treatment is attached to the files.'

'Yes, we put a copy there for relatives when they ask. Gray – wasn't there something odd about that? Didn't she change her

376

name when she came in? I believe Mrs Ford, my predecessor, told me something about it.'

'The file wasn't under G,' said Lucy helpfully.

'Oh, they may have put it back wrongly then if the doctor saw it recently. I think her solicitor was in too, about her pension – Have a look – they're confidential though.'

'I only wondered about the name. You see – I've met someone who thinks they once knew her – they'd like to visit – ' said Lucy rapidly casting an eye on the folders in the top drawer where A–J had a home. She went through the covers, and there it was, M L G Crichton – see Gray – except that the file was there under C where it should have gone back to G. They hadn't cross-referenced it either.

'Oh, there it is,' she said, trying to sound not especially interested. 'Yes, it is the name my friend knew her under. I wonder why she changed it?'

'Some people don't like anyone to know they've lost their independence,' said the secretary severely. 'I don't suppose a young person like you can imagine that.'

'Well, they need not have visitors unless they want them,' said Lucy.

'That's true – but most appreciate visitors.'

Lucy hoped that this one would. She would not reveal she knew her name though. That might set off an extremely adverse reaction.

M L G Crichton it had said on the file, then crossed out to M L Gray. She would write to Mrs Vallés and tell her she was right: Old Dr Gray *was* the Young Woman in Green. She felt a shiver of excitement. This unearthing of the past of her patient was so strange.

That evening it was her turn to put the non-ambulants to bed. Then the sleeping pill trolley came round. She dare not upset Dr Gray with any new information, so said only – 'You remember I told you yesterday that an old friend of yours was hoping to visit you one day?' This was not exactly what she had said, but it pushed things a little further on. Dr Gray, whom Lucy had decided she would now think of as 'Maud' – she thought the name suited her quite well said: 'I remember we were talking about Calum – how can you know Calum?'

'His granddaughter is a friend of mine.' She did not say 'I told you'. – 'His wife would like to see you – if you agreed of course.'

'Why should she want to see me? I would like to see Calum though,' said Maud.

'I'm afraid Calum died a long time ago – in the war – my friend Isobel told me – he was her grandfather,' said Lucy gently. Maud did not appear to take it in. Then, cautiously, Lucy said – 'Jackie has rescued a portrait of you Dr Gray. So nobody else could see it. I think she would give it to you, you know, if you wanted it.'

At the word 'portrait' Maud's head reared up from the pillow. 'How do you know this, Xanthe?'

'Because I've seen it and I recognised you! You were very beautiful. It is very like you.'

'The portrait is *like* me?' said Maud slowly. 'No – I dinna think it's like me – there was a woman who wanted it, she wrote me a letter and I told her I wanted nothing to do with it. I sent her a letter and she never gave me the courtesy of a reply.'

Lucy looked baffled, but said: 'Try to sleep. Jackie – Mrs Fyffe – Vallés now, is a very nice woman who wants to see you – you need not see the picture. She will keep it safe.'

'They are all spying on me,' said Maud. 'Go away, Xanthe – I dinna want to talk about pictures.'

Lucy drew the curtains to and said: 'Goodnight then, Dr Gray.' Just as she had her hand on the light switch Maud said again: 'You saw the picture – and it was *like* me?'

'Yes, very like,' said Lucy, and shut the door. The woman's memory was seemingly sound – when she wanted it to be.

'Dear Mrs Vallés,

Yes, I was right. Your friend Maud Crichton is my patient, but she has changed her name to Gray! She remembers you and your husband, but says she does not want any visitors. However, she may change her mind. She was peculiar about the portrait – says someone wrote to her about it and she replied but never got an answer. She is very forgetful and I am never certain how much she remembers, though she mentioned your first husband by name. I have not mentioned

378

to her that I now know her name – I found it in the files. I do not suppose there is much anyone can do unless she herself wants to see people. I think she fears intruders upon her life, even though she must be very lonely. When I said the portrait was very like her, she cheered up a bit. But she has bad dreams and talks about an old woman in black. Did she ever have some sort of shock when she was young to do with an old woman?

I loved seeing you again – and all the family – I don't feel there is anything more I can do now for Dr Gray except try to look after her. Everyone is very kind here to her. I have only another month or two to go and am worried that she will react badly when I leave. I suppose I'm flattering myself! There is some "mystery" about her, which I expect you would understand better as you are a writer!

With love from Lucy Eden.'

Lucy also wrote to her mother, whose reply was quite unexpected

'Dear Lucy

It was lovely to hear from you. I hope the work is not too depressing. I know I could not have done it at your age. Pa sends love and Giles writes that he is working "quite hard". Don't rush into any decision about Medical School, darling – it's a long and gruelling course and I've always thought that you'd be better off doing something like anthropology with your academic background.

What you say about your old lady – Maud – is very strange, but even more strange than you know because I'm sure this is the person who once taught me many years ago – though not as long ago as your friend's grandmother's time! Ask her one day when she seems lucid if she remembers "Hero", will you? Lots of love – M.'

Lucy was intrigued. It seemed that everyone connected with her had known Maud Crichton/Gray. But her mother had not lived in Scalby – it must have been when Maud was teaching somewhere else.

379

Jackie Fyffe had not been mentioned again to Maud. Lucy was reluctant to do anything more about that since it obviously upset her. But it would surely not do any harm to mention her mother?

They had persuaded a few of the inmates to sit in wheelchairs in the garden and at the last minute Dr Gray had consented to join them and stay in the sun with a woollen stole draped round her shoulders. She had also insisted upon having her best shoes on and Lucy had had to shine them. The woman had clutched the arms of the wheelchair tightly when Lucy wheeled her out to the air. It was, however, progress. Maybe mention of more of the past would give her a new lease of life?

Lucy took her book in case she did not want to talk and then went to greet some of the others, leaving Maud alone like a small doll in a big pram, her feet in their black shoes looking as though they did not belong to her.

On coming back to her Lucy sat down and remarked: 'Are you awake, Dr Gray?'

The woman had the book on her lap, but it was upside down. 'I should think so,' was the reply. 'Why did you not bring my gloves – my hands will suffer.'

Lucy stood up. 'I'll get them for you then.' She went indoors and opened all the windows in Maud's room wide to the fresh air. The gloves were in a drawer and she returned with them. She helped her draw them on, noticing that the bracelet was on her wrist. Then: 'Did you ever know someone called "Hero"?' she began.

Maud looked baffled and then took off her glasses and wiped them on her sleeve. 'The sun hurts my eyes,' she said.

' "Hero"?' said Lucy, feeling like an inquisitor rather than a therapist. But this afternoon she seemed lucid.

'Oh, aye, I used to know Hero – but she was only a young girl – younger than you, Xanthe, a lot younger – aye I used to know Hero.'

'When was that then?'

'Oh, a long time ago. She went away.'

'What was she like?'

'A clever girl,' said Maud after a pause. 'A very clever girl – and a good-looking girl.' Lucy waited. Should she say it? *Was* this "Hero" her own mother, who was called Milly. 'Why – do *you* know her?' asked Maud.

'I think she is my mother,' said Lucy.

Maud stared and stared at her till Lucy felt quite uncomfortable. What was going on behind that stare?

'You taught her,' Lucy said.

'I taught Hero a lot, I remember,' said Maud. 'But she didna want to learn all I could teach her. She went away,' she said again.

'She is my mother,' Lucy said once more. 'Truly. Of course Hero is not her real name, just as Xanthe is not mine.'

'You are Xanthe,' said Maud in astonishment. 'How can she be your *mother* – she is younger than you.'

'It was a long time ago,' said Lucy. 'I expect you taught hundreds of children.'

'Hero wrote poems – and stories,' said Maud.

'It was Jackie who wrote stories,' said Lucy, before she could think what she was saying.

'Jackie Fyffe had bairns. She had no business writing stories,' said Maud. 'Hero loved me, you know.'

'Oh!' said Lucy.

'You met her then?' asked Maud, seemingly having forgotten that her Xanthe had laid claim to her female parent.

'Was her name Milly?' Lucy asked, since this time the reminiscences were not upsetting her.

'I forget,' said Maud. 'Probably.'

'Did you have a nickname for Jackie too?'

'A nickname?'

'Like you called my mother Hero and me Xanthe?'

'You are Xanthe and Hero was Hero,' said Maud, closing her eyes. 'Aye, the air is quite good out here.'

Matron looked approvingly at Lucy when they were wheeling their patients back to their rooms. 'You'll all have appetites tonight,' she said cheerily. She was thinking it was a pity that the Eden girl was not permanent – she was a good little worker.

Lucy knew nothing of it. No bell was rung and there were no screams, but in the night Maud Crichton had a slight stroke or something similar. At least that was what the other doctor, Dr

381

Simpson, said when he came along later in the morning. They could not wake her for her breakfast, but she was breathing, if rather roughly. Lucy was distraught. Was it her fault? Should she not have told her all that yesterday? She didn't say anything to Matron, but the latter came up to her as she was picking at her lunch.

'Don't worry, Miss Eden – these things happen – maybe a lack of oxygen to the brain – she'll come round. When she does we'll give her some treatment.'

'There was somebody who used to know her who wants very much to see Dr Gray,' she said. 'Do you think I should let her know – I mean, when she does "come round"?'

'Doctor Gray has never had any visitors – except her niece – it might do her good, if she's a bit better tomorrow – I don't know – ' Matron looked vague.

'Or it might be a shock?' said Lucy. 'If she comes all the way from Scotland she'd want to see her, I think. She's an old friend – an old lady too.'

'Tell her the circumstances,' said Matron. 'I don't believe in putting things off.'

Did she mean Dr Gray might not recover? Lucy felt cold and anxious. She telephoned her mother. The reassuring voice calmed her a little. 'She did remember,' she said to Milly. 'But she's had a little stroke – at least that's what they think. But she said you were a clever girl! It was *you*, "Hero" then?'

On the other end of the telephone Milly plunged in. 'You say she knew your friend's grandmother? Isn't it a small world?' She hesitated – 'Once upon a time she meant a great deal to me. Let me know what happens.'

'Would *you* want to come and see her too, then?'

'After all these years? I don't think I could bear it.'

Lucy was not surprised at this answer. She had guessed that Dr Gray did not want to see pictures of herself because she feared the changes time had brought. Perhaps her mother feared the same. How well had they known each other, her old patient and her mother? Suddenly she thought, Mother will die one day too.

'Let me know – if anything happens, won't you – ?' The usual words for dying, Lucy thought.

But Maud recovered and in a few days was sitting up. The 'stroke', or whatever it had been, seemed to have cleared her memory for she said: 'Xanthe, you were telling me about Jackie Fyffe, weren't you? I will see her perhaps – if she can spare the time from her family.' No mention of 'Hero'.

Lucy telephoned Isobel and then Mrs Vallés. 'She *will* see you – she said so just now. But she's had a sort of stroke – I don't think it can have been a real one – the doctor talks of "vascular accidents", but she's not paralysed or anything and she can speak. There's a very good hotel near here if you want to come. I think it should be before I leave. The other nurses don't know her so well.' There was no hesitation from Jackie.

'I'll come at the end of the week – book me a room for Friday. I suppose I can get a taxi to the Home? Isobel might come with me – she's due some leave – they work her too hard.'

Lucy had hoped that it would be her son who accompanied her, but said nothing. In the morning she hardly dared go into Maud's room for fear she might have changed her mind. But she looked rather peaceful.

'At the weekend your old friend, Jackie, is coming to visit you, Doctor Gray,' she said without preamble.

Maud opened her eyes. 'Why? Does she think I am dying?'

'No – of course not – but you said you might see her, you know. She could come and see you on Saturday morning, if you like.'

Maud did not reply, so Lucy took this for a sort of grudging consent.

She was sorting linen with Nurse Dobbs later that morning who said: 'I hear yon Doctor Gray is to have a visitor?' Word spread round the Home very quickly. 'She used to tell the nurses to go away when she first came, you know, and would not eat. But Matron says she's improved a lot since you came.'

'I expect she's got used to the place,' Lucy replied. But she felt pleased nevertheless.

Jackie Vallés left Edinburgh on the Friday morning accompanied by her granddaughter. It would be a tiring journey, though nothing like it had used to be in the old days. Isobel had wanted to drive, but Jackie had been adamant. 'You need a rest – driving is exhausting – we change in York and after that take the train down the coast.' Jackie had paid for a first class compartment for the first part of their journey and so they were left alone in it.

'I love train journeys,' said Jackie as though she were a child, not an old lady of over eighty.

'Are you looking forward to seeing your old friend? It must be strange after all this time?'

'Well – looking forward, and rather frightened too, if you want to know – and one always feels a trifle guilty if one is fairly healthy and someone else is not.'

'She isn't actually ill, is she? I mean, apart from this stroke they say she might have had?'

'I can guess from what your friend Lucy tells me that Maud must have become a bit of a recluse,' said Jackie. 'Not because she can't get about physically, but more that she doesn't want to – go out. Yet she used to be quite active, and people don't change on the whole unless they just give up on life.'

Isobel, who could not imagine her grandmother ever giving up on life pondered this.

The journey to York was uneventful. Jackie was still able to get in and out of trains, though her walking pace was slower than it had been and she was glad and grateful that Isobel had come with her and told her so.

'I'm just curious,' said Isobel.

But when they finally reached the market town and arrived at the Lamb and Bay Tree, a message was waiting for them. 'Miss Eden rang,' said the receptionist and handed them a note before they even went up to their room. Lucy's message was brief – 'Dr Gray has had another stroke, I'm afraid. I'll ring you at nine tonight with news – Matron says you may come round anyway.'

Jackie sat down in distress. 'Oh dear, – I should have come as soon as Lucy said Maud would see me.' But she was a philosophical old lady and insisted on going down to dinner before resting in her room and waiting for Lucy's call. There were some things you could do nothing about and for some time, as far as her friend Maud was concerned, she had felt she was in the hands of fate.

Lucy promptly rang at nine, sounding extremely upset. 'It was this morning when we went in to her – she wouldn't wake up,' she said. 'The doctor thinks it's what he calls another "Cerebro-vascular accident", which is, I suppose, a stroke. She's still unconscious – but no worse. Matron says don't come now – leave it to the morning and then they'll be able to see better how it's going to go.'

'I'm very sorry,' said Jackie. 'I'll come along at ten unless I hear from you – they have told the niece?'

'Oh, yes, but she's not coming till tomorrow afternoon. Dr Gray recovered from the other thing – if it really was a stroke – I don't know. I couldn't let you know this morning. Your housekeeper said you'd already left.'

'Don't worry, my dear – I know a bit about strokes – it's out of our hands. See you in the morning.' She put the phone down. 'Maud was always elusive,' she said to Isobel, who was sharing the chintzy sitting-room the extremely posh hotel had provided them with.

'Take a sleeping pill, Gran,' suggested Isa, worried that she might have another invalid to deal with.

'Oh, I am all right – I'll get my usual four hours in. I'll go to bed now. You must have a look round the place tomorrow – they say there's an interesting market here – I'll order a taxi for quarter to ten.'

Isobel left her sitting up in the vast bed. Her tall grandmother looked small in it and she kissed her goodnight and went into her adjoining bedroom.

Jackie did not sleep straightaway. She did not like pills and as you got older you needed your routines, but whenever she felt upset she put her Walkman on and listened to the music that always calmed her. It brought back Carlos too, but as he was never far from her thoughts she was used to that, had stopped mourning him in the dreadful way she had first reacted to his sudden death and now found solace in the fact that he had lived and they had loved each other and that he had died as bravely as she hoped to herself, one day. Not yet though. First she must see Maud Crichton who was unaware that she had come hundreds of miles for that very purpose. *Had* Calum and Maud ever . . . ?

*　　*　　*

Jackie was sitting by the bedside of her long-ago friend Maud Crichton, covering the loose white hands that lay on the coverlet, palms down, with her own. She had had a word with the doctor on her way in. 'We can only wait and see,' he had said. Apparently such a 'cerebro-vascular accident' could kill straight off, but sometimes people lingered on until they had another or, less commonly at Maud's age, recovered, often left with paralysed limbs.

It was such a terrible shame that she had come too late – yet in some ways she was relieved as she watched and waited. She had spent a reasonable night in the circumstances and then come over straight after breakfast to meet Lucy. How little she now enjoyed departures from habit. Yet she had felt compelled to come for Maud's sake. What would she say to her though, if her old friend returned to life?

'They told me to take you in – I think they're surprised she's still alive,' Lucy had said in the foyer, taking her arm firmly, but gently. Jackie thought, not for the first time, what a pretty young woman Lucy was with her long, blonde hair and green-grey eyes. Small frame, but wiry-looking. Strong she thought. Charlie liked her too.

Together they had gone into this room. The blinds were half up and the October sun was fitfully gleaming under them, the wind from the half-open window rattling the acorn of the blind. The room was tidy and did not have that invalid smell; evidently the Home was a superior one.

'They had to put two enormous trunks full of her things in store in the basement. Even when the solicitor sold up the house, she wouldn't be parted from some of her stuff,' whispered Lucy, not quite knowing what to say. On the bedside table Jackie saw a bracelet and a bottle of scent.

'You can leave me here for a bit – it's been so kind of you to arrange everything – I'll just sit by the bed. Perhaps they might bring me a cup of coffee?'

'I could take you out for a drink and a sandwich at lunch-time,' suggested Lucy – 'You'll need a change – nothing so tiring as sitting like this – I know, I've done it – and I ought to be sitting with you, but we're short-staffed again today – more nurses down with 'flu, so I can't. People will come in and check how she is. There's a bell if anything happens.'

'Isobel will come over at three o'clock,' Jackie told her.

She stroked the hands, remembering the ring on the little finger of the right hand from long ago when they were both young and strong and proud of themselves. It did not really seem all that long since. Such a 'scene' as this was what it all came to in the end – she had always been aware of that. Yet it seemed unfair that it should not be herself lying in a coma, that she should be still alert and *compos mentis* (she smiled to herself, thinking – well I *think* I am) – even if she had one or two ailments – whilst she who had always had the clearer head should have been felled.

Jackie composed her thoughts as she was wont to do when alone and sat on as the sun went in behind a cloud and the wind quietened. It would be nice if she could have a cup of coffee, but she was reluctant to trouble them; she hadn't been able to swallow much breakfast. 'We are frail,' she thought. 'Even at times like this we can feel thirsty . . . our bodies let us down.'

But she sat on, and the woman whose hands she held and stroked did not stir. A long life, a woman's life, like her own lived through two world wars and the shadows of slumps and unemployment, and the benison of hard work. Yet had they not been lucky, the two of them, to have been both born with intelligence and good looks? 'Neither of us had exactly easy lives,' she thought. 'I wonder if she was often unhappy?' She looked at Maud's old face, but saw instead the face as it had once been, as it still was in her portrait.

She looked again at the white, waxy forehead and the pinched-in nose and pale lips and this time saw them as they were. You'd have thought she was scarcely breathing, except that a little rasping sound came rather irregularly from the back of her throat. She did not appear to be in pain. Perhaps they would give her morphine? If only a person could reach into the innermost recesses of another's mind to say – 'You're not alone' . . . But the stark truth was that we were all alone in the end.

She had left it too late, should have come straightaway, even if she had not been sure of a favourable reception. But she had never known what had been going on behind those closed eyes.

387

How little you ever knew another person. It was a fact that we were all in the same lifeboat and should help each other if it foundered; hold tight to each other if we were to drown, – but some people didn't want to be saved.

'Maud,' she whispered. 'Maud – hold on Maud. It's Jackie.'

Jackie went out with Lucy for half an hour to have a bite of lunch – 'Only a sandwich, but you must have something,' Lucy had said. 'The doctor is going to have another look at her, I think.'

When they came back Matron was waiting in the reception area. 'Please come into my office,' she said. Then – 'I'm afraid she's gone,' she said. 'I'm very sorry as you'd come all this way – there is no telling. It happened only twenty minutes ago.' She sounded very upset. This old friend of Dr Gray's was an imposing looking lady. Lucy Eden had said she was a writer. She hoped she was not going to make a fuss. But Jackie only said: 'May I see her – ? Or will the nurses – ?'

'Of course – I'll come with you, if you can wait. I'll telephone the niece. She may not have left home.' An hour later she led the way up the stairs to the rooms above, where Maud Crichton now lay. 'I'm sorry there is no lift,' she said, noticing that the visitor climbed rather slowly.

Jackie thought, so this is how it happens. They must be used to it. Poor Lucy, she is upset. At the landing she got her breath and asked the usual questions – how, and why, and when – but the answers were immaterial now. Then at the door, which was closed with an incongruous 'Do not Disturb' notice hanging from the knob, she turned to the Matron. 'I shall not be long. Can you let me have ten minutes? and then I think I shall go back to my hotel for a rest.'

'Certainly – I'll ring you a car as soon as you wish.'

Jackie went alone into the room. She came out ten minutes later, looking no different, but she held on to the banisters as she walked slowly down the stairs.

Mrs Vallés had gone back to her hotel and Lucy had promised to join her that evening there with Isobel. Now Lucy was alone in the room where Jackie had already been. Death had not appeared to frighten *her*. But she hasn't seen Dr Gray for years, thought Lucy – I've been with her every day almost for several months – how can the others really feel anything? She felt unsteady, drained, and only a cup of tea in Matron's office had given her the strength to confront her dead patient. Matron had said: 'Are you sure you're all right? Death is always a shock – even to us, you know.' But Lucy had insisted on going in alone to say Goodbye. Suddenly she remembered that she must tell her mother what had happened. How well had *she* known this woman?

'You were so lonely,' she said silently to the body of the woman lying there on the familiar old bed in the familiar room. Even the scent bottle was standing on the dressing-table almost empty. And she had been going to buy her another, she thought. How stupid. She must concentrate, not avoid looking by thinking of silly little things. 'You were so lonely,' she said again, this time out loud. 'And now everybody has come to see you and you don't know anything about it.' But would she have been pleased if she had known?

She stood looking at the face on the pillow. The layer-out was to arrive any moment – it seemed the nurses did not like this job and somebody came from Scalby to do it. There was only a rough sheet covering the rest of the body but the arms were outside it. She saw the well-kept hands and nails which she had so recently tended. The face was uncovered, the eyes closed. It was the second dead body she had seen, but it looked very different from her grandfather's. Granddad had somehow looked more dead than this. It seemed to her that at any minute the eyes of Dr Gray, who was not really Dr Gray, would open and she would demand some service, make some complaint or call her 'Xanthe'. At this memory Lucy's own eyes filled with tears. Nobody else would call her that now. Dr Gray had been a difficult woman, but she had liked her; she had herself known that her mind wandered, Lucy felt sure, and the knowledge must have been a torture to her. She stared at the cheekbones and the forehead, polished like smooth marble. Now anyone could see she had been a beauty, even if the mouth was sunken. The long greyish white hair was awkwardly caught under the neck again, some of it spread on the pillow; the straight nose was a little pinched, but there were few lines on the face, unusual for such an old lady. Under the hair she could see the little gold sleepers in the ears and that green ring was still on the little finger of her right hand where they had folded them. Perhaps Mrs Vallés had done that. The heavy silver bracelet had been removed and was on the bedside table. Dr Gray had wanted her to have it. What should she do? Dr Gray had said – 'I don't want Janet to have it,' and Lucy knew Janet was the niece who would soon be arriving. She would ask Matron. And tell Mrs Vallés. She picked the bracelet up and put it in her pocket.

The face seemed to grow less familiar as she stood there, and suddenly she felt, rather than grief or fear, a sort of anger that all human beings came to this in the end and a feeling almost of shame that a person was reduced to a dead animal. Dr Gray had been so full of a sense of self, even when she had been clearly only half herself . . . but that was better than nothing, the physical embodiment that had to be put in a shroud and disposed of, now the mind had stopped giving it directions.

Lucy braced herself, and touched the cold hands.

'Goodbye,' she said. And then awkwardly, and she did not know why, she said: 'God bless you,' and she went out of the room. She went into the staff tea-room where they were now talking of the dead woman with a sort of grudging admiration.

Then she found she could not drink any tea so she went and tapped on Matron's door.

Matron was filling in a form: 'Janet Dalston, Dr Gray's niece, is coming from Birmingham tomorrow morning now' she said. She looked tired.

'May I ask your advice?' said Lucy.

'You look exhausted – sit down.'

Lucy knew that she would soon be leaving in any case, so that was perhaps why Matron was being so obliging.

'It was – Dr Gray told me many times she wanted me to have this of hers – and I *would* like to have it – but I don't suppose I may?' She took the bracelet out of her overall pocket and placed it on the desk. 'It was on her bedside table – I suppose it will have to go to her niece?'

Matron looked at her thoughtfully before replying. 'As a matter of fact,' she replied, 'Dr Gray mentioned the matter to me when you were on weekend leave – on one of her good days it was. I took the precaution of getting her to sign this, which Mrs Marshall typed out.' She looked in her desk drawer. 'Here it is.' She handed it over to Lucy. 'So you may keep it. I don't think Mrs Dalston, between you and me, takes much interest in jewels – and I expect she's getting the bulk of the estate as she's the nearest relative.'

'She said she hadn't made a will,' Lucy ventured, still not picking the bracelet up again, but looking down at the tiny signature.

'No – I expect she thought it was less trouble to leave things as they were – funny though – I expect she was once a stickler for everything signed and sealed.'

Lucy thought, she was afraid of dying, that was why. 'Did she suffer much?' she asked impulsively.

'It's one of the easiest ways to go,' replied Matron dryly. 'Take the bracelet and don't mention it to any of the staff – she was quite clear about it, if about little else!'

Lucy picked it up and felt the smooth silver against her fingers. 'She said I could look inside one day,' she said. 'It seems awful to take it like this, but I think she did mean me to have it. Thank you, Matron.'

Later she went over to the hotel in the taxi Jackie sent for her, when the layer-out had been and then the undertaker (at the back entrance so as not to disturb the other inhabitants of the Nursing Home) and when she had been persuaded to have a drink of brandy and a sandwich by Isobel, she took it out of her pocket.

'Why – that's Maud's bracelet,' said Jackie. 'I saw it on the table. Sir Hector gave it to her. She showed it to me once.'

'She wanted me to have it,' said Lucy and burst into tears.

'I'm glad about that,' said Mrs Vallés. 'You were the one I expect who did most for her recently. Look inside – your young eyes will be able to read it, I'm sure.' They were sitting in the room that adjoined the two bedrooms and Isobel was looking rather anxious. Her grandmother might be young for her age, but she must have had a shock and she wanted her to go to bed.

Lucy looked inside the silver rim worn smooth against

Maud's arm for so long. 'It says "Time will unite us",' she said eventually.

'I thought it said that', said Mrs Vallés.

'She said her *mother* gave it her!' exclaimed Lucy.

Later still, when Jackie had retired, Isobel said: 'This didn't unite *them* did it? I mean Gran and your Dr Gray.'

'People always die alone,' Lucy said. 'It was that I was feeling. Even if I'd been there when it happened. But she was always alone.'

'Will there be a service?' asked Isobel. 'I think Gran wants to stay here for it – the funeral, I mean – no point going home if she needs to come back soon.'

'Her niece – a Mrs Dalston, I think Matron said – she will arrange it, I expect.' Flowers, she was thinking, before the burning of the dead. Most people were cremated nowadays. All that part she found horrible. Isobel was probably tougher, dealing as she did with other sorts of deaths – animals, not human beings. 'I must ring my mother,' she said. 'I forgot to tell you both – it went right out of my mind – but my mother says *she* knew her too!'

'Your *mother*? I can't believe it. How?'

'She taught her, ages ago – Dr Gray remembered her. Isn't it weird? It seems I was just meant to look after her, doesn't it? It was a shame we were not there – we'd only gone to get Mrs Vallés a bite to eat,' said Lucy.

'Yes – she is sad about that – but she says "Maud would have known I'd come if I could," – she even said she'd played her last trick on her. I wonder what she meant?'

'That Time would not quite unite them,' said Lucy.

Chapter Seventeen

Lucy had been puzzled by her mother's reaction on the telephone when she heard of Dr Gray's death. 'I ought to have come to see her when you told me at first – but I just could not bear to. I wanted to remember her as she was. But I'll come to her funeral, Lucy, if you'll tell me when. Then you can tell me more about her.'

When Lucy, about to ring off, said 'Goodbye' to her mother, Milly said: 'I never said Goodbye to Maud Crichton, you know – I called her Helena – but I suppose I shall be able to now.'

Lucy had not yet mentioned the bracelet to her mother.

The funeral was to be on the Thursday at a Presbyterian church in a nearby town and then there was to be the cremation. Lucy wished it were over. But when she was told that Jackie's son Charlie was to come down also for it she was puzzled. '*He* never knew Dr Gray, did he?' she asked Isobel. She still kept thinking of her as Dr Gray, which after all was her name, though Mrs Vallés always called her Maud.

'No, Charlie never knew her, though I expect Gran mentioned her to him. I expect he has other fish to fry,' said Isa, mysteriously.

Charles Vallés was coming: Lucy hoped it was not a sort of disloyalty to the dead that thoughts of Dr Gray were by the Tuesday before the funeral displaced by thoughts of the handsome Charlie. She tried to resist speculating that he might, just might, have come partly because she was there. On the Wednesday morning she was called to see Matron who introduced her to a small, wispy-looking woman of about fifty who was the niece, Janet.

'Mrs Dalston just wants to know if you would clear those

trunks for her, Lucy,' said Matron. 'She's had a look and there's nothing valuable there. You might get some black plastic bags and do the job for us.'

'I am the executor,' said Mrs Dalston apologetically. 'Anything valuable was seen to when we moved. And the jewels are in the Bank.' Lucy tried not to look guilty.

Thus it was that she found the wallet marked 'Letters from HH' in a briefcase under a pile of yellowing and disintegrating German newspapers. Maud had evidently not wanted to reread the letters recently. Lucy burned them as she had been asked to, and the rest of the trunks' contents – folders of what looked like Latin exercises and old school registers, a pair of white kid gauntlet gloves, several packets of moth balls, old postcards, wallpaper samples, an iron with a burnt flex, several address books and at the bottom, wrapped in what looked like an old nightdress, a large studio portrait. She kept the last and left it for Mrs Dalston.

'It's Mrs D's grandmother,' said Matron later. 'Mrs Dalston says she never knew her well – she died before she was old enough to remember, I suppose.'

'Dr Gray's mother then? Does she not want it?'

'No, she doesn't seem to have much interest in her family,' said Matron. 'Why not give it to Mrs Vallés – she may have known the lady.'

Thus it was that Jackie Vallés saw for the first time the picture of Maud's Ma, a word which she was sure would have been the last on the lips of her old friend before she lost consciousness. A good-looking woman, rather like Maud.

By the time of the funeral Lucy felt it was weeks rather than days since Dr Gray had died. When Charles arrived the day before in Scalby, she could not help a sudden feeling of happiness, in spite of the event that had occasioned his arrival. Her own mother was to arrive on the day of the funeral itself, but the evening Charlie arrived she was free to observe him as he talked to his mother in the lounge of the hotel over a drink. Lucy had to be back at the Home by ten and was hoping he might drive her back there, since he had come in a large, old-fashioned car in which he was to take his relations back to Scotland afterwards.

He was a tall man, yet he did not look tall as much as large – and rather foreign. It was his eyes that drew you to his face. They were almost black, with eyebrows like firm strokes of dark ink under a wide forehead. *Was* he handsome? She thought so, but they were not conventional good looks. His nose was broad and his mouth wide and generous with large teeth. He laughed a lot and looked as if he enjoyed life. Not the face and body of an intellectual, she found herself thinking, though she knew he was a clever man. He had presence, that was it. When he did offer to take her back at ten o'clock and when he did say 'I hoped we'd see each other again, Lucy,' and when he actually kissed her hand when he said 'Goodbye till tomorrow,' her cup ran over. But perhaps being half Spanish or Italian or whatever he was, he did such things without thinking. 'Uncle Charlie is a love,' Isobel had said. Lucy wondered why he had never married. Perhaps he was always as attentive to young women as he was to his family? She knew she was not ugly.

Maud's funeral tired Jackie. She found herself thinking rather grimly that she was too old for other people's funerals. She saw her son Charlie looking across at little Lucy Eden as the preacher intoned that in the midst of life we were in death. If anything lay beyond the grave, doubtless she would soon know. But not yet, please, not just yet. Meanwhile it was an old lady's dream that her son should be attracted to a young woman like Lucy. She then chastised herself for being an incurable romantic and thought instead of Maud Crichton, who had not been one, before making a few prayers to that God they were invoking; one for Maud herself and one for Carlos Vallés and one for Calum Fyffe, whose granddaughter stood next to her now, Isobel, a little remote from all the emotion generated by Maud's death, but pleased that she had led her to the famous portrait and pleased, she thought, that her Gran liked her friend Lucy. Isobel would be all right. She had Calum's practicality and some of his idealism, a rare mixture.

Lucy was holding Dr Gray's bracelet in her hand.
' "Time will unite us",' said Milly.
'Yes – ! How did *you* know?'

395

'I've seen it before. She always wore it. She told me what it said.'

She had seen it hundreds of times on Helena's arm, but when her daughter handed it to her it was the first time she had held it. She felt most peculiar. Silver rubbed for sixty years by Maud's skin, words which though not meant for any of them, fate had led them to read together.

' "Time will unite us",' she read again.

'Time has certainly done that for me,' said Jackie. I wonder whether she kept Sir Hector's letters.'

'She told me there were letters in one of her trunks,' replied Lucy. 'She asked me to destroy them when she died. I found them and burned them – they were in a leather wallet with HH on the outside on a little label.'

'Those would be his,' said Jackie.

They were still in Mrs Vallés's sitting-room at the hotel. Matron and the niece had gone and Milly and Jackie were eating sandwiches of thin brown bread and cucumber and drinking coffee. Not what you might call a funeral tea, but necessary to bring them back to life after the cremation. Lucy and Isobel and Mrs Vallés's son were somewhere else in the hotel. Milly had decided to stay the night. She had not had much time to talk to her daughter and felt a little nervous with this imposing lady whose books she had read and admired. She wanted to see more of her, hoped she would, now that she had met someone else who had actually known Maud Crichton.

'Lucy said that Miss Crichton often had nightmares,' said Milly, plunging in. No point in putting this conversation off. 'She talked about an old lady in black – she said she was frightened of her – '

'I didn't know anything about that,' said Jackie – 'I don't suppose I ever knew her well enough to understand her, though I think I knew her at one time better than most people did.'

'Yes – I felt that too, once,' said Milly, looking frankly at the woman who had known her Helena in an ordinary way and could tell her quite a lot if she wanted. 'I used to call her Helena,' she added.

'Of Troy? Yes – there was that. Sir Hector did too, the one

who had the picture painted. Look, you must come and stay with me and have a look at the portrait and then we can have a longer talk, – if you would like – '

'I'm sorry – you're tired – now I must go – but I'd love to talk – '

'Just stay a little longer. The young people will be enjoying themselves somewhere – there's nothing like funerals for making people want to make the most of life, I've found.'

'She would never tell *me* her Christian name,' offered Milly. I found it out, but I invented another. I think Maud suited her – I could never decide whether she was a virgin or a – well not a whore – ! – a courtesan, a Camille – '

'Oh, I don't think she was a virgin,' said Jackie. 'Neither was she a Messalina. She was beautiful though, certainly that. I think Maud saw herself as a sort of *femme fatale* – but she didn't look like a vamp or a siren, did she? Or the Venus of the Sleeping Cars!'

Milly Eden smiled, said 'There were other aspects – not just to do with the effect she had on men. When I knew her – it was in the forties – she was a sort of *Belle dame sans merci*. She enchanted *me* anyway.' Would the old friend be shocked?

'I expect she had that effect often on some women – but she was not awfully fond of women, you know – ' said Jackie.

'Did you always call her Maud?'

'Oh, yes – there was nothing mysterious about that! She once told me that she used to call herself Isolde – she confessed that she'd told her first admirer that that was her name.'

'But Isolde died for love!'

'Yes – and Maud certainly did not. You know I looked up her thesis in the university library out of sheer curiosity. It was extremely interesting – and rather witty – not at all stuffy – quite brilliantly researched.'

'I always wondered why she never got a post in a university. She really was wasted on us,' said Milly.

'Thereby hangs a tale – it made me angry the way they rejected her after encouraging her to go to Germany and do all that work.'

'Was the thesis on Germany then – in German?'

'Oh no, no – it was a classical piece of research into the late Roman Empire!'

Milly was astonished. Why hadn't Maud ever told her that? 'There are so many things a girl doesn't ask – when I think how well I knew her and yet was completely ignorant about other parts of her life!'

'Maud always told you only what she wanted you to know or think,' replied Jackie. 'Look, I mean it about visiting me – will you come soon? – there's plenty to see in Edinburgh – unless your husband doesn't like you to travel without him?'

'Oh, George can look after himself very well – he *likes* being left alone – we've only just got back from a cruise – and he's "getting himself up to date", which means reading all the papers he missed. He's only just retired from the Civil Service – I'm sure he could spare me for a few days.'

'Promise to come and stay then?' said Jackie.

'Yes, I'd love to.' She lingered by the door for a moment. 'Maud Crichton used to call me "Hero",' she said. 'Like she called my daughter Xanthe.'

'She never called me anything but Jackie,' said the old lady, laughing. 'But then I was her age, you see – she didn't want to mythologise me!'

'I think she needed a real hero to love her,' said Milly, and went out.

Jackie was thoughtful. It was not surprising that Maud had attracted women as well as men. Even the usually sensible Lucy had been affected, she thought. Then, *I* was loved by a hero, she said to herself. The thought of Carlos Vallés was with her as she fell asleep but when she woke in the night she thought of his son, her son, and of little Lucy, and smiled to herself.

Milly felt strange talking about her old love all those years later. She had never said much about her to her husband, except that she had had a *grande passion* when she was a schoolgirl. Every now and again she had thought of her old feelings and wondered how they would now be classed. But Lucy's actually meeting Maud Crichton! – if only for her to be snatched away once more, and the words Lucy had reported: 'She says you were good-looking and clever,' had given her a curious sense of sadness. That Maud had evidently not forgotten her and yet chose to remember her just as a pupil, if a bright one, made her wonder what memory did to the past. How much had Maud Crichton remembered? If only she could ask Mrs Vallés – Jackie she must call her – more.

It was late and Lucy and Charlie were in his car parked in the Nursing Home Drive. They had been having a long talk.

'So you see I had to grow up rather quickly,' Charles had been saying. They were at that delightful stage when every small detail of another's life holds a monumental significance for each other. He had told her how his father, Carlos Vallés, had suddenly died after the best performance of his life in *Lucia di Lammermoor*.

'He sounds like a hero,' said Lucy.

'He was a most wonderful man. I so missed him – I was only twelve when he died. Not more than Mother did, but even so . . . she never made me feel I ought to take his place or any of that nonsense some women sometimes feel is necessary when they're widowed and left with a growing boy. I'm not a bit like him. I mean, I know I *look* a bit like him. Why am I telling you all this?'

'Because I like to hear it – and to listen to you,' said Lucy. A real man, not a memory, or some unhappy botched love . . . Charles was so solid and, she thought with a small smile, just what the doctor ordered for a young woman who had had rather a lot to cope with recently. But she also felt he might be what the older generation called 'serious' about her. Another 'hero' too, who 'went about doing good', from what Isobel said. When they said goodnight she was already looking forward to the next day in a world that contained him, even if he was off to Scotland.

Jackie decided, once home, that she would write straight away to Milly Eden and give her a definite date for her stay in Scotland. She wanted her to see the portrait. There was also something else nagging her about that, a feeling that as Maud had never seen it again it ought to go now to Christina, whose son was apparently not only a collector like his grandfather, but determined to buy back Garvits to live in when he married for

399

the second time. Part of the house had been used by the Red Cross as HQ and was dilapidated. They had moved out and the whole place was on the market. He had told his mother he wanted to demolish the servants' quarters and sell off part of the land and then rebuild the old wing. As he was an extremely successful business man she was sure this was what he would do, and told Jackie this in her reply to the older woman's letter, in which Jackie had described what had happened to the elusive Maud. Maud seemed more real now to her now she was dead, Christina replied, than she had been for years as a kind of figment of her father's imagination. Other people had actually known her recently; it seemed to bring her father back to her in a strange way. Jackie had told her also about the bracelet which had been given to the young woman who was looking after her, Lucy Eden, Isobel's friend. Wasn't it all rather weird, wrote Christina, how Jackie had found out where she was?

In her letter to Milly, Jackie wrote: 'I suppose we all see people differently when we come to think about it. But Maud would have been, I feel, the same sort of person when I knew her as when you did. It's nice for me that I can talk about an old friend with you. So many of my friends are dead, you see. I have the feeling that my son Charles would be awfully pleased to see Lucy too – he may have arranged that already. Such a cheerful girl. I'm so glad that Maud saw fit to leave her that piece of jewellery!' Milly read this with a smile and arranged a long weekend before Christmas, and told Lucy she had accepted. Lucy, who was now back from her labours at Dedlock Grange and still uncertain whether to apply or not for the following autumn at Medical School said, trying to sound guileless, 'How nice! Isobel thinks *I* need a holiday too, so I shall stay with her.' They arranged therefore to go north together when the freezer had been stocked for Giles and his father. Lucy's brother Giles was already down from Cambridge for the Christmas vacation and Milly said how practical it would be for the two of them to do a bit of housekeeping together.

Jackie had taken Milly in to see the portrait, which was still hanging in her dining-room. Then she left her there saying Mrs Thomson would be bringing up drinks to the next room as soon as Milly felt like one. Milly looked round at the high-ceilinged room before cautiously lifting her eyes to the portrait. She felt like an interloper in this house, though that was silly, for Mrs Vallés seemed really grateful to her for coming. But there were still old feelings buried in her somewhere, of inadequacy, or envy . . . *Did* she envy Jackie Vallés? – Oh, perhaps, but because she was creative and had gone on being so after her youth.

She went closer to the picture and put on her reading glasses. They made it a bit blurred. She fished in her bag for her TV specs and put them on instead. The green dress clarified itself and then the young woman with the long neck, her hair parted in the middle and looped around her ears. It was a sumptuous picture of a person who had been very beautiful. She had not been wrong, could recognise her 'Helena' as she had been twenty years before she had taught 'Hero', the Helena from the time before Milly Hargreaves was born.

Milly thought, she was quite, quite separate from me; she had a life before I met her, quite a long life, and then half her life after that. Why did she never want to see this again? But she knew the answer. This woman was young, and though Miss Crichton had been a person who looked especially ageless, the sheen on the skin, the curve of the arm here, were young. Milly had a lump in her throat, mourning now her own lost youth rather than that of Maud Crichton. She thought, love reminds us of ourselves, egoists that we are – and she went into Jackie, who was waiting by the fire, a small black cat curled up on a chair beside her.

'I knew her as an autumn rose,' said Milly. 'But that picture is of a spring blossom. I ought to have gone to see her when Lucy told me at first,. but, you know, I was afraid – just like *she* was perhaps afraid of seeing herself sixty years later.'

'Her looks were of paramount importance to her,' said Jackie. 'Help yourself to a glass of sherry, Milly. Will you come and sit by me?' The cat stared at Milly as she sat down with her drink.

'You loved her very much didn't you?' said Jackie.

'Oh, yes.' A silence. Then 'I don't think she would ever lose her faith in her power to attract – women as well as men – girls anyway.'

'What do you think of the picture – as a picture?' asked Jackie.

'It's difficult to separate my feelings from my "aesthetic reactions", if I want to be pompous,' said Milly. 'But I think it is the sort of picture the man who loved her would want.'

'I've been thinking about it,' said Jackie, sipping her drink and looking in the fire. 'You see Christina Gordon's father – Christina is the daughter of the man who loved Maud – Sir Hector Heron – *he* would see it as a work of art from a certain period – by an artist consciously making a statement about a woman he saw as belonging, even then, to another age. Hamish Gordon – that's the son – will see it just as an "object" – not an effigy from a personal past. That's how I think the picture ought to be now that Maud has gone. I feel it should go to him now especially if, as he says, he's going to do up a wing of the old place. What do you think?'

'I think you're right – see it as something separate, a finished piece. Yes.'

'You're sure – not just saying it to agree with an old woman?'

'No, Mrs Vallés – I do think it would be best. It might please Maud too, if she knew. Not to be named, but to be seen as an example of beauty.'

'You know,' Jackie went on, 'What you said about not wanting to see a person change – and Maud being like that about herself – our wanting to remember ourselves as we were, holding on to old feelings, that touches a chord in me. I've never stopped loving my second husband, you know – Charlie's father – I try to live in the present, though there may not be much of that left now. But there are parts of one's life one knows one was so incredibly lucky to have lived that one can't let them go. You "work through" your feelings as they now say when they go in for "therapy" – but it's only to understand them better, not to lose them or forget them, don't you think?'

Milly felt she had a good deal in common with this woman who talked like a young person. How she'd like to have known her when she was younger. Jackie would have sorted her out!

'I think you are a romantic – as I was,' Jackie went on. 'I believe the new generation of women thinks it has more sense than we probably had – you know how they *say* they'll marry the man who would be their "best friend" if the man had been a female. But then they fall in love and everything is forgotten. I know I couldn't have written my later stories without experience of love. And I was lucky because Carlos, whom I loved, also loved me and was also a man who let me be myself. We're often told that women should make more of themselves in the career line and I'm all for that – as I'm sure my granddaughter Isobel is, – but I hope she'll have children too. I am biased I expect.' She laughed. 'Of course he became my "best friend" too, later' she added.

'I suppose Miss Crichton – Maud, wanted to have a successful career? But she didn't, did she? – and no children either. It's sad.'

'Not many women managed both in those days,' said Jackie.

Milly was thinking, her Charlie and my Lucy did not meet through Maud. It was Lucy who knew her and was a sort of vessel to bring things about before Maud died, through the picture. 'Did she ever admit failure to herself, do you think?' she asked

'Maud? I wonder. I expect so. Probably ashamed, you know – they treated women very badly then. If she had got the lectureship she wanted – set her heart on – but she'd never have married in any case.'

'She used to hint to me about men, you know. There was someone she called "Moltke" – '

'How odd! – that's what the man I met said when I met him at a party. He'd known Maud in Germany and he told me she went about with a man who wanted to marry her – "Moltke" she called him, he said.' She looked thoughtful, then said:

'He was killed at Alamein, like my first husband Calum. Did she talk about other men too?'

'Oh, I think a film star – and an older man – that must have been your Sir Hector.'

'I don't know anything about a film star,' said Jackie. 'How glamorous!'

'She was always hinting things about men who gave her presents or made confidences to her,' said Milly, thinking she had perhaps better not mention the man in the train.

403

Jackie said: 'She had an awful experience once in a train – she told me, swearing me to secrecy – a man exposed himself to her.'

After a pause Milly said 'She told me her mother told her "they couldn't help themselves", but then she often said – when she would not dance with anyone at parties – that she "couldna bear to be touched".'

'That sounds like Maud – '

'But she allowed *me* to touch her – I even kissed her – several times,' said Milly.

'I expect you were very bold,' said Jackie.

'On the other hand she might very well have had a few affairs at the time I knew her. I just dared not ask.'

'She'd want to keep you guessing – That old idea of a Messalina of the suburbs, I expect – though why the suburbs I always ask. People are so snobbish.'

Milly was laughing. 'You put it in perspective,' she said.

'Yet – there you were – you loved her – she'd like that – was she lonely?'

'Yes, very – but I never knew whether she'd have wanted to be any different. In the end I couldn't give up everything for her, you see – I was too young.'

'Of *course* you could not.'

'In the end, before she went away, after three years – a long time when you are young – I wanted her to set me free, but she would never say the word, so I never felt it was over. I suppose it never was, in one sense.'

'But you fell in love again later?'

'Oh yes! – often – and with men. Do you think she would have thought I'd played with her affections? I hope not. I'd love to have talked to her as I'm talking to you, but it was impossible. Later I could have done, but it was too late. Tell me about when you knew her.'

'I think Maud was very proud, and a proud person gets wounded – and then wounded pride turns to cynicism – grows a protective shell – do you think that sounds like the person you knew?'

'Yes – but a long way down and hidden even from herself. I had the impression, even when I was only about sixteen, that she was chained to some idea of herself, not free – stuck in a groove – and that I might have rescued her from it; but I wasn't strong enough . . .'

'I expect you *did*, Milly – she'd be fond of you, you know. A person like Maud needs other people in a way we don't. I know we *do* need people, but not to affirm ourselves as real. If people like Maud lose touch, they turn in on themselves.'

'Lucy says she was told Dr Gray was almost a recluse before they took her off to that Dedlock place.'

'It's an unfortunate name, isn't it? – yet it didn't seem too bad. I was there just before she died – Lucy will have told you – and I thought, just before I went out with your daughter for a drink of coffee, that her lips moved and she was going to wake up. Instead she had another seizure.'

'Did you hear what she said?'

'I thought she tried to say Ma,' said Jackie. 'Her mother adored her – I do know that. I must show you the picture Lucy found of *her*. I think Maud was always a child at heart – that's the conclusion I've come to. Sir Hector might have made her life different, but he died – of course his wife came back – she was said to have been an invalid for a long time. He was to have his cake and eat it and then try to be noble and give her up and I expect the strain killed him. But her mother was always there.'

'I think something broke in her when her mother died.' Milly said.

'Mother love sets us going, but we have to escape in the end,' said Jackie. 'Do help yourself to another drink. I haven't had such an intimate talk for years.'

When Milly came round with the sherry, Jackie took another half glass saying the doctor said it was good for her 'in moderation'.

'She didn't want to see anyone she'd ever known, didn't want to be traced, did she? Even before she went a bit peculiar?' Milly asked.

'We'll never know. Perhaps they're mourning her in the town – there were one or two people Matron couldn't place at the funeral – there was a whole life there, and at her other schools, I suppose.'

405

'No story ever ends, does it?' said Milly. 'But in the "end" we can't help people who don't want to be helped.'

'Just think now, if she had been a man, people would have thought it absolutely normal – they wouldn't have thought her all that eccentric. She wasn't popular, of course, not even up here at university – at one time I wondered if my first husband, if Calum, had had a little thing with her – after we were married. I was awfully caught up with the children then – but I'll never know that either.'

'I think she'd always be loyal to you,' said Milly.

'Do you? She tolerated me, but castigated my taste just as often. Said I was a "romantic," which I was. She was loyal to her own lights, though, I feel, whatever they were. Maud was a catalyst, that's another conclusion I've come to – the way people reacted to her taught them more about themselves than about her.' Milly looked thoughtful.

'She was very clever too,' Jackie went on. 'You know, really *awfully* clever. And you see it in the portrait, really awfully beautiful, too. I was a callow girl at the time, I think, scarcely rational – Maud was always rational – or am I mistaken and she lived in a dream of herself? The only way to live with the loss of self-esteem is either to become deluded or confect a myth about yourself in which you come to believe. People like Maud, however, really need hard objective facts to live by. I was never "in love" with her – just rather admired her, and was intrigued – as you were, my dear, and I sympathised with her because others thought her eccentric. She was from a very strange family, what with the preacher and all. If she'd had my parents she might have been happier. But we don't always deserve the parents we get, do we? "In our stars or in ourselves?" as the bard wrote. – Maud always called him The Bard!'

'She liked her games of power, though,' said Milly, wanting to lay the ghost once and for all. 'Why are people like that? – and why do they cut themselves off from others? That's why she was so lonely – I felt there was a pathos there in all that perfection, all that obsessive attention to detail, all that love of intrigue so long as *she* could control it. And yet also this great need to be looked after – Lucy said she still had that – not just because she was old. I was a body servant and an amanuensis, you know –

I suppose I was a great help to her. I was there just when she needed me most, or a person like me. She could be touchingly grateful too – and self-protective as well as self-denying – '

'Passive yet scheming?'

'And sarcastic and witty – '

'Silent and inscrutable – '

'But sometimes expansive and talkative as well.'

'Superstitious – '

'Gullible, though? Women must try not to see themselves the way they want men to see them,' said Milly finally.

'We seem to agree upon the effect she had,' said Jackie laughing. 'What do you think she'd make of us sitting here analysing her? I hadn't actually seen her, apart from the day she died, for over fifty years – and you for what? – almost forty? Women are faithful creatures, aren't they?'

'I think she'd be enormously flattered,' said Milly. 'I can't imagine anyone ever discussing men in this way. But would she really want us to understand her.'

'The dead can't choose,' said Jackie. 'Would you have wanted to be her?'

'No.'

'Not with all that beauty, all those brains?'

'No – would you?'

'No – I used to think that it was easier to love than be loved – what a burden to be desired for something that was only a superficial part of yourself. Then, later in my life, I found it quite wonderful to be loved.'

'Dr. Crichton – Helena – your Maud – she thought she had power – she *did* have some but in the end it was men who wielded power over her, I expect,' said Milly. 'Though lovers are usually in love with their own feelings.'

'Adoration without conquest, is what Maud wanted, I think,' said Jackie. 'We'd better go in to dinner, as Mrs Thomson so grandly calls it.' She got up slowly.

Over dinner, presided over by the portrait of Maud, Jackie told Milly more about her earlier life and Milly told Jackie about her children and about her work as a translator of modern French novels. Before they went to bed they went over once more to look more closely at the picture. 'She didn't die

407

because she was beautiful but because she was old,' Jackie said finally, and kissed Milly Goodnight. 'Our children would think we were mad, I suppose, but I've really enjoyed this autopsy,' she added.

Milly went out in the morning to explore Edinburgh, where she had not been for years except for a flying visit to the festival. In the evening Jackie showed her the notes she had taken from Maud's thesis and they agreed she should have written a book about her empress. 'It was actually witty, which is extremely unusual for a thesis,' said Jackie. 'That man I told you about who knew her in Germany – he died some years ago – made the *DNB*,' she went on. '*He* made it and I'm sure he wasn't as good a historian as Maud. She wasn't "vain about her brain". But nobody wrote *her* biography.'

'What was he like? Did he fall for Maud, do you think?'

'Oh, the sort to have scores of women – and men like that get worse as they grow older, I've always found.'

If Jackie Vallés and Milly Eden had found each in the other a new friend, and it seemed that this was the case, their respective children were discovering something equally important. They met each day and walked and talked. It was Charlie's vacation already, but he showed her his departmental study and spoke of his work. 'There's an interesting post-graduate qualification we do here you might like to think about,' he suggested. Lucy had said she had now decided that medicine was not for her. 'Research in Anthropology,' he said. 'Takes you abroad to the same places I visit!'

'My mother suggested anthropology too!' said Lucy.

They had dinner at his mother's on Lucy's third day there and found their mothers chatting as though they had known each other all their lives. 'All this has given Mama a lease of life,' he whispered to Lucy – 'She looks younger already.'

Milly was to leave on the Friday, but Lucy announced she was staying on a bit, though she'd come home for Christmas. Both Milly and Jackie tried to look suitably disinterested at this decision, but could not help catching each other's eye. It was with real regret that Milly finally left Edinburgh. They were going to meet again in London when Jackie came for her annual visit to her agent and publishers.

Jackie was just as sad when Milly departed, but already had the idea for a story which she was itching to write. She'd have to start it soon. There was never enough time left.

Lucy and Charlie had climbed King Arthur's seat and were sitting on a wall in the December sunshine.

'I'm very old-fashioned,' Charlie said. 'But I should like you to marry me. Would that be a good idea, do you think?'

Lucy, who had never had a proposal before, only a proposition, hesitated out of surprise that he was already thinking of that.

'Don't say we don't know each other! You can get to know me and I can get to know you – give it six months, eh?' said Charlie. 'I just wanted you to know I've decided after thirty-six years of debauchery that I am the marrying sort. You can live up here, can't you, whilst we do the getting to know part – and register for that thing I told you about? Will you, Lucy, please – I do love you.'

'I love you,' said Lucy.

After some time had elapsed in which Lucy felt she would never want to leave the shelter of those big, comfortable arms, but knew she must, and during which Charlie Vallés felt he could not bear to be parted from her even for one night, but knew that life was not so easy, they drew apart. Then he said: 'There's no name in-laws can call each other, is there? Mother and your mother – they'll be related when we get married, won't they! Then they can dissect your Dr Gray as much as they like.'

Lucy laughed. 'Mother's a bit of an obsessive type,' she replied. 'But it was just *so* peculiar, the whole thing.'

He stroked her wrist under the heavy overcoat, for although the sun shone, it was Scotland, and it was nearly Christmas. 'Shall I call you Xanthe too?' he asked.

'If you like.'

'Show me that present she gave you. Let me have another look.'

Lucy unclasped it and he looked inside at the words Hector

409

Heron had engraved so long ago. Then he said 'Time has united *us* – death unites only the dead.'

Lucy shivered at his words, but as he put the bracelet gently back on her wrist, the black hairs on his own wrist standing up in the cold, she had that sudden conviction, so strong when it first comes in youth, that life, whatever it all meant, was going to continue through the living now not the dead, and that it would continue through her.

It is summer again and Lucy and Charles are married and are walking one warm afternoon in the grounds of Garvits. Maud's portrait is now hanging there and is the most talked about picture in the new gallery Hamish Gordon has built for his collection. Lucy feels the warm stone of the garden wall under her fingers and Charlie puts his big hand over her small one. How happy they are, how contented; how joyous and pleasurable their love-making always is. Lucy sometimes feels old and wise and sometimes young and lusty, and Charlie feels the same, and their moods mingle and match. How lucky they are. They both know it. We shall leave them there, for the rest of their story is yet to be told. Maud's is over, and she has taken her secrets with her.